To Greta & Jim

Enjoy the escape!

Andrew Hunkins
Serial #34

# NO SUCH THING AS EVIL

BOOK 1

CIRCLE OF SIX

This is a work of fiction. The people, corporations, organizations, institutions, circumstances, and events depicted are fictitious and a product of the author's imagination. Any resemblance of any character to any actual person, either living or dead, is purely coincidental.

ISBN 13: 978-1-59298-999-7
LCCN: 2015952949
Printed in the United States of America
First Printing: 2016

20 19 18 17 16     5 4 3 2 1

Book design and typesetting by Tiffany Daniels.

Beaver's Pond Press
7108 Ohms Lane
Edina, MN 55439–2129
(952) 829-8818

www.BeaversPondPress.com

To order, call (800) 901-3480. Reseller discounts available.

*To my wife, Jen, who, with unconditional trust,*
*always supports my dreams*
*no matter how crazy they seem at the start.*

*There's no such thing as evil. Just as there's no such thing as cold. Cold is merely the absence of heat. And yet, absolute zero is very cold indeed.*

*Or very, very evil.*

# ACKNOWLEDGMENTS

FAMILY MEMBERS AND FRIENDS SHOWED LOVING tolerance to many versions of my unfinished manuscript.

First, I would like to thank Holly O'Brien for her detailed written comments on multiple drafts as well as hours of feedback sessions. She was the wall to which I could toss my undercooked spaghetti.

Second, I would like to thank my test readers who provided significant feedback on one or more drafts: Stan Hunkins, Jen Hunkins, Marin Johnson, Brian Hunkins, Judy Brown-Wescott, Marlys Widmark, Matt Hunkins, Jeffrey Hill, Laurie Graves, Matt Geurink, and Stasa Fritz.

Third, I would like to thank my test readers who provided feedback: Charlie Roberts, Shiloh Jackson, Cori O'Brien, Julianne Hunkins, Phil Moen, Paul Hunkins, Jim Hunkins, DeeDee Ogren, Allison Krogstad, Jonathan DenHartog, Andrea Hoerr,

Mike Boyle, Kenny Wolf, Tony O'Brien, B. Richard Vogen, Whitney Dierks, Marlene Egge-Hunkins, Natalie Bauleke, Abbey Geurink, Beth Geurink, Rob Feinholz, Harold Slawik, and Kevin Bruce.

I would also like to thank those that could not finish the first draft yet still provided critical feedback about how it could be improved: Kathy Flynn (mother of the late Vince Flynn), Becca Hunkins, Penny Ryan, Alice DiFilippe, and Gordy Koehler. I hope they'll give the published version a try.

And of course, this book would not be possible without my team of professionals. From Beaver's Pond Press: Lily Coyle, Hanna Kjeldbjerg, Wendy Weckwerth, Tiffany Daniels, and Amy Quale. Kellie M. Hultgren from KMH Editing. Sara and Chris from ScriptAcuity Studio. From Peter Hill Design: Megan Junius, Whitney Dierks, Hannah Bakke, Allison Krogstad, and the late Peter Hill. Flip Crummer from FlipCrummer.com. And from New Counsel: Harold Slawik and John Roberts.

# Chapter 1

AT THE STREET CORNER ACROSS FROM THE UNIVERSITY campus, Professor Laura Richards stood waiting for the light to change. She pulled out her percomm and thumbed to the message with the photo. The girl was twenty-two. The age and gender matched the other missing girls, but otherwise, Laura couldn't see what someone would want with one of her students. *Lisa ... yeah, that's her name.* Laura looked into Lisa's eyes in the photo and tried to imagine what she was going through. *Is she alive?*

Students pressed in around her as the traffic braked for the changing light. A guy bumped her from behind—at around six foot four, he blocked the morning sun, and Laura felt the cool summer air on her neck.

Laura was shorter than most of the students, and her thin frame only made her look more like a student instead of a faculty member. She backed up to get out of the guy's shadow just as the light turned green. She let the crowd of students pass around her before crossing.

A black metal fence surrounded Benjamin Franklin University, except at the main gate where it joined a tall concrete wall. She counted more security guards than usual for summer term. *Do they really think more guards can prevent another abduction?*

After passing through the biometric scanner at the main gate, she gave a start at the sight of student protesters preparing in the plaza. Then she remembered, *It's Saturday—protest rallies are only allowed on weekends.*

She hurried to Ben-U's poli-sci building while keeping an eye on the protesters. There weren't many yet. One had a stack of signs and was passing them out. The guards were keeping their distance.

Inside her office building, the air conditioning brought more relief than usual.

"Laura! I can't believe you came in for this," said Professor Nick Hinkle when Laura entered the conference room.

She took a seat at the opposite end of the conference table. Large vidcomm displays covered one wall. "You said we had to come in person."

"Yup. How else can they drop water on your forehead?"

"Don't start, Nick."

"It's just such an honor. You never come in on the weekend."

"I'll do anything for these girls."

"Coming in on the weekend … wow, really above and beyond."

"I said don't start."

Hinkle sneered. "I know how much you like the demonstrations."

"We only have a few minutes until the police interview starts. Let's just sit and wait quietly for the detective to arrive. You can do that, can't you?"

"Interview? How about interrogation? Inquisition? You know they insisted we come here in person so they can look in our eyes. I'm sure they'll bring a lie-detector machine." Hinkle laughed when he saw her reaction.

Ignoring him, she pulled out her percomm and scrolled through her messages. Marian Lumière was asking for a ride home from a doctor appointment at 10:30. Laura tapped the screen, which displayed Saturday, August 11, 2040, 8:54 a.m. *The interview won't take more than an hour. That'll work.* Laura replied to her friend, confirming she'd be there.

Scroll … scroll … scroll. Nothing interesting. She put away her percomm and rubbed her arms; the air conditioning seemed especially chilly now.

The display screens glowed to life, showing two people. On the right was the dean of students. On the left was a man she didn't recognize.

"Thank you all for meeting on a Saturday like this," said the dean. "Let's get started. Detective, please begin."

"Thank you. Now, I just have a few questions—"
*By vid conference?*

Hinkle put his hand over his mouth, almost falling out of his chair as he tried to contain his laughter.

"Is there anything wrong, Laura?" asked the dean.

The detective had stopped talking, and they were all looking at her.

"No. Well, I was told to come in person. I—"

"You're Laura Richards?" asked the detective. "The victim's political science instructor? Are you aware of any affiliation she might have had with the Hoods? Was she politically active?"

"No, nothing like that."

He seemed to weigh her answer, and then he turned to Nick. "Professor Hinkle, did you notice anything unusual?"

Laura looked away and blinked. *The way the detective is phrasing his questions … putting Lisa in past tense.*

After only a few more questions, the detective said, "Thank you for your cooperation."

"What?" The word had jumped from Laura's mouth.

"Excuse me. Do you have something more to say?"

"No. I mean, don't you have anything to go on?" Laura looked at each of them in turn. "I mean, she's missing. You can find her."

"She disappeared. Forensically, that is. That's what makes these cases so unusual."

"Then you're assuming she's one of the girls … in the news … never to be found?"

"Fits the profile."

The displays went dark. The interview had taken all of six minutes. She rubbed her arms again.

"Want me to escort you to the gate?" Hinkle laughed and walked out of the room.

110 110 110

ON THE LOWEST LEVEL OF THE MEGARON—A LUXURY ESTATE located in southern Nevada and a labyrinth of ornate glass, polished concrete, and brushed steel that might appear on the cover of an architectural design magazine—Aeron Skotino stood before the open door to a staircase leading down.

He felt a thrill unlike the countless other times he'd crossed from the world above to his destination below. *Finally … after millennia of toil.* He brought his hand to the knot of his red silk tie, pressing his fingers into the tight folds of the perfectly shaped knot and elegant dimple. The movement exposed the French cuffs of the white dress shirt under his British-tailored business suit. The gold cuff links were in the shape of a circle with six diamonds evenly spaced along their circumference and one larger diamond in the center. His hand glided down the front of the tie, ensuring its perfect alignment.

After descending the stairs, he reached the threshold to the oubliette—he preferred that term over dungeon because it emphasized the solitary point of egress. Before stepping in, he treated himself to a favorite Shakespeare quote: *And you all know, security / Is mortals' chiefest enemy.*

The man-trap causeway separated the oubliette from the immaculate showcase above. He took a moment to inspect the threshold. *I'm not overconfident, I'm meticulous.* He stepped across, and his broad shoulders brushed the sides of the deliberately narrow doorway. The door closed—vertically from above, like a portcullis—moving so quickly it seemed to simply appear.

Inside the causeway, Skotino looked up to the security camera over the sealed door at the other end and waited until Victor Tyvold, one of the Circle of Six, approved entry. With a click and the hiss of equalizing air, the far door opened.

The main hallway of the oubliette was cold, bare, and dimly lit. Skotino heard a satisfying moan. *That's Lisa*, he thought. *Tempting. But no, not today. Today will be Stephanie.*

Just to the left of the causeway, in the oubliette's security substation, Tyvold was monitoring a dozen displays showing status information and vid images from cameras in and around the compound above.

"Report." Skotino's deep voice reverberated against the walls, eliciting more moans.

"Six pharmakoi today, a full house," said Tyvold. "Lisa is still fresh; she's in room two. Sarah won't make it through the week. Who'll have the honor?"

"Stephanie."

Tyvold nodded. "Room four."

Walking down the hallway, Skotino heard another moan and felt the first tingling of the clarity sensation. *It is time.*

Outside Stephanie's room, he placed his hand on the doorknob. The clarity was building. He closed his eyes, tipped his head back, and embraced the feeling. In his mind's voice, he recited the ancient hymn.

*Hear me, god of gods, once one of twelve, now ruler over six*

*Hide the before, peer to beyond, our fate unfix*

*Humanity's false beauty, infected with the disease of mortality*

*For thee, I wield the threat of pain, now and unto eternity*

*Open my eyes and reveal future's grip*

*For the chance of reality's path doth tip*

Skotino prepared himself, knowing his next move often yielded a tantalizing result. He turned the doorknob, fraction by fraction.

||0 ||0 ||0

LEAVING THE CLINIC'S FRONT DOORS, MARIAN WAVED TO LAURA IN her pertran and started waddling over. She had one hand on her back as she teetered from side to side with each step. They were the same age, about thirty, but today Marian looked older somehow, probably the summer heat.

Laura got out and rushed to Marian's side. "Here, let me help you." She got Marian settled in the passenger compartment, took her own seat, and gave the pertran's navigation system the destination.

Once the vehicle pulled away from the curb in normal autopilot mode, Marian said, "Thanks. I didn't think I was ever going to get out of there … all their poking and prodding." She reached up to the vent, adjusted the airflow to her face, and closed her eyes. Her light brown hair bounced in the air—somehow her curls were surviving the summer humidity. Marian had curled her hair since grade school. *Such an extravagance these days.*

"The prenatal scanner still doesn't work?" asked Laura. "I thought they replaced it."

"They did. Twice. With a different model, even. And it still doesn't work. Remember when they had to draw a sample of amniotic fluid with a needle? It took all morning."

"Yeah. The sonogram was the same way, right?"

"Uh-huh. They smeared gel all over. Ruined my blouse. And after all that, they learned nothing. They have to send the results to a lab to be processed. It takes weeks." Marian pushed herself up in the seat and shifted to a more comfortable position.

"Well, you were so insistent you were having twins. The sonogram ruled that out on the spot. And they told you it's a boy."

"Who can trust their witch doctor ways? I'd swear at this very moment that I'm carrying two. Next they'll have me squatting on the prairie." Marian wiped her forehead. "Thanks for picking me up. When you said you had to go on campus to meet the police, I was concerned. They hold rallies on the weekends, right?"

"Yeah, no problem. I was happy to go. They haven't found Lisa. She'll probably turn up soon. The police said they always do."

IIO IIO IIO

SKOTINO HEARD STEPHANIE GASP FROM INSIDE THE ROOM. IT WAS thrilling the way the simple act of turning the door-knob generated such intense fear. He visualized her beautiful face with her forehead suddenly wrinkled in fear as his sensation of clarity intensified.

He opened the door to see her in the chair that was anchored to the floor, her arms and legs bound.

"No!"

Her scream invoked involuntary cries from several other pharmakoi. The clarity grew stronger, swelling almost to completeness. But not quite.

He entered the room and focused his attention on the young woman. *Do they ever stop crying?* Her head was turned away from him, and her eyes were clenched tight. She was wearing a shirt and under-wear but no pants.

He stepped to the table along the left side of the room. The wall above had instruments organized in neat rows. He pulled a pair of extra-large latex gloves from a dispenser and pulled one over his hand, fin-ishing with a snap. While putting on the second, he perused the assortment of instruments. The selection could make all the difference in the speed and intensity of the clarity. Some instruments, like the razor blade he'd used during his last visit, generated immediate fear. He took pride in the esoteric diversity of the collection, which included options that evoked memories of common, familiar pain. Like the cheese grater. But not this time; this visit required a special tool, so special he carried it with him.

Skotino picked up a clean towel from the stack, placed it on the floor in front of Stephanie, and knelt.

Her head was still cranked to one side as far as possible, eyes shut.

Inch by inch, he leaned forward, allowing his breath to pass across her bare legs. The ever-present crying changed to convulsive sobs—no sound, just the jerking of her torso. Her fists were white-knuckled balls. The fear was intense, and so the clarity was almost complete.

He examined the left knee. The scab there was perfect, about the size of a quarter. Very hard on the surface and curled up on the edges. *Perfect*. In a smooth and practiced motion, he withdrew the knife from its sheath at his waist. It had a six-inch double-edged blade, serrated on both edges. The black hilt had a gold circle with six dots evenly arranged along its circumference and a dot in the middle. Special indeed.

He brought the knife tip to the crusted edge of the scab and paused to look at her. As expected, she was looking at him with an expression of complete disbelief. He looked back to the scab, and then, with the tip of the blade, delicately lifted the edge.

She shook her head and, in barely a whisper, repeated, "No." Blood trickled down her calf as the brittle wafer separated from the skin.

With the scab fully extracted, Skotino admired the underside, which was crimson, milky translucent, and velvety—exquisite. He placed the scab in his mouth, savored it.

She was staring at him with utter disbelief.

He shifted his attention now to her opposite knee and said, in his gravelly voice, "Let's start the next one."

Stephanie's limbs yanked at the constraints, yanking again and again. She shrieked in terror.

Then, just at that moment, the clarity was complete. Skotino froze and allowed the feeling to penetrate his very being. The liminal presage seeped into his conscious mind.

> *Tell, told, and so foretold*
> *Future's fickle promise to seize and unfold*
> *A hint, a glimpse, a whisper from thy lip*
> *For the chance of reality's path doth tip*

Remembering where he was, he opened his eyes, looked directly at Stephanie, and said, "Sorry. My manners. What are we waiting for?"

The task took only a few minutes. Skotino stopped at the security substation.

Tyvold's face conveyed his anticipation.

"The location of the next fetus is clear to me," Skotino said to Tyvold. "Host of my god's brother, convene the Circle."

"I hear and obey."

||0 ||0 ||0

LAURA'S PERTRAN TURNED ONTO THE LONG DRIVEWAY TO Marian's house. The driveway led to a detached four-car garage in back, but the vehicle turned off to the circular drive in front. Laura helped Marian out of the tran and up the front steps.

The door didn't open.

"Oh, fiddlesticks," said Marian. She stepped closer to the seccomm camera. The door swished open.

"What was wrong?" asked Laura.

"Oh, I have no idea. Stupid thing's been acting up."

Laura guided her to a seat in the living room. "Here, you rest. I'll get us some water."

"Ahhh, thanks." Marian rolled into the chair and adjusted herself.

In the kitchen, Laura opened the cupboard and took out two glasses. She knew where everything was because they usually chatted in the kitchen around the island. But Marian would be more comfortable in the living room, now that she was so close to having the baby. Laura filled the glasses from the water dispenser. Even the kitchen was a treat. The cupboards were made of real wood, and the glasses were made of real glass.

"So Chris is still your favorite name for the baby?" Laura handed Marian the water.

"Yes, that's what Joe and I discussed, before … you know … once we decided to start a family. And I know it's what he would've wanted."

Laura got comfortable on the matching love seat as she listened.

"I know I've got to move on. On one hand, planning for the baby creates so many reminders that Joe's gone. On the other, it was such a blessing to discover, after the accident, that I was pregnant. I have a part of Joe that will live on. But it's so hard. Like the silly security system. Joe would have someone fix it. Now it's up to me. Everything's on me."

"It'll mean a lot of changes." Laura noticed the coffee table and flower arrangement were gone. The picture frames, delicate sculptures, and vases, which had all been within reach of small hands, were gone too. Laura couldn't imagine the house fully baby-proofed. Joe had inherited his wealth, and Marian had poured herself into his lifestyle, like bourbon into eggnog.

"How's Ben doing?" asked Marian.

"Fine."

"What's his latest project?"

"I have no idea. But he's been putting more equipment into the lab at home and spending more time there in the evenings instead of working late. So that's nice. I don't see him any more minutes in the day, but he's home more."

"Just research or does he still teach?"

"He still teaches advanced computing."

"What does he think about the missing girl? Are any of his students concerned?"

"Well, we haven't discussed it. I'm sure Lisa will turn up soon."

110 110 110

SKOTINO HELD HIS EYES CLOSED AND HIS ARMS OUTSTRETCHED. HE listened as each of the six men moved into position around him. Hearing that each was seated, he opened his eyes. Tyvold had once again prepared the circular sanctuary for the gathering of the Six inside the megaron. Six candles, one behind each seated man, provided the only illumination. Skotino faced Tyvold, in deference to the host of his god's brother.

At the center of the circular room and directly in front of Skotino, a podium supported a small wooden box with holes on all six sides. The holes on the top and bottom were smaller than the ones on the sides. Tyvold had flawlessly prepared the sanctuary for the ritual, as usual. The apparatus of needlelike spikes was aligned with the small holes and poised above. Skotino peered through the air holes on the side but couldn't see any movement, and no sound came from the box. *Probably sleeping—not uncommon for the young canines*. He appreciated the quiet.

"Host of my god's brother," said Skotino, "we begin."

"We hear and obey," said Tyvold.

"Another fetus has been conceived," announced Skotino. "The location is clear to me now."

The six together chanted, "We thank the gods."

Skotino stepped around the podium to face Erik "Big Vega" Mathers while keeping the small box between himself and Vega. Vega's apelike frame completely obscured the stool on which he sat. "Host of my god's son, you will go to the mother. You will determine the gender of the fetus."

"Host of my god's father, I hear and obey," said Vega.

Skotino noticed the childlike eagerness and wondered if Vega actually heard the command. *His skull is thick in so many ways.*

Skotino shifted his position, always facing the center of the room, until Mark Spire was on the opposite side. Spire wore black denim jeans and a black nylon shirt. His skin was so black that only a bluish sheen was visible, like raw coal. He kept the tight curls of his black hair trimmed to the scalp. All this combined to make him nearly invisible in the darkness.

"But if the fetus is female ..." Skotino allowed the words to hang.

None of the men gave the slightest indication, but the potential for disappointment was palpable. This wasn't the first time they had prepared, only to resume waiting. *Frustration feeds vigilance,*

Skotino thought. He didn't care how long it would take to find the first male. "Host of my god's son, if the fetus is female, you will eliminate the fetus and the mother."

"Host of my god's father, I hear and obey," said Spire. The words were nearly a whisper and difficult to tell from which direction they came.

Skotino had considered letting Spire find the woman, but he didn't want Spire engaged for long periods. Always best to keep Vega busy. Regardless, Spire would be the one to handle the elimination.

Two years before, clarity had finally revealed the presence of the first fetus. Maryellen Lizbottom of Ottawa had conceived the first child with the long-awaited genetic alignment. Big Vega had reached her and determined that, regrettably, the fetus was a female. He handled the elimination. He used an unmarked van. The extracted surveillance footage captured the impact perfectly. She bounced off the front of the van and then rolled against a parked vehicle before hitting the pavement, dead even before the next truck, brakes screeching, flattened her chest. The authorities were unable to trace the van without the surveillance footage. Vega's elimination was successful, but clumsy.

Four months later, a woman from the Congo had conceived the next fetus. Again, female. This time, it was Spire's turn. He took the woman silently during the night and made sure the body would never surface from the ocean floor. Spire was professional, discreet, and efficient.

Improper disposal of the bodies represented the greatest vulnerability to their plans. *Macbeth, the fool.* Skotino made a mental note to address this growing disposal problem.

Skotino now turned to Rick Anderson, CEO of TerraStore Information Storage. His gray hair—close cropped in military style—and tanned skin were the perfect image for the leader of a company with critical government and defense contracts. "Host of my god's son," said Skotino, "you will harvest the haoma."

"Host of my god's father, I hear and obey," said Anderson.

Anderson's response was sharp, reflecting not only the precision with which he handled all his responsibilities but also his defensiveness about the haoma harvesting. Harvesting delays had also threatened the Circle's preparation. *Anderson might be the only one of the Six who will be relieved if the fetus is female yet again.*

With arms still outstretched, Skotino addressed the entire Circle of Six. "Host of my god's brother and hosts of my god's sons, for millennia we have toiled. The emergence has begun. We must prepare fecund Terra. From haoma, we will concoct the para-haoma—the nectar to transform ripe fetuses into my demon horde."

The Six together responded, "May our offer please the gods."

Skotino brought his outstretched arms together over the set of spikes looming over the small box.

He thrust his arms down, forcing the spikes into the holes, through the box, and out the bottom, completing the expiation.

| | 0  | | 0  | | 0

LAURA SAID GOOD-BYE TO MARIAN AND LEFT FOR HOME. HER pertran cruised the grand, curving streets of Marian's Ivyland neighborhood, exiting at the automated security checkpoint. The navigation computer calculated the shortest route home, taking Laura through some unsafe parts of town. Laura selected a different route that was a bit longer, taking her through the Philadelphia suburbs of Fort Washington, Whitemarsh, and Lancasterville. In these neighborhoods, like her own, the streets ran in a strict grid pattern with each block packed with the prefab residential units. The government had razed most areas with winding streets and sprawling homes. *What kind of neighborhood does Marian want for her son? Does she want him to be a target?* Reaching Wynnewood, her pertran turned onto the alley of her block.

"Pedestrian obstruction," the navigation system announced, and the vehicle decelerated to a stop.

Laura leaned forward to see the couple who lived in the corner house arguing in the middle of the alley. The husband was enraged. His face was flushed, and his belly fat jerked as he waved his arms. The wife looked exhausted, defeated, and embarrassed. Her eyes never met his. She looked like she wanted to run home, but he was in her way. She was pregnant and pretty far along.

Suddenly, the husband turned to look directly at Laura. He held the stare.

Laura leaned back and pressed the door lock button. A beeping sound indicated the doors were already locked. She reached for the tran's manual override switch.

The husband dropped the stare, turned, and grabbed the wife by the hair.

An involuntary sound escaped Laura's lips at the sight of it. She covered her mouth and looked away when she saw the wife's humiliation as he pulled her into the house.

The tran resumed its customary pace. Laura sat low in the seat and watched as they went inside. Rooted to the seat, she kept her eye on their back door through the rearview mirror.

The tran slowed again, this time on approach to the Richards home one house down on the opposite side of the alley. Ben had backed the university's van into the driveway, blocking the ramp to the garage level below their home. The pertran politely announced a new warning and came to a halt in the driveway.

Laura parked manually in the driveway. Before getting out, she looked back down the alley. She hesitated before unlocking the door. Marian lived so ostentatiously, but was it safer? With two incomes, Laura knew she and Ben could do better. No, on second thought, there was nothing wrong with the prefabs. They had elevators to be fully accessible to the elderly and handicapped—a nice convenience—and they were equipped with the state-of-the-art sec-comm home-security systems. But was all that better than a gated community?

Laura unlocked the door and got out. Looking into the back of the van, she saw computer equipment but no Ben. She walked down the short concrete ramp from the driveway into the open garage. The pocket door leading to the house opened with a swish.

"Ben, I'm home," she called out.

She took the elevator up to the first floor and into the kitchen. She sat down at the kitchen table and tapped the pubcomm display screen in the table's surface. A vid image of Ben's basement lab, three floors below, appeared on the screen. He was in the far corner, hunched over some of the same type of equipment that was in the van. "Ben, I'm home."

"Yup, I heard the seccomm announcement," he said without looking up.

"Do you want any lunch?"

"You go ahead," he said.

She tapped the screen, ending the comm. From the refrigerator and freezer, she took out her lunch ingredients. She scooped a serving of chia seed gel into the bottom of the blender and added frozen strawberries, frozen blueberries, fresh spinach, and a banana. She blended the ingredients and poured the slurry into a plastic glass, took a sip, and sat back down at the pubcomm.

She typed in a query about Lisa and the other abductions reported over the years. The articles described the particulars that made the cases similar and unusual. The missing persons were all young women ranging in age from late teens to midtwenties. In each case, the abductions seemed to occur just beyond the recorded forensic evidence—small areas where security-camera angles had a blind spot, where cameras were broken, or when security doors failed to log entry and exit. The aberrant circumstances made the cases impossible to investigate.

Scroll ... scroll ... scroll. She found a recent article and tapped it. A warning popped up on the screen saying the information was restricted. Her eyes widened. She stabbed at the display to close the connection, missed, stabbed again, and then logged off completely. The chair scraped the floor as she jumped up and backed away from the screen until she bumped into the counter. Through the window, she scanned the street and pulled the shade closed.

IIO IIO IIO

THE LIGHTS CAME BACK ON IN THE SANCTUARY. SKOTINO STEPPED back from the podium and looked down to make sure none of the blood dripping from the small box had splashed on his shoes or trousers. Tyvold got up from his seat to clean up the mess, as usual.

"Come to my office when you're through," Skotino said to Tyvold. Then to Spire, he said, "You, come with me."

Spire followed him into the adjoining office. Skotino walked to the floor-to-ceiling windows and took in the view as he contemplated. Miles of orange sand dotted with clusters of rock and brush surrounded the Nevada compound. Anyone who approached the megaron would have to cross open ground. He watched two birds of prey circling high in the clear, blue sky. The intense sunshine illuminated the room, yet the energy-efficient glass blocked the warmth.

"Vigilance is paramount now," Skotino said, still looking out the window.

"How?" asked Spire with his omnipresent whisper.

Skotino turned to him, just to know the point of emanation. "Statistically, finding the first male is inevitable. But after we take the males, we still need to dispose of the mothers. And as the emergence grows, we'll have more female fetus–mother pairs. The sheer volume. From now on, bring the bodies here to be disposed of in the same manner as the pharmakoi."

Spire nodded.

Tyvold entered the office with his shirtsleeves rolled up, wiping his hands with a towel.

To Tyvold, Skotino said, "Secrecy has aided us to this point, but it will only fuel suspicion if any part of our plan becomes exposed. We need a positive public image. Arrange a philanthropic gift. Very public. But the secrecy of our disposal site is more important than ever. Spire will bring the bodies here. What's the remaining capacity in the cavern?"

"We should have plenty of room—hundreds more, I think," said Tyvold. "But I'll ask Alvarez for a report when he comes to pick up the next expired pharmakos. It won't be long."

"So we'll need a fresh pharmakos?" Skotino asked rhetorically.

"Yes," said Tyvold. He flipped the bloodstained towel over his shoulder. "I think you'll be pleased."

# Chapter 2

CHELSEA PITT WATCHED THE EARLY MORNING LIGHT PEEK through the window shade, creating long shadows across rough imperfections on the bedroom ceiling of the London flat. Evangelos tugged at the duvet. He shifted and then shifted again. Chelsea remained still, feeling the heat of her body reflect off the quilted fabric. *It was a three tog night*, she thought, grinning at the cleverness of her own humor.

The alarm sounded, and Evangelos snapped out of bed. "Chelsea, we need to talk." His tone was sharp and intentionally loud. He rubbed the palm of his hand across his eyes and thick black eyebrows and then scratched the heavy stubble shadowing his deep olive skin.

Chelsea didn't move right away. She rolled over to face him—not rushing it, letting gravity do its magic—and then gently propped her head up on one elbow. Strands of blonde hair cascaded down, cover-

ing one eye. She guided a fingertip across her forehead and behind her ear to put the strands in place.
She smiled.

"Don't do that," he said.

"Why?" Her gaze drifted down his naked
body … the square pecs of his broad chest … and
down farther where it all tapered to his waist. His
six-pack was more like a four-pack, but still it was
clear why they used Greek men to pose for all those
statues. Her view of that cute little strip of black
curly hair, beginning just under his belly button, was
now somewhat obstructed. "I like the reaction I get."

"Argh." He stormed off to the shower room.

"I'm listening," she called after him playfully. She
swung her legs out of bed and pulled her percomm
from the nightstand. There were precious few messages from girlfriends—the ones who'd remained her
friends, anyway, once she'd started dating Evangelos.

She went to the wardrobe. Evangelos had relin-
quished about six inches of space on the left end of
the rung. *That will change*, she thought. *Soon, I'll
have whatever I want*. She reached into Evangelos's
side and pushed a hanger over, examined the shirt,
and then pushed again. She yanked a T-shirt off its
hanger and threw it over her head. Reaching behind
her neck, she pulled her hair up and out of the
shirt's collar and allowed it to spill down her back.
The neck of the shirt dipped on one side, shoulder
exposed. The shirt's bottom draped nearly to her
knees. Hearing the water run, she danced to the
shower room.

"Come on, tell me. What is it?" Her tone was sensual yet respectful.

"I've been thinking," he said, standing outside the shower stall. Noticing her gaze, he pulled a towel from the edge of the sink and wrapped it around his waist. "I love you dearly, Chels, you know that. And I don't want you to take this the wrong way. But I can't live this way anymore."

"I agree."

"You don't even know what I'm about to say. You are so frustrating!"

"Just tell me what you want, love."

"I want us to be married."

"I agree. See, I did know. Now, how is that frustrating? Do you think I should feel otherwise?"

"No, that's not the point."

"Right. The point is, if you want me to marry you, then you should ask me."

He didn't respond.

She continued, "You own this. If you weren't such a perfectionist, we'd be married by now."

"I'm not being a perfectionist. You need to understand my family's traditions. I can't propose before our families have been formally introduced."

"I do understand. Mum hasn't recovered yet. Your Greek upbringing isn't her fault. It's so far away. Why can't your family come here?"

"Your mum is perfectly fine. The cardiologist said so."

"Physically, yes, but she's still not herself. It was one thing to deal with the depression after

Father died, but now the stroke has given her a new excuse. She's a recluse. I'm tired of fretting with it. You ask her."

"I will."

"Fine." Steam billowed from the shower stall, clouding the top of the mirror. "You're still frustrated," she said, her tone sultry once again.

"That's the other thing. Do you have any idea the disgrace it would bring if you became pregnant?"

"Obviously, you're referring to yourself."

"Chels, you're not taking this seriously. I—"

"We've discussed this. Contraceptives are out of the question. They're not 100 percent effective. Celibacy is."

"Exactly! What about last weekend? Celibacy means no intercourse."

"That was just a leg over."

"Look, you keep saying that celibacy is 100 percent effective. But celibacy means 100 percent no intercourse. Leg-over spunk included!" he said. "Be honest with me. You're constantly reading that rubbish online about how all the celebrities are against contraception. It's a fad, Chels. Do you really believe anything online? It's pure swill! They all run about touting celibacy and then go on and on with intimate details of romantic relationships. It doesn't work that way for real people in real life, Chels!"

"That's entirely unfair."

"Unfair? You want to talk about fairness? You don't have any brothers. You don't understand how difficult it is—"

"Who suggested I move in with you?"

"I did, but—"

"And who's driving this marriage timeline?"

"We both are, but—"

"Both?"

"Well, I want it to be right with my family and your mum, and—"

"I know that. But don't say I'm creating all this pressure. Own it!"

||0 ||0 ||0

ON SUNDAY MORNING, BEN WAS ALREADY WORKING IN THE BASEment lab when Laura awoke. From the kitchen window above the sink, looking out over their tiny backyard, Laura could see it was going to be another hot and humid day.

The pubcomm announced an incoming comm. She sat down with her coffee and tapped the display. Her friend's image appeared on the screen. "Marian, good morning." Marian's expression looked unusual. After marrying Joe, she'd adopted a regal air, like she had a permanent audience to impress. But now she looked more like the teenage girlfriend Laura remembered so well from high school. Her expression was contrite, even desperate. "Is everything all right?"

"Yes," Marian said. "You know ... we had such a great time yesterday, I thought, well, I thought I would ask if you would help me pick up my groceries."

"You have your groceries delivered."

"Yes, I know." Her eyes glanced away for a moment. "But I thought we could go together."

Laura agreed and said she would swing by in an hour. Then she began to organize her own shopping list online.

From out in the hallway, she heard the elevator door open. Ben walked in to the kitchen wearing a white T-shirt and shorts. He'd obviously rolled out of bed and gone straight to the lab. Typical. He crossed to the counter and refilled his coffee cup.

He was so different from Joe. The four of them had never really gotten together as couples. Ben, being the polar opposite of materialistic, couldn't relate to Joe. Joe and Marian's lifestyle broadcasted their wealth—incredibly offensive behavior since the economic collapse following the health-care crisis. Joe had liked to impress people. But he'd made no impression on Ben. Nothing intentional. Such things just didn't reach Ben's conscious mind.

Ben crossed the room again, back to the elevator. She could tell he was engrossed in his work. She'd learned not to take it personally. Mostly.

"Ben," she called to him, "I'm going to pick up groceries. Is there anything you want?"

"No. Whatever is fine," he called back from the hallway.

She heard the elevator door open. "Say, before you go—is it bad if you get a search-denied warning?"

At first she wasn't sure if he heard her, but then he popped his head around the corner. "What kind of warning?"

"One that says the information is restricted."

"No. It thinks you're looking for restricted information. Just rephrase the query."

"Is the query attempt logged?"

"Yes, but that's not bad. Well, I suppose if you kept at it, the authorities might take notice. Why?"

"Just curious. Oh, one more thing—the scanners used in doors and gates, do they have logs?"

"The biometric scanners? Yes."

"Does anything prevent a log entry?"

"No. Unless it's broken, I guess."

"Yeah, that's what I thought too. Thanks!"

He seemed puzzled.

"Technology. Fascinating stuff, huh?" she offered.

He smiled and disappeared.

She tapped the submit button on her grocery order.

110 110 110

CARLOS ESPINOZA MOVED QUICKLY DOWN THE AISLE BETWEEN THE expanses of workstations on either side.

"Hey! Carlos! Hey, I've got the updated list of guests for the RKC event," came a voice from behind the cube wall as he passed.

"Yeah. Send it to me," Espinoza said without looking back.

"Will do," said the voice, "but, hey, I thought you were out of the office for the afternoon. Look, I've got a couple more—"

"I know!" Espinoza yelled. "I wasn't planning to be here. Just send it to me!"

Entering his office, Espinoza addressed the pub-comm display on the wall. "Computer, did my original three o'clock appointment get rescheduled?"

The pleasant female voice replied, "Yes. However, a subsequent message from the sales representative suggests dissatisfaction with the change."

"Great," he said sardonically. At his desk, with the few remaining minutes, he tapped out notes from his previous meeting. "Where is my visitor for the new three o'clock appointment?"

"Visitation status: cleared security. Visitor location: in transit. Escort enabled."

"Visitor summary," Espinoza demanded.

"Victor Tyvold is executive assistant at TerraHoldings, LLC. The TerraHoldings account was established six years ago. We have completed two previous public relations projects; both received a high rating. Average project revenue is—" The audio summary cut short automatically as the office door opened. Espinoza rose from his chair but stayed behind the desk.

The escort announced, "Sir, Mr. Victor Tyvold is here to see you."

The man stepped in and glanced around the room. It was difficult to judge Tyvold's age. His style of dress suggested tech-savvy elite—the type of person who could afford to look younger than he was. The title of executive assistant didn't seem to quite fit. *This guy is more executive than assistant.*

Tyvold approached Espinoza's desk and extended a hand.

Espinoza hesitated and then briskly shook his hand. *A lot of nerve.* Espinoza wasn't about to make this meeting pleasant. *Keep him off balance.* He let the tension hover, like the last two competitors in musical chairs—motionless, both anticipating the start of the music before circling the remaining chair.

"May I sit?" Tyvold asked.

Espinoza nodded.

Tyvold unbuttoned his sport coat, sat, and crossed his legs. Espinoza remained standing.

Finally, Espinoza said, "I'm sorry you felt the need to come down in person. I thought I was clear on the comm. We can't meet your requirements by your requested event date."

"I don't think that's true," said Tyvold.

"I don't expect you to understand."

"I understand perfectly well. You think the promotion of an event announcing a charitable donation isn't worthy of your firm's time."

Espinoza sat heavily. "Look, Mr. Tyvold, you're a good customer. I want to accommodate you ... but our business has grown. You must understand ... we accomplished our growth through careful advancement in the stature of our engagements, and thereby profit, not by taking on as much business as possible. Donations by organizations are certainly less common these days, but from a practical standpoint, I can't drive press to such an event that is ... lackluster, in the public's opinion."

"Your firm drives attention to events announcing new products. Unknown products. No luster. No opinion."

"Yes, of course, but we use veiled secrecy as a lure. The press and the public trust that the topic, once revealed, will be worth their time. In this case, however …"

"It has to be sexy? Something groundbreaking? Something novel? Something the public would find amazing?"

"Yes, exactly. Now, I realize you've offered to pay a premium. But you see, it's just not in line with the strategic direction of the firm. I'm sure another agency would be happy to take your business."

"The donation will be sizable."

"Sizable, huh? Are you a Hillite, Mr. Tyvold? Is that what this is about? I don't have the security for that. The protestors will be bad enough. You rub two pennies together, and you'll have a mob. But flaunt? You'll piss off a lot of people doing that. You want a riot on your hands? You'll have to cut the donation just to afford the tear gas."

"My employer is not a Hillite. He's a philanthropist."

"Sure."

"TerraHoldings is a conglomerate," said Tyvold. "TerraStore Information Storage, TerraLectric Solar Power, TerraProperty Real Estate, TerraMed Biotech. It's simple."

"It's boring." Espinoza leaned forward. "Look, I'm sorry. We covered all this on our comm. Nothing has changed. I don't know why you insisted on coming here. You're wasting my time."

Espinoza became aware of Tyvold. What a strange thought. *Of course I'm aware of him, he's sitting right in front of me.* The many business concerns in Espinoza's mind faded from his consciousness. Tyvold was looking directly at him, penetrating him, as if the man could see his own upside-down image on Espinoza's retina. The walls of his office seemed slanted somehow, distorted around Tyvold's face. The credenza on the far wall stretched into the distance.

Espinoza struggled to make sense of his feelings. A surprising rush of thoughts entered his mind. *How callous can the firm be? Maybe it should be named Scrooge & Marley. Is life just about profit? And how have I been a party to this? I'm no innocent bystander.*

An incident from Espinoza's past barged into his consciousness. *The old lady ... at the masstran station. She was unsteady, clinging to a pole, the torrent of people coursing around her. She needed help to sit down ... to rest. The look on her face ... fear ... desperation. I ignored her. I passed right by, and I ignored her.*

Then the memory of Espinoza's nephew flashed into his mind, vivid and corporeal. *My brother kept telling me, "It's cystic fibrosis." Cystic fibrosis? I didn't even look it up. Doctors can fix anything, right? Dear God, the years my brother had to watch the boy struggle for every breath. I was too busy to visit. I ignored him. I ignored both of them.* An image crashed into Espinoza's mind. His nephew, gasping for air. From memory? No, he never visited. The boy ... gasping for air. The last moment. No strength to move a breath in or out. Mouth open. Open wider. Then he *was* his nephew.

Mouth open as wide as possible, gaping. The burning in his chest. Neck straining. Mouth open even wider. *Oh my god, the end was horrible!*

"Please! Stop! Don't! I …" Espinoza began to sob.

"You'll promote my donation," said Tyvold. He stood.

"Yes," said Espinoza. "Yes, of course." The dimensions of the room returned to normal. His mind and memory cleared of the past few minutes except for a deep yearning to work on the event. To douse the flames of guilt. To make things right. To find a way to live with himself. Commit himself fully. A salve for his blistering self-disgust.

"You'll send your plan to my office?" Tyvold turned for the door.

Espinoza nodded. "Yes."

||0 ||0 ||0

ARRIVING AT MARIAN'S HOUSE, LAURA'S PERTRAN ROUNDED THE circle drive. She got out and noticed the garage behind the house. All the doors were up. She walked to the corner of the house for a better look, but Marian's two pertrans were nowhere in sight. And the rest of the garage space looked unusually empty, no tools and only a few things on the shelves. The garage could hold four vehicles, but the largest thing in there was the trash container.

Laura walked back and up the front steps.

"Visitor arriving. Quantity one," she heard the seccomm announcement from inside.

Laura waited for Marian to come to the door. With the pregnancy, she was moving more slowly.

"Visitor arriving. Quantity one."

Finally, the door swished open.

"Ready?" Marian asked, waddling out of the door, purse in hand. Her demeanor was just like the comm that morning. *Is it the pregnancy or something else?* She seemed in a rush to get in the tran.

Laura hardly got the tran moving before Marian said, "Say, have you and Ben thought about starting a family? I mean, I've never really sensed a strong feeling from you. Is there anything … wrong?"

"Uh, well, I don't think there's anything wrong with the plumbing—that I know of, anyway, if that's what you mean," said Laura. "Ben and I haven't spent much time talking about it. Neither one of us thinks of ourselves as the parenting type, I guess. Well, maybe I shouldn't speak for him. But we both like our work. I don't have a huge maternal drive."

"But it's not that you don't like kids or any-thing?" she asked, hesitantly.

"No, no, no. You know I can't wait for you to have your baby boy. Is that what's worrying you? That I'm not going to want to be friends after he's born?"

"No, not exactly." She shifted in her seat.

"What then?"

"Well, what do you think about the idea of you and Ben being the baby's godparents?" Marian squinted, like a balloon might pop in her face.

"Uh, well, I don't know," said Laura. "I guess I don't have any idea what it means to be a godparent.

You know I'm not very religious. Ben isn't, either, I'm pretty sure."

"Well, it doesn't have to be about religion." Marian shifted in her seat again. "It just means you would support him if I couldn't."

"Oh, everything's going to be fine. We're happy to help without all that formality."

Marian didn't say anything. She picked at the upholstery with her fingernail and looked out the window. She had the look again, like a little girl. No, not young, she was like she had been before meeting Joe. Joe had been the kind of man who took care of everything. Once they were married, Marian had no worries—and it showed in the way she carried herself, the way she viewed the world. That was all cracking now. Laura looked at Marian's purse. So offensive to carry one these days. Marian was oblivious. Now, it didn't fit her at all.

"Sure," said Laura finally. "We'll be the baby's godparents. I'll talk to Ben. I'm sure he'll agree."

| | 0   | | 0   | | 0

MARK SPIRE ARRIVED AT LAS VEGAS INTERNATIONAL AIRPORT under orders from Skotino to prepare their equipment for transport. They needed to move quickly once Vega determined the gender of the fetus.

Inside the airport's passenger terminal, Spire approached the checkpoint to the private gates. The crowd of protestors was bigger than usual. He kept his distance. He tapped a message to Tyvold, letting him know he'd arrived and now needed a few more minutes to prepare before mixing into the crowd to reach the checkpoint.

"Enough is enough!" yelled a protestor in Spire's general direction. Other protestors took notice.

Thankfully, they weren't looking at him but rather behind him, farther down the airport corridor. He turned to look too. A small group of men approached, heading for the checkpoint. Spire took a close look at the group as it passed. A VIP and his entourage. The bodyguards tightened the protective envelope around the man in the center strutting toward the checkpoint.

"Enough is enough!" chanted the protestors. Individuals lifted signs into the air. The words GREED DESTROYS appeared on one, while another read CHARITY IS SALVATION. Airport police pushed the crowd apart, creating a narrow gauntlet. As the bodyguards advanced, they pulled out batons and swung at the arms reaching over the shoulders of the police line. Jeers erupted from the crowd: "Hillite bastard!" and "Enough is enough!" among others.

Spire watched the VIP and his entourage pass single file through the checkpoint's biometric scanner and across to the other side. Getting through the scanner himself was simple, thanks to Tyvold's computer wizardry, but first he had to get to the checkpoint without drawing attention. He needed to relax. *Concentrate*, he told himself.

*Hear me, god, cloud victim's eyes*

*Naught escape a familiar guise*

*Intimacy without foundation*

*Familiarity before acceptation*

*In victim's mind, recollection thou shall flip*

*For the chance of reality's path doth tip*


Ready now, he meandered toward the crowd. The protestor closest to him turned, residual anger from the VIP incident still visible on his face.

*Concentrate*, Spire coached himself. *Take it slow.*

The protestor's expression changed from anger to recognition, even giving a nod of acknowledgment. "Hey, Horowitz, didn't expect to see you here."

"Yeah, go figure," replied Spire, confident the sound of his voice, like the image he projected, was received warmly—the appearance and voice of a friend, a person Spire had never met, stolen from the man's mind.

The protestor waved to Spire and then looked past him, ignoring him, eyes darting, evaluating anyone approaching the checkpoint, the determined expression returning to his face.

Spire inched his way through the crowd, allowing familiarity to penetrate each individual. A police officer stood by the biometric scanner. *Tyvold's turn*, Spire thought.

The barrier swished open, and Spire stepped across to the protected terminal area, leaving the raucous crowd behind. He proceeded to TerraHoldings' private gate.

LAURA OPENED THE SMALL STORAGE COMPARTMENT NEXT TO HER seat after arriving at the parking ramp next to the grocery warehouse. "I've got an extra grocery bag for you. I hope your order will fit." She pulled out two nylon sacks.

"Sorry. I didn't think about that," said Marian anxiously.

"It's all right," said Laura. "I can manage both bags." The pertran door glided open. Laura hopped out, turned, and offered her hand.

Marian didn't move, her eyes huge with exaggerated alertness.

"Jeez, Marian. Now you're making me nervous."

"You learned to live with it. I hid behind Joe. He's gone now."

"Living? More like a cold war in a dystopia. It's coping. I just don't like conflict."

"Don't get academic with me. I don't like it, either. It's why we're friends. Help me."

"When was the last time you picked up groceries?"

"Years ago. Not since I started dating Joe."

Marian still seemed paralyzed. Laura took a moment to really look at her. Her hair was curled as usual, her makeup was fresh, and her maternity outfit was more fashion than function. She still wore her wedding ring as well as a bracelet on each wrist.

"Let's review it first." Laura got back in the pertran and sat next to her. "When you walk through the door, it sends a message to the warehouse in back to start picking your order. You did place your order online, right?"

"Yes," said Marian. "That's the way it works when they deliver the groceries."

"OK, good. Then we get in line at the register. The bins will come on the conveyer belt from the warehouse. The customers in front of us will transfer their items to their bags and pay. Remember, the important thing is, keep your head down or look away while the other customers are packing and paying."

"Why? What will they do to me?"

"Nothing. Don't be ridiculous." Laura recalled the determined look on the students' faces during the rally on campus. "It's just polite, that's all."

"Are they going to stare at me? They always stare at me."

"Marian, most people are unemployed, right?" She still seemed confused. "Marian, honestly, put yourself in their shoes. The food and clothing they can buy with the federal subsidy is a set list—"

"I can't do this!" Marian's eyes started flitting in all directions.

"No one's going to hurt you," Laura said as she hopped out again. "Come on."

Marian leaned forward in the seat, jerking unsteadily.

Laura grabbed her arm, not sure what she was trying to do.

Marian clung to her, hugging her arm, weeping now.

"Marian, what is it?"

"You said I should put myself in their shoes," she said. "I don't have any choice!"

"I don't understand."

"He left me nothing! Joe left me nothing! We have debt, Laura. Did you know that? I had no idea. I told you I hid behind Joe, but it was his wealth I hid behind. The life insurance money is gone now. I had to sell everything." She cried into her hands. Then she lifted her head and gripped Laura's arm. "Do you know why I asked you to pick me up at the clinic? I had to take the masstran. A filthy, stinking pig-pen on wheels. Everyone stared at me. I'm pregnant, and no one would give up their seat. They were all Hoods! They can tell I'm not one of them! Like they can smell it!"

"Shhhh! Keep your voice down," said Laura, scanning the parking ramp. *Unemployed people don't own pertrans*, she reminded herself, *usually*. "Pull it together, or I'll take you back home."

||O ||O ||O

*OH MY GOD, I CAN'T BELIEVE I'M ACTUALLY HERE*, thought Chelsea. *This is fantastic!* The public appearance by James Lovejoy was under tight security. It took her nearly an hour to make her way down to the underground garage of London's Hotel Branson. At the parking garage door to the hotel, velvet ropes stretched across six sets of poles extending out to the point where James would arrive at any moment. The ropes straddled a crimson carpet where James would actually walk, in person, just a couple of meters in front of her. *Fantastic!* Dozens of girls crammed into the area on both sides of the crimson carpet. Chelsea had arrived too late to be one of the lucky ones in the first row, but she could still see the path in the center and the group facing them, pressed up against the ropes on the other side.

Lovejoy was returning to the hotel after a music recording session. The buzz of the crowd was intense as the sound reflected off the gray concrete walls of the enormous underground parking garage. At the far end, Chelsea could see the garage door his tran was expected to pass through. Several security men lined the short route from the door to where the crowd waited.

Chelsea always dreamed of an opportunity like this. Her father, while alive, had a few years of employment, but not enough to make a difference. Growing up, she could only read about the celebrities online. She was thrilled when Evangelos said he could get her credentials. Once they were married, she would do this sort of thing all the time, or better yet, she'd be famous for marrying such a wealthy man, and she'd be the one walking down the carpet. *Fantastic!*

Girls around her tittered in anticipation with their friends. Chelsea had come alone. Evangelos was angry when she'd asked for a second set of credentials. She didn't mean to be ungrateful. It would just be more fun with a girlfriend. *They're never going to believe it!*

She watched the girls talking and giggling. She scanned the crowd. She might be the only one alone. Then she saw a man, a very big man, in the crowd on the other side. He also seemed to be alone. A plain-clothes security man, probably.

A loud mechanical sound muted the crowd instantly. The huge steel garage door at the far end began to roll up. The girls screamed. Chelsea screamed too. Girls in front of her thrust their percomms into the air. Chelsea pulled out her own, started a vid recording, and raised it above her head. A large black limousine cruised down the ramp and approached the frenzy. Chelsea struggled to see through the sea of arms. The vehicle came to a stop at the end of the carpet, and the door opened as girls screamed even louder.

"James! Here, over here!" yelled the girls.

James Lovejoy looked just like his pics and vids online. He waved to the crowd and touched hands as he passed. Chelsea wasn't close enough to reach, but she angled her percomm as best she could.

"I'm here! Over here!" Chelsea yelled, jumping now. If only she could catch his glance. *I can't believe I'm actually here. Oh my god, he's gorgeous!* She felt tears stream from her eyes and saw several others with mascara smeared across flushed cheeks.

James walked up the hotel entrance steps, turned, blew a kiss to the crowd, and then disappeared. It was over.

Several girls continued crying, holding each other. The crowd began to break up. Chelsea wiped her eyes and looked at her percomm. She couldn't wait to post the vid online. *They're not going to believe it!* She tapped to find the recording.

"Virgin," came a man's voice from behind.

Startled, Chelsea looked up and turned. The large security man was right behind her. *Talking to me?* He was even bigger up close.

"What?" she said.

"Do you know how the hotel got its name?" he asked.

"Excuse me? I don't know you. I—"

"Sir Richard Branson," he said. "The names of all his businesses used the same word. Did you know that?"

Chelsea put away her percomm and backed up.

"Virgin," said the man. "The word that Branson used was virgin."

||0 ||0 ||0

SPIRE PROCEEDED TO TERRAHOLDINGS' PRIVATE GATE AND WENT directly to the cargo staging room. The containers in the room appeared to be as he'd left them. He accessed the manifest from his percomm. He opened the first shipping container and started his inspection.

An incoming comm interrupted him. It was Tyvold.

"Well?" asked Spire.

"It's a male."

"Finally," said Spire. "Skotino must be relieved."

"No, he's in a rage."

"Why?"

"Vega actually spoke to the mother," said Tyvold.

"What!"

"Yeah, he thought he was being witty."

"Dumbass," said Spire.

"Exactly. Finish up. We need to get over there."

110 110 110

"WE DON'T HAVE TO DO THIS," SAID LAURA. TOGETHER THEY rounded the street corner from the parking ramp to the grocery pickup warehouse. She wanted to at least hold Marian's hand, but she'd resisted. The heat of the day was in full swing. Laura felt sticky. The door to the grocery warehouse was only half a block away now, but with the sun beating down, it seemed much farther.

"I do," said Marian.

"Huh?"

"I have to do this, or I'll starve," said Marian.

Laura heard the inner frailty—the voice of her teenage girlfriend. "Oh, nonsense." Marian seemed to be on the edge. Before leaving the pertran, Laura was able to convince her to at least take off the extra jewelry. That seemed to provide some assurance that this would go better than the masstran ride. But she'd refused to leave the purse behind. It dangled from her elbow now, bobbing back and forth like a middle finger in the face of every unemployed person.

"Not so fast," said Marian.

"Sorry."

Laura went through the security door first. The seccomm panel emitted a beep and a green light. Marian walked through next and followed Laura to the line of customers. The grocery clerk at the register smiled in greeting.

Laura watched the next plastic bin slide down on a track of metal rollers through the opening in the wall from the warehouse. The bin coasted to a stop by the customer at the front of the line. Laura and the other patrons looked away respectfully as the man packed his items. Laura glanced to Marian. She was staring. Laura touched her shoulder, caught her eye, and gave her a disapproving look. Marian's eyes grew wide, and she dropped her head like an anchor.

"Pull it together," whispered Laura.

The beep from the register was the signal to look up again. Idle conversations resumed until the next bin appeared.

When it was Laura's turn, she unfolded her grocery sack. The bin rolled down the conveyor and bumped to a stop. In her periphery, she saw everyone look away. She packed her items, filling the insulated section of the bag first with the frozen peas and frozen chicken breast. Then she loaded fresh lettuce, almonds, quinoa, soy milk, and tofu.

What had Marian ordered? She didn't know and didn't want to know. That was the point. Laura and Ben selected products from the federal subsidy list out of respect to the unemployed, even though they could order any product they wanted. One income gave them all the freedoms that employed people enjoyed. Two incomes was extremely rare. But nothing like the way Marian and Joe lived. To think it all suddenly collapsed. Laura couldn't imagine what Marian was going through. There was no telling what innocent faux pas might spark resentment and anger in an unemployed person.

Laura pressed her percomm to the display counter. A beep confirmed the payment—there was no way to tell if the funds were from earned wages or food credits.

Everyone looked up. Laura lifted the sack, smiled to the clerk, and waited as Marian went next.

The bin stopped in front of Marian. Before glancing away, Laura saw a look of panic on her face.

*Not now!* thought Laura. "What? What's wrong?" Laura whispered as discreetly as possible.

"It's not my order," Marian said. She put her hand over her mouth, and her eyes were huge.

The clerk frowned and read the register display screen. "Peter DeJannet?" the clerk asked, confusion in his voice, knowing it was wrong.

The customer behind Marian cleared his throat. "Uh, that's me."

"No. It should be Marian Lumière! I'm Marian Lumière. It's not my order," she said, her eyes wild.

The patrons all looked away. The discomfort from Marian's embarrassment was tangible.

"Marian, it's OK. We'll—"

"It's not my order!" Marian yelled.

The customers backed away. Laura backed away too, instinctively. "Marian, please, don't—"

"It's not my order!"

Marian pushed herself away from the counter, heading for the exit. She stumbled, reached for Laura, and faltered.

Laura tried to catch her, dropping the grocery bag.

Marian collapsed into her arms, still screaming, "It's not my order!"

Laura held on to her as they both went down. It was all Laura could do to keep her head from hitting the linoleum floor.

"Oh god, no!" Marian yelled out, gripping her stomach.

Laura felt warmth slosh around her knee. A pool of clear fluid expanded across the floor.

"No!" Marian cried hysterically. Then the saturated material of Marian's dress darkened. Red streaks of blood streamed into the liquid.

"Call for help!" Laura yelled.

Marian grabbed Laura's shirt, pulling her close, the look of agony on her face.

Laura, only inches away, said, "Hold on!"

"Reviver ... level ... tirrit," Marian's back arched grotesquely. "Murdrum ... redivider ... solos."

"What? I don't understand."

The sight was nearly unbearable. Marian's eyes rolled back in her head, leaving only the whites. Then, like a light switch, her body relaxed. "Nun ... mom ... deified." The contortions in her face vanished, and the brick-red color began to recede. Marian looked at Laura now, as natural as could be, like a conversation they might've had as teens, and said, "We're OK now." Her neck went limp, head tilting back, eyes still open.

||O ||O ||O

LAURA PUSHED THROUGH THE ELEVATOR DOORS AND RUSHED through the hospital corridor to the maternity ward. She ran to the nurses' station and then saw Ben at the end of the hall. She ran to him.

"Thank you for meeting me," she said.

"Sure."

"It was horrible. I tried to come as soon as I could, but the paramedics kept asking more questions. I thought it would never end. Have you been waiting long?"

"No, no problem."

"I just can't believe she died."

Ben wasn't looking at her. She wasn't sure if he was even listening. He had that distracted look. Then, remembering, she followed his gaze. Behind the glass was the nursery. Medical personnel were attending to several infants. Ben was looking at one nurse rocking a swaddled infant.

"Is that her baby?" she asked.

"Yes."

"Is he all right? I mean, is he healthy and everything?"

"Seems to be," he said. "The ER doc came up to talk with me." Then he added, "After your comm, I got another from the police. Did you know Marian listed us as next of kin? Not just in case of emergency, but next of kin?" Ben was speaking without taking his eyes off the rocking baby on the other side of the glass.

"Yes," Laura said, "I mean, sort of. Marian talked about us being godparents. I was going to ask you about it." Unable to resist it any longer, Laura put her arms around her husband. "I never thought it would come to this!"

He put his arm around her clumsily.

She cried uncontrollably and buried her face in his chest. She took a deep breath.

Ben was still looking into the nursery.

"Are you upset?" she asked.

He turned to her. "No. I mean, I guess you're telling me he's going to be ours."

"His name is Chris," she said.

"OK." He looked back to the baby.

"What is it? Is something wrong?"

"You said they had questions."

"Yes. The paramedics were doing their best. There was a complication, I guess. There was a lot of blood." She squeezed her eyes shut at the recollection. "My god, Ben, it was horrible. Marian started screaming nonsense words. I didn't know what to do."

"The doctor told me that the paramedics couldn't get the medical scanner to work."

"That must have been it," said Laura. "I remember now. For some reason, the doctors could never get those silly things to work." She waited for Ben's expression to clear, but it didn't. He was still looking away, through the glass.

"Did Marian ever mention the scanner problem before she was pregnant?"

"I don't know. I don't recall. She was always healthy. I can't think of a reason that would ever come up. It doesn't matter now, right?"

Ben didn't say anything. He didn't move. He just watched the baby.

"What is it? You're scaring me."

"The doctor said they should know very soon now exactly how Marian died." Ben finally looked down into her eyes. "They will know because the scanner is working perfectly on her now. But ..."

"But what, for god's sake?"

"The postnatal scanner," he said, returning his gaze to the baby. "It doesn't work on *him*."

# Chapter Three

**P**ETE RASMUSSEN, SENIOR RESEARCH DIRECTOR AT
TerraStore, waited with the other members
of his team in the control room eight hundred meters
underground. The security monitors showed the elec-
tric cart, essentially an industrial golf cart, departing
from the main tunnel junction. It held two riders: the
driver wearing a white hard hat and the passenger
wearing a green hard hat. The unique green color
was reserved for the CEO alone, Rick Anderson. The
cart seemed tiny as it glided through the enormous
tunnels, like a single blood cell flowing through a
vast network of arteries.

*Damn! What does he want now?*

"Listen," Pete said, turning to the group, "he's on
his way. Let's walk through it one more time." Pete
nodded to his staff, the several scientists in white
lab coats sitting at control stations around the room
and the half dozen technicians in protective clothing standing by. They looked like kids on a baseball

diamond, waiting for the owner of the house with the broken window to come out.

The appointed scientist straightened in his chair, cleared his throat, and looked around the room. "Well, we've detected neutrino bursts consistently. The average interval has been seventy hours. However, six days ago, we failed to detect a burst at the expected interval. Initially, we were unable to determine the cause. Then we found an error in the detection subroutines—" The scientist reached for a trash can. He leaned over it with a sickening heave, his mouth opening wide, uncontrollably, his face beet red. His eyes bugged out as he shuddered under the convulsive strain. Viscous strings of bile dripped into the basket.

Pete could almost taste the sourness at the back of his own throat. The only sound in the room was the scientist gasping and spitting into the basket. Pete gave him time to recover.

*What does Anderson want? What is he going to ask that he hasn't already? Anderson doesn't want excuses.* But there were plenty. The laboratory's location was far from ideal: deep under Yucca Mountain in Nevada, built secretly at the same time as its closest neighbor, the infamous Yucca Mountain Nuclear Waste Repository. The government needed a place to store material of any type—for any reason—without prying eyes. *Working under the veil of secrecy made everything difficult.*

The laboratory tank, used to harvest the unbihexium, was originally built to store crude oil as a fail-safe for the Strategic Petroleum Reserve. It could hold 1.5 million cubic meters of oil. But as the US energy industry converted from oil to renewable forms of energy, especially solar, oil lost its strategic significance, and the tank remained empty. As reliance on oil and nuclear fission declined, the government's secret complex became obsolete. The cost of maintaining the facility became a liability. Anderson's firm had agreed to take ownership, ostensibly as a geologically stable vault for the world's data. TerraStore always seemed to be at the right place and the right time.

Unbihexium, atomic number 126, didn't exist on Earth, but serendipity revealed a reaction that yielded a few atoms. Liquid $CH_2O$, commonly known as formaldehyde, catalyzed a reaction between a neutrino buildup lasting only a fraction of a second followed by a perfectly timed discharge of high-energy electrons at the peak of the buildup. The reaction formed trace amounts of unbihexium-310, a stable isotope.

Out of work for two years, Pete didn't hesitate to take the job to modify the tank and build a fully automated process to produce unbihexium. *Anderson should be grateful to have me. I'm the only one who could come up with this design. Between the refrigeration system and the extraction filters, I've done everything right.*

"But we fixed the computer code. Harvesting of the unbihexium has resumed," the scientist concluded, looking toward Pete.

Pete glanced at the security vid feed. The cart pulled up to the door outside the lab. *What the hell does a company that stores data need with unbihexium, anyway?* It was a question he didn't have the courage to ask. The display switched to a different camera showing Anderson walking down the access tunnel to the control room.

Pete opened the door at just the right moment. With an overly enthusiastic smile, he said, "Mr. Anderson, please come in. We've been expecting you."

Anderson slowed as he crossed the threshold. His face passed a mere inch in front of Pete's.

Pete's smile vanished.

Anderson entered the control room. He walked in a circle, surveying each person in the room before facing Pete. "Well?"

Pete felt his face flush red. All eyes were on him—eyes registering his humiliation, his embarrassment, his fear. He felt as though the heat from his flushed forehead and cheeks radiated to everyone in the room, like the sun in winter when it emerges from behind a cloud.

"Report!" yelled Anderson.

As rehearsed, the appointed scientist began the explanation.

He'd uttered only a few words before Anderson yelled, "No!" He looked at Pete and demanded, "No. This time, I want it from you."

Losing bladder control, Pete pressed a hand to his crotch, pinching off the stream of urine. He felt the warmth against his leg followed by the coolness of moist cloth. Most of his team had to look down or away. One scientist cradled her face in her hands.

"Everything's fine now," he blurted out, forgetting completely the organized explanation they'd rehearsed.

"Last time, it was because you lost the connection to the detectors."

"We've checked everything."

"How do you know the detector system won't fail again?"

"There's no way to test the sys—"

"I don't care about what you can't do!" exploded Anderson. "Is the detector system redundant?"

"No, no, that wasn't part of the design. We—"

"Not part of the design? You mean, not part of *your* design!"

In Pete's mind, Anderson's voice took on a haunting tone, reminiscent of a bully from his childhood, taunting him. The dimensions of the room distorted.

*Of course it's my fault. I'm supposed to be in charge. I let everyone down.* An image appeared in Pete's mind. A scientist from his team was explaining to his wife how he'd lost his job. The look on the wife's face ... the disgrace, the loss of pride, the inevitable humiliation that would follow once family and friends found out. Scenes flashed in Pete's mind showing the devastating experience for each member of his team. *Their lives are ruined! It's all my fault.*

The intense emotion lifted, and Pete realized, like waking from a nightmare, that he had a chance to avoid that future. The room was quiet except for the sound of soft sobs coming from someone in the back.

Anderson surveyed the group and said, "You have forty-eight hours to get it fixed." Anderson moved to the exit and left.

Pete looked down at his wet trousers and heard more sobs.

||0 ||0 ||0

ON THE RIDE HOME FROM THE HOSPITAL, LAURA WATCHED BEN FLIP through messages. "Do you have to do that now?"

"Why not?" He didn't look up.

"Well … what are we going to do? About Chris?"

"Right now? Nothing we can do right now." He gave her a quirky kind of smile, a smile she couldn't remember ever seeing before. "Marian was your close friend," he said. "I assume you'll be sad for a while." He looked down again.

Facts. That was Ben—always correct, rarely helpful. She searched her own feelings. "Marian was your friend too."

"Fine." He sat up.

Moments passed. The sun was just starting to set. A brilliant orange curtain stretched across the sky behind long pink clouds.

"I'm going to visit Father Arnold," Laura said finally.

"OK. Tell him I said hi."

||0 ||0 ||0

THE TERRAHOLDINGS CORPORATE SCRAMJET CAME TO REST IN THE private hangar at London's Heathrow Airport at dusk. The hatch opened like a clamshell, the bottom half with steps. Skotino descended to the hangar floor.

Big Vega had already hopped out of the corporate van and started to unload crates from the jet's cargo hatch.

Spire emerged from the jet holding the silver briefcase and joined Skotino.

"How much unbihexium-310 did Anderson harvest?" Skotino asked Spire.

Spire hefted the case comically, as if he could tell by weight. "Barely a gram. How much do we need to transform the haoma to parahaoma?"

"Tyvold will continue clarity communions. The gods know. We should learn soon."

Spire nodded, walked to the van, and placed the briefcase inside.

Vega lifted a huge crate to his shoulder and carried it to the van.

Spire called to Vega, "There's a hand truck, dumbass."

"Help yourself, dumber-ass."

Their bickering grated like dueling calliopes. Skotino walked to the open hangar door. Navigation lights lined the taxiways across the tarmac, stretching out to the horizon. He watched the faint glow of pink and orange fade to indigo. Darkness had descended upon London.

| | 0 | | 0 | | 0

LAURA HADN'T BEEN BACK TO THE CHURCH SINCE HER MARRIAGE. She peered out the vehicle's window at rows of three-story prefabs as she passed. Each house was nice but ordinary and nearly identical to the one before. It was impossible to tell which families had employment. Pertran ownership was a determining factor, but with the garages one story below ground, who could tell? Anyway, the neighborhood seemed safe.

Her pertran slowed its approach. The church was just as she remembered: an old stone structure complete with stained-glass windows in brilliant colors. Beautiful landscaping surrounded the little building with even more color. Nestled in the row of larger, taller prefab units, the church looked like a Boy Scout standing in a line of soldiers in gray uniforms: sharply at attention but shorter and more colorful, neckerchief and merit badges arranged neatly with great care. The church decorations were gifts from nature, not fabricated; the beauty was from hard work, not a catalog.

After the tran completed the auto-park cycle, Laura walked up the short stretch of pavement. The last time she'd been here was her wedding day. She remembered coming down those steps, smiling and holding Ben's hand. *It's all still the same.*

Someone had just watered the flowers and sprayed the pavement clean, and beads of water glistened along leaves and petals. The air was heavy with the humid fragrances of earth. Bees gracefully visited the blooms. She remembered the sense of peace she'd felt on her wedding day, the feelings of exhilaration and anticipation about her future with Ben.

Inside, unlike her wedding day, the church was empty and quiet. She allowed her eyes to adjust. Father Arnold waved to her from across the sanctuary.

"Laura! It's so nice to see you again. I was so pleased to take your comm. I'm terribly sorry for your loss. Please, come in and sit down." He ushered her into his office just to the right of the altar.

"Thank you, Father."

After hearing the events leading up to Marian's tragic death, Father Arnold said, "So you said over the comm that Marian had asked you and Ben to be godparents. What are your thoughts?"

"Well, I was hoping you could help me figure that out. To be perfectly candid, I don't know what I think."

"OK." Father Arnold pondered a moment. "Let me ask you some questions. Let's start by taking the word apart. Godparent. We'll start with the word *god*. Who is God to you, and how does he fit in?"

"I was afraid you were going to ask me something like that. You see, I work at Ben-U. I'm a professor of political science. It's very academic, naturally. I'm married to a professor of advanced computing and astrophysics. I live in a world of science, a black-and-white world. God isn't a part of it, at least not on the surface."

"I see. Have you ever asked Ben about God or how God is related to the scientific world he works in?"

"No," said Laura.

"This involves both of you." He paused. "Let's flip it around. How do you think it would be if God had no influence in your life or in the lives of others around you?"

"Part of me wants to say that nothing would be different, and another part of me thinks that everyone would be mean to each other or something. Lots of crime? Chaos or anarchy maybe? I'm sorry, Father; I feel so ashamed for not having more of an opinion about this."

"It's quite all right. Now, let's talk about the word *parent*. Obviously, Marian was to be the mother, not you, but now you need to think about how the word *parent* fits you."

"I guess Marian was thinking she was going to be overwhelmed when the baby arrived—that she'd need help."

"Yes. After losing Joe, I'm sure that's true," said Father Arnold. "Hmm. Just now, you said she expected to need help, but think beyond the obvious. What do you think the child needs that you could help with?"

Laura thought for a long time. "Love?"

He smiled and nodded. "Do you see a relationship between the two words, *god* and *parent*?"

"I think so," she replied.

"Excellent. Laura, I'd like you to come and see me again after you get through these immediate challenges. If there's anything I can do, please let me know. And I have homework for you. I'd like you to ask Ben about his beliefs."

TYVOLD ENTERED ROOM NUMBER TWO BUT HELD THE DOOR OPEN
as he evaluated the sight in front of him. Lisa was
secured to the chair in the middle of the room, asleep,
her head tilted all the way back. Her mouth was
open, and she was breathing gravely. Her left eyeball
had been punctured during a previous visit, and the
viscous juice within had long ago streamed down her
face, the aqueous humor dried and matted in her hair.
Black, purple, and green bruises covered the left side
of her face. The skin of her left cheek had been torn
open, making her look as if she had two mouths. Her
left arm was twisted backward, dislocated completely
at the shoulder, the forearm and hand bent at an
unnatural angle, as well. The nails of her exposed left
foot had been ripped off, and each toe was crusted
with rock salt and blood that was black with age. The
big toenail remained in place, but a drill bit stuck out
of it like a toothpick through an olive.

Tyvold felt the anticipation of clarity arousing him in a vaguely sexual way. He slammed the
door shut.

Lisa's head jerked forward. Her one eye blinked
and squinted his way.

He could tell she was close to the end. She hadn't
eaten in days. The physical weakness and dehydra-
tion were apparent. He took the cup of water with the
straw from the counter and offered it to her.

Leaning her head down and to the side, she
plugged the hole in her cheek with her tongue and

sipped. Then she spit the water at his face. The water didn't go much beyond her lips. Mixed with dried blood, it dribbled out of her mouth and ruptured cheek.

Tyvold smirked. "I think your left side needs some more work." After setting the cup down, he evaluated the variety of tools along the wall above the counter like a child peering at shelves in a toy store.

"Why ... left?" she asked, her words sloppy.

"You don't get answers while you're here. Only I do." *She'll expire soon. But such a unique girl. What's the difference*? he thought. "If you must know, it's more effective. It has to do with how pain affects the brain in the opposite hemisphere, where specific feelings are processed."

"Effective?"

He tried to decide if she was stalling or truly curious. Lisa had lasted quite a while. Her will to live was strong. Reaching clarity was straightforward with her. "Communion with my god ... the stimulation on the left side creates a clearer connection. Historians believe pharmakoi were executed. No, they were just stoned or beaten. It's about communication, not penance. The left side works best."

Her eyelid blinked heavily, and her head drooped.

"I don't expect you to comprehend," he said loudly.

Her head jerked up again.

From the assortment of instruments, he selected a ball peen hammer. *Skotino's the real master. Fear is more valuable than pain. The scab eating really sets the mood for all the visits that follow.* "Let's break a rib this time."

Her eye opened wide.

The clarity sensation swelled. Standing in front of her, he placed his left hand on the back of the chair and leaned forward to let his body tower over her, invading her space. The wave of fear filled him, but the intensity was disappointing. He looked across her rib cage, analyzing. Conveniently, her left arm was twisted out of the way.

In one swift motion, he grabbed her shirt at the shoulder and yanked. The spandex ripped, exposing her bra and rib cage.

She cringed and gurgled.

Again, the wave was disappointing. Fear—the anticipation of pain—prior to actual pain was the path to reach clarity, not pain alone. Sinistraspherical pain completed the pathways for communication, but more importantly, it served to create memories for the next encounter, a form of self-fulfilling prophecy.

Hammer at the ready, he selected the target rib, pulled his hand back, and struck hard.

She screamed, but the rib didn't break.

Her fear response lagged and waned. Her usefulness was coming to an end. He swung again, harder.

The sound extracted from her this time was more of a grunt. Again, the rib didn't break. The waves of fear were cresting but not curling.

He pulled back and struck even harder. He heard the snap. Tyvold shuddered with satisfaction as the sensation overtook him, filling him and allowing him to commune.

Recovered from the trance, he knew the steps to transform the unbihexium as haoma into parahaoma, and he knew the ritualistic conditions that must exist at the exact moment the first dose is administered.

Tyvold looked at Lisa. She was slumped forward. By her hair, he lifted her head. One open, blank eye. He put his finger to her throat. *Expired*. Reaching to the back of the chair, he found the restraining harness latch and popped it. Her body sagged, rolled off the chair, and slapped onto the tile floor on its right side.

Tyvold needed to get the information about the dosage to Skotino, but proper disposal of the expired pharmakos was even more important. *Not dispose— no, the correct word is* hide, *he reminded himself. Using the incinerator was so much easier.*

||0 ||0 ||0

A DOZEN FACULTY MEMBERS OCCUPIED THE STAFF ROOM OF THE political science building at Ben-U. Vending machines, sink, counter, microwave, and refrigerator lined one wall. Laura worked alone at one table.

"What are *you* doing here?" Hinkle asked as he entered.

She ignored him.

At the vending machine, he placed his percomm against it and then set his cup under the dispenser.

Hot coffee poured into the cup. He blew across the top and took a sip.

"What are you doing here so late?"

She let out a sigh. "I work here."

"Work? Sure, you're all about the grindstone and midnight oil." He took another sip.

Laura kept her head down, reading the document on the screen in front of her, trying to ignore his hovering.

"You know," he said, "you never know who you might run into on campus this time of night. It'll be dark soon."

Laura stole a peek at the windows and then cursed herself for taking the bait.

He laughed. It was so easy for him press her buttons. He scanned the room and the staff milling about. "Aha … no one else on your floor this late, huh? I bet it's quiet up there … I bet you can hear every noise."

"If you must know, my best friend died yesterday. I've got some catching up to do and … and being around people helps. Ben's working late too. We're going home together."

"Sorry about your friend." He cocked his head. "Well, I'll check on you later. Your absent-minded professor could even teach Fred MacMurray a thing or two about forgetfulness. If the hubby doesn't show, you can come home with me." He growled like a leopard, laughed, and walked out.

Laura pulled out her percomm and sent a message to Ben saying she wanted to leave immediately, and then she gathered her things.

On the ride home, Ben continued his work, and so she tried to do so, as well. It was no use; she couldn't stop thinking about Chris. She felt paralyzed. She tried to put a word to it. *Denial*.

The incoming comm startled her. It was Dr. Williams. He started with the autopsy report. "I confirmed my presumption regarding Marian's cause of death; internal bleeding precipitated a catastrophic drop in blood pressure. The hemorrhage erupted from one of several fibroids in the wall of the uterus. We discovered the fibroids early in the pregnancy; they were getting large, but this is not uncommon. What *is* uncommon is that the growth of one fibroid appears to have intersected with one of the uterine arteries, consuming more and more of the fetus's blood supply. Fibroid tissue is similar to heart tissue; a lack of blood causes great pain, just like a severe heart attack. Unfortunately, Marian died in tremendous pain, and it wasn't quick. I'm sorry to have to tell you that."

"It's all right, Doctor," said Laura. "I wanted to know."

"It's fortunate that the paramedics arrived in time to free the infant and rush him here; he wouldn't have lasted long. The good news is that Chris is a very healthy boy. There's no detectable stress from the emergency cesarean section. Mrs. Richards, I received the documents from the court. So if it's all right with you, since Chris is officially yours, I've made arrangements for you to take him home tomorrow. A hospital is no place for a healthy boy."

| | O | | O | | O

EDUARDO ALVAREZ DROVE THE OLD PICKUP TRUCK ACROSS THE Nevada desert on his way for the retrieval, transport, and disposal. The ball of ice in his stomach had formed the moment he got the comm.

What at first was a sweet gig had gradually morphed over the years into a hellish enslavement. He'd assumed he was dealing with drug smugglers. Tyvold had offered a stream of steady jobs. The guy was all about secrecy, he never rushed him, and he paid better too. Then, little by little, Tyvold got leverage. Now Alvarez was trapped. He felt like he was in a busted elevator, in a free fall, waiting to hit bottom.

He turned left onto the long entry road leading to Tyvold's place. There had to be other people there, but he'd only ever seen Tyvold. *Smart*. The location was secluded, nothing around except flat desert. Surprise was impossible. *Really smart*.

He drove up in front of the garage doors along the side of the complex. Tyvold was waiting, as usual.

The ball of ice in Alvarez's stomach seemed to climb up his throat. He jumped out and walked around as Tyvold pushed the wheelbarrow to the side of the truck. Alvarez looked at the body. *Always a girl*.

"What's the capacity at the site?" asked Tyvold.

"It's fine ... at least a hundred more. The lake is huge." Alvarez checked the fit of his plastic gauntlets and plastic apron.

"You seem more pensive than usual."

"Why are they always young women?"

"You don't want to know that, Ed."

Alvarez kept his eyes on the girl's body, wrapped in the plastic sheet. Tyvold watched him from the periphery.

"Don't think too hard, Ed. Monitor capacity. Don't surprise me."

"The lake in the cavern is huge. I told you," said Alvarez, and he knew his tone had gone too far.

Tyvold didn't respond immediately. Then he spoke, with each word hitting like a bullet. "You transport, your family lives."

Alvarez didn't need to be told what his job was. He was good at clean transport, best in the trade. He had selected one of the vehicles prepared in advance. The cars and trucks were junkyard derelicts. He rebuilt them to minimum working order. The key was to destroy all the serial numbers and all forms of tracking information. It was possible with older vehicles. Yes, old cars and trucks had serial numbers etched on primary parts, but he knew every spot. Modern trans were manufactured with microscopic filaments forged into the material itself. It was impossible to have an untraceable vehicle from parts produced over the past two decades. Alvarez *had* to think hard; it was a difficult business.

"If you ever cross me, Ed," Tyvold whispered, "I won't just hunt down your family and kill them; they'll all go through the same hell she did. And I'll make you watch."

Alvarez closed his eyes and then opened them. He shoved his gloved hands and arms under the body. Even through the clothing and layers of plastic, he could still feel the warmth of the body. *Tyvold didn't let this one sit around long.* He threw the body into the back of the pickup. Avoiding Tyvold's penetrating stare, he got behind the wheel, drove back along the entry road, turned on to the main road, and headed for the mesas.

||0 ||0 ||0

NOT FAR OFF THE COAST OF GREECE, A SEAPLANE CIRCLED FOR A landing. It was a spectacular day with a blue, cloudless sky.

"Mr. Anderson, we'll be landing momentarily," announced the pilot.

Anderson looked up from his work and peered out the window. Surrounded by turquoise water, he identified the *Balkan Beauty*, a 105-meter superyacht, white with swept features and black-tinted glass.

After landing, the plane maneuvered alongside. A dinghy departed from the yacht and picked up the solitary passenger.

Anderson climbed the short ladder from the dinghy to the deck. A man in uniform was waiting.

"Mr. Anderson, I'm Captain Alexiou. Welcome." The language was English, but the accent was a mixture of Greek and British. The captain's expression was jovial, and he continued his greeting with a broad smile. "We've been expecting you. Please, if there's anything I can do for you during your visit, I—"

"I won't be long," Anderson said, speaking in perfect Greek. "Your boss is waiting for me."

The smile fell from the captain's face. With steeled professionalism, he escorted Anderson inside to a grand room that spanned the width of the craft with windows on the bow, port, and starboard sides but open along the aft end. The opening allowed free passage onto the open upper deck where sunshine poured in. The luxurious room was appointed with a full bar, an entertainment area that featured an enormous view screen, and a dining area that seated twenty.

"Mr. Venizelos will join you in a moment. May I get you a drink to—" Anderson's glare stopped the offer cold. The captain simply closed the door.

It was less than a minute before a strapping man entered, followed by Alexander Venizelos. The security man stood at attention.

Although eighty-seven years old, Venizelos looked younger; the fine life had its benefits. He wore loose-fitting layers of ecru silk embellished with crimson velvet, cocktail in hand. Once seated, he motioned Anderson to sit also.

Anderson eyed the security man for a second before sitting.

"I want to know how you learned this information," said Venizelos.

"I told you I can provide information that your own security staff cannot. I made this clear when I first approached you. Our methods are not your concern," said Anderson. "You pay me to know."

"I'm paying you to find out—" He stopped himself, stared at Anderson, and then turned to the security guard. "Leave us."

After the door closed, in a more controlled voice, Venizelos asked, "Is it my grandson's child?"

"Yes."

Venizelos slumped in the chair.

"You'll want to know the mother's background," said Anderson. "You'll want to make sure your great-grandson, as heir to your fortune, has the kind of mother who will prepare him to be a Venizelos ... and the kind of mother that will protect him." He waited while the senior Venizelos consumed the words. When the old man nodded, Anderson stood and stepped to the door. "She has not told your grandson yet. Once she does, he will come to you. You will then instruct him to cooperate."

Venizelos nodded again.

||0 ||0 ||0

"MORNING," SAID BEN, OPENING THE CUPBOARD. "YOU TOSSED AND turned all night."

"Sorry. Too much to think about," said Laura. "Everything's happening so fast."

"You have the list of items from the doctor? We can pick up the essentials on the way." With a cup of coffee, he sat down at the kitchen table across from her. "Do you think any mother feels totally ready? Regular parents have more time to get used to the idea of bringing an infant home. But on the actual day the child arrives, do you think they feel any more ready?"

"My brain tells me no, but my fears tell me yes," she said. "Ben, I'm not a mother. I'm a college professor."

He didn't say anything.

"How can we protect him?" she said. "Will he get beat up at school? Will they call him a Loyd?"

"You're letting all that political science get to you again. The economic divisions between Pogers, Loyds, and Hillites are only that—economic divisions. It doesn't have to be violent. You of all people know that."

"No, you're wrong. The protests are real. The Robin Hood terrorists are real. The Hoods are snatching those young women ... some twisted new form of terrorism. I'm sure of it. Then they'll snatch young men ... little girls ... little boys. We can't protect him."

"That's a non sequitur."

Laura opened her mouth to respond but closed it again.

"We'd better get going. Don't forget to order the items."

| | 0   | | 0   | | 0

THE EVENING CROWD WAS JUST BEGINNING TO ARRIVE AT THE London dance club. Music blasted across the dance floor, but only a few bodies undulated. Spire slunk to the back, away from the entrance as the throbbing bass created vibrations across his body.

He'd copied the drab grunge look favored by the spoiled offspring of the financially independent, but the similarity stopped there. The young people showed their individuality through fashion, by accentuating some unique aspect, such as exceptionally long hair over the face or sleeves ripped up the arm and dangling. Spire conveyed no such individuality. He wore a charcoal sweatshirt with the hood over his head, framing his dark skin in shadow.

She wouldn't arrive for another thirty minutes. He needed to prepare. He needed to adapt to these surroundings. He needed to control her perceptions. He needed to be close to her once she arrived. He needed to remain unseen until he was ready, until it was time.

| | 0   | | 0   | | 0

"WE'RE HERE TO COLLECT CHRIS LUMIÈRE," LAURA SAID TO THE hospital receptionist. Laura had decided not to change his last name and to share the knowledge of his real mother when he became curious. Ben followed her to the elevator and up to the maternity floor. Checking the room numbers, they headed in the direction of the assigned room. Laura noticed a group of med techs outside one of the rooms next to the nursery. It had to be the room where Chris was. She gave Ben a concerned look. He frowned and shrugged.

When they got closer, several of the med techs turned. They were smiling. Relieved, Laura smiled too. She recognized several of the people as nurses who'd been caring for Chris in the nursery.

"There they are!" chimed one of the nurses in the singsong voice of someone accustomed to talking to infants. Two others broke away to greet them; one wrapped Laura in a hug, and the other shook Ben's hand. More hugs followed, and Ben looked terribly uncomfortable. Finally, the group parted to let them into the room, and a nurse gently placed Chris in Laura's arms. The feeling was utterly amazing. It felt so comfortable, so natural. His head rested gently at the crook of her elbow. He was warm and soft.

"There you go, little guy," said the nurse. She folded the swaddling blanket away from around Chris's face. Now Laura could see him better. His eyes were closed, but one hand was pushing against the blanket in sort of a stretch, or maybe he was just getting comfortable again. He smelled of soap and faintly of dried formula. Everyone was beaming. Laura took a few steps back to the corridor so Ben could see.

Touching his little hand, Ben said, "His fingers are so tiny. And it looks like he needs a nail clipping already." The nurses chuckled.

Chris pushed again against the blanket while his lips curled into a snarl in a cute baby kind of way. Ben smiled.

"Can I hold him one last time?" asked one of the nurses.

"Of course," said Laura. She and Ben became spectators as the group crowded around. The conversation swelled into remembrances of Chris's short stay and a mixture of well wishes and good-byes.

"Oh, Doctor, hello. Sorry, I didn't see you there," said Ben. "I didn't expect to see you today."

Laura noticed Dr. Williams standing next to them too.

"No, I wasn't planning to be here."

"Oh?" said Ben.

Dr. Williams was watching the nurses chattering about, and so Ben returned to watch also, smiling. But the doctor's demeanor seemed oddly businesslike.

"It's rather unusual," said Dr. Williams.

Without looking away, Ben said, "Well, we certainly appreciate you coming yourself to see us off."

"That's not what I mean," said Dr. Williams.

Ben turned his attention. "Excuse me? What *do* you mean?"

"We have only one tech assigned at any given time. You would've been greeted by that individual and that would've been that. Yet, since Chris arrived, he's often had more than one caregiver. Some stayed late while others came in early. Some weren't even in the rotation; they heard about Chris and wanted to see for themselves. Four of these people here are off work today. They came in just to say good-bye."

"Sounds like a dedicated staff to me, Doctor," said Ben. "I'm still not sure what you mean."

"I'm not sure, either, Mr. Richards," he said, smiling. Then, in a lighter tone, he offered, "You've got a remarkable kid there. Take good care of him. Let me know if there's anything I can do before his first checkup."

During the ride home, Laura watched Chris as he slept in the child-restraint basket.

"How are you doing?" Ben asked her.

"Really great," she said. "He's all scheduled for his first checkup appointment. The nurse gave me several online courses to take for infant care. She went through his feeding, eating, and bathing schedule. Maybe it was all the unknowns making me nervous before, but yeah, we can do this. How about you? How are you doing?"

"Great. Yeah, it's going to be very different, and I'm sure challenging at times, but I'm looking forward to it. I've got a lot to learn too."

She laughed. "What an adventure!"

# CHAPTER 4

LISA'S BODY SLID FROM ONE SIDE OF THE TRUCK'S FLATBED to the other. Her raw left side smacked against the protruding metal wheel well. Pain shot across her nerves and pushed her into consciousness. Lying on her stomach, she felt the bumps and vibration. She opened her one good eye but could only make out rough shapes in the darkness.

Her entire body stung with pain, but pain had become such a constant that she no longer cared. She didn't know where she was or what was happening. She wasn't in the room anymore, and that's all that mattered. There was still a spark of fight deep down inside. *Nighttime ... outside ... traveling. The end of the ride will bring nothing good. Get out of the truck!* She assessed her condition. Did she have the strength to get out or even to survive the fall to the ground? She put those thoughts out of her mind, because there was no alternative.

Gripping the metal ridges on the bottom of the flatbed, she dragged herself toward the side of the truck. Her mutilated left side simply dragged behind, but the bumpy road helped lessen the friction, so she made fairly quick progress to the side.

The minor success fueled her strength. She groped over the wheel well for the edge of the truck. With one pull, she hauled her torso up onto the wheel well and immediately felt light-headed. *Almost there.* Another heave sent her body over the side. Her leg and dislocated arm caught momentarily on the spinning edge of the tire—burning into her flesh and yanking her to the ground. She smacked down, rolled, and came to rest on her back beneath the starry sky.

She lay still as the rumble of the truck became more distant. Finally, surrounded by silence, the peacefulness overwhelmed her. Exhaustion enveloped her very existence, and she slipped out of consciousness.

||O ||O ||O

THE GUEST ROOM OF THE RICHARDSES' PREFAB DIDN'T RESEMBLE A nursery. Ben had set up the crib, but that was about it. Laura paced in the darkened room with Chris in her arms until she was sure he was asleep. Leaning over the crib, she lay him on his stomach and placed her hand on his back, feeling the patter of his heart.

"You have two parents now," she whispered. "Trust me."

She adjusted the pubcomm settings on the bedroom wall panel so she could monitor Chris from anywhere in the house. No telling how long he would sleep until he was hungry or needed a change. She realized she was starving.

In the kitchen, she opened the refrigerator to peer inside but then closed it. From the pubcomm, she tapped for a vidcomm to the lab. Ben was sitting at his computer console. *Trust me*, she thought. She watched him tinkering for a moment and then canceled the comm. Opening the freezer, she dug down under layers of plastic-wrapped items. *There they are.* She pulled out two boxes, unwrapped the contents, and popped them into the microwave.

Meals in hand, Laura rode the elevator to the bottom floor and stepped into the hall leading to the basement lab.

"Feeding time at the zoo," she said when the door opened.

"Thanks," said Ben. "I meant to finish earlier … so I could help get him—"

"Save it," she said.

He reached for the plate, but she held it back.

"I thought we could eat together," she said, and then she handed it to him.

"Wow. Chicken potpie? Is it really? Where did you get it?"

"Wasn't easy. I only know one store that carries them. I've had them awhile, waiting for the right time."

"The fat content alone probably violates some kind of federal law," Ben joked. He pulled over a chair, pushed a cardboard box off a second, and wheeled it over too. "You first, my dear."

"Thank you." She sat down, crossed her legs, set the plate on her lap, and unfolded the napkin.

He sat and shoveled chunks of chicken, crust, and gravy into his mouth.

"So tell me, what've you got down here?" she asked, assessing the menagerie of equipment.

"Well …" He marshaled a mouthful of food into one cheek. "My local calculations are still taking a long time, so I added some more computing power and memory. From a pure hardware standpoint, my processing power increased fivefold, but because of the programming techniques I use in my work, it's an effective increase of almost a thousand times." Gravy lingered on his lower lip.

She handed him an extra napkin.

He wiped his mouth and then blew the steam from his next bite.

"I went to visit Father Arnold," she told him.

"Oh, right, I remember." He shoveled another load. "How did it go?"

"Fine. I think it'll help me deal with Marian's death. It was nice to see him. He hasn't changed much." She recrossed her legs. "I just don't consider myself very religious, and I know Marian wasn't, either, but it made me think about the commitment of being a godparent. Father Arnold asked me why I wasn't very religious, and I found myself explaining about the academic environment you and I work in. Your work, for example, seems to be the polar opposite of religion. Father Arnold said I should ask you what you think. We've never spent much time talking about religion, so maybe I just assumed. In any case, the godparent thing involves you too. What are your thoughts about religion?" When she looked up, she could see he was frozen in midchew.

He blinked his eyes and swallowed. "Wow. OK ... uh ... let's see. Well, for starters, I draw a line between religion and spirituality. There are aspects of religion I believe were created by mankind without God's blessing—lacking grace. However, with regard to spirituality, I take that pretty seriously. As for the godparent invitation, I'm glad Marian asked us."

"Father Arnold gave me some homework. He wanted me to ask you about your work as a scientist. The academic nature of your work seems so devoid of religion, or spirituality, or everything about the basic human stuff you just said, like all the laws of nature confirm that God doesn't exist. Father Arnold wanted me to ask you if that's how you see things."

"No, not at all," said Ben.

"Really?" she said excitedly. "I thought scientific discoveries tend to disprove religious teachings."

"Well, that's where I get into trouble, trying to interpret religion. Let's stick to spirituality. Call it a higher power or the reason why making the right choice matters. Some scientific discoveries support the existence of forces outside our physical universe. And many scientists, myself included, believe these discoveries provide evidence that these forces are not indiscriminate but instead have a purpose—an intelligence, you might say."

"Really! Like what?"

Ben chuckled, and he seemed excited too. It reminded her of the lectures she'd seen him give when the students really got into the subject at hand. It had been a long time since she'd sat in on one of his lectures.

"OK, let's see, how about the entanglement of light. You know that the photon is the basic unit of light. But did you know that photons have properties that change at random, like rolling dice? Interestingly, when you examine a property, it becomes fixed, as if a die came to rest. By the way, light can be entangled, meaning the photons originated from the same source at the same time. Here's the fascinating part: consider a pair of entangled photons going in opposite directions. When you look a property of one photon—forcing that property to become fixed—miraculously, the same property of the other photon becomes fixed also, instantaneously, even if the two have traveled a great distance apart."

"How can that be? There must be something that connects them."

"Maybe," agreed Ben. "We don't know yet. But even a very simple type of energy like light has the ability to connect across great distances. Einstein's formula, $E=MC^2$, tells us the relationship between mass and energy, so it seems reasonable that matter is also connected in ways we don't understand."

"But you said the photons needed to be, uh …"

"Entangled?"

"Yeah. Wouldn't the matter need to be entangled to be connected?"

"I think so," he said, and then he paused. "When we were married, I'd like to think it was a form of entanglement." He smiled.

She smiled too and said, "But marriage seems like one of those religious things made up by mankind."

"Right. The ceremony part. But marriage is between two people who love each other, a form of entanglement."

Laura giggled.

"And when I say that, we both think of romantic love, yes, but there are other forms of love. The Greek word *agape* is used for a kind of love shared between friends, family, even pets. Is it possible that all living things have the ability to affect matter at a distance? Mankind has identified a small set of individuals— such as Jesus, Buddha, Muhammad—believed to possess pure love and responsible for miracles that demonstrated control over our physical world. I think new discoveries will help us harness the ability to affect matter at a distance through linking energy. Maybe even an energy like love."

"Is all this part of your work?" she asked.

"Not directly, but much of my success has been the result of unconventional techniques from what you might associate with the softer sciences. Conventional scientists make computers go faster by processing bits faster, like making the analytic side of your brain really big. I modeled my techniques after human intuition. For example, how you can tell someone is sad versus knowing two plus two equals four. My techniques allow computers to solve entire classes of problems that were once considered impossible to solve and also to solve traditional problems in a dramatically faster way." He took another bite. "What do you think?"

"Wow," said Laura. "All this time, I never understood the impact of your research. Everyone I talk to knows you from your work on dark energy."

"It's part of my hypothesis. The concept of dark energy explains observable physical effects in our universe. Dark energy makes up 68 percent of the mass in the universe. I believe dark energy creates linkages between regular matter in ways we can't see. The force could be as powerful as the gravity that binds planets to stars and stars to galaxies."

"Oh," said Laura in a small voice. "So dark energy is the connection?'

"Yes, like a wire between entangled pairs." He burped and then noticed her expression. "Sorry," he said, and he belatedly put his hand over his mouth.

llO llO llO

THE TRUCK'S HEADLIGHTS PIERCED THE BLACKNESS OF THE NIGHT, illuminating orange rock and sand along the canyon between the mesas. Alvarez slowed down as he approached the designated dumping site. The gap in the canyon wall was sizable but natural, and it wasn't

obvious that it led to a cavern inside. Carefully, he
steered the truck through the narrow gap, the vehicle
tilting drastically as it went over the slanted ground.

Once inside, the light reflected off the ceiling and
walls, revealing the subterranean lake completely
enclosed and hidden by the surrounding rock. The
headlight beams barely reached the far edge of the
enormous lake.

He eased the truck up to the edge of the lake.
The front tires went over the crest at the depression's
edge and started down the gradual slope to the water.
Alvarez allowed the rear tires to also pass over the
crest before pressing the brake, and the old truck
creaked to a stop. Gravity would do the rest. Time to
move the body to the cab of the truck.

Alvarez put the truck into neutral and set the
parking brake. Leaving the driver's-side door open,
he walked back to the truck bed for the body. He
froze at the sight of the empty truck bed. *Shit! Where
the hell … ?*

Blood smears ran across the bed and over one
side. In several smears, he could make out the impression of a handprint. *Shit!*

Panic flashed. He circled the truck and then back
along the path, zigzagging, looking in every direction. No blood, no sign of where she had gotten out.
Nothing. He sprinted out of the cavern, retracing the
course until the truth was obvious: he had no idea
where she was or when she'd gotten out. *Shit, shit,
shit!* Panting more from fear than exertion, he turned
back. *She was dead. Tyvold must have made sure. Her*

*body was totally mutilated. How could she be alive? If she wasn't dead, it's Tyvold's fault, not mine. She can't survive for long. Maybe she didn't survive the drop to the ground.*

He imagined himself explaining to Tyvold what had happened. *Put the blame on Tyvold. No. Bad idea.* Maybe just plead? *No.* He couldn't bear what would happen to his family. Maybe he could find the girl, kill her, and dump the body as usual? It was the middle of the night. *Too many miles to cover. Too risky.* He had to hope the coyotes and vultures would do the job.

*No choice.* He'd dump the vehicle as usual and not deviate from the routine. If Tyvold had some way of tracking his progress, Alvarez would do nothing out of the ordinary. He'd sink the truck, walk the six miles to his own vehicle, and then go home to his family. Just like always.

At the truck, he reached inside the cab and released the parking brake. The truck rumbled forward into the water with a gentle splash, sending ripples across the mirrorlike surface. It glided out into the lake and then, after the engine died, submerged completely. Bubbles foamed at the surface, and a blue-green glow danced along the ripples until the head-lights winked out.

llo llo llo

THE HACKNEY PUBTRAN ROUNDED THE CORNER HEADING FOR THE nightclub. The crowd had already formed a queue down the street. The pubtran driver—the title *driver* was just an endearing English tradition for the attendant—asked, "Miss, shall I drop you off at the end of the queue?"

"Yes, please," said Chelsea. "Thank you. Sorry for the trouble."

"Oh, no trouble at all, miss."

As the taxi came to a full stop, the driver rotated his chair to face the passenger area, reached across to open the door, and in one smooth motion, hopped out and offered his hand.

Chelsea pressed her percomm to the screen and selected a generous tip. She accepted the driver's hand and stepped out onto the curb.

"Are you sure you'll be safe alone, miss?"

"Yes, I'm meeting a friend," she lied. Evangelos was so sweet to get her two passes to the club. None of her girlfriends had accepted her invitation. *Forget them.* She'd always dreamed of living this life. Wealthy and famous. Well, at least the wealthy part, once Evangelos got his act together. Tonight she might see a celebrity at the club. Maybe even James Lovejoy.

"Very well then. Evening, miss."

Chelsea gave a friendly wave good-bye and took her place at the end of the queue. *Miss, miss, miss! If I were married, would he still call me miss? Ugh, probably.*

It was a busy night, and the queue to get through security was long. Evangelos was studying late, as usual. But even if they were married, that wouldn't change, not until he passed his exams. And even then, he still had to finish his thesis.

Security personnel directed patrons through the screening gate to detect any manner of weapon, drug, or anything else illegal or against club rules. Once she passed through the inner doors, the beat of the music penetrated her bones. Couples and singles crowded the huge dance floor, flaunting extreme and sexy styles. She'd spent all afternoon primping and hoped she fit in. Roving spotlights highlighted one couple in motion, wrapped around each other. The sight of their bodies pressed together intensified the longing she felt for Evangelos, and she allowed herself the fantasy that he would arrive out of nowhere and whisk her out onto the dance floor. The crowd would part, followed by percomm flashes, and the pics would be online in moments. Her ex-friends would turn green.

She glimpsed a few male eyes admiring her as she passed. One guy admired too long, and it earned him an angry nudge from the girl on his lap. It made Chelsea feel good, special, and sexy. Her choice of outfit, at least, seemed to do the trick.

She wanted a drink. She found an open stool at the back bar, tended by a pair of young women in identical fishnet body suits and knee-high black patent leather boots with stiletto heels. Smoky shadow sparkled like diamonds on their eyelids, and their lips looked like molten glass. Chelsea admired their professionalism. They moved with the elegance, speed, and precision of Olympic athletes.

One bartender paused in front of Chelsea, her uniform basically transparent but for three small, strategically placed panels of fabric.

"Tequila cruda," said Chelsea.

The shot, lime, salt, and a glass of water appeared even before Chelsea could take in the other people at the bar. With her tongue, she moistened a spot between her thumb and forefinger, sprinkled salt there and then picked up the slice of lime. In a series of practiced motions, she licked the salt, swallowed the shot, and bit the lime. The liquor warmed her throat, ending in a glow at her tiny waist. Looking up, the bartender caught her eye, and Chelsea nodded.

Finally getting an opportunity to look around, she noticed that the man next to her had his back to her and was chatting intensely with the woman across from him. Farther down, two other men were watching the dancers. There was another couple next to them. On the other side of her, the seat was open. At the corner of the bar and along the far side, six girls were well on their way to a good time. Chelsea guessed one was having a birthday. The six girls were laughing and giggling, and one wore a silly hat.

The bartender set down the second round. Lights flashed across writhing limbs on the dance floor. Relaxing, Chelsea tried to see if she recognized anyone. As the second shot followed the first, she focused on the twisting bodies under the light, ignoring the shadows around her.

BEN STOOD TRANSFIXED, LOOKING OUT THE WINDOW OF HIS UNIversity office. The baby—*Chris*, he reminded himself to use the boy's name. The whole situation was becoming very real very quickly, and it was constantly on his mind. Laura had taken the remainder of the week off to get the house ready. He'd offered to work from home and help too, but she insisted it wasn't necessary. He felt off balance, and being in the office didn't seem to help.

"Good morning, Ben. You busy?" It was Rajiv Gupta from the Australian team, via vidcomm.

"No, not really. What's up, Raj?"

"Did you run the model yet? The guys from the last shift expected to see the results by now. We decided to wait until morning your time before checking in."

"Oh, Raj, I didn't. I'm sorry. I'll run it right away."

"No problem. Is everything copacetic?"

"Yes, just some personal stuff I'm dealing with." Ben wasn't prepared to explain how he had become a parent overnight. "Nothing to burden you with, Raj. Thanks for asking. I'll get the results of the run right over."

After he sent the completed report, Ben questioned his own ability to concentrate. The events that brought Chris to them were extraordinary and unexpected, but he was still surprised at his inability to put it aside mentally. Parents all over the world got up and went to work every day. Just having a kid shouldn't derail one's career; raising a kid was completely normal. *Normal? Something doesn't fit.* Was it scientific curiosity, or did he suddenly have a paternal urge to know for sure that Chris was healthy? *The medical scanner.*

"Computer, contact Dr. Williams, West Philadelphia Hospital."

"Connecting." After a moment, the computer voice continued, "Dr. Williams is unavailable. Do you wish to leave a message?"

"No. When is he available?"

"Dr. Williams is available for live communication at 11:00 a.m."

*Ninety minutes from now.* "Book it."

Once the ball was rolling on the scanner mystery, Ben found his focus again.

At the appointed time, the computer offered to initiate the comm to the doctor.

"Dr. Williams, this is Ben Richards calling about Chris Lumière."

"Of course, Mr. Richards. Is there something wrong?"

"No, nothing like that. But I wanted to ask you about the problem with the postnatal scanner and wondered if it got fixed."

"No. We ran the tests manually. It just takes a little longer," said Dr. Williams. "You know, we had the same problem with Marian. It must be hereditary or something, although I've never heard of such a thing."

"Tell me, did Marian experience this her entire life?"

"Hmm, well, Marian only became my patient once she became pregnant. Let me check her records from her general physician … no, her file has data from many successful scans. Strange."

"Did the inability to use the scanner create any concern for you initially?"

"I contacted the manufacturer, and they sent a technician, but he was unable to determine the cause. I assumed they'd fix it eventually, but I never heard from them again. To answer your question, though— no, many rural locations haven't converted to the exclusive use of the scanners, so the lab method is still available. The tests are equally accurate."

"I see. Would you mind if I contact the manufacturer? I'm curious. Maybe there's a new model or something."

"Not at all. I'll send you the contact information right now. Mr. Richards, if you do learn of a fix, please let me know. We should've been notified."

"Yes, of course. Thank you, Doctor."

Ben contacted the manufacturer immediately and spoke with several people who directed him deeper into the organization. Finally, he reached someone who sounded like he could help.

"Yeah, I handled this one. Unfortunately, I don't have any good news. This anomaly remains unresolved. It's the only such occurrence, and we still don't know the cause."

Ben conveyed the information about Marian's death and that the postmortem scanner apparently worked on Marian's body but the postnatal scanner didn't work on Chris. "Do you know if both scanners use the same technology?"

"Yeah, it's the same device. The software is different, and it's a different market, of course, but they operate using the same principles."

"Forgive me; maybe my ego is out of line, or maybe I'm too personally involved now, but I wanted to ask if you could spend a few minutes and explain to me how the device works."

"I'll try. The device relies on the Compton Effect; it's when energy becomes scattered when it passes through matter. The signal is—"

"Yes, sorry to interrupt. To save you some effort in explaining, let me say that I use the Compton chamber here at Benjamin Franklin University for my own work on brain function."

"Ah. Well, the device is basically a Compton chamber without the chamber."

"But your device can read precise information about the body, including chemical composition. Our chamber only gives information about brain function."

"Correct. Your chamber has only one ray emitter. Our device needs a true three-dimensional image. Two rays would do the trick, but we need to measure processes over time. A third ray provides temporal fidelity."

"Amazing. I've used a Compton chamber for years, but I wasn't aware of this three-ray technique."

"It's a trade secret. Under the circumstances, I'm happy to share the information if I can count on your discretion."

"Of course," agreed Ben. "Tell me, how do you emit three rays? With no chamber, you just have the device. Three rays coming from the same location wouldn't provide enough lateral perspective, right?"

"Correct. The device emits one ray. The solar wind and the cosmic background radiation are the sources for the other two."

"Really," said Ben in admiration.

"Yup. Pretty tricky, huh? Our challenge is crunching the data uploaded in real time to our processing center. Think of the number of cells in the human body. Every strand of DNA is made up of … oh, never mind, you understand the magnitude of the problem."

"Yes, I know that end of it quite well. In fact, I may be able to help you there. But back to Chris— what could prevent your device from working?"

"I really don't know. Our tech on-site tried everything we know to get any kind of reading. The error from the device means no Compton scattering was detected. Nothing. Even if you made your son available for testing, I wouldn't know where to start. And frankly, I don't have the budget. Unless this shows up again, we're not going to pursue a solution. It's only one case. It's too expensive. I'm sorry."

Ben concluded the comm with thanks and an offer to collaborate on software techniques if the company was interested. Somehow, he was sure the strange behavior of the medical scanner wasn't a meaningless fluke.

||0 ||0 ||0

CLOSE ENOUGH NOW, SPIRE CONCENTRATED ON CHELSEA AND probed her mind for images of Evangelos: the way he carried himself, his scent, his speech, and his attitude toward the world—but most importantly, how she perceived him. She was watching the dancers. Her mood was mellow. It seemed she'd purged all worries from her mind.

Certain that no one was paying attention to him, Spire pulled a piece of folded paper and tweezers from his pocket. He carefully unfolded the paper, revealing a tiny capsule about the size of a grain of sand. With the tweezers, he delicately picked up the capsule and placed it on the tip of his tongue. He had to move now; he had only a few moments before the capsule dissolved.

Chelsea was watching the dancers and listening to the music, tapping her foot to the beat. "Evangelos! You came! What a splendid surprise!"

He walked up to her, took her chin in both hands, and kissed her.

||0 ||0 ||0

*HE CAME! HE'S HERE WITH ME!* THE KISS WAS DEEP AND penetrating, just what she needed at that very moment. It continued, becoming even deeper and then unsettlingly rough. She tried to pull away, but he held her face. *Stop!* She pushed him away, hard. Seeing the stranger, Chelsea screamed, but the sound was lost in the blaring music.

The man fled, melting into the crowd.

*It was Evangelos! I swear it was!*

"Are you all right?" asked the bartender, yelling over the music.

"What?" said Chelsea robotically. She replayed the moment in her mind. It happened so quickly. She felt violated. Guilt washed over her. Could she be so pickled that any man could walk up and take advantage of her?

The bartender leaned close to Chelsea's ear. "For a moment, I thought you knew the bloke, but then he started hurting you."

"Hurt me?"

"Here." The bartender dabbed a cocktail napkin on Chelsea's mouth. "Looks like you split your lip."

"What?" Chelsea pulled the napkin away and saw blood. She felt a fat lip forming.

Picking up the glass of water, the bartender motioned for her to take a drink. "Are you all right? Should I call security?"

Chelsea took a sip. *What have I done? How could I be so foolish?* "No. Thank you. I'm fine."

||0 ||0 ||0

SPIRE WEAVED HIS WAY ALONG THE BACK ROADS. SIX BLOCKS FROM the club, he got into the tran where Skotino was waiting.

"It's done."

Skotino smiled and tapped out a message, letting the Circle know that Spire had successfully administered the first dose of parahaoma.

# Chapter 5

SHE MADE SURE SHE HAD EVERYTHING READY FOR THE walk after getting Chris strapped into the stroller and then took a moment to look at him. He was certainly a handsome young man, with bright blue eyes and wisps of dark hair. One arm bounced off his round belly with what might be excitement in anticipation of the walk.

Things were starting to fall into a rhythm. In all the material Laura had studied about childcare, the consistent theme was to develop a regular schedule. At first, she was concerned about so much to keep track of, but once Chris came home with them, everything seemed manageable. She'd taken time off initially. Then after some discussion with Ben, she'd decided to leave her job permanently. It wasn't an easy decision. She'd always viewed herself as a career woman, but she had to admit her maternal instincts had kicked in. Raising Chris was something she wanted to do.

Laura pushed the stroller down the alley. At the corner, the neighbor woman she'd seen having a confrontation with her husband was sweeping the back sidewalk leading to their house. When she switched her grip on the broom, she had to maneuver it around her belly. She flinched when she heard Laura passing.

"Good morning!" Laura called, waving. The woman smiled and nodded but didn't slow her sweeping. *I guess now's not a good time.*

At the park, Laura found an open bench. She lifted Chris up, supporting his head and holding him against her chest. It was a beautiful day. The sun was still low in the sky, but it was already warming the air. A dozen kids were running, jumping, laughing, and playing. *What will Chris be like at that age?* The song of the cicadas was starting. Wave after wave of their clicking sounds carried across the park. She placed a cloth on her shoulder, lifted Chris a little higher, and patted his back gently, hoping for a reasonable burp after the morning feeding.

Laura had been stashing away little memories of special times with Chris, like this one. Now she realized why—to share with Marian the next time they were together. She had to accept reality. *She's gone.*

*Marian was so stressed at the end. Is the woman on the corner stressed too? Is that why she's so reserved? I did everything I could for Marian. She needed me, and I was there for her.* Laura looked to the sky. *Marian, now it's my turn. I need you.*

Holding Chris close to her, Laura cried—a healing, releasing cry, the kind ending with a shudder and a deep breath. *I'm your mom now, Chris.*

On the way home, Laura looked for the neighbor woman, but she wasn't outside. She pushed the stroller to the back of the woman's house and waited at the back door. She could barely hear the repeating seccomm voice announcement coming from inside the house. "Visitor arriving. Quantity one."

Leaning over the stroller, Laura brushed the strands of Chris's hair to the side. "That's OK, buddy. You certainly count in my eyes." Still, no one came to the door. *Maybe she left?* No, the seccomm wouldn't announce if nobody were home to hear it. In a window, Laura glimpsed the drape fall back into place.

*Well, maybe just the attempt to get formally introduced is good enough for now.* Laura took Chris back home. *There'll be other opportunities.*

IIO IIO IIO

THE PEOPLE IN THE WAITING ROOM AT THE COMMUNITY CLINIC reminded Chelsea of cattle heading for slaughter. A mother tried to corral her snotty-nosed kid. One man held a surgical mask over his nose and mouth. The queue was long today, at least sixty people. Chelsea touched the scab on her lip. It was still tender.

*Soon, I won't have to deal with this ever again. I'll go to an actual doctor. Maybe two.*

When she reached the head of the queue, the scanning chamber door opened with a swish. She stepped into the circular booth, and the door closed behind her. There was no perceptible change—no sound, no light flickering, no puff of air, nothing. After a second, the exit door opened.

*Maybe Evangelos didn't have a doctor? Maybe he went to a special scanner just for rich people?*

Her percomm vibrated with the confidential results. Scrolling through the message, she found the section titled Communicable. *Thank goodness, no sign of herpes or anything else from that creep.* Flipping through the rest of the report, she noticed a red circle symbol with an exclamation point in the middle, next to the section titled Reproduction. She tapped to expand the section. *Oh my god.*

"Pardon." A woman bumped into Chelsea, pushing roughly as she passed.

Chelsea realized she was blocking the clinic exit. "Terribly sorry." She bolted outside. *It can't be right.* She crossed at the corner. *Leg-over spunk. Evangelos said as much.* She needed to get back to the flat. *I need to think.*

She followed commuters down the steps of the tube station and made her way to a spot on the platform behind the yellow line. Her eyes settled on the concrete wall across the tracks. The words STAY CLEAR were painted there along with a stick figure falling onto the tracks. And painted over that was a big red circle with a slash. The rumble of the approaching train preceded a gust of air out of the tunnel. She steadied herself against the resulting vacuum that tugged at her toward the platform's edge.

When the doors opened, she stepped across the gap and found a seat. *What am I going to do?*

Passengers hurried in and out. As the door began to close, a man dashed through sideways, setting off the automated warning: "Please allow the doors to close." The man grabbed the ceiling strap next to her. "Please hold on. The train is leaving the station." She felt the car lurch, and then shafts of light flashed across her face.

*What will Evangelos say? Will he leave me?* She remembered the mother in the clinic with the sickly child hugging her thigh. For a moment, Chelsea was the mother. Her thigh wasn't slender and silky anymore but instead stubbly and fat. *How does the silver spoon taste? Scrumptious, no doubt. I'll never know. Not now.*

At her stop, she stepped off and merged into the stream of pedestrians at street level. She concentrated on the flat's lobby entrance when it came into sight, like a ship in dense fog toward a lighthouse.

"Chels! Chelsea!" Evangelos was practically on top of her.

"What are you doing here?" she asked.

"My class was canceled," he said. "What kind of a greeting is that? Love, you look positively lost."

"I'm fine." She walked across the lobby to the lift and waited.

He followed, trying to keep up. "Where were you?"

"No place special. Just time for my physical. I was at the clinic," she said, aware her smile lacked the usual drama.

"The community clinic? You mean the public scanner?"

"Yes. And you can keep your pretentious attitude to yourself."

"Chels, I just can't believe you go there. It's so ... Amexican."

"There's nothing wrong with it. Besides, it's Mexican."

"The Americans invented it. The Mexicans manufacture it ... and are the ones getting stinking rich."

"Fine thing for you to say. The spoon has to be Greek silver?" Her words carried no fight. She could hardly concentrate. *I need time to think.* "We should be grateful for the public scanners. Preventable diseases are a thing of the past." Watching the numbers count down, she willed the lift to go faster.

"There's your tabloid education again. Everything's made in Mexico now. Even with our staggering trade deficit, the prime minister—that spineless puppet—gives away our quid to the American gluttons and their money-pit economy. The Amexican parasite sucks us dry." The lift door opened, and he followed her in. "My point is, I don't like you going to that part of the city. It's not safe. You don't have to mix with those people, Chels."

"They're my people, Evangelos. I'm unemployed. They're unemployed."

"I don't mean it that way."

Once inside the flat, she went to the kitchen. He followed and watched her in silence. She placed a cup under the dispenser, and hot water drowned the tea bag. She sat down at the table.

"Something's different," he said finally.

"Everything's fine."

"What is it?"

The tears pooled, and there was nothing she could do to stop them.

"What is it? What's wrong?" He put his arm around her.

"I'm pregnant! All right? I'm pregnant." She felt his embrace slacken. "Don't do this. Don't you make me face this alone. You just said I don't need to be with *my* people. You're implying we're together. Are we?"

"This is no time for an I-told-you-so," he said, hugging her tightly. "This is wonderful news, of course. I'm just— Chels ..." He shook his head.

"I know ... your family ... their reaction."

"No, you don't understand. It's more than that."

# Chapter ΣΤ′

"**F**ANTASTIC! A LIMOUSINE!" SQUEALED CHELSEA. SHE RAN to the curb, pivoted so her back was against the shiny black metal, and flung her arms out wide. "Take my picture! Take my picture!"

"Oh, honestly, dear," said Chelsea's mom from her wheelchair as Evangelos pushed it out the airport doors.

Judging from Evangelos's smile, Chelsea knew *he* didn't mind the performance.

"Oh, Mum, don't be so sour." Chelsea dashed forward, thrust her percomm in Evangelos's hand, dashed back to the limo, and took up the exact same pose.

Gregory, the Venizelos family chauffeur, had greeted them at the VIP gate. Now he stood by, flanked by a small army of porters hauling luggage. *Gregory must be fiftyish, judging by the silver hair at the temples, like strokes of pencil on black paper.* Chelsea knew she had a body that could make old men cry, but there wasn't a crack in his professionalism. The young porters behind him, however, were another story.

"Again! Again!" Chelsea bent one leg and put her hand on her hip, achieving a dramatic curve, one of her favorites. Two of the porters exchanged appreciative glances.

Evangelos lowered the percomm. "All right, that's enough." To Chelsea's mom, he said, "Here, Margaret, let me help you up."

Gregory opened the boot, and the porters got to work.

"She's just like her father, you know," said her mom, holding Evangelos's hand as he guided her to a seat inside the limo.

Chelsea stepped to the middle of the sidewalk, threw her arms out, and twirled. "Greece! I can't believe we're here!" A group of weary travelers gave her a wide berth as they passed.

Gregory held out his percomm to the porters, and each took a turn touching their percomms to his. They seemed thrilled with the amount of the gratuity.

*This is going to be fabulous!* She twirled again.

"Quite right," said Evangelos. "Come now; there's more to see." Like the string of an escaping balloon, he caught one of her hands and pulled her to the limo.

"Sir, we should get everyone inside," said Gregory as he collapsed the wheelchair.

"Doesn't he work for you?" she asked Evangelos discreetly. "Bit of a hen."

"No, it's not like that. Come on, get inside."

The limo pulled away from the curb and headed for the exit checkpoint. The limo was just as Chelsea had imagined it every time she'd seen a celebrity get in or out of one. Gregory sat in front, but he wasn't really driving, of course. He was tapping away at his percomm. *Anticipating Evangelos's every whim, no doubt.*

"Margaret, I hope the flight from London to Thessaloniki wasn't too exhausting," said Evangelos.

"Not at all. Evangelos, we've only just arrived, and I simply can't tell you how magical this trip has been already."

"May I offer you a refreshment?" asked Evangelos. A panel opened, revealing a wide array of spirits.

"Oh yes! Let's have a refreshment!" said Chelsea. Her mom rolled her eyes.

"For goodness' sake, Mother, your attitude is fit to mix with whiskey." Chelsea sat up on the edge of her seat. Just the word *refreshment* was intoxicating.

"Your lifestyle is certainly different from ours," said her mom. "I simply can't imagine what it was like for you to grow up in such grandeur. And to know what a kind and considerate young man you've grown up to be. My respect for your family grows with every passing moment. I can't wait to meet them."

"Oh, don't let him fool you, Mum," said Chelsea. "His head is enormous!"

"Thank you, Margaret," said Evangelos. "I'm thrilled that the trip—"

*Crack!* Something hit the window. Chelsea screamed and looked around. The limo was in a queue waiting to pass through the security checkpoint. "What was that?"

"A stone, I believe," said Evangelos. "Gregory, was it this bad on the way in?"

"Yes, sir."

"You'll be quite safe inside," said Evangelos.

There wasn't even a mark on the window. "Who threw it?" asked Chelsea.

"This is the VIP checkpoint," said Evangelos. "The fence keeps the protestors away, but, well, not far enough, apparently."

Chelsea pressed herself into the leather seat. *Will they hit us again?* She accepted the gin and tonic from Evangelos.

"It's Beefeater gin," he said. "Your favorite."

She smiled, rested the drink on her knee, caught his eye, and patted her stomach.

With the shock of realization, he said, "Oh, I—"

"But so sweet of you to try to recapture the mood," said Chelsea, covering for him.

No one said another word until the limo passed the checkpoint.

"Please, Evangelos, tell me about your family, your home, and what it was like growing up in this beautiful country," said Chelsea's mom.

"Well, Thessaloniki, a port city, is one of the oldest harbors in the world. It's where my grandfather's grandfather started our family shipping business. I have fond memories of growing up. Unfortunately, I didn't see my father often when he was alive. He was always working. After he died, my mother raised me and my two little sisters while my grandfather became my father figure. You'll have the opportunity to meet him, my mother, and my younger sister Triana. My other sister, Adrienne, is attending university and won't be able to join us."

"Everything's so beautiful," said Chelsea's mom, gazing out the window.

The limo traveled up along the mountainside, providing a breathtaking view of the sea—the Aegean Sea, Evangelos explained.

"At this point, we're entering my family's property. The village you see here is where the workers who farm and care for the grounds live." As they turned onto a long parkway leading up a hill, with trees on both sides, he continued, "Over there, you can see the oldest standing family home. We simply call it the old house."

"Oh, my eyesight isn't what it once was," fussed Chelsea's mom. She leaned forward with her face nearly pressed against the glass. "Oh yes, I can see it now."

There was a mansion in the distance, and it looked abandoned. An enormous tree, just to the left of the house, had long since died. It reminded Chelsea of a mansion one might see in an old American horror vid.

"There—there's the main house," said Evangelos, pointing.

Black iron fencing atop a low brick wall surrounded an opulent estate. Chelsea wanted to see the house in person. She'd only seen pictures. The guardhouse at the checkpoint, with its razor wire, didn't appear in any of the family photos.

A man in a neat, short-sleeved uniform, percomm in hand, jogged from the guardhouse to the driver's-side window. Gregory lowered the window, and the men exchanged words. The gate opened.

The limo edged forward up to yet another gate inside. More guards were visible now, maybe half a dozen. One guard passed a long pole with a mirror on the end under the limo. Another guard walked around with some kind of probe attached to a percomm, like searching for lost jewelry on the beach.

"This won't take long," said Evangelos apologetically. "You can't be too careful these days."

"Has your family ever experienced any trouble?"

"Mother!" exclaimed Chelsea.

"It's quite all right," said Evangelos. "Yes, at the beginning of the century, when religious terrorism ended and economic terrorism began, the Robin Hood terrorists took hold here in Greece after decades of austerity. There've been a number of attacks on my family over the years. One of them succeeded. They murdered my father."

"I'm so sorry," said Chelsea, and she took his hand with both of hers.

"Margaret, it's a shame to share this information with you before you've even had a chance to meet my family."

"I'm terribly sorry for you, dear. A tragic story. I had no idea, but thank you for your candor. It's the world we live in. Not like the old days. Chelsea needs to understand how to support you. The extraordinary conditions of everyday life that you take in stride ... she must be under no delusions."

Chelsea scowled. "Stop talking like I'm not even here." Changing the subject, she said, "Evangelos, tonight we're having the party you talked about, yes? And I can wear the new dress?"

| | 0 | | 0 | | 0

### "LISA? LISA, CAN YOU HEAR ME?"

The eyelid of Lisa's one good eye fluttered, and she squinted at the harsh fluorescent lights.

"Take it easy."

She could hear a repeating tone she recognized, a heart rate monitor.

"Don't try to move. Just let me know if you can understand what I'm saying."

Her mouth was dry, and her throat felt thick with phlegm.

"Yes." The word came out as part choke, part whisper, and part cough. She tried again. "Yes."

"Good. Now just relax. You're safe now. You're at Las Vegas Community Hospital. I'm Dr. Sinclair. We're taking good care of you," he said. "Lisa, can you repeat back to me what you understand?"

"Yes," she said. "I'm in a hospital."

"Good, very good," he said. "You've been under heavy sedation. We needed to induce a coma to allow your body to heal. You're stable now, and I've allowed you to become conscious so I can assess your brain function. Your parents are here from Pennsylvania. They've missed you terribly. When you feel up to it, I can invite them in."

He waited, but she didn't say anything.

"Lisa, can you tell me what happened?"

Her lips parted slightly.

"The nature of your wounds, Lisa … trauma like this—"

Her body began to tremble. She gripped the bed railing. The heart rate tones quickened. An alarm from the device sounded. Her head pressed back into the pillow, body rigid.

"Lisa, please, you're in a safe place. Try to relax."

*Could it be over?* She focused on the present, to do what he was asking. The tone slowed its pace, ending the alarm.

"I'm sorry. I needed to assess your memory. Your parents and the police are going to ask a lot of questions. I'm giving you time to prepare."

*Prepare? What does that even mean?*

"We don't have to do it now. You can rest if you like." Sitting on the bedside, he waited.

"You said trauma. Is that what they call it when you've been to hell and back?"

# Chapter 7

"**S**O THAT CONCLUDES THE OLD BUSINESS," SAID DR. Heinrich Miller. "Do we have any new business?"

There was a long pause. They'd been having weekly meetings on the dark energy project for ten years and, knowing there would be no new business, they always pushed it right to the end. But *new business* was on the agenda, and the group always waited respectfully—a formality—and Ben could feel the others' anticipation of the meeting's end. On one of the large wall-mounted vid screens, Ben watched as Heinrich started pulling his notes together at the research center in the UK, and on the other, Rajiv Gupta stood up, not fully in the camera's view now.

"Well, I do have something," said Ben.

They stopped. Heinrich looked up and said kindly, "Out with it then."

"Well, I know we're out of time, but I—"

"I've got time."

"Of course," said Raj, sitting back down.

"OK," said Ben. "I have an idea to use the Compton Effect to get better resolution."

"That would require a separate signal," pointed out Raj from the satellite downlink facility in Australia.

"That's right," said Ben. "Actually, I'm proposing three signals. The idea is to use the cosmic background radiation and the solar wind as the two additional signals."

"Hmm, interesting," said Heinrich. "Neither is stable or predictable. Both vary substantially. Neither source is one signal but rather an aggregate of billions of signals."

"Yes," said Ben enthusiastically. "The method takes advantage of the variability. Medical scanning devices use the same technique. I spoke to the company in Mexico that manufactures them, and I learned how their process leverages the signal variation. So using the same principles, I developed a prototype and fed it archive data. The results look promising. I'd like to ask the team to review my work."

"Ben, if you're right, this could be a tremendous breakthrough. What are you waiting for? Send it on!"

Ben had the message cued up. He tapped *send* on his surface display. The link to the centrally stored information raced across the globe to his colleagues.

||0 ||0 ||0

CHELSEA PUT HER MOM'S PURSE ON HER LAP ONCE SHE WAS SET-tled in the wheelchair. Gregory wheeled her out of the guest room to the hallway.

"Are you sure you'll be all right?" asked Chelsea.

"Of course, dear," said her mom. "You finish getting ready."

"I'll take good care of her, miss," said Gregory.

The door swished closed behind them. *Ugh! Miss, miss, miss! He said that on purpose. I know it.* Chelsea crossed her mother's guest room to the adjoining door to her own guest room. Standing in front of the full-length mirror, she tried to see what Evangelos's family would see. *Mrs. Evangelos Venizelos.* She turned and admired the reflection. The dress was spectacular. Sleeveless, with a beaded bodice. The ivory color was ... magical. The beads shimmered like opals with bits of rainbow dancing about. The skirt hugged her hips and thighs. Not too short, she hoped, although bending over would be tricky. The bodice supported her breasts beautifully, creating a dramatic décolletage. The necklace was a gift from Evangelos—thin as thread, ending with a single strand that lay in the valley between. Her blonde hair was up, a masterpiece of its own. Large flowing curls reached the nape of her neck. Turning to see the other side, she imagined herself walking with Evangelos down a red carpet at a premier event, blinding flashes from the crowd as she waved, blowing kisses at just the right time, just like James Lovejoy. Vids would be online in seconds.

Standing sideways, she put the palm of her hand to her tummy.

Evangelos had delayed asking her to marry him because he wanted the moment to be just right, and he wanted to be respectful to his family, and he wanted them to be present when he asked. No one was going to be surprised by the proposal, but she was still nervous. His family was so traditional. She was the furthest thing from the traditional girl he was supposed to marry. *I should be Greek, not English and, well … proper!*

The fact of her pregnancy would have to come out at some point. She wanted the family to know the truth now so they would fully accept her as she was. Starting the relationship based on deception was wrong, but Evangelos insisted they wait until after he proposed to break the news. If outsiders accepted pregnancy after engagement, he reasoned the timing of the baby's birth would be close enough.

Chelsea pressed her eyes shut and opened them, but nothing had changed. She would be meeting Evangelos's grandfather at dinner too. *What will he say when he finds out? Oh, why did it have to happen this way?*

She gathered her things, walked down the hall, and turned to the sweeping staircase down to the main doors where they were all waiting. Evangelos, in his smashing dinner jacket, came to the foot of the stairs.

The six-inch platform heels would be a challenge, yes, but they also created a delicious opportunity. With one hand on the banister, she placed each foot expertly, allowing her hips to strike a rhythm. The lotion on her tanned legs contained a tasteful amount of glitter. The skirt did most of the work, with enough stretch to ride up ever so slightly. From their vantage point, she was sure it was a treat.

Evangelos took her hand at the last step. "You look absolutely gorgeous," he said. The intensity of his eyes confirmed as much.

She glanced at Gregory; his professionalism was unbroken.

"Chelsea, dear," said her mom, "look at the surprise Evangelos arranged for us." Both sides of the double doors were wide open to the advancing summer evening.

Chelsea stepped closer for a better look. The warm breeze drifted across her legs. Outside, she saw a carriage drawn by two horses. It was the old kind of carriage with large, spoked wheels and elaborate embellishments of yellow metal—brass, probably; she couldn't imagine it could be gold.

"Oh, how grand," said Chelsea.

"Dinner preparations aren't quite ready," said Evangelos. "We'll take the long way."

Chelsea leaned out the door. No audience. No one to record it.

||0 ||0 ||0

UNDER A BLANKET OF GRAY CLOUDS, RAIN SPRINKLED DOWN across the Ben-U campus. Laura gripped her umbrella, with her grocery sack folded up under the same arm—she used it to carry just about anything. Walking to the political science building, minding the puddles as she went, she heard the chant leader from the plaza: "Enough is enough!"

The group of protestors was small. The one leading the chant stood on the concrete edge of the central fountain. "Enough is enough!" came the response. They weren't holding signs, probably because of the rain.

One of the protestors waved his percomm in the air. Laura couldn't make out what it said, only the glow of the screen as it went back and forth. A student held out her own percomm. The protestor stopped waving, touched his percomm to hers, and then continued waving. The student found a spot off to the side and began to read.

Laura took out her own percomm and walked up to the protestor.

"Don't miss the Sunday comic," he said when the percomms touched.

"Thanks." Laura stepped out of the way and looked at the transferred file. It was a newsletter of sorts. She flipped through several pages and found the comic. It was a political cartoon from a popular satirist. The series was called *Poge and Loyd*. Poge was the name of the unemployed character, and Loyd was the employed character. The cartoon showed Poge lying on a lawn chair eating a taco with an entire tray of tacos in reach. Over his fat belly, his shirt had a big American flag on it. Nearby, Loyd was bent over with his head in a hole in the ground. His arms resembled ostrich feathers.

At her desk, she unfolded the grocery sack. She picked up a picture frame and looked at it before putting it in the bag. It was a picture of her and Ben before they were married. *Why don't I have more pictures of Ben? More recent pictures?* She wiped the dust off the frame before putting it in the bag and then started on the contents of the top drawer.

"Took you long enough to come and get your crap out of here," said Hinkle, uninvited.

She ignored him.

"Did you hear the big news?"

"Yeah. Since I've decided to leave for good, it means I don't have to put up with you anymore."

"Ha ha. That's old news. Seriously, they found Lisa."

"What? When? Is she all right? Where was she?"

"They won't say. Hush-hush and all that. But it wasn't the police; it was the FBI. Kidnapping across state lines is a federal offense. Found her in Jersey, I bet."

"Well, aren't you the clever sleuth. Will she be coming back to school?"

"Who knows? The whole thing's an information black hole. If you ask for information, you don't get any answers, but they record the fact that you asked," he said. "Why don't you ask, Laura? Wouldn't it be great to have all your communications monitored for the next six years?"

"No, thank you." She continued to pack her things.

"So you're off to enjoy life as a Poger, huh?"

"Hardly. Say, have you seen today's *Poge and Loyd*?" She pulled out her percomm and angled it so Hinkle could see.

"That's the protest newsletter. Where did you get a copy?"

"From one of the students. They're outside."

"I know." He cocked his head. "You? You just walked up?"

"Sure. What's the big deal?"

Hinkle finally left her alone. The bag was heavy, but she was able to manage both it and the umbrella for the walk back.

"Enough is enough!"

The rain hadn't let up. *They sure are determined.*

Scanning the crowd, she noticed one young man with his hands jammed into the front pockets of his jeans and a scowl on his face. Rain droplets hung from his hair and fell onto his shoulders.

She walked next to him, raised the umbrella to cover both of them, and said, "You're soaked."

"I'm fine," he said. "Enough is enough!" he chanted back. He noticed she hadn't. "Why are you here?"

"Uh, the Sunday comic."

He seemed satisfied with her answer.

"Are you a regular?" she asked.

"No." He wiped the rain from his eyebrows and shoved the hand back into his pocket. "You're faculty, aren't you?"

"Yeah."

The troubled look on his face was unmistakable.

"Well, I should say I *was* faculty. I came to clear out my desk."

He seemed to mull it over. "So you're unemployed now?"

"Yup."

After a moment, he said, "I was awarded one of two internships for next summer. The award was based on merit, but because so many students qualified, they had to pick the winners by lottery. I couldn't believe my luck when they picked my name." He paused. He didn't look like a lottery winner.

"That sounds great," she said.

"Yeah, well, my professor had me come in today—so he could tell me to my face—the company had cutbacks. There's only one winner now. I'm the loser." He glanced at the umbrella. "Thanks." With an expression that was less scowl but still melancholy, he ducked out from under the umbrella and walked off.

||0 ||0 ||0

DURING THE SHORT RIDE IN THE HORSE-DRAWN CARRIAGE, CHELSEA had hoped to wave to droves of adoring workers, but they all seemed to go about their business, not even looking up as the carriage passed.

At the main house, Gregory and a servant helped her mom up the stairs and into the wheelchair.

A woman emerged from the opening doors, arms outstretched. "Evan!"

"Mother!" Evangelos hugged and kissed her. They exchanged words in Greek that Chelsea took to be something like "How are you?" or "It's been so long." His mother looked as she did in the pics and vids, maybe a bit plumper, but she wore it well under a sophisticated-looking evening dress. Chelsea tried to judge if the dress was conservative, but the differences in age and culture made it impossible to know.

Evangelos turned and—in English this time—said, "Please let me introduce you to Mrs. Margaret Pitt and her daughter, Chelsea."

Chelsea received an even warmer welcome. The hugging and kissing was more than Chelsea was used to. Brits weren't quite so familiar so quickly. *I'll have to get used to this.* And they were speaking so loudly now. This was all very natural for Evangelos, like he could switch between British and Greek at the snap of a finger. Yet the energy was contagious.

His mother offered apologies for Evangelos's grandfather, saying he'd join them shortly and added that he spent much of his time on his yacht but that he was on his way. Then she led them to a sitting area to have cocktails. Servants offered drinks and *mezethes*. "That's the special name for hors d'oeuvres," Evangelos explained.

*How grand! My first dinner party with wealthy people. And in a foreign country!*

Chelsea watched the exchanges between Evangelos and his mother, imagining herself in his family. The nervous feeling returned, and she questioned her worthiness to be his wife in the eyes of these sophisticated people with their rich traditions. Evangelos's mother was so warm and engaging. Was it possible for her to become angry? *I'm practically a street whore compared to the family's expectations.* A shock wave flashed across her body as the memory of the night at the dance club replayed in her mind—the black man with his tongue deep in her mouth. She'd felt violated and ashamed at the time. Ashamed for allowing herself to become so vulnerable. The shame continued even now, because she couldn't ignore the conflicting thought that he was so incredibly good looking. The primal thought, combined with the embarrassment, lodged in her brain. *Did I desire Evangelos's affection so completely that I lost my sense of reality? Was my outfit too sexy? Did I invite the kiss somehow? Or was it just an innocent pass at me? Then why didn't he stay and try to talk to me?* Chelsea put her fingertips to her lip.

"Chels, is everything OK?" Evangelos asked.

Everyone was looking at her, including a distinguished-looking gentleman.

"Chelsea, Margaret, I want you to meet my grandfather Alexander Venizelos, my father's father. Pappous, let me introduce you to Mrs. Margaret Pitt and her daughter, Chelsea."

"Welcome to my home. It's wonderful to meet you at last," said his grandfather in heavily accented English. When Chelsea stood, he crossed the room deftly and confidently, like a man half his age. He held her at the shoulders, gently but firmly, and kissed her on each cheek. Not too close; he seemed to sense the right amount of space she was comfortable with. His motions were so smooth and natural. He was the kind of man who could pull you out onto the dance floor and make you look amazing even if you'd never danced a step in your life. His dinner jacket was deep crimson over ivory silk. His cologne, enchanting.

After a servant announced that dinner was ready, Chelsea took Evangelos's arm. The large dining room was just as luxurious as the sitting room. Gregory assisted her mom up and out of the wheelchair to a seat at the table. Servants poured champagne. Evangelos's grandfather looked around the table and raised his glass.

Evangelos interrupted, "Pappous, if you don't mind."

"Not at all. Please."

Evangelos stood and looked around the table and then to Chelsea's mom. "Margaret, I want to thank you for making the long trip to my family's home to meet my mother and my grandfather. Such a long trip can be a burden, and I wouldn't have asked you to do so if the purpose weren't so very important to me—and to Chelsea." He turned. "Chelsea, I wanted to have all our loved ones together so that I might ask you a very important question." He knelt to one knee and took her hand. "Chelsea, ever since I left home for boarding school in London, I've felt a sense of isolation. Odd, since I've never had trouble making friends; I've met so many wonderful people in England and have many close relationships. Still, I felt alone until the day we met."

"I joined you under your brolly," she said.

"Yes. A sudden downpour. You came straight under. Brash as ever. And stunningly beautiful." He squeezed her hand. "From that moment forward, the aloneness was gone, and the sense of family returned. I knew then that I wanted to spend the rest of my life with you. Chelsea, will you marry me?"

"Yes!" She leaped off the chair into his arms and kissed him.

Everyone clapped and chuckled.

Chelsea realized how it must have looked, and she pulled herself away.

Evangelos sat down too, but he continued to hold her hand under the table. He gave his grandfather a deferential nod.

"To my grandson and my granddaughter-to-be," he said with glass raised, "may you find joy and happiness in all that life brings."

Glasses touched, the champagne was tasted, and hugs were exchanged, even cheek kisses. The conversation erupted around the idea that the announcement was hardly a surprise and how thrilled the family was that Evangelos would be settling down.

Chelsea felt elated. Evangelos's mother and grandfather had accepted her warmly. She was the center of attention, and her mom was enjoying it too.

The servants entered the room with the first course.

"Now, Chelsea," said his mother, "I realize that it's traditional for you to be presented with an engagement ring. I don't want you to feel that my son has neglected you. The truth is, our family has a set of rings that have been passed down through generations to the eldest son. Naturally, we would want you to have the engagement ring tonight, but, well, I don't know how to say this any other way—the gems are really quite valuable and only worn at special events with proper security. The rings are held in a vault at our bank in the city. Evan has arranged to take you there tomorrow."

"Yes," said Evangelos, "and once we return to London, I'd like to pick out a ring with you, one that you can wear safely in public. You won't be disappointed."

"So," continued his mother, "it would be our honor if you would accept the rings to represent your bond."

"The honor would be mine, truly. I wouldn't dream of anything else. It sounds magnificent." Chelsea wanted to ask if they had a picture. *No, that might be rude. Maybe later.*

The joyous tone continued throughout the dinner. Before dessert, Evangelos's grandfather excused himself, saying he had some work he needed to finish. Servants offered after-dinner drinks. Chelsea wanted a drink in the worst way, but she refrained. Her mom, blaming the eventful day, asked to retire and, after catching Chelsea's eye, said that her daughter should get to know Evangelos's mother better.

It seemed like only a few minutes passed when a servant asked if Mr. Venizelos would be able to talk with Evangelos and Chelsea privately, in his study. Evangelos's mother took the cue and said good night.

Hand in hand, the couple followed the servant through the beautiful halls of the estate. Evangelos seemed apprehensive.

"Maybe you're not the only one capable of surprises?" Chelsea giggled, trying to lighten the mood.

"Maybe."

Stepping inside the study—an enormous room with a very high ceiling and rich masculine furnishings—Chelsea felt Evangelos's grip tighten. He was focused on his grandfather, sitting at a desk. Books lined the wall behind him from floor to ceiling. Directly across from the doors, the entire wall was glass, providing a commanding view of the grounds. Landscape lighting illuminated the trees and shrubs under a clear night sky full of stars. To the left was a large sitting area with a couch and several large wing-backed chairs facing a grand fireplace. Chelsea could just barely make out a man sitting in one of the chairs holding a snifter of brandy or liquor.

"Sit down," his grandfather said without smiling.

Evangelos, realizing the force of his grip, stopped crushing Chelsea's hand. Once they were seated, Chelsea expected Evangelos to ask, "What's this all about?" But he simply waited.

His grandfather stood and walked along the bookshelves and then back. "When were you going to tell me about the baby?"

||0 ||0 ||0

THROUGH THE OPEN DOOR, SOUNDS OF BUSY HOSPITAL PERSONNEL drifted in from the hallway. The pubcomm was playing a news program, but Lisa wasn't interested. She wasn't paying attention and didn't care. Her life would never be the same, but she wasn't defeated; she wanted revenge. *Justice, optional.*

The FBI was no help. The agents seemed eager at first. Naturally, the forensics would lead them right to the guilty party. *Bastards.* No one got away with crimes in this day and age. And only nut cases actually committed crimes, because the concept of logical consequences was no deterrent to crazy people. But the DNA evidence from her case had come back as inconclusive. The FBI's interest in finding the culprits had evaporated at that point. *Inconclusive?* No one could explain what that meant.

"Lisa! Good morning. Today's your big day," said Dr. Sinclair, entering the room.

She didn't acknowledge him.

"Your parents are making arrangements to take you home. Aren't you excited to finally get out of here?" The sunshine gone from his voice now, he said, "Lisa, I can't imagine how difficult this is for you. I think the therapy sessions are helping, don't you?" He waited for her to respond. "Well, you'll be discharged this weekend. Keep up your walks. Two each day. You'll get more comfortable with the crutch. You need the exercise and fresh air."

Her face softened. "Sure. And thank you for everything, Doctor. Really."

"OK then. Talk to you in two weeks." He patted her shoulder and left.

*Being home won't change anything.*

Out of the periphery of her eye, she caught a glimpse of an image on the pubcomm display. *One of the bastards!*

She flailed and tried to give the hand gesture to rewind. With almost unbearable frustration she remembered, yet again, that she was left-handed—but now with no left arm! In frantic desperation, she managed to rewind the vid using her other arm.

"At a press conference today in Sacramento, California, Rick Anderson, CEO of TerraStore Information Storage, announced the donation of $750 million to build a new medical research facility aimed at finding cures for the six most deadly diseases. TerraStore is one of several enterprises controlled by Aeron Skotino."

A still image of a businessman appeared superimposed next to the anchor's head. Skotino's unforgettable black hair and bronze complexion, pocked in the way that remained after bad acne as a teen.

*"That's one of them!"*

"A spokesperson for the organization confirmed that the recent charitable activity is a direct result of Skotino's personal philanthropic goals."

*"That's one of them!"* She gestured *nurse call* and simultaneously pounded the manual nurse call button again and again.

The pubcomm switched to show the face of the duty nurse. "Lisa, what's up?"

"I know who did it! I know the name of one of the bastards who tortured me!"

"What? Hold on, I'll be right there."

*Payback, you bastards. Payback.*

||0 ||0 ||0

WARMTH FLUSHED ACROSS CHELSEA'S FACE. *BABY?* SHE PUT HER hand on her tummy. It was like his grandfather had x-ray vision. "How did—"

His grandfather interrupted in Greek, yelling at Evangelos. Not knowing the language, she felt cut off. At one point in the exchange, Evangelos turned to look at the strange man in the winged-back chair.

"Please ... Evangelos ..." Chelsea tried to get an explanation, but the lip lashing continued.

Finally, his grandfather said to her in English, "Chelsea, my dear, I realize all of this is very new to you. You must understand what life as a Venizelos entails. The limitations—limitations placed upon us by our station in the world—are necessary because of the unrest across the globe. Dear Chelsea, my son was taken from me, murdered by cowards. It was my own fault. I was complacent, unprepared. I will *never* take the safety of my family for granted again. You have no idea of the personnel in place to protect Evangelos. This has largely been invisible to you, for good reason."

His grandfather seemed older now, his charisma fractured somehow. "Chelsea, you have put me in a difficult position. You're worried I will pass judgment on you for becoming pregnant out of wedlock. No. You clearly love each other, and I believe my grandson has made a brilliant choice. But the heir to the Venizelos family fortune requires protection. What has been invisible to you will now become apparent. Unfortunately, you have robbed me of the time to prepare for the protection of both you and your unborn son."

*Son?* she thought. *How could—*

"There will be demands made of you. Both of you." His eyes flitted over her shoulder. "You will cooperate."

She didn't know what to say. Her entire world had turned upside down.

"Go now," said his grandfather. A smile appeared on his face, and his tone had softened; the smooth confidence had returned. "Get a good night's sleep. Don't fret. You'll have a wonderful time tomorrow. The ring is special. I hope you'll agree. My granddaughter Triana will be home from her studies for the weekend. She wants to meet you with a passion. You can all go together. Enjoy it. I'll take care of everything."

# CHAPTER 8

LAURA LEFT THE HOUSE WITH CHRIS IN THE STROLLER— the way she did each morning if the weather wasn't bad. And like all the mornings before, she looked for the woman who lived at the corner house. *There she is.* Laura was beginning to think the woman was deliberately avoiding her. After all, Laura left the house at the same time each day.

The woman was sweeping the walk again and had her back to Laura. Laura decided to be more direct this time. She waited before speaking until she was only a few feet away.

"Good morning! My name's Laura—Laura Richards. I live there, on the right."

The woman turned and smiled meekly. "I'm Sue Avenir …"

It sounded like she would say more but didn't. The silence became awkward. Laura started to speak, but then the woman added, "Oh, your baby is adorable. A boy?"

"His name's Chris. He was born in August, on the fourteenth. It looks like you'll be having yours soon too."

"Yes." Sue caressed her protruding midsection and rested her hand across the top. "It could be any day, really."

"Only a few months apart; maybe they'll be playmates."

"Maybe."

More awkward silence.

"Look, if you need anything. If there is anything, *anything* at all I can do to help, you let me know. OK?"

"OK." Sue smiled, but there was no acknowledgment of the subtext.

"OK." Laura waved good-bye and pushed the stroller on toward the park.

Sue did look genuinely pleased and thankful, but if a friendship was possible, it was going to take a while to break the ice. *I'll look her up online.* Some people were more comfortable with online relationships.

||0 ||0 ||0

IN THE STREAM OF PEDESTRIANS, CHELSEA MADE HER WAY ALONG the street to the café to meet Evangelos for lunch. Normally, she would saunter down the street and watch the eyes of the men walking the opposite direction to see if they noticed her and to see the expressions on their faces. Now she didn't want to think about anyone watching her.

Once they had returned to London, Evangelos told her about the security precautions. Their movements were monitored 24-7, either electronically or by special personnel. These people were very good and would remain unseen unless needed. Disappointed, she'd imagined a security detail. She wanted to visit her friends in her old neighborhood. Her convoy would pull up in front of a friend's house with a motorcycle cop in front, lights flashing.

She scrutinized the trans traveling on the street. Nothing out of the ordinary. No one was blatantly following her. It was creepy to think someone was watching her at all times, but she also remembered the incident at the club. *If that happened again, what would be the consequences? Surely he wouldn't get away with it. What would they do to him?*

Evangelos was already at a table, and he waved her over.

"I have wonderful news," she said, sitting down after a kiss. "I've found the perfect baby doctor. You'll adore him! He comes highly recommended. I have my first appointment next week."

"Pardon?" said Evangelos. "An obstetrician? Highly recommended? Really. By whom, exactly?"

"He earned five stars out of five in the online directory. I read all the reviews. His patients always comment about his nurturing approach. And several women who had dire situations credited him for saving their child's life! Impressive, don't you think?"

"Yes, absolutely smashing," he said dryly. "Um, so, we're still on for this weekend? We'll go ring shopping?" There was excitement in his voice now. "I want to get you a spectacular ring to show off to your girlfriends."

"Oh yes. I can't wait. And I've looked at the plans to convert the extra bedroom into a nursery. The designer for the nursery is taking care of everything!"

"OK. And the wedding … I know things are a bit rushed since you don't want to be showing in the pics, but … Chels … the wedding just couldn't be soon enough for me."

"Oh yes, the wedding coordinator is taking care of all the arrangements. But if I was showing a little by that time, well, it wouldn't be the end of the world."

He looked at her blankly.

"What?"

"Well … I don't know … everything seems to be rather … intermingled," he said. "For the past year, I've thought about nothing but spending the rest of my life with you. God, you're so sexy. We've had to control ourselves for so long. I don't know. I'm excited about the baby, of course, but—"

"Sex? You're not excited about the baby because of sex?"

"Shh, keep your voice down. No. I don't know. I guess I'm feeling, well, almost jealous. I want *you*, Chels. And I want you to want me. I'm sorry, I feel horrible for saying it."

"No. I'm glad you said it. You're right. There's been so much change so quickly. I love you desperately, Evan, and I can't wait to be married. The baby has opened up so many possibilities. A baby shower! It's all so incredible!"

"Oh, so now you're calling me Evan?"

"Yes, just like Triana and your mother. It was so cute! Do you mind?"

"Being addressed by you with the same name my mother uses is a little unsettling, but I guess I'll get used to it."

||0 ||0 ||0

LAURA TRIED TO STEAL AWAY A FEW MINUTES TO GET THE HOUSE picked up while Chris was down for his afternoon nap. It seemed like she never got a break. Her life now was so different—a selfish thought, maybe—but it was definitely easier before.

From the window, she saw the university van pass by on the alley, and then it backed into the driveway.

"What are you bringing home this time?" she called from the back door.

Ben hopped out of the van. "More equipment." The loading door of the van rolled up.

The equipment he'd brought home in the past was mostly computer stuff, but this load looked like building material.

"Is that *all* going downstairs?"

"Yes," he said, maneuvering a power hand truck under a pallet.

"What is it?"

"A Compton chamber."

She waited for more of an explanation. The hand-truck motor groaned as it lifted the pallet off the ground. "What is it?" she repeated.

He stopped, turned, and walked over. "You know the algorithms I develop in my work are the result of analyzing brain functions, right? A Compton chamber is what I use to perform brain scans."

"I know that. You use the psychology department's chamber. Why do you need one here?"

"This one's different."

"How?"

His shoulders slumped. "Look, I'm sorry. This is another communication failure on my part. We should have discussed it together. I know the lab takes up a lot of room in the house."

"Yes, people with our model prefab use that basement level for an entertainment room or exercise area. We need that kind of functional space now. It could be a playroom."

"I know. Having the lab at home was a compromise, and now the situation's different because we have Chris."

"Yes."

He looked at the equipment and then back to her. "Do you want me to take it back?"

"I don't know," she said. "Yes, I feel resentment. That's not fair to you, because we agreed to have the lab here. But the deal was that you were going to spend more time at home. You're physically here, but I assumed you would be *present*."

"You're right. I can do better."

She let the point linger for a moment and then said, "But I sense something's different with you—about the lab—you seem ... driven."

"You're right, I guess. You know how there was that weirdness about the doctor unable to scan Chris's vital signs?"

"Yeah."

"And those first weeks we had Chris, how we got those strange errors from the seccomm in the pertran and in the house?"

"Yeah, but that stopped. It's not a problem anymore."

"No, it's still a problem. The scanners are still throwing off warnings; I adjusted the system to ignore them for now."

"What's the error? What do the warnings mean? And what does all that have to do with this—this chamber thing?"

"Well, the seccomm system uses a biometric scanner to locate and identify people. Society uses these scanners for everything—security, advertising, even to properly size clothing. Chris is going to have major issues growing up if we don't figure out what's going on. At the very least, I'll need to make some modifications to the house. I'm sure he's fine. The more I understand what's going on, the more we can be confident about that and the better I'll feel. I learned how the scanners work, and I want to use the chamber as a programmable scanner. I'm going to figure out what's going on." He took a deep breath. "Laura, when Chris is within sensor range, the scanners don't see anything. Nothing. Like he's not even there."

# CHAPTER 9

"**H**ONEY, ARE YOU SURE YOU WANT TO KEEP LOOKING AT it?" asked Lisa's mom on the pubcomm display on the hospital room's wall.

Lisa stared into the hand mirror. The image was grotesque. She wouldn't be fitted for an ocular implant for another few months, and more plastic surgery for her cheek was scheduled. The empty eye socket was revolting, but she preferred not to wear the eye patch the doctor gave her. She wanted the constant reminder, and she wanted there to be no confusion for others about what happened.

"Please, honey, put it down, just for now."

"No," she said, tilting the mirror for a better angle.

A small vid image popped up, superimposed in the corner of the display. "Lisa, you have a visitor. He's on his way up," said the duty nurse.

"That's the officer now. Please, honey, put down the mirror so you can talk with him. He's trying to help you."

"Mom, he's just going to take my statement. Again. He's not going to *do* anything."

"But you recognized that man. They have to take you seriously now."

"Detective Fontain is fat and old. He's a slug, Mom."

"Please, honey, don't you think—"

Fontain entered the room. Seeing her mom on the display, he said hello, and they exchanged pleasantries.

"How are you doing, Lisa?" he asked.

She put the hand mirror down. "How's it look like I'm doing?" She let the sight of the eye socket make its impression.

Unflapped, he said, "Lisa, I came here to talk to you about your claim that Aeron Skotino is allegedly one of the people who held you captive."

"Claim? Alleged? Are you fucking kidding me?"

"Oh, honestly, dear. Your language. Be respectful and—"

With a gesture, Lisa ended the vidcomm.

"Fine," said Fontain. "I'll give it to you straight. Do you know who this Skotino character is?"

"Who cares? What counts is what he did to me."

"He owns and operates one of the largest companies in the world. A conglomerate. We're talking hundreds of billions of dollars, Lisa. While you were so busy comming my office, did you pay any attention to the news story? Huh? The guy is giving money to charity, Lisa. In a big way."

"So he's a goddamn saint? Is that what you're saying? So, again, you're going to do nothing? You came all the way out here to tell me that?"

"Just think for a minute about the likelihood."

"Fuck you."

"Lisa, your forensic data are inconclusive. If the guy was within ten feet of you, we could pick up some kind of DNA evidence that—"

"I can't even believe it. I'm the victim, you idiot. *I was there*, asshole. Get out! *Get out!*"

||0 ||0 ||0

UNDER THE DARKNESS OF NIGHT, MARK SPIRE MOVED SILENTLY along the street leading to the medical center building in London. From his percomm, he tapped a command, and the display showed verification from Tyvold that the security system was now disabled.

He moved in behind the building to the back entrance next to a loading dock door. The light above the door went dark. In the shadows, he waited until the pocket door swished open, and then he slipped through. He went to the sixth floor and found the designated examination room. Inside, he surveyed the ceiling tiles and selected a location for his perch.

||0 ||0 ||0

"OK, BUDDY, YOU'RE ALL SET." LAURA GOT CHRIS SETTLED IN THE pertran's child restraint seat as the tran pulled out onto the main road from their home. He had a good grip on the ring of plastic keys, which had quickly become his favorite toy. *Keys?* Funny how old-fashioned concepts like choo-choo trains and keys were used for infant toys. She couldn't recall the last time she'd seen a real key. Chris's fondness for the plastic keys was so ironic. *You couldn't open a door if your life depended on it.*

"Let's go see Father Arnold and see what kind of grade I get on my homework, shall we?"

Chris just stretched his fingers around the keys into a small fist and added a few kicks of his legs.

During the drive, Laura took a moment to check for messages on the pubcomm in the pertran. "Look, Chris! Our friend down the street had her baby. A girl. She named her Hope—Hope Avenir. What a pretty name. Well, we'll have to stop by and say hello. I guess I should pick up a baby gift. That'll be fun, won't it?"

The pertran completed the auto-park cycle, and with Chris in the detachable restraint seat, Laura carried him inside.

"Now that things have settled down a bit," said Father Arnold, "I wanted to ask if you had a chance to ask Ben about his thoughts about God and parenting."

"Yes. And your suspicions were right. He made a distinction between religion and spirituality and considers himself to be a spiritual person. He also doesn't see a conflict between science and the belief in a higher power. In fact, he gave me some examples of areas in science where experts believe that our knowledge of the physical universe intersects with belief in a higher intelligence. Actually, I think *intelligence* is the wrong word … higher power still fits, maybe, but he emphasized the emotional side."

"Good," said Father Arnold. "Now, I have some more homework for you. But this may take a long time—years, maybe. I want you to think about your life as it's been up to this point. Think about the time before you met Ben and after you were married. I want you to fix in your mind your outlook on life, its purpose, and what it means to you now. In the future, I'm going to ask you to compare your memory to life in the future with Chris in your life. Of course, I know your life has changed tremendously already, but I don't mean that; I don't mean the day-to-day stuff. After enough time passes, I'll want you to tell me what's different at a deeper level."

"Yes, Father."

"Wonderful. Now, I can see Chris is starting to get antsy. Mind if I hold him?"

"Oh, of course not," she gushed. She unstrapped Chris and lifted him into Father Arnold's arms. Chris went easily with big eyes.

||0 ||0 ||0

"CUESTA? ELIZABETH CUESTA?" CALLED THE ADORABLE YOUNG Asian woman at the open door next to the reception desk. She was wearing a cute surgical blouse—not the green kind but rather white with a purple flower print. Chelsea looked around the waiting room of the

146    ANDREW HUNKINS

baby doctor's office. She had plenty of time; she'd arrived twenty minutes early. She couldn't help it. She'd filled out all the registration forms and questionnaire paperwork online and read all the posted information for first-time mothers. Dr. Opum had a stellar reputation—five out of five, in fact. *I'll show Evan I can make good decisions.*

The waiting room was neat, clean, and well decorated. The other patients looked like they came from wage-earning families. *Didn't they? Hard to be sure.* Chelsea glanced at the clock. Ten more minutes and it would be her turn.

At almost exactly the time of her appointment, the same woman opened the door and called Chelsea's name and then led her to an examination room to change into a gown. The woman performed the biometric scan in preparation for the exam. Everything looked fine. "The doctor will be in shortly," said the nurse on her way out.

When the door opened again, Chelsea recognized Dr. Opum from his pic online.

"Hello. I'm Dr. Nigel Opum. You must be Miss Pitt."

"Yes," she said. "Uh, soon I'll be Mrs. Venizelos. I'm engaged to be married," she added. *Oh, this isn't starting off well at all.*

"Well, that's wonderful," he said.

Sitting on the examination table, she offered her hand in greeting, and he shook it gently. But before letting go, he said very directly, "You know, we don't make any judgments around here. I'm your doctor, and I want to you feel like you can share anything and everything with me. OK?"

"OK." He was so very genuine and confident. She relaxed.

"Brilliant. Now then, let's get started. I want to learn your history and get to know you better. Your medical transcript is on file here now, and I reviewed your medical log. Today, I'll assess your condition. Please, lie back." He placed his hands on her abdomen and pressed gently at various spots. "You've been feeling well?"

"Yes, Doctor."

"All right. The pelvic exam is next." He placed the stirrups in the mounting holes. "OK, just scoot down to the edge." He helped her place her legs up into the stirrups. "That's it."

Looking up, she squinted from the harsh room lights. She could hear him as he wheeled a stool around to the end of the table and positioned himself between her legs. Just then, she heard a notification chime.

"What's this?" he said. "I shouldn't be disturbed during examinations. I know this was set to silent. I'll turn it off. I'm so sorry, Miss Pitt."

"Oh, no bother." She heard him fumbling under his lab coat for his percomm as the chime persisted.

"That's odd; it *is* on silent. Hmm, let me see. Oh my. Unfortunately, the message is an urgent one. Miss Pitt, if you don't mind, I really should handle this. I'll be back in just a moment."

"Of course, Doctor. I'm fine."

She sensed him brush past the exam table and heard the door open and close. *Dr. Opum is certainly conscientious. If I ever need his urgent help, he'll be available to me too. He's the kind of doctor that cares about his patients.*

"I'm so sorry for the wait, Chelsea. Let's continue."

"Oh, you're back. I … OK." She heard the stool roll into position again.

"I'm going to insert the speculum now. You may experience some discomfort."

She sensed him get closer and felt the warmth of his body against her thighs in the cool air of the examination room. After a moment, he seemed unusually close, she could feel his breath across her pubic hairs. *Is this normal?* She prepared herself for the speculum. But it didn't feel the way she remembered; it was very gradual—almost nothing at all. Maybe it was nothing at all. *Did he even start?* She waited. *Is he finished?* The sound of the opening door made her jump.

"So sorry, Miss Pitt." She heard the stool roll into position yet again. "No excuse for it. Entirely unacceptable. I'll be having a word with my staff. If it's an emergency, I should be notified by a knock on the door, not this ridiculous device. A thousand apologies, Miss Pitt. Now, please relax, I'll finish your examination."

*There*, Chelsea felt the speculum, uncomfortable as usual. *Did he leave twice?* She considered asking, but he had resumed the questions about her history. He was no doubt embarrassed; his apology was so sincere.

After the exam, he assured her that everything looked normal and that she should expect a normal pregnancy. With a prescription for prenatal vitamins and an appointment scheduled for the following month, she gathered her things and headed back to the flat.

# Chapter 10

NOTHING ON THE PUBCOMM TO WATCH. ONLY A FEW MORE days until the weekend and she would finally be able to go home. Lisa gestured to change the channel. She'd gotten used to using her other hand. She gestured again.

Her percomm jingled. "Hey, Dad," she answered. "I didn't think I'd hear from you until tomorrow."

"I'm sorry, Lisa. This isn't your dad. Please don't hang up. I'm Detective Jones from the Las Vegas Metropolitan Police Department."

"I don't understand. Did my dad lose his percomm or something?"

"No. Please listen. Did a Detective Fontain visit you yesterday?"

*Fontain? Now what? These people have quite the nerve.* "I don't want anything to—"

"Please, Lisa, please listen to me." His voice was urgent, but she sensed compassion. "I know Fontain came to tell you that there's no evidence supporting your case. That's not entirely true. Look, I can't have this conversation over the comm network. Please, can you meet me outside the hospital?"

"How did you get my dad's percomm? Look, if you think you can just—"

"I don't have your dad's percomm. I spoofed the comm. I'll explain everything. Please, Lisa. We can't talk this way. The hospital parking lot—there's a bench at the far end. Do you know it?"

Maybe she wasn't the only one who thought Fontain was an idiot. "All right. When should—"

"Now, Lisa. Can you meet me outside right now?"

"Uh, give me a minute. How will I—"

"You'll know." The connection ended.

With her crutch, she hobbled out of her room.

"Where are you headed, dear?" asked the duty nurse from the nurse's station.

"Going for a walk," she said. "Doctor's orders."

"Good girl!"

She was getting the hang of the crutch. They had to amputate her left foot and left arm—too much infection. Eventually, she'd get a prosthetic foot and not need the crutch. But the crutch was fine; it just took a little longer.

Sure enough, a vehicle was parked at the far end of the parking lot with the unmistakable characteristics of an unmarked police vehicle—too plain—and a man waiting on the bench along the walking path. He was the only person that far from the hospital entrance. He was young, maybe a few years older than herself.

When she finally reached the spot, he stood up.

"Coulda parked a little closer, dontcha think?" she said. "I'm not quite ready for Cirque du Soleil."

"Sorry," he said. He was wearing a suit, not unlike Fontain's, conspicuously plain. But where Fontain's neck bulged with fat and his gut hung over his waist, this guy was tall, lean, and fit.

"Let me see some identification."

He pulled his percomm from his suit pocket, tapped the display, and held it up. Lisa aimed the camera of her percomm at him. The display flashed green, confirming the credentials matched his image.

"Sorry to have to talk with you this way. I'm here against orders." He looked from side to side. "Lisa, the people who hurt you are powerful and have the ability to track information that you would find hard to believe. The hospital surveillance cameras are recording us even now. A trail of evidence is getting longer by the second. I can purge the data, but there is only so much I can do before I create suspicion. Please, can you come with me to my vehicle so I can explain?" He held out his arm.

She paused and looked in his eyes. The compassion in his voice was evident, even the way he looked at her. She took his arm.

He helped her to the tran and opened the door. For a moment, the scene made her think of a boy she once knew, and just as quickly, she reminded herself that no man like this would ever find her desirable again.

"Now what's this all about?" she demanded once he was in the tran too.

"Skotino—the guy you ID'd—he controls some very influential companies. One of them, TerraStore, stores data for most of the global network—the US government, the Mexican government, the FBI, and most state and city agencies, including mine, the Vegas police. They receive every kind of real-time streaming data you can think of, including security feeds. Every transaction you make and every sec-comm you pass, it's all recorded. Lisa, I have security authorization as part of my job to manipulate the hospital seccomm. Yes, it takes a court order, but as you know from press reports, it happens all the time without one. I've prevented the seccomm from recording my presence here, and I can keep them from tracking my vehicle's location for short periods. But I have to get back to my normal jurisdiction. Lisa, we need to drive around while I explain more. Will you take a drive with me? I have more to tell you."

She looked at the stub at her ankle and the left sleeve of her shirt neatly folded and pinned to her shoulder. "Well, OK. I guess."

"Good." He tapped commands at the console, and the tran backed out of the parking space.

"So these companies, part of Skotino's TerraHoldings, have government contracts—not just city and state but military too. These guys are completely wired. So when the report came in that you identified Skotino, it must have tripped a slew of alerts." He sat back in his seat. "Lisa, I'm ashamed to say that the FBI are not going to do anything. And as far as I know, there's no authority that you could appeal to hear your case."

"Well, I kind of figured that. But why? I don't understand why they did to me what they did."

"I don't, either," he said. "It doesn't make any sense. Not yet. But I'm worried for your life, Lisa. If you press forward, they'll kill you. No investigation. No one will care."

"Why are you doing this? Why don't you just let them spread their story—that the whole thing was some delirious hallucination following an accident after being hit by a speeding tran along the highway? Just another drugged-out college student ... completely ignore the obvious nature of my injuries. Why not just let them snuff me out if I keep complaining?" She wanted him to say, "I care! I care about you!" She wanted someone to believe her, care for her, protect her, and help her bring the bastards to justice.

"When I started with the force, I had such an altruistic determination about the kind of professional I would be. But it didn't take long before I realized how little influence I have. Everything about modern police work comes down to forensics. Between the physical evidence left behind and the surveillance evidence logged in the seccomm and pubcomm devices that saturate our society, no crime can be committed without generating mounds of evidence—even serious crimes like murder. We track every conceivable method known to destroy evidence. Air filters register the signature of burned human protein. We monitor the sewer systems, lakes, and streams for human remains, even if they've been destroyed by chemicals. The only known way to get away with crime is to hide the evidence beyond the lifetime of those responsible. My profession is point-less. Before long, I'll be just like Fontain." He looked away from her.

None of it was about her. She scolded herself for risking the thought, that he could be some kind of white knight to save her. "You didn't answer my question," she said.

"No, you're right." He continued, "I wish I could tell you that I'll help you go after Skotino ... that I can avenge your hellish ordeal. But I can't. I'm sorry. I'm doing this because you said in your statement that there had to be other people held captive. You said you heard them sometimes. Is that true?"

"Yes," she said. "I don't know how many. I never saw anyone else, but I could hear them."

"Lisa, I don't know if it's possible to save those other victims, but I see no reason to believe that the torturing will end. I'm doing this because they must be stopped, but it can't be done in connection to your case. They're watching you. Everything you do, everything you say, and every move you make is monitored. I can't hide you from the grid for any significant period. Your life is in danger if you pur-sue this. And anyone else who has information that could aid your case is also in danger. You must stop going after Skotino for your own sake and tell me everything you said to family or friends that would put them in danger. I can use the information to investigate on a different path. They won't be monitoring me."

"I told the police and the FBI everything. I don't know how I got away. I can't remember anything but the room. My first memory was waking up in the hospital." Looking outside, she noticed they were traveling across the desert, away from the city. "Where are we going?"

"I'm assuming you weren't supposed to survive. Skotino wouldn't let you see his face and allow you to live. So that means you escaped somehow without them knowing. It's really just a stab in the dark, but I'm guessing the location where you were found is important, because they had no chance to control that. Working backward, I figure the place they held you might be on the road ahead. The terrain might trigger a memory even if you have no direct recollection of events. I'd like you to tell me if anything looks familiar for any reason at all."

"Honestly, I can't remember a thing."

"I know. Consciously you don't, but the terrain might jog a memory—even a fragment—anything that might tell us we're close."

"OK," she said.

The road sliced between foothills rising to tall mesa cliffs in the distance. The surroundings became more rugged, but nothing seemed familiar. The tran climbed the winding road, and then halfway up, it pulled over along a stretch with rock faces on either side.

"Why are we stopping?"

"The only buildings or structures in this area are off the road, and I don't want to go directly toward them. There's a spot here where you can look out over the entire range and see the homes. I'd like you to have a look. It's getting dark. This is our last chance."

"OK," said Lisa, feeling useless, as if she was letting him down.

He helped her out of the tran. With the crutch under her good arm, she walked with him to the break in the rock overlooking the range. When she was close enough to peer around the gap in the rock, she sensed he was no longer following.

A few feet behind her, he'd stopped. Glancing back, he had a strange grin on his face and was looking over her shoulder.

Turning again, she saw a parked vehicle ahead— an old truck—and men coming toward her. *Skotino!* She backed up.

The young detective grabbed her from behind, kicked the crutch away, and forced her to her knees.

Skotino walked up, flanked by two other men. One, she recognized, had tortured her too. That man and Skotino were both well dressed and staring at her with a look that was part sneer and part resolve. The last man was dressed like a farmer and cowered behind the other two, paying more attention to them than to her.

"You've been a naughty girl, Lisa."

The voice rumbled across her psyche. Most of the torture had occurred with her eyes shut, but there was no way to block the sound of his voice. It seemed to make the ground shake. She didn't answer; she just stared back at him.

Skotino looked up at the detective. "What does she know, and who did she tell?"

"Nothing," said Jones. "So she had nothing to say to anyone."

The smirk was obvious even though she couldn't see his face behind her. He sounded confident and pleased with his elaborate deception, eager to win praise from Skotino.

"You asshole, Jones!"

He tightened his grip on her shoulders. "Oh, that's not my real name, Lisa, but I want to thank you for a most enjoyable date." His laugh was laced with sarcasm and ridicule.

Skotino looked back down. His left hand slid up along his suit coat, withdrawing the familiar knife from its sheath. He grabbed the back of her head by the hair. She screamed. He twisted her head back and to the side, providing a good view of her one good eye.

The sight of the knife alone was nearly unbearable. She forced herself to keep her eye open. He positioned the blade—double-serrated edge, six-inch blade, with the gold circle emblem on the handle—and pointed it directly at her remaining eye.

"See, Lisa," Jones continued, "I told you—a stab in the dark."

"Do you think you can properly transport the body this time?" asked Skotino.

The man dressed in denim nodded.

"Say it."

"Yes," he squeaked and looked away.

"No. You watch."

The other well-dressed man added, "Because if you screw up again, Ed, this is what will happen to one of your plump little babies ... and your wife will watch. Do you understand? Because we like it when you watch."

The man's gaze settled back. "Yes," he said again, clenching his jaw.

Skotino plunged the blade into Lisa's head, piercing the eyeball, slicing through the socket and into her brain behind. He twisted the knife. Her body twitched and went limp.

# CHAPTER 11

ഇന്ദ്ര

*Chelsea Victoria Pitt*
*&*
*Evangelos Venizelos*

*Have chosen*
*The first day*
*Of their new life together.*

*You are invited to share*
*In the joy of their wedding*
*At four o'clock in the afternoon.*

*Venizelos family compound*
*Thessaloniki, Greece*

*Guest travel and accommodations courtesy of*
*The Venizelos family.*

"NOW, JUST LOOK UP AT THE CEILING WHILE I DO YOUR EYES ..."

In her flat's sitting room, Chelsea remained very still. She wore a large paper bib around her neck. The makeup artist applied the proper color to best accentuate Chelsea's features, she'd explained, because of the bright lights and the meticulous eye of the high-definition vid camera. A technician was setting up studio lighting with what looked like large white parasols and rectangles of white fabric at precise angles. The director was hunched over a display screen making adjustments of some kind. Selby Hancock, her interviewer, should arrive any minute.

"Almost finished," said the makeup artist, dabbing a triangular wedge of sponge.

Chelsea could hardly contain her excitement. She'd dreamed of this life since she was old enough to use the pubcomm. The request to be interviewed by Ms. Hancock, publisher of the most prestigious online social registry network, came as a complete surprise. She'd said she wanted to capture—in Chelsea's own words—the scope and spectacle of one of the most exciting events of the year: her exotic wedding to one of London's most eligible bachelors. London's Nouveau Social Season would begin just after Christmas, and the interview would be a striking launch to kick off the season, now that she was officially Mrs. Chelsea Venizelos. *Oh, the sound of it! Mrs. Chelsea Venizelos.*

Ms. Hancock had said that the mystique of the Venizelos family shipping empire—not to mention the couple's stunning good looks, especially Evan's tall, dark, and handsome physique—had become a top sensation in London's social circles. Combined with the Greek venue, the story was irresistible.

"Visitor arriving. Quantity one," announced the seccomm's pleasant female voice.

"I'll show her in," offered the director. "She'll freak if she has to wait even a second."

Selby Hancock rushed in. Chelsea, keeping her head steady, strained to get a look at her. The *Selby Hancock!*

"All done," said the makeup artist with a final stroke to Chelsea's eyebrow, yanking off the paper bib.

Selby darted across the room, set her briefcase down without slowing, and landed in the chair across from Chelsea. The artist pulled out a fresh paper bib and tucked it under Selby's collar.

"Ms. Hancock, it's such a pleasure to meet you," said Chelsea. "In person, I mean. I've followed you online since I was a teen. I'm your biggest fan."

"The pleasure is all mine," said Selby, beaming. Then her expression snapped to one of exasperation. "That's fine. Enough!" She waved her hands. The makeup artist backed off and snatched the bib away. Selby's smile returned.

The director gave final instructions and called for quiet. The technician held a slate in front of the camera. Digital clock digits raced across its face. The technician pressed a button on the slate. *Clap!*

"Action!"

"Mrs. Venizelos, thank you for appearing on my show. You've just returned from your honeymoon, which followed your decadent wedding just six weeks ago. Our viewers are excited to hear the details. How does it feel to be married to Evangelos Venizelos?"

Chelsea described the wedding, the dress, and the luxurious honeymoon on a secluded Greek island. The interview then went on to topics more relevant to Chelsea and Evan's place among London's elite.

"Chelsea, now you must know that you've become somewhat of a role model for many young women—a girl of modest means swept into the lap of luxury. If that weren't enough, you've been very open about the circumstances of your pregnancy. Women all across His Majesty's kingdom—and indeed the world—are looking up to you for your maternal individualism."

"Well, my generation objects to hormone manipulation or any other artificial control over conception. Evan and I practiced celibacy—to our best ability." Chelsea gave her subtle but sexy little smile to the camera. "And I want to be very candid when I tell you that we didn't plan to get pregnant so soon. It just happened. Love will do that, you know." She giggled.

"You certainly are the quintessential mother image, with glowing skin and a baby bump. How have you managed?"

"Splendidly. Not even a touch of morning sickness. Now, I'm passing my sixth month, and he's really starting to grow. I just didn't expect him to be so heavy. I guess it's just more than my little frame is used to." She giggled again.

Selby finished the interview with a few more questions.

"That's a wrap. Nice work, people."

The technician began dismantling equipment.

"Brilliant!" Selby popped up from her chair and dashed for the door.

"Did it go well?" Chelsea called to her.

"Marvelously. We should have this edited by evening and posted online before midnight. I'm sure it'll get a million views." She waved and disappeared just as quickly as she'd arrived.

IIO IIO IIO

"DID YOU GET THE REST FINISHED?" ASKED BEN WHEN LAURA entered the kitchen, rubbing her cold hands after shoveling the walk.

"Yeah. All cleared off now. Just nice to be out-side," she said. "How's Mr. Hungry Man?"

"Great," said Ben. "Hard to say if he was really hungry or just sick of watching us shovel snow."

In the high chair, Chris's cheeks were still red. Ben scraped the bottom of the dish of smashed peas and slipped the last bit into Chris's mouth. Gathering the dish and spoon, Ben stood and then rolled a handful of whole peas onto the tray for Chris to play with while he prepared the next course. Chris cor-ralled the peas in his chubby fist and pushed them into his mouth palm-first. He had smushed peas on his cheek, on his chin, and between his fingers.

"Say, I've been meaning to ask you," Laura said as she washed her hands. "I signed up online for a newsletter. It's supposed to be a weekly subscription, but I'm not getting the messages. Could it be getting stuck in the filter?"

"Maybe," said Ben. "What kind of newsletter?"

"The one the kids hand out on campus. You know."

"Oh, that? It was blocked for sure." Ben stirred turkey puree with the little rubber-coated spoon. Chris flailed his arms and legs. Pea paste had migrated to his hair. "Why do you want to read that?"

"Why not?"

Ben shrugged. He sat down again, facing Chris.

"I mean," she continued, "why let people sign up for the newsletter if no one can get it?"

"Well, the people who want to read that sort of thing don't use their own accounts," he said.

Laura turned off the water and pulled out a fresh towel. "What do they use?"

"They use an untraceable account," he said, putting a spoonful of turkey into Chris's mouth. Most of it made it.

"There is such a thing?" she asked. "Why?"

"Human nature, I guess. The Internet was built on pornography, after all," he said. "What did Adam Smith call it? The invisible jerk-off?"

"Not funny. And watch your language, please."
She used the damp towel to wipe off as much pea
from Chris as possible. "But why use an account like
that just to get a newsletter?"

"The authorities track that kind of thing."

"Oh, those kids aren't dangerous. It's not like
they're Hoods or anything. They're just frustrated
because there're no jobs."

"I'm sure you're right," he said. "Still, people
don't just wake up one morning and decide to become
a Robin Hood terrorist."

| | O   | | O   | | O

CHELSEA ARRANGED SIX WALLPAPER SAMPLES ON THE DINING
room table. She wanted Evan's opinion. He was
studying late again. Or was he having a Venizelos
Shipping meeting? She wasn't sure.

The notification announced his arrival, and she
went to the door to greet him with a kiss. "Evan, I
know you're hungry, but come with me, just for a
second. I want you to look at the wallpaper choices!"
She took him by the arm and pulled him to the
dining room.

"Very well, but I've been told wallpaper paste
is edible, so I may not be able to control myself," he
said, giving mild resistance.

"Oh, come on, you'll love them," she said. "Look,
here they are. I'm going with blue, of course. This one
has pictures of trains. This one has pictures of bunny
rabbits. There are kangaroos, dinosaurs, and kites—

and this one has no pictures at all, just this enchant-ing design." She lifted the sixth one under the light so he could see it clearly.

"Well, you know I'm very partial to trains and bunnies," he said playfully. "But I agree the design on this one is intriguing. Do you think our son can survive the first few months of his life without knowing what a kangaroo looks like?"

"Seriously, do you like this last one?" She held it against the dining room wall for perspective.

"Yes, Chels, I do."

"Look at the wallpaper, silly, not me. I'm blowing up like a balloon." She put her arm back under her tummy. "Or maybe a wrecking ball."

"Could anything be more beautiful?"

"Oh, nonsense. But thank you for indulging me with my wallpaper selection. Everything will be just perfect! I'll let the designer know our choice. Now let's get you some dinner." Keeping one arm under her tummy, she took his hand, and they went to the kitchen. "I'll reheat some pasta for you while you relax."

"You know, I just love our flat," she said while he poured a glass wine and took a seat. "I know the baby will be very comfortable in the guest room once it's ready. But don't you think it would be nice to have a tad more room?" She tried to gauge his expression. "I don't mean we should be off on a large estate, but I'll be busy caring for the baby. Wouldn't a private chef be tremendous help?"

He picked up the fork and arranged the noodles on the plate, spreading and repiling.

"See?" she said. "You wouldn't have to put up with reheated leftovers."

"No, it's splendid," he said. "Chels, I think we do need to make some changes. I mean—well, I want to make sure we share the same values."

"Values?"

"Yes. Safety, for one. Safety is important to you, right? It's important to *us*. We want the best for our family when it comes to safety, yes? That's not an area where we want to compromise, is it?"

"No, of course not," she agreed tentatively. "What do you mean by change? Of course safety's important."

"Well, there're some bad people in the world, Chels. You're wealthy now. People will try to swindle you. Do you know how they do that? They find information about you, and then they use that information to create false trust. They wait for a time when you're vulnerable, and before you know it— bam—they've stolen money from you. Or worse. You don't want that."

"Of course not. I'll be careful."

"Chels, this online interview, you—"

"Oh! I completely forgot! Is it up? Oh, I want to see it! How did it turn out? How do I look? Oh, I can't believe you saw it before I did!"

"Chels, this is what I'm talking about. The information you shared ... the whole planet can see it."

She pouted.

"And another thing—I know you're very happy with your doctor. But it's not just *your* doctor; it's the baby's doctor too. I wasn't included in selecting the doctor."

"Well, you're so busy. And Dr. Opum is highly respected, and—"

"You found him online, for Christ's sake."

She opened her mouth to defend herself but held her tongue and frowned.

"Look," he said, "you're right; I'm not around as much as I'd like, but I need ... I mean, I want to spend the time on the really important decisions. Like safety. And I want the decisions to be ours, together."

She heard his words but really wanted to see the vid.

"Chels, I got a recommendation from the university. Dr. Brandon Cornelius. He's the head of the human genetics department, fully certified in obstetrics, his reputation is—"

"My doctor is just fine!"

"Please, listen to me. Prominent families go to him because he's the best. We can't compromise on safety."

"Dr. Opum is no compromise!" she shot back, and then she organized her thoughts. "Evan, you're right about our values. You're right about not airing our personal information too. I can see that now. But I've already started seeing Dr. Opum. He's wonderful. You still need to meet him and see for yourself."

"That's true," he said. "I'm sure he's an excellent doctor, and I have no reason to think he isn't the best in the world." He stabbed several noodles, put them in his mouth, and then stabbed several more. "OK."

She watched him eat. *He communicates, shares his feelings, values my thoughts, and is willing to compromise.* She felt closer to him each passing day, even after a heated discussion like this one. *This is marriage,* she thought. He was rich, *and* she loved him.

| | 0 | | 0 | | 0

LAURA FINISHED CHANGING CHRIS'S DIAPER AFTER HIS NAP AND carried him to the kitchen. Along the way, she saw the baby gift sitting by the back door. She'd initially brought the gift along on trips to the park, thinking she would see Sue outside, but no such luck. She'd nearly forgotten about it. *I'll just go over there and give it to her. Good thing I didn't buy an outfit; her baby girl would never fit into it now.*

It was a typical February day—the kind where it was hard to find the sun behind a featureless gray sky. She crossed the alley with Chris in her arms all bundled up warm and snug. As the wind buffeted them, she pulled the little knit cap down farther over his ears.

The Avenir house looked occupied, but no one was visible. She waited, but no one came to the door.

"Visitor arriving. Quantity one," she heard the seccomm repeat from inside.

*A real introvert. Maybe I'm forcing this. Maybe I should just leave the gift with a note and forget about friendship.* With a knock at the door—the old-fashioned way—she called out, "Sue, it's me, Laura. From across the alley. Chris and I have a gift for Hope."

When the door finally opened, Sue was holding her daughter. "Hi."

Hope was a beautiful baby, but Laura immediately noticed bruising down the side of Sue's face. "Hi. Uh, we just wanted to say congratulations. Well, actually, Chris, Ben, and I. Ben's my husband. Oh, never mind. Here. This is for Hope."

"Thank you." Sue accepted the package and set it down just inside the door. Shifting Hope to the other side, the bruised side of Sue's face was hidden now. No eye contact.

"She's beautiful," said Laura.

"Thank you."

"She has dark hair, like yours."

Sue brushed the wispy brown strands with her fingertips.

Admiring Hope politely, Laura held her smile through the sound of a distant siren and dog barking from down the street.

"Thanks again," said Sue, backing inside.

"Look," said Laura, "if you need help, you come to me. You got that? Anything. Anytime. Day or night. Understand? You come to me, and I'll help you."

"Thanks. I'm fine, really. Thank you." The door closed.

"Well, buddy," Laura said, turning for home, "I think that's about all we can do for now. But the next time I see that bozo husband of hers, well ... I'm not sure what I might do."

| |0 | |0 | |0

CHELSEA LAY IN BED LISTENING TO EVAN CLEANING UP HIS BREAK-fast dishes before leaving for class. She hadn't slept well, preoccupied by the argument from the night before about the interview posted online.

"Chels, love, I'll be working late," Evan called from the front hall. "I may be home after you're in bed. Bye!"

"Bye!" she called back just as the pubcomm chimed.

"It's for you," he said. "The doctor's office. Can you take it?"

"Yes, I've got it! Bye!" She gestured to the pub-comm. "Hello, Dr. Opum."

"Chelsea, good morning. I hope I'm not reaching you too early."

"No, not at all. Is there a problem?"

"Not really. I was just reviewing your progress in preparation for your appointment tomorrow. The biometric scanner reported errors during one of your prior visits. We planned to just run it again, but from your last visit, I see now that the problem persists, and in fact, several measurements failed to register. I wanted to ask if you would visit the community scanner. I'll get our equipment repaired, but in the meantime, this will give us full results. If it's not too much trouble, could you get the scan before your appointment tomorrow?"

"Of course."

"Excellent. So sorry for the bother. See you tomorrow at ten o'clock. Cheers."

Chelsea visited the community clinic later that day. Just like the times before, she received the results on her percomm after leaving the scanning booth. Everything looked fine. Satisfied, she completed her other errands before returning back to the flat for dinner.

Startled, she found Evan in the kitchen. "Is everything all right? I thought you were working late tonight." She kissed him.

Kissing her back, he said, "I had a cancelation and thought I'd come home to be with you."

"How marvelous. Have you eaten? Let's go out, shall we?"

"Could we have dinner here, darling? I think we should talk."

"Certainly," she said, sitting down.

"I was thinking about our agreement. You know, that we share the same values and work together on important decisions? Right? And it occurred to me that I need to do *my* part. And I haven't. So I've arranged a meeting for us tomorrow with Dr. Cornelius at the university."

"But, Evan, no, you agreed. I mean, *we* agreed. It's water under the bridge. I have a doctor, a good doctor, and you still haven't met him."

"We agreed we wanted the best for our family. And it's true we can't make a decision together if we haven't shared the information. That's why I made the appointment with Dr. Cornelius for both of us. Have you arranged a time for me to meet the online doctor?"

"His name is Nigel Opum. He's not the online doctor; he's *my* doctor. He's *our* doctor. It's too late to change."

"But we agreed we want the best. If it turns out that Dr. Cornelius is better, well, then—"

"He's not!" she yelled. "You just can't—"

"*You don't know that!*" he yelled back.

Chelsea was stunned. *I can't remember him ever raising his voice, much less screaming at me.* In a calmer voice, she said, "That's true; I don't know that. But that's not the point. The decision has been made, and changing doctors now is unnecessary."

He said, also in a calmer voice, "I'm asking you to meet him. And I'll meet with the other doctor. If you're not convinced that Dr. Cornelius is significantly better and worth the risk of switching, then we won't. We'll be true to our values, and we'll have made the decision together."

*He's willing to compromise.* "All right," she said. "I guess that's fair. When?"

"Ten. I'll miss my class, but this is important."

"Ten? But that's right when I have my appointment with Dr. Opum."

"You'll have to reschedule; Dr. Cornelius doesn't take new patients. He's seeing us as a favor to my grandfather."

"Your grandfather? He knows your grandfather?"

"Yes. Pappous has his personal physician in Thessaloniki, but he has an arrangement with Dr. Cornelius for when he's traveling here. He has a similar arrangement with another doctor in Amexica when he travels there."

"Oh," said Chelsea in small voice. "And don't say Amexica; you sound like a Hillite."

"Well, maybe you should start sounding like a Venizelos. So you see, he's practically our family doctor."

"Apparently," she said. "It's late. I'll send a cancelation to Dr. Opum's office now, and tomorrow I'll arrange a new time."

"Brilliant!" He hopped up from the chair and kissed her. "Dinner out sounds wonderful."

"Sure." He seemed energized and relieved, but now she felt drained. *Is this marriage too?*

The following morning, Chelsea tapped on the pubcomm display for Dr. Opum's office and initiated the comm.

"Good morning, Mrs. Venizelos. How can I help you?" answered the receptionist.

"Yes, I wanted to follow up on my cancelation from last evening. I hope it's not an inconvenience to reschedule."

"Sorry. I don't have any record of a message from you. Dr. Opum was expecting to see you at ten. I'll let him know. One moment while I review your records and see what you had scheduled for today."

"It was just my routine exam," Chelsea offered as she waited.

"Yes, however, I do see a note about the biometric errors."

"Oh yes, Dr. Opum asked me to get a community clinic scan. I did that yesterday. Everything's fine."

"You only get a summary of the full analysis. Yesterday's scan was also incomplete. Dr. Opum wanted to talk with you about that today. I'll need to check with him before I can reschedule."

Chelsea finished the comm. *The community clinic is so ... unsophisticated. And the way he fumbled with his percomm—who doesn't know how to use a percomm? Why do I have to go to this extra trouble? I'm Mrs. Chelsea Venizelos.*

|  |0  |  |0  |  |0

"YOU SHOULD BE ABLE TO SEE IT NOW," SAID TYVOLD, HIS VOICE coming over the tran's comm. "On your left."

"I see it," said Vega, tapping a button on the dash. The pertran initiated the parking cycle and came to rest at the curb of the residential street.

"Now don't think so much this time," said Tyvold.

"Shut up. Just distract him. Do your job."

The homemade sign in the front yard read: PUPPIES $10. A big cardboard box, open at the top, was next to the sign.

"Hey, mister." The kid was already up on his feet. He'd been sitting in a folding chair behind a card table.

*Pretty nice set up. Quite the salesman, this one.*
"Hey," Vega replied casually, peering into the box.

The kid was bouncing on his toes, swinging his hands together. Huge smile on his face. "You lookin' for a pet, mister?"

"Maybe," said Vega.

Inside the box was a blanket and six puppies. Five were sleeping, and the other was chewing on the bottom flap of the box.

"Ten bucks is a lot of money," said Vega. "Not purebred. That one there—his coloring is different. The white paws and the ears—not the same father."

"Yeah, we're not sure how that happened." The kid was still bouncing and swinging. "But they're all real healthy, mister."

"I'll tell you how it happened," said Vega, locking eyes with the kid. "The bitch was humped by two studs in quick succession, one right after the other, when she was in heat. That's how."

No more smile. No more bouncing.

Vega picked up the oddball. "You see here, kid?" He pulled the puppy's leg and pressed his thumb into the paw, spreading the toes apart. The puppy yelped. "Here on the side: the dewclaw. It's so the stud can get a good grip. You know, when the pink thing comes out? He digs in and holds her. Real deep like. Boy, you need a fire hose to get him off her at that point."

The kid, mouth open, backed up and nearly tripped over the lawn chair.

"Robby," a woman called from the house, "you got a comm. Some man's asking for you."

"You go on and take your comm, kid," said Vega. "I'll just look at the others 'til you come back."

The kid turned and ran.

Vega waited until the kid reached the house and inside, and then he gripped the mutt by the loose skin at the neck and held it high. *Yup, female.* "You're coming with me, little bitch." Returning to the tran, he said, "We have a nicer box for you."

ǀǀO ǀǀO ǀǀO

THE BUILDINGS OF THE UNIVERSITY'S LONDON CAMPUS WERE centuries old, gray stone with ornate detail. Evan and Chelsea checked in at the security desk where they were required to leave their percomms behind. Evan said it was to keep people from stealing intellectual property. *Don't rich people have their own property?* thought Chelsea, but she didn't object.

Entering the lift, she fully expected to go up a few floors. But Evan explained that while the surface buildings had great historical significance and contributed to the prestigious image of the university, most of the university's facilities were underground and very cutting edge.

When the lift doors opened, she understood. The corridor was extremely modern with an interior design similar to some of the most elite shops in

London catering to the tech-savvy neo-bourgeoisie. Chic cove lighting created dramatic illumination on curved surfaces.

Alcoves and small gathering spaces with designer furnishings invited passersby for thoughtful collaboration. The environment was visually inspiring. *What did all this cost?* The people walking through the halls or chatting off to the side were smartly dressed. *Faculty? Or students? Both, probably. Maybe some are visiting patients too? No unemployed people here.*

Dr. Cornelius was waiting at the door of his office to greet them personally. He was an older man with white hair, a full white beard, and a pink face. He looked like the American Santa Claus but without the jelly belly; he was slender and tall. Chelsea had searched for a pic of him online, but hardly any information was posted. *Private physician. Such a nice ring to it. Maybe Evan's family had one on each continent.*

Dr. Cornelius invited them to have a seat in his office, which was neat and modestly appointed but still had the designer look of the entire facility. It was amazingly bright. The entire ceiling was illuminated, providing very natural light with no shadows. Even the surfaces of the walls—the ones without display screens—also shone. She didn't feel at all like she was six stories underground.

"Chelsea, when I received the request from Alexander, I was only too happy to honor it. But I want to reassure you that in no way do I underestimate the seriousness of switching physicians. It's a decision for both of you. There's no risk as long as your current condition is good. Do you have any present concerns?"

"Well, there is one small thing," said Chelsea.

"What?" said Evan, turning to her.

"It's nothing, I'm sure," she said. "My other doctor, Dr. Opum, said his biometric scanner had errors. He had me visit the community scanner. When I contacted his office this morning, they said the clinic scan was also missing data. Does that sound strange?"

"Hmm. Certainly, it's highly uncommon. Of course, I can't know for sure without examining you, but there's a condition called teleparallaxus. Just like the common parallax effect you experience when looking at an old-fashioned needle gauge—since the needle is a few millimeters away from the face of the gauge showing the graduation, the needle will appear to point to a slightly different point on the scale depending on the viewing angle. The phenomenon is possible when two individuals occupy the same physical space, superimposed on one another. Pregnancy is the only known situation to cause the effect. Modern equipment can compensate, but there are rare circumstances that may prevent an accurate reading. I certainly wouldn't fault your doctor for being unaware of it. This is one of the advanced areas of research we perform here at the university."

"Is it dangerous?" asked Evan.

"No, teleparallaxus itself is not something that will harm the mother or the baby, but it creates a kind of diagnostic blindness. The manual tests are just fine."

"Chels? What do you think?"

"I'm relieved … and impressed," she said. "Doctor, I hope you can give us some time to think about this."

"Of course. And please, if you have any other questions or would like more information to help you in your decision making, please don't hesitate to contact me."

Evan could have been gloating about Dr. Cornelius's apparent triumph over Dr. Opum, but he was very respectful and simply let the facts speak for themselves.

After returning to the flat, she took out her per-comm to contact Dr. Opum's office and noticed it was still off from when it was left at the security check-point. She turned it back on and waited as it powered up. She would arrange a time to introduce Evan, hopefully at her next appointment. On the screen, she saw she had a missed comm.

"Dr. Opum, I'm sorry. I didn't get your message until just now. I do apologize for canceling today."

"Yes, I was hoping to see you tomorrow if pos-sible. There's no need for alarm, but I would like to resolve the issue of the biometric scan. I understand you're aware that the community scan was also unsuccessful."

"Yes, well, Doctor, I must tell you, I've sought a second opinion. It turns out this is a rare condition," she said unapologetically.

"I beg your pardon. To which condition are you referring?"

"It's called teleparallaxus. It only happens with pregnant women, and it's very rare. I learned this today."

"Mrs. Venizelos, I can assure you there is no such condition as teleparallaxus."

"As I said, it's a rare condition. I only know of it because I visited the university today, where advanced research is performed. It's perfectly under-standable if—"

"Madam, with all due respect, there is no such condition as teleparallaxus. If I may ask, who gave you this information?"

"Dr. Cornelius. He's the—"

"I know exactly who he is." There was a pause. "Mrs. Venizelos, it is certainly your prerogative to see whomever you wish. Please, I'm only looking out for your well-being and that of your child. Let me speak frankly. The wealthy and powerful seek out Brandon Cornelius because of his work in genetic manipu-lation. You need to understand with whom you're dealing. He's a licensed physician to practice obstet-rics, that's true, but he's a scientist. I can't phrase it any other way; Brandon Cornelius makes designer babies, Mrs. Venizelos. Please, look up teleparallaxus for yourself. You won't find any such reference."

"I don't know what to say." *Teleparallaxus? Biometrics? Genetics? Evan will know what it all means.* "My husband should hear this."

"Of course, yes, excellent. Please, I need to explain to you what you're getting involved in. Promise me you'll both come in at ten tomorrow morning. If your husband has difficulty changing his schedule, I can come to you. We can perform your routine exam at another time. Please, you must hear me out."

"Very well, Doctor. I'll talk to my husband. I'm sure we can be there. I'll confirm in the morning."

Chelsea ended the comm and went to tell Evan what happened.

"Chels, his reaction is totally predictable. Naturally, he's defensive. Honestly, darling, I don't want to keep calling him the online doctor, but these people will do anything to protect their reputation. You might give him only two stars out of five."

"But you can go tomorrow? We can talk to him together. You're probably right. We can decide together."

"Of course. This is very important. We'll meet with him tomorrow."

The next morning, Chelsea contacted Dr. Opum's office to confirm the appointment.

"Mrs. Venizelos, thank you for ringing," said the receptionist. "I was about to comm you. I have dreadful news. Dr. Opum passed away last night, apparently from a heart attack. He died in his sleep."

# Chapter 12

TWO MONTHS LATER, CHELSEA PUT HER HAND ON THE wall to steady herself, exhausted from walking the short distance from the kitchen to the den.

Ingrid, the young nurse Evan hired at Dr. Cornelius's recommendation, held her opposite hand and forearm. "Just take a deep breath," said Ingrid.

Chelsea was convinced her stomach was larger—no, not larger, just heavier somehow—than it should be, even for thirty-eight weeks. Dr. Cornelius had reassured her that each pregnancy was different and that it was normal for first-time mothers to be sensitive to the many changes occurring in their bodies.

Reaching the chair, Ingrid supported her as she eased into it.

"Your vitamins, madam," said Ingrid, nudging the glass of water.

"Can't it wait? I don't think I can fit anything more down there. It'll make it that much heavier."

"Doctor's orders."

"They're only vitamins. Let me skip it."

"Don't forget the folic acid. Dr. Cornelius said it prevents congenital birth defects. You don't want that."

Under any other circumstances, Chelsea wouldn't let a woman like her even be around Evan. Ingrid was only a few years older. That fact, combined with the nurse uniform, made quite a package. Chelsea was sure that, in the eyes of any warm-blooded male, only a French maid uniform could top it. Yet Ingrid was very professional. Chelsea liked her and even wished they could be friends. But it was clear she was there for the baby, not for her. Chelsea reminded herself that was a good thing and not to take it personally. Evan's course load had been lessening now that he was approaching the end of his graduate work. He was spending more time on his thesis, which meant he could spend more time working from home. He still worked for Venizelos Shipping, of course, but that was part time during the day and some evenings. She had to admit, Ingrid was an enormous help.

"Here now." Ingrid handed Chelsea the water and pills.

Chelsea swallowed them dutifully.

Evan dashed into the room and gave her a peck. "Sorry I wasn't able to join you for dinner, love," he said. "I had to take that comm. No choice. How are you this evening?"

"The baby's heavier than ever," she said wearily.

"You know, I've been thinking. I know you've invested so much time preparing, especially the nursery, but I'm worried about your ability to manage things until he's born."

"What do you mean? Ingrid's been an absolute dear. And Dr. Cornelius says everything's fine."

"Yes, I know," he said. "Your pregnancy is normal, but he didn't say it would be easy. He prescribed a private nurse for a reason. You need more help. What do you think about going to Thessaloniki? Just until the baby's born."

"What? Nonsense. We have everything here. Everything's ready. The baby could come any day now."

"Yes, but if you were home—I mean, in Greece— my mother could help, and even my sisters."

"No, Evan. Our life is here. I like being independent from your family. I don't want to have to rely on them."

"Very well," he said, raising his hands in surrender. "I just want to be sure you have the best care available. Look, I have to work tonight. I'll eat something there. I'll see you tomorrow morning." He kissed her good-bye and left.

Her percomm jingled. It was Selby Hancock from the social registry.

"Selby. What a pleasant surprise. It's been a long time."

"Chelsea, thank you for taking my comm. I regret not keeping a tighter acquaintance. I've been terribly busy. How are you?"

"Excellent. I'm doing very well, thank you. Now, Selby, your reputation precedes you," she teased. "I'm simply not convinced that you commed just to engage in small talk."

"No, you're quite right, Chelsea. I'll never fool anyone. My viewers are keenly interested in a fresh interview with you. They want to know how your marriage and pregnancy are progressing. Your independent style is such an inspiration."

"Well, I'm flattered. What did you have in mind?"

"Wonderful," said Selby. "Unfortunately, the publishing pressures never cease, always a deadline. Could you come by the studio tonight? No vid this time, just an audio interview. I promise not to keep you late."

"Now? Oh my ... well, yes, I think I can make that work."

Ingrid, who'd been standing by throughout the conversation, now looked at Chelsea with consternation on her face.

"Yes. Give me half an hour, and I'll be right over." Ending the comm, she said, "Now I don't want any disapproval from you."

"Madam, I don't think this is prudent."

"Ridiculous. I'm going to Ms. Hancock's studio, and you're coming with me."

Ingrid helped Chelsea with her coat, and the two took the lift to the ground floor.

By the time they reached the street, Chelsea was already fatigued. Using both hands to hold her stomach, each step was exhausting. Outside, the evening was getting into full swing, and pubtrans would be scarce. The tube station was too far. Searching up and down the street, she saw only one tran with the distinctive hackney shape pass by, and its light atop was dark. *Better luck at the corner by the pub.* The distance seemed daunting. *I can do it.*

Ingrid at her side, Chelsea concentrated on each step. Ahead, an unsavory character in the shadows between two storefronts took interest. The streets were populated yet also chaotic. Chelsea had walked here many times—sometimes much later at night—and never had a problem. It was so public, it had to be safe.

The man watched as they passed.

Chelsea remembered the boys that used to admire her when she crossed the dance floor at the club. This was different.

In a blur, the man lunged with arms outreached. At the same time, Ingrid's firm hand pulled Chelsea away. Ingrid's forearm caught the man in the throat, and then her foot smashed into his knee, forcing it back with a sickening pop. The man went down silently, clutching his throat.

Ingrid held Chelsea protectively.

Another man, wearing a dark suit and dark coat, came up from behind them. "You good?"

"Yeah, I'm good," said Ingrid.

"Was she harmed?"

"She's fine. Get rid of him."

The man turned toward the street and waved. A black tran roared out from a parking spot, executed a U-turn, and careened to a halt in front of them. Two more suits jumped out and grabbed the scruffy man, who looked alive but wasn't fighting, dragged him to the tran, and sped off.

"Watch our backs," said Ingrid to the first man.

"Yes, ma'am."

Once inside the lobby, the man was gone—or not really gone, Chelsea guessed, merely out of sight again.

"Who are you?" Chelsea asked Ingrid.

"I'm here for you and the baby, madam. You know that. You've always known that. Now let's get you upstairs."

||0 ||0 ||0

JIMMY SQUINTED FROM THE BRIGHT TORCHLIGHT SHINING IN HIS eyes from the open door of the vehicle's boot, yet he could still make out the faces of the men, the same men that hired him.

"What the hell are you doing?" Jimmy screamed at them. "Didn't you hear me yelling? How long have I been locked in here? My knee is totally fucked! We'd better be at a goddamn hospital. Shit, it hurts! Get me the hell out of this thing!"

"Shucks, Jimmy," the man with the torch said sarcastically, "you know how cities have gunshot-locating systems? Firing a gun anywhere near London would draw too much attention, Jimmy."

"Gun? What gun? I had no gun. That wasn't the plan! The deal was, I grab the prego and rough her up. That was it! You said nothin' about that other wench goin' all special forces on me. Get me outta here!"

"Oh, we'll get you out, Jimmy, don't you worry. In fact, we've taken you to a place here, out in the county, where you won't have no more worries at all, Jimmy."

"And you owe me. This is gonna cost you extra."

The other man pulled a gun from his coat. "Yup. Time to get out, Jimmy. I don't want to dirty my ride."

"No! That wasn't the deal. *No*—"

||0 ||0 ||0

"WE PUBLISHED ANOTHER INTERVIEW INSTEAD," EXPLAINED SELBY on a comm the following day. "Unfortunately, the window of opportunity has passed. But I was so alarmed by your message, I wanted to make sure you were all right."

"Yes, the whole episode was quite frightening, but I'm completely fine," said Chelsea.

"I'm glad to hear you weren't harmed," said Selby. "There may be a publishing slot in the future. If you have a moment now, I'll take a few notes. Perhaps on the topic of health, fashion, or lifestyle?"

Chelsea gave a synopsis of her life since the interview. She talked about preparations for the baby, Evan's increased involvement, and how the baby was so dreadfully heavy.

"So heavy, but ... everything is normal?"

"Yes. My doctor says everything's fine. I must admit my stomach doesn't look any bigger than it should; the baby's just so heavy. I have to put my arms underneath just to move. I guess I'm just a complaining weakling. The doctor says each pregnancy is different."

"I see. Would you mind telling me the name of your doctor?"

"Oh, not at all—Dr. Brandon Cornelius from the university here in London," she said proudly.

"Chelsea, I must say this is a bit of a shock."

"What do you mean?"

"Please forgive me; I'm not known for skirting around an issue. Let me be perfectly blunt. Cornelius has a reputation of working with couples who wish to tamper with their baby's development—the well-to-do who wish to give their child an unfair advantage in life. You've married into a wealthy family, but frankly, Chelsea, your charm came from your fresh perspective and independence—doing things in a down-to-earth manner, avoiding artificial anything."

"No, you don't understand. Dr. Cornelius isn't like that at all. He's wonderful. He's taken wonderful care of me."

"Chelsea, I have no experience with him myself. I only know the gossip."

"What gossip?"

"There's suspicion that his methods are illegal. You must know the university receives generous funding from Parliament—for education, naturally—but, Chelsea, the university also supports weapons development. Cornelius works on research for genetically engineered soldiers, specifically MI8. That part's not gossip."

"MI8?"

"His Majesty's Signal Intelligence Service, the part of the Ministry of Defence responsible for cyber-terrorism defense. You know MI8—from the vids? Secret agents who fight the Hoods."

"You mean like the Omega Force?"

"Yes, that's the American equivalent."

"They're not real people. That's Hollywood."

"Hollywood? Yes, Chelsea, but MI8 is quite real."

Selby's tone had become like Evan's when he corrected her from his pulpit. *"Tabloid education," he calls it*. Her mom did it too.

"The US media hype Omega Force. Blockbuster vids exaggerate their abilities, but they can do things no normal human can do. Cornelius is at the heart of both MI8 and Omega Force," said Selby. "Or perhaps I should say at the DNA of both."

"What's the gossip part?"

"That he uses the same genetic manipulation for the benefit of his patients in his private practice. For a fee," Selby added. "Chelsea, his nickname is Dr. Frankenstein." She paused. "Now, I'm sure that label is used by people who covet of his financial success, but think about it."

*Like Dr. Opum's warning?* "No, Dr. Cornelius is a brilliant baby doctor. I actually switched to him because my first doctor was having trouble working the scanner. Dr. Cornelius knew what the problem was straight away. It's because of his research that he knew about the rare condition." *The whole scanner thing seems so silly now.* "And he's made sure I'm getting the best nutrition. He's prescribed extra folic acid because a deficiency during the development of the fetus can cause birth defects."

"Chelsea, those aren't even your words."

"Don't talk down to me! Online is fake, and Hollywood is real? I can't trust anything anyone says!"

"Chelsea, you're in your third trimester, yes? Folic acid is indeed an important nutrient, but only immediately following conception, or even just before if a woman is trying to get pregnant. There's folic acid in standard prenatal vitamins. Chelsea, I'm no expert, but—"

"Well, you certainly sound like one!"

"Look, there's no reason you should be taking extra folic acid now. Are you sure that's what you're taking?"

"I can't discuss this any further."

"I didn't mean to upset you. I'm sure—"

Chelsea ended the comm and sat in silence. *Selby said it herself; it's gossip. Dr. Cornelius has access to important research, and that makes him a better doctor. Maybe the best, just like Evan said. That's right, Mizzzzz Hancock, he's the doctor to the rich and famous, and he's my private physician.*

# Chapter 13

CHELSEA LAY IN BED WITH PILLOWS PUSHED UP AROUND her stomach. The bulge pulled her skin so severely she had to support it at all times. The baby's kicks didn't help, either, causing sharp pain across her spine. Holding her stomach, she tried to fall back to sleep.

Evan, Ingrid, and Dr. Cornelius barged into the bedroom.

"Oh, I'm not asleep; just come right in," Chelsea said cynically.

"Chels, Dr. Cornelius thinks bed rest isn't enough," said Evan. "You're going to need more. Around-the-clock care. Ingrid can only do so much. We're all going to Thessaloniki so my family can help. It'll be safer too. You'll have the baby there."

"What? No! Evan! Everything is fine here."

"No. You could have the baby anytime now. I've made the decision. We're going home to Greece."

"*You've* made the decision? That's not the way we do things, Evan. You don't just—"

"*No!*" he said. "No, you're right, that's *not* the way we do things. *You* made the decision to stay here without taking my opinion into account. You never consider anything but what you want. You are judge and jury when it comes to the baby. There's never been any question in your mind. Now it's *my* turn. We have to think of your proper care and security now. It's Brandon's—it's Dr. Cornelius's recommendation that—"

"So you're on a first-name basis now, is that it? Well, I don't care what Dr. Frankenstein says!"

Cornelius gave Ingrid a furtive glance, but she didn't even budge. Ingrid was amazingly calm for the situation. Unbelievably calm.

"Chels, you're becoming irrational," said Evan. "Ingrid is going to pack your belongings. We leave in the morning."

They turned and walked out of the room.

"No!" Chelsea yelled after them. "You've wanted to control me and my baby from the beginning!" She was yelling at a closed door. Enraged, she allowed her head to rest back on the pillow. *I have to tell someone. Who can help me?* She reached for her percomm and made a connection to Selby Hancock. *Please, please, please pick up.*

"London Social Registry. How can I help you?"

"I need to speak with Selby Hancock."

"I'm sorry, Ms. Hancock is no longer employed by the Registry."

"What? Why? I need to reach her. It's desperately important."

"I'm sorry. I have no forwarding information. Can someone else assist you?"

Chelsea ended the comm. *What's happening?* She looked down at the mass, propped up by pillows. *What are you?*

Ingrid came in with a glass of water and pills.

Chelsea stared at her. "What is that?"

"Your vitamins, of course."

"No. Really. What are those? What's in it? What's in the small pill?"

"Folic acid," said Ingrid.

*Play it cool.* Chelsea accepted the glass and the two pills and then paused and looked into Ingrid's eyes. "Maybe I'll just drop this down the heat vent." Chelsea moved her hand over the edge of the bed and watched for Ingrid's body to tense or a widening of the eyes. Nothing. Ingrid was strangely calm. Yet somehow, Chelsea sensed a woman-to-woman connection that confirmed an alertness behind the steel facade.

Chelsea threw the pills and the water glass across the room. "Evan! *Evan*! You have to listen to me!" Rolling back, she tried to get one foot on the floor.

Ingrid's hands moved in a flash, burying a hypodermic needle in Chelsea's arm, plunging the contents into her bloodstream. The world went black.

# Chapter 14

OPENING HER EYES, CHELSEA SAW EVAN'S FACE AND smiled. But the room was unfamiliar. The memory of the struggle with Ingrid came back.

"Relax," Evan said. "Everything's fine."

"Where am I?"

"Home. In Greece. In my family's old house. It's ours now," he said.

*Oh my god.* She moved her hand to her stomach. *Flat!* "What have you done?"

"Relax. Everything's fine," he said again. "We had to keep you sedated for the trip here, and once we arrived, Brandon said it would be best to induce labor. Our son is just in the other room. You can see him. He's perfect. We just want to be sure you're well."

*Could it be true? The baby's fine? I'm a mother?* "What's his length and weight?"

"Fifty-six centimeters," said Evan. "About average. He's perfect."

"You didn't say how heavy. What's his weight?"

The door opened. Ingrid came in holding a swaddled infant, followed by Dr. Cornelius. Everyone had smiles on their faces. Chelsea couldn't help but smile too.

"How's our new mother doing?" asked Dr. Cornelius. He came to her side and helped her sit up.

Ingrid stepped forward.

Chelsea tried to see the baby's face, but he was completely swaddled.

"Careful. He's a solid boy," said Ingrid, transferring the shrouded bundle to Chelsea's arms. Immediately, Chelsea felt the weight—like a boulder. "How heavy?" Without waiting, she freed her left hand, struggling to hold his entire weight with the other arm, and parted the folds from around the face.

He looked normal. His eyes were closed, sleeping. The weight was so very strange. Also, something odd about his skin. She touched his cheek with the back of her finger. The skin was firm. Very firm. Dense was a better word.

"What—is—the—weight?"

"He's 22.6 kilos," said Dr. Cornelius. "Magnificent, don't you think?"

"That's—that's about six times normal birth weight," said Chelsea. "How can that be if he's normal size?"

"He's very special," said Evan. "Brandon explained to me how unique our son is. He'll explain it to you too."

She looked down at her son as his eyes opened. Chelsea screamed.

# CHAPTER 15

"SO WHAT DID HINKLE SAY EXACTLY?" BEN ASKED HER.

"He said the girl just vanished. Her bike was found alongside the road in Florida, where she lived, backpack untouched. No surveillance vids, no percomm ping, nothing. Just vanished, like the others."

"How does he know these details?" Ben asked. He stood, stretched, and flattened the hair sticking up on the back of his head.

"I don't know. Probably one of those private accounts you told me about. He's the creeper type."

Ben put his coffee cup in the dishwasher.

"It's so troubling. Why don't we hear about these cases in the news? I can't believe it's still happening. They question me every time," she said. "Now I regret going back to work."

"You went back to work when Chris was five. They questioned you equally before and after. They have to check any possible connection."

"There is no connection. Chris is eleven now. That's a whole decade. When will they be convinced?"

"After Lisa's disappearance, I guess you're lodged in the system." He closed the dishwasher and looked out the open kitchen window through the screen. "Looks like it'll be a beautiful day. Any big plans?"

"That's just it. Lisa turned up."

"Hinkle told you that. You're too gullible. He plays you like a fiddle."

She swallowed her last bit of coffee. "Anyway, no, no big plans. I'm still adjusting to the summer schedule."

"OK, I'm going down to the lab. Still on for our walk before lunch?"

"Sure," she said, putting her cup in the dishwasher too. Out the window, she saw Chris's friend Al Fuentes sprint into the backyard from the alley. Al's real name was Geraldo, but no one ever called him that.

"Hey! Migo! Let's go!" he called up to Chris's open bedroom window.

She heard Chris's scrambling feet run to the window ledge above. "Comin'!" Then the sound of his feet dashing across his room to the stairwell. He never took the elevator and only used three of the steps on each flight of stairs. With a thud, he hit the ground-floor landing, banked a turn past the kitchen, and shot out the back door.

"Where are you going?" she yelled after him.

"To get Katie and then to the park!"

Al began his sprint up the alley. Chris caught up with him, and they both went to full speed.

||0 ||0 ||0

"WHICH WAY?" AL ASKED, PUFFING AS THEY RAN.

"Diego's yard, if he's out," said Chris between breaths.

Diego, a neighbor's dog, had a fence around his backyard. There was no way through to the street on the other side without going over the chain link fence, but that meant dealing with Diego, who was very territorial, which made the challenge that much greater.

Chris slowed to a jog. *Yup, there's old Diego.* The dog spotted them and moved to the closest corner, ready to bark. The neighbor had a large shed in the back, set right up against the fence along the alley. Diego could be on either side, but he had to run back and forth to bark at people.

Chris and Al jogged right along the fence, Diego barking as they passed. But halfway to the other side, they both stopped and pressed their backs against the shed wall, motionless. Diego ran to the other end, ready to bark.

They caught their breaths.

Diego, confused now, ran back to the first corner.

Chris smiled to Al and whispered, "Ready?"

Al nodded, sidestepped to the far edge of the shed, and hit the fence with his fist. Diego barked and raced to the noise. Chris turned, jumped the fence, and sprinted across the neighbor's backyard to the front. Diego reversed course diagonally across the yard and chased him. Chris took the front fence with both hands and vaulted over it.

Al timed his move and jumped the back fence too. Diego turned hard to catch him. Blades of grass flew as Diego skidded to a stop, snapping after Al with his paws up against the fence. *Bark! Bark! Bark!*

Joining Chris in the front yard, Al matched pace behind him, like a jet-fighter wingman.

They ran down the street and then crossed, running up past a few more houses, between two others, and emerging at the alley on the next block right at Katie's backyard.

"Ready, miga?" Chris yelled to her open window.

Katie darted from her back door. The two boys turned and ran toward the park. She caught up, matching their pace.

"Did you get it?" asked Al.

"Yup," said Katie.

Aside from Katie's dark hair in a ponytail, the three kids were hard to tell apart. Their denim shorts, T-shirts, and sneakers were nearly identical and well worn. Al's hair was shorter than Chris's. Chris thought it was jazz, because it made Al look like a soldier. Mr. Fuentes had the same haircut, and Al looked like a little version of him.

The kids slowed to a walk as they approached the park. It was early still, and the area looked pretty clear. They crossed the playground and went to the far end of the park, which backed up against a line of shrubs with woods behind that.

Chris reached it first. After looking around casually, he kneeled down at a gap in the bushes and crawled under the branches. Katie and Al followed the hidden path to a space between the bushes where the branches arched over top like a dome. Enough light penetrated that they could see, but otherwise, no one would ever know about their hidden meeting place.

Each found a spot and sat down cross-legged.

Chris looked to Katie with anticipation.

"Let's see it," said Al.

She dug a hand into her pocket and pulled out a rectangular device. It had two wires coming out of one side—an old photoflash capacitor. Katie had planned for over a month to get one. It'd be an antique if it had any value.

"Jazz," said Al as if it were made of gold.

"Top jazz, baby," said Katie. "Let's get started."

Al reached to the edge of the enclosure and brushed away the dead leaves concealing the large box they used for storage. He set the box in the center of the space and opened it. Inside, there was the battery and the heavy wire in the shape of a coil mounted on a block of wood. Along with some tools, switches, and other miscellaneous parts and components, there was the thick metal rod, nearly an inch in diameter, with a point on one end. Altogether, parts for their coil gun. Electricity from the battery applied to the coil created a magnetic force that shot the rod through the coil. The more electricity, the faster the rod would go.

Chris pulled out a piece of lumber and positioned it at the other edge of the enclosure. One side of the board had a bull's-eye painted on it with gouges that matched the shape of the tip of the metal rod.

"So the capacitor is going to store up power from the battery?" asked Al.

"Yup," said Katie. "We put it in the circuit with a second switch. This time, when we press the second switch, instead of just the power from the battery, the capacitor will discharge."

"And the rod will go faster?" asked Chris.

"Oh, migo, you're not gonna believe it," she said.

Chris watched Al and Katie as they put the components together. He'd known them both his entire life. The three weren't just best friends; they did everything together. They shared everything.

Katie was brilliant. She knew all kinds of science stuff. Chris thought she was the smartest kid in the fifth grade, maybe in the whole school. Chris wasn't dumb himself, and he knew Al wasn't, either, but they were no match for Katie, though she never talked down to them or made them feel stupid. She explained everything.

Al was the class clown, always wanting to have fun, around the clock, seven days a week. His ideas were amazing, and he was always coming up with new things for them to try. The coil gun was his idea, and Katie knew exactly how to build it.

"Remember how we had to make sure the base was anchored well? You know, because of the kick?"

asked Katie. "That's really important now. Make sure the base is right up against the trunk of the bush."

Al had the base well anchored. He leaned down with one eye closed and looked through the coil to the target a few feet away. He nudged the base slightly before leaning back up.

"Good?" asked Katie.

"Good," said Al. He loaded the rod into the coil.

"OK. Move back and get ready," said Katie. "When I press the first switch, the capacitor will charge. Then, when I hit the second switch, it'll fire."

The three got into position to watch. Katie pressed the first switch. Chris heard a high-pitched whine that went higher and higher, so high he couldn't hear it any longer. Then Katie pressed the second switch.

Everything happened at once. With almost no noise at all, the rod shot from the coil, not just hitting the target but blasting straight through it. The board exploded in a burst of wood chunks and splinters. Sparks flew from the coil, and the wires leading from the capacitor burst into flames, igniting the dead leaves around it.

"Holy crap!" yelled Al, slapping the flames with his hand, extinguishing them.

Chris smelled the burned leaves and smoldering wire insulation as bits of wood drifted to the ground across smoky rays of sunlight beaming through the canopy.

They howled with laughter, laughing so hard Chris thought his sides would give out.

Once the laughter died down, Al said, "Maybe we should use heavier gauge wire next time." And they laughed some more.

||0 ||0 ||0

HOPE AVENIR TAPPED AT HER DISPLAY IN THE DARK CORNER OF HER basement where she spent most of her time. Today was Saturday and her father was home. *Best to stay out of his way.*

Her favorite online network was called BlisterPool. The name didn't really mean anything, but she liked the people on it. It was one of the paid networks, which meant she didn't have to put up with any advertising. She'd learned on another network how to get in without paying. She supposed that was stealing, but others were doing it too. After the government shut down the network where she'd learned the trick, she found the same people on another network, a new network with new identities, so she'd also learned how to create and dispose of identities without leaving any trace. The authorities eventually caught up with anyone who wasn't good at keeping their activity hidden, but she and her online friends, the careful ones, were like cockroaches in the night: turn on the light and—*snap*— gone without a trace.

The pubcomm speaker on the wall crackled. "Hope, get your ass up here!" came her dad's voice.

*Great, now what?* She took the elevator up and walked to the kitchen. Her dad was standing over the open trash bin. He had a smear of mustard on his lower lip and a half-eaten sandwich in his hand. At the sink, her mom stood with her back to both of them, motionless.

"Look here," he said, pointing into the bin.

Hope didn't move.

"Get over here and look, I said!"

She shuffled over.

The slap on the back of her head nearly knocked her into the bin. "What part of 'when it's full' don't you understand?"

She didn't move.

"*Now!*"

Her shoulders jumped. She grabbed the bag, heaved it up, and carried it out the back door. After setting the bag down next to the large trash container in the alley, she twisted the top of the bag and got a fresh grip. That's when she saw them—the trio walking down the alley—the Lumière kid and his two friends. *Oh my god.* She wanted to look away, but she just had to get a glimpse. From this distance, she couldn't make out his blue eyes. But the way he carried himself—he was so confident, so carefree.

"What the hell are you waiting for!" yelled her dad from the door. The trio stopped their conversation. First they looked at her dad and then at her.

She lifted the bag into the container and walked back to the house. She felt like the universe had put a spotlight on her. Her cheeks burned, but she wouldn't cry. She got over crying a long time ago. *Best to stay out of his way.*

# Chapter 16

LAURA TOOK THE ROAST OUT OF THE OVEN WHILE BEN SET the table in the dining room. "Notify Chris that dinner is ready, and ask him to invite his friends," she said to the pubcomm.

"Message sent," replied the female voice. A moment passed. "Recipient acknowledged. Recipient replied. Quantity two."

Laura carried the platter heaped with pot roast into the dining room. Ben set the pitcher of water on the table. She heard the three kids race up to the back door.

"I win!" said Katie.

"You always win," said Chris.

"Wash up," called Laura, and she went to the bathroom to supervise.

The three kids were crammed into the bathroom, all at the same time. All three pairs of hands went under the water at the same time. Each grabbed for a corner of the towel at the same time.

"It's not a race," Laura said.

"Tell her that," said Al.

Katie stuck out her tongue.

They dashed into the dining room.

"Hey, Mr. Richards," said Katie.

"Hey, Mr. Richards," said Al.

"Hey, kids," said Ben.

The three took their usual seats. Laura loved having the kids over for dinner on Saturday night. It had become a tradition over the years. Their parents appreciated the help; both households were unemployed.

"Yes! Pot roast! My favorite!" said Al, accepting the platter and skewering a chunk.

"I thought strawberry-rhubarb pie, fried chicken, cheese fondue, and pizza is your favorites?" asked Ben.

Laura caught the deliberate use of bad grammar to emphasize the comedy of Al's claim.

"Yup," said Al. "But I like those only 'cuz we can't have them at our house."

"How come?" asked Chris.

Ben's eyes flashed Laura's way, and he started to answer, but Katie got it first.

"It's the law, silly. You can't use food credits for that stuff."

"My dad says we won't have to use food credits after the Mexicans take over," said Al.

"Take over what?" asked Chris.

"The Mexicans are not going to take over," said Katie.

"Why not?" asked Chris. "Will we still get pot roast?"

"Say, Katie," said Ben, "do you have a vocabulary word for us today?"

*Nice diversion.* Laura gave Ben a thankful smile. She loved the little dinnertime rituals he created when they were younger. He would ask Katie for a new word she'd learned, and then she'd explain the word's definition. Laura hoped some knowledge would rub off on Chris.

"Yes. My word for today is *ferromagnetic*. It describes something that can be influenced by a magnetic field," she said. Then she added, "Like a metal rod."

Stifled laughs erupted from the boys. Chris nearly lost his mouthful of milk. Katie had an overly innocent look on her face.

"Your turn, Al," said Ben. "Do you have a joke for us tonight?"

Al didn't care much for vocabulary, but he liked jokes.

"Yes," said Al. "Here goes. Why did the photographer get arrested?"

"I give up," said Ben.

"Because he shot all his customers and then blew them up."

"I get it!" said Chris. "Al, I wish I were funny as you."

"He's not that funny," said Katie.

"I am too funny," said Al. "I put the *h* in funny."

"Chris," said Ben, "I finished the adjustments to the Compton chamber today. I was wondering if you wanted to try a scan tonight."

"Aw, we were going to watch *Dragon Fighter Three* tonight," said Al.

"Martial arts again?" said Laura. "Haven't you seen that one at least five times?"

"I know, but it's the best one of the series. Hai-ya!" yelled Al as he sliced the air with a chop of his hand. "Or we could watch an *Omega Force* vid!"

"Yeah!" said Chris.

"Oh, come on," said Katie. "It'll be fun. We haven't done a scan in a long time."

"Sure, it's fun for you," said Al. "You get to run the scan sequences. I just sit around."

"Well, I certainly understand if you don't want to," said Ben. "And you're right, Al, I imagine it's kind of boring for you. But I received a suggestion from the people who make the biometric scanner, and they said there might be too much ambient moisture in the chamber. The human body is 57 percent water, and if we reduce the surrounding water, it should improve the chamber's ability to get a reading on Chris's body. I made the corresponding adjustments to the scan program, and I got a portable dehumidifier. You can set it up, Al, and suck the water out of the chamber."

"Well, OK, that sounds pretty good," said Al.

"Great," said Ben. "We'll start right after dinner."

"Did you all have fun today? Anything interesting?" asked Laura.

"Yeah, we had a great time," said Al. "And we saw that weird girl who lives on the corner. Her dad was yellin' at her."

"She's not weird," Chris snapped.

"Oooo!" said Al. "I forgot you like her."

Chris kicked Al under the table.

"Ouch!" said Al in manufactured pain.

"It's a tough situation over there," Laura said, rescuing Chris from further harassment. "Now, finish up and get to your project."

| | 0 | | 0 | | 0

LATER THAT NIGHT, BEN SHOWED AL HOW TO OPERATE THE DEHU-midifier while Katie tapped commands into the computer to program the scanners and to process the captured signals, just as Ben had taught her. The chamber was the size of a large closet and had top-to-bottom windows on three sides and a glass door. One side was up against the laboratory wall.

"We need to reduce the absolute humidity to three grams per cubic meter or less," Ben explained. "That's about as low as we can get it since Chris will be exhaling in the chamber. Al, let me show you how this works." Al followed Ben into the chamber. "This is the display that says how dry the air is. It needs to be three or less before we start."

"Got it," said Al.

"OK, everyone, here's the plan. After Chris opens the chamber door to enter, the moisture in the outside air will mix with the dry air inside. Once

Chris closes the door and sits down, the dehumidifier reading will have jumped up because of the added moisture. Al, you watch the dehumidifier display and announce when the reading has dropped back to three grams per cubic meter. Katie, at that point, you can begin the scan sequence as usual. Ready? Let's do it!"

Chris entered and closed the chamber door. Al kneeled down outside the chamber and watched the dehumidifier display. They all waited.

"Three! It says three now!" said Al.

Katie's fingers danced across the input display. "OK, that does it," she said. "Let's see what we have."

Ben and Katie looked up at the large wall display for the results. Chris opened the door of the chamber and came to the console to watch too.

On all previous attempts, the words *Null Scan* would appear. This time, however, the display simply showed *Complete*.

"*Yes!*" Al exclaimed. He raised his arm high into the air.

"Dad," said Chris, "it's called a high five. You're supposed to slap his hand with yours."

"Oh," said Ben, and he did his best.

"I can't believe it!" said Al. "It worked?"

"That seems to be the case," said Ben.

"Now what?" asked Katie.

"Yeah, is Chris full of crap?" asked Al.

"Ha-ha. Very funny," said Chris.

"I don't know," said Ben thoughtfully. Then, see-ing Al snicker, he added, "Oh, sorry, Chris. I mean …

I don't know what the results mean. We have to send the data to the scanner company. I helped them with their software algorithms, and in return, they said they'd process the results for me. We probably won't know until Monday at the earliest."

# CHAPTER 17

"SIEGFRIED, MARSHA E.," ANNOUNCED THE SECCOMM SYStem of Laura's university office.

"Enter," said Laura, and her office door swished open. "Have a seat, Marsha."

Marsha was dressed summer sporty, with her spandex sports bra and shorts—very different from her usual clothes during the normal academic year. She sat down, keeping both feet on the ground and back straight.

"So you want to skip next term. Taking a trip?"

"Yes. If you think I can still get the classes I need when I get back."

"It should work out fine," said Laura. "Learning doesn't just happen in the lecture hall. May I ask what you're going to do?"

"Cave diving."

"Really? That sounds exciting," said Laura. "Also dangerous."

"Yeah. My brother and I. We've been doing it for a while. We're pretty experienced. Going with some friends."

"Wow," said Laura. "You must be fortunate to be able to do that kind of sport."

"Yeah. My dad pays for it." Marsha glanced at the wearable display on her left wrist, a subtle combination of "Look what I have" and "Are we done yet?"

The boldness reminded her of Marian. "Huh. Well, so you get to go scuba diving often?"

"Not scuba diving; that's for wimps. The biggest risk to scuba divers is running out of air. Cave diving is swimming laterally through caverns connected by long, narrow tunnels. If something goes wrong, you can't just swim to the surface."

"I see. Narrow tunnels?" Just the thought of it made Laura nervous. "Aren't you afraid your equipment will get stuck or something?"

"We use a rebreather. It's smaller than scuba tanks. It filters out the carbon dioxide using chemicals. We carry a tiny oxygen tank to replenish the oxygen we need. We can get through very tight spots."

"Well, sounds like you have it all figured out," said Laura. "And that goes for your class plan too." She tapped the button to close Marsha's file. "I'll see you back here for winter term."

||0 ||0 ||0

CHRIS SHOT BASKETS IN THE DRIVEWAY WHILE WAITING TO MEET up with Al before going to Katie's house. Al came around the corner on a red bike.

"Whoa! Migo! Where did you get that?"

"My dad got it for me from the thrift store," said Al, hopping off. "It's not new, but it's in good condition."

"I'll say." Chris was happy for Al but also for himself. He and Katie rarely rode their bikes because Al didn't have one. Now they could all ride together.

"All right, let me get mine, and we'll ride over and show Katie."

When they arrived, Katie was just as surprised and pleased about Al's new bike.

"What's the plan for today?" asked Katie. "Whatever it is, we're bikin' there," she added.

Al seemed to stand just a little straighter. "I think it's about time for another stock market day."

Chris had almost forgotten about Al's elaborate scheme. The idea was to convince someone—a neighbor—that they could predict the stock market. The scheme took a month or two to fully unfold. Each weekend, they would pick a stock exchange symbol at random and make a prediction for that stock to go up or down in price. In order to have a single neighbor become convinced that they could predict the stock market, they started with a list of thirty-two neighbors. Each week, they would divide the neighbors into two groups. They would tell one half that the stock would go up and then tell the other half that the stock would go down. On the following Monday, the stock would have gone either up or down in price. Of course, none of them were actually able to predict which direction the stock price would move. The trick was to only return to the group of neighbors where the so-called prediction happened to be correct. As far as that set of neighbors knew, the prediction *was* correct. Each week the group became smaller by half: thirty-two, sixteen, eight, four, two and finally one. This last person would be convinced the three kids could predict the stock market. The only catch was the possibility that the neighbors might talk to each other. Al reasoned that human nature—greed and then shame—would keep the neighbors from talking.

They were down to a group of eight now, so four in the winning group. The next step was to deliver a new stock pick to those four houses.

Katie ran into her house to get the slips of paper showing the list of predictions to hand out. She came back out with the slips—and something else. "Hey, before we go, I want you guys to try something." She held out her open hand with three morsels wrapped in wax paper.

"What are they?" asked Chris.

"Chewing gum," she said. "My uncle sent me a kit that lets you make your own flavors of gum. It mixes and then extrudes the gum into pieces. It uses micro-bead encapsulation, so the flavor lasts for hours."

"Jazz!" said Al.

Chris unwrapped it and examined the bright blue color. "What flavor is it?"

"Blueberry," said Katie. "I can mix the color and the flavor independently. Blueberry is the only flavor that went with the blue color. I like the blue."

"Delicious," said Chris. "Thanks!"

"Yeah," agreed Al. "All right, let's get to the first house. Who's our first victim?"

Katie pointed to the address on her percomm.

"That's the place on Al's street," said Chris.

The three kids arrived at the house, just down the street from Al's. Chris parked his bike on the sidewalk.

"What do we do if someone finds out?" asked Chris.

"Same thing we always do," said Al. "Give 'em the slip."

"*Bwaaaah-ha-ha!*" Chris did his best maniacal laugh.

"Shhhhh!" warned Katie.

The door of the house had opened even before they reached the front steps. "I've been waiting for you kids," the guy said. The neighbor stood outside his front door, arms folded.

"Oh, good," said Chris, "Uh, I guess you know we were right again. Here's our stock pick for Monday." He handed the guy the slip of paper.

The man examined it carefully. Then he looked at the kids. He seemed to be examining them too. "I want to know how you're able to do this."

"We've got a stock-picking algorithm," said Chris.

The man tilted his head. "How could three kids come up with such a thing?"

"His dad's a science professor," said Al.

Chris smiled pleasantly, as if the connection should be obvious.

The guy looked at them for a moment longer and then said, "Thanks." He went back inside.

The kids jumped back on their bikes and then burst out laughing once they were far enough away.

"Are you sure this is a good idea?" asked Chris.

Katie and Al peddled in front of him. "We're not lying, and we're not asking for money," Al called back.

"OK. Where to next?"

Katie took her hands off the handlebars and pedaled no-handed as she pulled out her percomm to check the list. Al watched Katie with fascination. He took his hands off the handlebars too. Before Chris could say a word, Al's bike veered right, swung back, and then hard right again. The front wheel jackknifed, sending Al over sideways.

Chris slammed on the brakes, but it wasn't enough. He went over the handlebars, pushing the bike back as he went and preventing a crash with Al. Chris flew through the air, floating, almost as if held by a wire, completely missing Al, and then he skidded to a halt, flesh on pavement.

"Chris!" Katie ran to his side. "Are you all right? How did you do that?"

"Do what?"

"That's like thirty feet," she said. "You flew through the air."

"No, I just didn't want to hit Al."

"How bad is it?"

"Me? What about Al?"

Al trotted over. Looking down at himself, he said, "A scrape on my knee, that's all. Migo, I'm so sorry. Let's take a look at that."

"What? What are you talking about?"

Katie pulled his wrist, examined his arm, and then pushed his leg to the side and looked at his knee, thigh, and hip.

"I'm fine," said Chris. "What's the big fuss?"

"How can that be?" she said. "You should have major road rash. Like ground beef." She continued to poke and prod.

Chris yanked his arm away. "I'm fine. Enough already."

||0 ||0 ||0

THE KITCHEN PUBCOMM JINGLED FOR AN INCOMING COMM. BEN glanced at the sender's name; it was his contact from the scanner company. *So soon?* He set down his coffee, accepted the comm, and switched on the room speaker so Laura could listen too.

"I didn't expect to hear from you until Monday. Are you working weekends now?" Ben asked jovially.

"No, I was just going through my messages this morning and saw yours," said the technician. "I figured I'd run your data, but when I saw the error, I thought I'd let you know in case you had time to do another scan yet this weekend."

"So the results are no good? After so many years of trial and error, I was excited when the scan completed normally for the first time. What was the error?"

"Well, you know your son has to be in the chamber alone," said the technician. "Did you just forget? That's why the scan was successful this time; it was picking up the other person."

"No. He was in the chamber alone."

"Well, the results show two sentients out of the billions of identified candidates."

"I don't understand," said Ben. "Sentients? Billions?"

"The program has to sift through all the data to separate the life-forms from everything else in the chamber—like the chair, for example. Plus, you've got some dead insects in the corner, stuff like that. But the human body has entire communities of life teeming on the skin's surface, not to mention the intestines. Flora and fauna from fungi to skin mites, there are billions of individual organisms—all microscopic, mind you—but all with unique DNA. The program identified two sentients in your data. A sentient is a term we use for the candidates that are thinking and feeling. You know—people. One candidate has good data; the other is full of errors. I'm assuming the latter is your son and the former is whoever was in the chamber with him. Sorry, it looks like we still can't scan your son, but I thought you'd like to try again with him in there alone this time."

Ben didn't respond immediately. Laura had a questioning look.

"Hmm. Maybe you're right; maybe I made that mistake. Or maybe there's some other variable that allowed us to get a good scan. Maybe the other … sentient—the data set with the errors—is not a sentient at all, just bad data. Maybe we were finally able to isolate the bad data. Would you humor me and look at the set of good data? What do you see?"

"That's possible. Let's see here." There was a pause as he read through the report. "Bingo. I've got a male the same age as your son. If we can trust the data, he looks healthy." There was another pause. "Oh, I spoke too soon. I see an error here too. I don't know if we can trust the results. But we might be a lot closer."

"What's the error?"

"The DNA isn't right. There's no genetic connection to you. The system automatically correlates the DNA to the parents."

"He isn't our biological son," said Ben.

"Oh, I see. Well, but that's not all. The computer only found one match in the database, not two. That's impossible. They're not twins, because their ages are different. It must be an error."

"Who did it find?" asked Ben.

"One Marian Lumière," he said. "That can't be right; the DNA in the scan matches Marian Lumière exactly. It's like he *is* Marian Lumière—only male, of course."

Laura's questioning expression had urgency now.

"Can you tell when the boy was conceived?" asked Ben.

"Sure, it can be determined precisely through reverse stem cell-generation analysis. Let's see ... almost eleven years ago. December fifteenth, at 2142 GMT, plus or minus three minutes."

Laura's eyes widened, and she opened her mouth to speak, but Ben raised his hand.

"Thank you so much. I'll try another scan and make sure he's in the chamber alone."

"OK. Sorry," said the technician. "Look, I'm going to send you a subroutine that will separate out the sentients so you can ignore the bad data. I'll also include instructions that will allow you to submit your data directly to our computers and get your report back automatically. You won't have to wait on me every time you try something different."

Ben thanked the technician again and disconnected.

Laura's hands covered her mouth.

"When did Chris's biological father die?" asked Ben. "When was Joe's accident?"

"November," she said. "Joe died three weeks earlier." Her voice trembled. "What does this mean? Is the report about Chris right or wrong?"

"I don't know."

"I don't like this, Ben. And I can tell it bothers you too. I don't like this! I don't know what any of it means."

"I'm going to get to the bottom of it," he said. "But I'm not sure how."

# CHAPTER 18

THE RICHARDSES'S PUBCOMM ANNOUNCED AN INCOMING comm, but it wasn't the usual jingle.

On the display, Laura saw a yellow caution triangle. Indeed, she didn't recognize the sender's name. "Hello?"

"Hey, can I speak with Chris Richards, please?" said the voice.

"I'm sorry, there's no one here by that name," she answered, cautiously but truthfully.

"I'm looking for a boy named Chris. Do you know him?"

"Who are you, and what is this about?"

"Sorry. This is Jerry Petters." The icon blinked, indicating the sender had added vid to the comm. She accepted the vid stream, and the man at the other end appeared on screen. "I live three blocks west of you. He's been helping me out. Great kid. I just have a question for him."

The credentials matched an address nearby; the guy was a neighbor. "Yes, my son's name is Chris. Hold on. I'll get him." At the back door, she called out, "Chris, you have a comm."

The three kids stopped playing immediately. She knew what was going through their heads. Any comm for Chris would ring on his percomm. As a minor, few people had the necessary permissions— only family, friends, and school officials. This had to be someone else. From the back door, she could practically see the gears turning in their heads.

"Who is it, Mom?" Chris yelled back.

"A Mr. Petters, a neighbor," she said, using her I'm-onto-you tone.

She saw Al mouth the words *holy crap*, and then they exchanged whispers.

Chris yelled back, "I'll take it out here! Can you forward it?"

"No," she said. "Get in here."

With Chris in the lead, all three trudged inside.

She tapped the button enabling two-way vid. "Is this the boy?"

"Yeah! Hey, Chris," said the man. "Listen, I need your help again. I wanna make a big play for tomorrow, see. So I need your help."

"Uh, well, we only come by on weekends."

"Yeah, I know. But I wanna make this big play, see. So I thought you could help me out for tomorrow."

"Sorry," said Chris, speaking quickly now. "We can only make it on the weekends. Sorry. Bye." Chris stabbed the display, ending the comm.

Laura glared at them. Before she could say anything, Ben's image popped up on the pubcomm.

"Laura, can you ask the kids—oh, I see they're all there. Hey, do you kids want to come down to the lab and play mind reader?"

"Yeah!" they answered in unison, way too enthusiastically, and bolted for the stairs. Chris called back, "Uh, we gotta go help Dad."

She heard them race down the steps and then burst into laughter.

| | 0    | | 0    | | 0

"HEY, *AMIGOS*, *AMIGA*," GREETED BEN AS THEY CAME OVER TO where he was working.

"Dad, I've told you before, you don't say the *a*. It's just *migo*," said Chris.

"Oh, right. Sorry." He watched the kids go over to the drawer where the deck of cards was stored. He couldn't help but overhear their conversation.

"I love it when your dad tries to act all jazz with us," said Katie.

"Yeah," agreed Al. "As a dad, though, he *is* pretty jazz. He just needs to act his age."

"I know," said Chris. "He means well."

Al got out the cards and called out, "Me first!"

"Actually," said Ben, "how about Chris goes first this time?"

"What?" said Katie. "He can't go first. The scans don't—hey, wait a minute! We got the good scan Saturday! So did it really work? Does it work on Chris now?"

"Yes," said Ben. "We don't even need the dehumidifier anymore. But I need more scans."

"Jazz!" said Al. "All right, here's the deck, Chris. Get in there!"

Katie went to the console and started the program sequence to prepare the detectors.

"So the computer can really read my mind?" asked Chris, sitting down in the chamber.

"Not exactly," said Ben, "It just interprets your brain activity and then correlates it to a set of known responses."

"Can we get on with it?" asked Al, bored already.

"OK. I'm ready," said Katie. "Pick a card, Chris."

He pulled a card from the deck at random and looked at it. Katie tapped commands to initiate the scan.

After a moment, the computer displayed *3 Spades*.

They smiled, and Katie called over, "Are you holding the three of spades?"

"Yes!" said Chris excitedly, finally able to enjoy the game with the others.

The kids' faces were beaming, but then their smiles faded. Ben looked at the display. It had changed. Underneath *3 Spades*, the word *Emergency* appeared.

| | 0 | | | 0 | | | 0 |

MARSHA, LESTER, TOM, AND MARSHA'S BROTHER, DON, CHATTED
on top of the metal cage, the entrance to Devil's Hole
Number Two, as they prepared for their cave dive.
The early morning commute from their Vegas hotel
along Highway 95 across the desert was identical to
the ride each morning during the first two weeks of
their summer-term adventure.

"Comm check," said Lester.

Marsha adjusted her mask and acknowledged. "Check."

Tom and Don went next. "Check."

"Check."

Marsha eyed her brother. She could tell he was
getting ready to confront Lester again.

"I want to make the dive plan next
time," said Don.

Marsha cringed. Her brother would never be a
politician or a salesman.

"We've been over this," said Lester. "You don't
have enough experience."

"My plans for Hole Number One were fine."

"Yeah. This isn't Hole Number One, is it?"
said Lester.

The stout metal cage on which they sat was
designed to restrict access to the cave system but
also to allow bats and other animals to pass freely.
The Death Valley National Park Authority controlled
access to the gate on top.

Lester was right; he *did* have the most experience. He'd rented the tripod and winch system they

used to lower themselves down the vertical shaft to the water's surface. He knew it all.

Lester added, "You can go join those other pussies at Hole Number One."

Marsha bristled but had to agree. The excitement had fizzled after diving at Hole Number One. It was safe—totally explored and regulated. But Devil's Hole Number Two was largely unexplored and, by most estimates, far more extensive; not even the geoseismic survey data from the old petroleum companies showed the whole system. No one knew where all the passages went.

"You should give him a chance," Tom chimed in. Tom was defending Don, as he usually did, but also avoiding Lester's line of fire.

"Maybe next time," said Lester. "Did you recharge the winch from yesterday?" He flipped the winch's power switch to standby, and the light turned green.

"Yes. Of course," said Don. "Don't change the subject. How am I supposed to get experience if you never let me?"

"Just a few more dives, and then you'll have enough experience." Lester looked at Marsha. "We all agree, right?" He yanked on the tripod legs supporting the winch over the hole, testing the stability. "Marsha, you're awfully quiet. Do we all agree?"

"Yeah," she said. She gave Don a one-battle-at-a-time glance. She couldn't decide if Don needed to get more of a backbone or if Lester was simply not worth the fight. Growing up, Don had always been complaining instead of doing. "Look, we need to finish the checks on the rebreathers. The sun's coming up. It's too hot for all this bickering."

Marsha's hands visited each tube and valve of her rebreather. She checked the internal computer system that controlled the filtration of carbon dioxide using the precise mixture of chemicals and then tested her helmet light and backup flashlights.

"Everyone ready?" asked Lester.

"Yeah," she said. "Get in position." She pressed the remote control button at her wrist, and once the cable unreeled a few feet, she attached it to Lester's harness.

Lester pivoted on his butt and placed his flipper-clad feet into the cage opening. He pulled his mask down over his face. They all used full-face diving masks instead of the old kind with the rubber breathing tube clenched between the teeth. The full-face mask allowed them to communicate with each other over radio transceivers. Pressing the button on his wrist control, the cable retracted, taking up the slack. He leaned forward, letting the cable take his weight, and then lowered himself into the hole.

Marsha went next. The morning sunlight from above shone through the hole at a sharp angle. Shadows flickered on the water's surface as Tom and Don came down in succession. Submerging, they left behind the last natural light she would see for the next six hours.

Lester secured the nylon cord to a protruding rock formation. There were only a few tunnel openings to choose from but many branches along the way. Lester indicated the tunnel to start with, the one they'd been exploring since they came to Devil's Hole Number Two. From the spool, the nylon line unrolled behind him. They each used a battery-powered propulsion system attached to the chest and could cover great distances with little effort.

Lester cruised away into the passage, his head lamp illuminating the tunnel walls as he went. Marsha waited until she lost sight of his flippers around a curve behind a fading glow, and then she activated her own propulsion system and followed.

After twenty minutes of travel, they reached the end of the system of passages they'd already explored. The goal was to explore new passages in each successive dive. They posted reports online and took credit for being first—in cyberfame, forever part of humanity's digital record.

"I'm at the junction chamber," said Lester. "Check in."

"I'm good," Marsha said, and she heard Tom and Don acknowledge too.

After attaching the line to a chunk of exposed rock, Lester selected an unexplored tunnel and kicked off, the line extending behind him.

Each time they emerged into a chamber, they took a few minutes to look around. The cavern chambers had air pockets at the top—or, more precisely, a combination of lethal subterranean gases. They always shone their lights around, in awe of the beautiful stalagmites and stalactites.

Two hours into the dive, they reached a chamber that was incredibly deep. It was like a flooded elevator shaft of a skyscraper, and they were floating at the top. Following Lester down, they passed several tunnel openings along the way. *Seriously, do we have to go all the way down?*

At the base of the shaft, six passages led away in different directions. Lester selected one, and Marsha followed. The tunnel made a gradual curve to the left. Ahead, she could see Lester had reached an opening. Normally, his helmet light would've illuminated the walls of the next chamber, but this time, it was like he drifted out into the ocean. She followed him into the vastness as the murky water consumed her light beam. Turning back, she saw the helmet lights from Don and Tom panning about, but the wall of the chamber was no longer in sight.

"Hey, guys, check this out," said Lester, shining his flashlight on a surface that wasn't rock.

Marsha fluttered over and saw metal, glass, and plastic. "Weird. These look like old trans—cars, trucks." She cruised horizontally, shining her flashlight. "It's a mountain of cars."

"There must be hundreds," said Tom. "How did they get here?"

Marsha floated up to one of the vehicles at the passenger-side window. With her gloved hand, she brushed away the accumulated silt and shone her light inside.

||0 ||0 ||0

"EMERGENCY? WHAT DOES THAT MEAN?" ASKED KATIE.

"I don't know," said Ben. "Katie, do you mind?" indicating the chair at the console where she was sitting.

"No, of course not, Mr. Richards. Please." She jumped off the chair.

He sat down and tapped commands. The kids watched as the display flashed with progress reports.

"The three of spades is from Chris's scan, of course," said Ben, still typing, "but I added the subroutine to separate out the readings. The new program has isolated the bad data. But now, it insists the bad data is from a second person in the chamber with Chris." He tapped in more commands. "We know that's not the case, of course, but now the mind-reader program is reporting the thoughts of the second person."

"Wow," said Katie. "So the word *emergency* came from the thoughts of the bad data? What does the word *emergency* mean? How did the computer come up with that word?"

"Let's see," said Ben. "The software maps the readings to a linguistic database and determines the word or phrase that best matches the interpreted thought or emotion."

"The bad data has thoughts and emotions?" asked Al.

"The computer seems to think so," said Ben. "To answer your question, though, Katie, I don't know what *emergency* means, or if it means anything at all."

"We have to do it again," said Chris.

Ben noticed an unusual amount of finality in his voice. Katie and Al seemed to notice too. Chris wasn't looking at them or the display; he was glassy eyed. But then he seemed to snap out of it.

"Mr. Richards," said Al, "you said the program gets better with practice?"

"Yes, that's true," said Ben. "But you have to train the computer. You have to tell it which responses are correct. It learns from the correct responses and ignores the wrong ones. Over time, the accuracy improves. There are people at the psychology department who've been test subjects for years. It's not mind reading, but the computer's interpretation is so complete you'd never know the difference."

"How often is the computer correct?" asked Al.

"Almost all the time, as you kids know from the mind-reader game."

"I see where Al is going," said Katie. "What if we tell the computer that it's right about the word *emergency*? Won't it get better and tell us more?"

"Yes, that's worth a try," said Ben. "OK, Chris, get back in the chamber."

After each scan, the computer determined the card Chris was looking at and then added the word *emergency*. And each time, Ben told the computer that *emergency* was the right answer.

After a while, Chris stopped using the cards and just sat and waited. Al and Katie thought it was pretty funny because the computer started coming up with words that described whatever Chris was thinking, like *hungry*, *sherbet*, and even *sore butt*. But the second line always displayed *emergency*.

"Let's take a break," suggested Ben. "Chris's thought about sherbet sounds pretty good."

After the break, they returned to the lab for a few more tries. On the third try, the second line on the display showed the words *feral emergency*.

"Hey, it's different!" said Al. "What does *feral* mean?"

"It's a word used to describe a domesticated animal that escaped back to its original habitat and turned wild again," explained Katie.

"That's right," said Ben. "The American mustang and the New Zealand wild boar are two examples."

"What would *feral emergency* mean?" asked Chris, coming over from the chamber.

"Your guess is as good as mine," said Ben. "It might not mean anything. Or the words might not be related. I'm not convinced this isn't just garbage results from garbage data." He wiped his eyes. "Look, it's getting late. I can do some more investigation, but you kids need to get home and get to bed."

110  110  110

UNABLE TO MAINTAIN SELF-CONTROL, MARSHA'S HEART RATE SHOT up, and her breathing quickened. "It's a person! A dead body!" She struggled to control her breathing; she was putting too much load on her rebreather and consuming too much oxygen.

Lester reached her first.

Holding the beam of light on the passenger-side window, she saw exposed bone under partially decomposed skin with clumps of hair still attached. The strands of hair swayed rhythmically, like a sea anemone in a snow globe of decayed flesh.

"It's a dead body," she repeated.

"Sure?" asked Lester. "Maybe we should take a pulse?"

"Hey, this is creeping me out," said Tom. "Let's get out of here."

That night, Marsha commed Lester. "It turns out the location of the chamber with the cars is not in the national park."

"So?"

"So? So we should report it to the police, not the park ranger."

"Marsha, don't worry about it. We can tell the police later ... you know, as if we just found it," he said. "We can't talk about this. Not to anyone. If it gets out, they'll lock it up and we won't be able to—wait, how do you know it's outside the park boundary?"

"I pulled the log from the inertial tracker."

"What the hell! You posted it!"

"No, stupid. I just pulled the log file for now. It's in my Ben-U account with the other logs. It's totally secure."

# CHAPTER 19

"I DIDN'T EXPECT YOU TO BE UP FROM THE LAB SO SOON."
Laura said, tending to the flowers by the driveway. She wiped sweat from her forehead with the back of her wrist, smearing dirt that was already there. "Any more clues?"

"Well, I think we should talk," said Ben.

Inside, while Laura got a drink of cold water, Ben said, "So I've been over the data again and again. Everything points to the same conclusion. It seems impossible, but there appears to be a separate intelligence of some kind in Chris."

Water dribbled when the cup came away from her lips.

"Don't be alarmed. There's no indication that he or we—or anyone—is in danger. I see no reason for concern."

"You're right," she said, wiping her mouth with her wrist. She saw the dirt but ignored it. "Somehow, it's not a surprise. I can't explain it, but I don't think there's any danger, either." Bringing the cup back to her mouth, she paused. "I don't know how, but the intelligence … I feel like I've known it was there all along. Like Dorothy waking up back at the farm." She took the drink. "What do we do?"

"I think we should concentrate on communication," he said. "The results from the computer are just a start."

"You mean the *feral emergency* phrase?"

"Yes. I did some more work on the program. It turns out, the word *emergency* results from the computer trying to make sense of two semantic meanings but expressing them as one. I've never seen anything like it. It's an entirely different form of cognition."

"What are the two meanings?"

"*Emergent* and *urgency*. So there is still the concept of urgency that we associate with the word emergency, but there is also the concept of emergent or emergence."

"Feral emergent urgency."

"Right. It doesn't make any more sense, really, but I'm hoping the adjustments I made to the program will help. I need Chris for more testing."

||0  ||0  ||0

"YES, FREEDOM, DR. CORNELIUS. THOUSANDS OF BRITONS HAVE died before you," said Anderson. "They fought and died for freedom. All for nothing? Because you're a control freak? You want to 'maintain artistic license'? Doctor, you're nothing but a *primo uomo* standing in a pool of blood from fallen freedom fighters mixed with the tears of their grieving mothers."

"No, please stop," Cornelius blubbered.

*Hear me, god, forked tongue unto forked conscience*

*Deposit your will in truth's absence*

*Mortal's resistance thou shall rip*

*For the chance of reality's path doth tip*

As the old man wept, Anderson stepped to the credenza in Cornelius's university office and picked up one of several framed photographs: a younger Cornelius shaking hands with the Minister of Defence.

"How could I be so selfish?" mumbled Cornelius.

"The boy will be the first of your next generation," said Anderson.

"Yes."

"Fine. My office will transmit the next payment."

| | 0 | | 0 | | 0

CHRIS TOOK THE LAST BITE OF HIS BREAKFAST AND SAID, "BUT I was going to play with Al and Katie."

"The animal shelter is visiting the church to promote animal adoption," said Laura. "You get a chance to pet the homeless dogs and cats. Father Arnold asked if some kids could be there right at nine, before it opens, to help out. You can still play with Al and Katie later."

"OK," said Chris. He cleared his dishes and then went to the garage, pushed his bike up the ramp, hopped on, and pedaled.

At the church, a large truck from the animal shelter was outside. A shelter staff member waved to him. Chris parked his bike and heard sounds of the animals in the church, mostly dog barks. He got in line at the church entrance and watched shelter volunteers as they carried cages up the stairs and into the church. Some had dogs while others held a puppy, a cat, or kittens.

Father Arnold came to the door and said, "Thank you all for volunteering today. Let me explain how this is going to work. Numbered signs have been placed around the church basement, the main floor, and the back lawn. Each sign identifies a small area that will have an animal for visitors to pet. The shelter doesn't have enough staff to monitor all the areas. We need your help to care for the pets at each area until others arrive. Once a few visitors have joined you, you can pass the responsibility on to one of them. You can then leave or get back in line to visit another animal."

When the church doors opened, Chris filed in.

"What kind of animal do you want to see?" asked the staff member behind the desk.

"I don't know. A dog, I guess."

The volunteer handed him a slip of paper with the number three printed on it.

He followed the signs to area three in the basement of the church and sat down on the floor.

Volunteers were taking animals out of cages and distributing them. A woman, holding a little red-haired puppy, came over.

"His name is Bruiser," she said, and she put the puppy in Chris's lap. Bruiser seemed to be half-asleep. "He's had a busy morning already. He might sleep for a while longer, or maybe he'll want to play." She took a rubber bone from her pocket and set it next to Chris. "If he gets bitey, give him that; his teeth are like needles."

"What kind is he?" Chris asked.

"Not sure. We don't know who the parents are. But he looks like he has some Lab in him. Well, I gotta get the rest. I'll come by in a bit. You OK for now?"

"Sure!" Chris stroked the soft fur. Bruiser was little but had big paws, big ears, and a big head for such a little body. His bright blue collar made a striking contrast to the orange fur. He still hadn't opened his eyes, so Chris just kept petting him. "It's OK, little guy. I didn't know my real mom and dad, either. But maybe we can find you nice parents like I have."

||0 ||0 ||0

HOPE AVENIR WAITED IN LINE OUTSIDE THE CHURCH. BY MIDMORNing, her dad usually announced he was going "job hunting." The moron frequently lost track of the days and even went job hunting on the weekend. She didn't care where he really went, but she needed to stay out of his way until he left. The shelter event would chew up time.

"What kind of animal do you want to see?" asked the person at the desk.

"I don't care," she said, and then she accepted the slip of paper with the number three on it.

"Around to your right and down the stairs."

Hope followed the signs, snaking through the bustle of people hovering over pets in little groups, and she found the stairwell. She walked to where the number three was posted on the wall. *It's him.* Right below the sign, the Lumière kid was sitting on the floor, legs crossed and a puppy on his lap. *Turn around.* Too late. He glanced up, and his eyes locked onto hers. *Those eyes.* She looked down and away. *Act natural.* She looked at the dog; it was all she could manage.

One of his hands was resting gently on top of the puppy. His long fingers were nestled in the puppy's fur. *Those hands! The eyes are bad enough; how could his hands be beautiful too?* She became aware that entire seconds were ticking by.

"His name is Bruiser. Do you want to hold him?" he asked, lifting the puppy from his lap.

She looked away completely, backed up, bumped into a person behind her, and then turned and bolted for the stairs.

# CHAPTER 20

"YOU CAN WATCH A VID UNTIL YOU FALL ASLEEP," BEN SAID to Chris. Ben had set up a cot in the chamber. "I'll work through the night."

Ben initiated scans and monitored the results as the hours ticked by. The computer continued to display variations of the phrase they'd seen already: *feral emergent urgency* or *feral urgent emergence*. He examined the underlying semantic meaning, but it was always the same.

"Dad, I'm tired," said Chris. "Can we at least turn off some of the lights?"

"Oh, jeez. Of course. Sorry." Once the lights were off, the console display illuminated Ben's face in the surrounding darkness as he continued to work.

*Maybe I should use the chamber the same way as the psychology department? Maybe I need to pose a question as stimulus, just like the mind-reader game?*

He found the deck of cards, selected a card, and held it up, facing the glass wall of the chamber illuminated by the glow of his display monitor. He tapped the scan button on the console.

*Queen Hearts* appeared on the display.

The card was indeed the queen of hearts. *It can see.* Inside the chamber, Chris was fast asleep. *The thought had to come from the intelligence.* Ben tried more cards, and each time, the display showed the correct response.

*Can it hear?* Ben checked the intercom setting. Chris wouldn't be disturbed if he spoke softly.

*What should I ask?* In a whisper, he said, "Who are you?"

||0  ||0  ||0

THE PUBTRAN PULLED UP NEXT TO THE RENTAL VAN AT THE entrance to Devil's Hole Number Two. Marsha, Don, and Tom got out, and the pubtran drove off. Marsha called out as she walked around the van, "I still don't understand why you had to leave without us." On the other side, Lester was with another man she didn't recognize. The other man was big, like a bouncer.

"Hey, Lester," she said, reservation in her voice.

"Hey," Lester said, unpacking gear. The other guy seemed to be helping.

She expected an explanation but wasn't getting one.

Finally, Lester said, "This is Erik. He's joining us on the dive."

"*What?*" said Don, taking a step forward. "Our dive plan is for four. You don't change the dive plan. It's an unnecessary risk."

"Risk?" Lester shot back. "You want to talk to me about risk? Migo, that's why we do cave diving. That's why we come to Hole Number Two. Remember?"

"Let me get this straight. You won't let me make the dive plan, and now you go and change it at the last minute?"

"It won't compromise our safety," said Lester. "It's better if I'm the one to guide us back to the graveyard chamber."

*I don't believe it*, Marsha thought. "You told him?"

"Yeah, I told him."

"You lecture me about secrecy, and then you go and blab to this guy? We don't know anything about him," she said. Then to the new guy, she said, "No offense."

"None taken," the guy said. He was just hanging back, organizing his equipment. She had to admit, he seemed cool and calm.

"Erik's up for the risk. Are you?" said Lester. He looked at Tom and Don and then back to her.

Tom gave Marsha a relenting shrug.

Don threw up his arms. "Whatever. Unbelievable. Un-fucking-believable."

From Lester's expression, Marsha knew he had the word *pussy* locked and loaded. "Fine," she said before he let it fly. "But I want to see this new dive plan. Now."

There wasn't much conversation over the next hour. Marsha handed the motor for the winch to

Lester, and he mounted it on top of the tripod and then stood back to examine the work. *Where's the new guy?* She found him at the back of the van.

"Hey, what are you doing?"

"Oh, just getting the rest of the equipment."

"The winch and tripod are already over there," she said. "We can handle the rest, thank you very much."

"Sure. I was just admiring your gear. You've got the Nelson CCR," he said. "And the model seven deco computer. Nice."

"Yeah, it's not bad." The sheer size of the man made a fresh impression. "You really are big."

"Yeah, that's how I got my nickname."

"What's that?"

"Big Vega." He stood back and put his hands on his hips. "Do you like *your* nickname?"

"Excuse me?"

"You know, Lester's pet name for you—pussy."

She felt the heat rise to her face. *This is going to be a long day.* Her percomm vibrated, a message from her poli-sci professor, asking how the adventure was going. *Well, there's at least one person in this world with decency and respect.* She tapped out a reply saying she was having a wonderful time. *I wish it was true.*

|10 |10 |10

BEN PULLED BACK THE COVERS AND CLIMBED INTO BED AS QUIETLY as he could. The sun was up now, but the house was still quiet. He might get a little sleep before Laura and Chris woke.

Laura reached over to the bedside table, put her percomm down, and then rolled to face him.

"Sorry. I didn't mean to wake you," he said.

"No, I couldn't sleep. Just checking messages. Anyway, what did you learn?"

"Extraordinary, really. I wasted a lot of time running more scans until I figured out I could simply ask questions. So I just came right out and asked who or what it was. The word I got back from the computer was *warden*."

"Warden?"

"Yes. The computer selected the word from three concepts: *steward*, *shepherd*, and *warden*. The word *warden* has several semantic meanings, and the particular usage is not like a prison warden—not like a type of guard over things trying to escape—but more like the warden of a nature reserve. Like a type of guard over things needing protection. So you can see how that fits with *shepherd* and *steward*."

"What else?"

"I asked the obvious questions like 'Why are you here?' or 'What's your name?' and just got the *feral emergency* response. I'm not sure if it can't understand those types of questions or if my program needs more work. So I decided to focus on only one question. I asked, 'Where are you from?' and then all the variations I could think of. Finally, I asked, 'What is your origin?' and the computer displayed *different world*. So I looked at the constructed meanings. The term *world* was constructed from the higher level meaning of *world* like *environment*, combined with the concept of *planet*."

Laura looked at him with a you've-got-to-be-kidding expression.

"Really."

"Do you believe it?"

"I don't know. It occurred to me that it could be a prank. Katie has completely mastered the software. And Al's creativity has no limit. It would be very funny. But I checked everything. Seems real."

"What should we do?"

"Well, I want to keep at it—as much as Chris can handle—but I also want to see if we can get some help. I mean, how do we know there isn't someone else like Chris somewhere—or this hasn't happened in the past and kept a secret?"

"Who can you trust?" she asked. "Who will believe you?"

"I know. I'm worried about that too. I'm going to use my government contacts through the university. My security clearance should give someone pause enough to at least listen."

"So you think there's some kind of government agency?"

"I think there was in the past. During the nineteen hundreds, there were UFO sightings. If I remember my history correctly, the government was worried about public hysteria over such things."

||0 ||0 ||0

IN THE ABSOLUTE DARKNESS OF THE TUNNEL, PASSING FAR BELOW the Nevada desert, Marsha's propulsion system thrust her smoothly through the water. The group had already traveled for more than two hours. Her helmet light panned across the rocky tunnel surface streaked with brown and yellow. She kept one gloved hand gently around the nylon line. As she approached a bend in the passage, she gracefully switched hands, putting as little stress on the line as possible. The cadence resembled Tarzan swinging through the rain forest, grasping vines and alternating hands at the top of each swing.

"Oh god." It was Lester's voice.

"What is it?" she called out.

No response.

"Lester, what's wrong?" She heard the click of Lester's transmitter and sounds of struggle but no words. "Everyone, check in!" She throttled up her propulsion system and kicked.

"Check," said Don.

"Check," said Tom. "But—"

"But what!" Ahead, Marsha could see the light from Lester's helmet thrashing about. She turned off her propulsion system and glided up next to him. He was twisting about, and his hands clawed at his mask.

"Marsha, we've got a problem." It was Don's voice from her helmet speakers.

"I know. Lester is—" The twisting was so violent she had to back up to avoid being kicked. She saw white fluid sloshing inside his face mask—a caustic cocktail of soda lime, sodium peroxide, and sodium dioxide, the unmistakable sign of a compromised rebreather.

Without warning, he yanked off the face mask.

"*No!*" she cried.

His jutting mouth, like a fish out of water, erupted huge white bubbles. The flailing slowed, and his body went limp. Milky whiteness billowed from the tube connected to his mask. His body drifted to the tunnel floor.

A tiny jet of white was coming from the edge of Lester's rebreather. She shined her light and saw a hole, no bigger than a pinprick, spewing a tiny plume of white.

"Don, what's your situation?" she called, and then she turned, kicked, and throttled up, back along the line toward the others.

"It's Tom! He couldn't breathe. He got the cocktail," said Don.

Just then, she noticed an acrid smell in her own air supply. She stopped the propulsion system and unstrapped her rebreather. Keeping the tubes to her mask in place, she swung the rebreather in front. *Damn!* A pinhole. Water had already started the chemical reaction with the sodium. She pressed her finger over the hole.

"Check your rebreather for a hole!"

Don's comm link opened, and she heard a horrifying scream.

"Don!" She throttled up but didn't kick, controlling her oxygen load to buy as much time as possible.

The gruesome screaming continued. She heard him gasping. The next scream was raspy and then turned to choking.

"I'm coming!"

The first few bubbles popped on her lower lip, burning. Froth squirted up, settling around her neck, burning the skin. Her body scraped against the rock wall, twisting like a bullet in a rifle barrel. She struggled to turn off the propulsion system, but all her attention was on the searing pain in her chest, chin, and neck. Her body bounced from side to side, ripping silt and debris from the tunnel wall.

The white foam splashed over her mouth. Instinctively, she breathed through her nose, causing an involuntary choking sneeze. Her face, mouth, nose, and lungs were on fire. Her body crashed into protruding rock and became wedged. Looking up, she saw two helmet lights in the distance some thirty meters ahead, both still, one huddled over the other. *Don and Tom.*

Then another head lamp turned, aimed at her, watching. "Hey, pussy, how do you like the pearl necklace?"

Her face throbbed as she held her breath, and tiny flashes of light appeared even though her eyes were pressed shut.

"Go ahead," the voice continued, "suck it up."

In total and complete surrender, she ripped off the mask and inhaled.

# Chapter 21

"**T**HANK YOU FOR TAKING MY COMM, MAJOR NOLAN," SAID
Ben, facing the vid image displayed on his
university office wall.

"Not a problem, sir. The request came through
channels."

"Yes, well, I traversed quite a chain of people, so
I don't know if you can help me or if you can point
me in the right direction." Ben paused conversation-
ally. "Well, you see, I don't know how to say this—"

"You believe you've detected an alien presence?"
said the major. "I see that here, in the notes attached
to the comm request. Your request came through
channels. I'm the right person."

"Oh, very good. Well, uh, so I was hoping to
get your help or—" Ben sat up straight in his chair.
"Forgive me, Major, but do you get calls like this
every day? You don't seem very interested."

"Professor Richards, I want to get the details. The
best way to do that is for you to fill out the paperwork. I'll send you the link."

ON THE FIRST DAY BACK TO SCHOOL, CHRIS, AL, AND KATIE STEPPED off the masstran after the short trip. Chris loved summer vacation, but there was also the excitement of a brand-new school year, a fresh start. Fifth grade was OK, but now they were the oldest kids in the school, their last year before middle school.

Kids gathered in small groups on the large front lawn as Chris, Katie, and Al walked the cement path leading to the main doors of the school. They exchanged waves with friends they hadn't seen over the summer.

"Over there," said Al. "The Queen's holding court."

The girls in the group were all wearing bright colors with an emphasis on pinks and yellows. "Yeah, the Queen and her royal subjects."

The Queen, Dawn Perkins, was waving her arms all over the place. *Must be some amazing story about her summer vacation.* The other girls were watching her like it was the greatest action vid they'd ever seen. *Now what? What is she looking at?* Something had caught the Queen's attention: Hope Avenir. The other girls turned their attention too, and they laughed. One mimicked Hope's walk.

Chris had to admit the girl captured it pretty well. Hope passed by, shoulders slumped. Her clothes were too big. The colors were drab—lots of brown— and her hair was messy. The girls laughed even louder at the one doing the impression. Hope walked faster, into the building.

Chris felt his hands tighten into fists. Part of him wanted to tell Dawn where she could shove it, and part of him wanted to run to Hope. *What would I say? She'd probably run away like the other times. What could I say to make her understand I'm different? I could say how unfair the world can be. Does she want someone to help? Or maybe just listen?*

He imagined himself like the heroes in the action vids, an Omega Force agent appearing from nowhere to restore her dignity. *I'll beat 'em up.* But that wouldn't fix anything, not really. *How can I help without making her situation worse?* He imagined himself telling Dawn what an awful person she was and to leave Hope alone. *Oh, how the girls would howl at that; they'd tease even more. Hope always tries to make herself invisible. Could that be the answer? Maybe she can take care of herself.*

The royals kept pointing at Hope even after she disappeared inside. But Dawn was now scowling at one specific royal, a girl who wasn't laughing along, one who looked ashamed.

"What's your problem?" Dawn said, so loudly that some kids stopped to look.

"She didn't do anything," the girl said.

"She didn't do anything," Dawn mocked. The other royals laughed. "Maybe you want to be her friend?" The girl didn't say anything back. "Come on, migas, I see Maria." The group moved on. The one girl started to follow. "Not you," said Dawn.

"I can't believe we have to put up with her for another year," said Chris.

"I know," said Al. "I bet she'll be elected class president again."

"She's been class president every year," said Chris. "Why do they have that stupid election, anyway? We've been doing it since kindergarten. What kindergartner even knows what a president is?"

"It's supposed to teach us leadership," said Katie. "They figure starting early is better."

"Well, it's just a popularity contest," said Al. "What I can't figure out is how she wins every year; she's a horrible person."

"It's because we have so many more girls than boys in our class," said Katie. "Girls vote for girls, and boys vote for boys. The Queen bribes girls to vote for her. Her dad's rich, I guess."

Chris's percomm vibrated, and all three pulled out their percomms for a glance. "First bell," said Chris. "Let's get this year started."

110 110 110

"MAJOR NOLAN, YOU'VE HAD MY SUBMISSION FOR WEEKS NOW. I filled out your forms, and I've heard nothing," said Ben.

"Yes, Professor, it all looks very compelling. Your case has been fully recorded."

"Fully recorded? Major, am I missing something? I'm reporting to you that an alien is on Earth. It's your job to respond to such a situation, is it not?"

"Yes, but you must understand, you don't have definitive evidence."

"What other explanation could there be?"

"That's just it. Your son could have a brain condition such that his neurons are able to support two separate identities—like schizophrenia, for example."

"But the medical analysis shows no such malady."

"I'm not saying your situation isn't unique. It might not be in the diagnostic database. I'm saying there are plausible medical explanations. There's no definitive evidence that you've identified an alien presence. You haven't ruled out other possibilities."

Ben was frustrated, but the scientist in him had to admit the major was right. "Look, I just need some help. Have you ever received similar reports?"

"No."

"Well, can't you help me with further analysis? Don't you have resources to investigate?"

"Yes, I have resources— I mean, Professor, my command is part of a contingency plan. Once first contact is confirmed, the plan is activated by executive order. Until then, the resources to investigate are minimal."

"How minimal? I don't need much."

"Professor," began the major, his tone shading toward a whine, "I get a lot of reports. Wild reports. It's impossible to pursue them all. I have to prioritize. It's my job to take each seriously, true, but think about it: we're talking about aliens. What are the odds? I have to prioritize."

"You don't have any resources, do you?"

"Professor Richards, you read the news. We're at war with the Hoods. The conflict is draining the country's resources. The Mexicans are losing patience. If we can't restore confidence in the financial system, the Mexicans will stop sending aid. We need all available resources to fight the Hoods. I have a team of signal analysts under my command. In the event of first contact, they would attempt to establish communication. But the war with the Hoods is a cyberwar, and my signal analysts have exactly the right skills to track terrorist activity by analyzing comm data crossing the global network. You have the required clearance to hear that, but that information is classified."

"So you defend the hoarded wealth of the Hillites?"

"The Hoods threaten national security. The Hillites don't."

"I'm not so sure."

"I'm not going to debate politics with you."

*This isn't going anywhere.* "Is there another group or agency that can help? I thought I'd end up talking to someone in the air force. But you're a marine. Doesn't the air force have programs to detect aliens, like SETI?"

"From space, yes. But you're claiming the presence is here on Earth, essentially a beachhead. That falls under the jurisdiction of the marines. I'm sorry, Professor Richards. I can't help you, and I know of no other place to direct you. If you get definitive proof, please contact me immediately."

I I 0   I I 0   I I 0

THE DOOR CLOSED, AND THE MASSTRAN GLIDED OFF. HOPE
replayed the pain of the public ridicule by the Queen
as she walked home. Inside, her mom was on hands
and knees, rag in hand, washing the kitchen floor.
She stopped scrubbing when Hope paused in the hallway. Her mom's hair was pulled back, but much of it
was stuck to her forehead in dried sweat, like spider
webs on basement window glass. She had a questioning look in her eyes, but she didn't speak.

Hope played out a scene in her mind. Her mom
would ask, "How was your first day back at school,
dear?" *Not going to happen today. Not ever.*

The scrubbing resumed.

Hope rode the elevator down. The display
screen glowed to life, and she logged on. *My friends
online understand. They're like me. They know what's
important.*

One went by the tag SalaciousFrog. Hope gave
SalaciousFrog more of her attention than any of the
others. SalaciousFrog spent time with her too, showing her how to access new areas of the network.

The funny thing about online tags was that they
shielded the user's identity, so you couldn't tell if the
user was a man or woman, boy or girl. Hope liked
the name SalaciousFrog because it made her think of
the frog prince she learned about in her History of
Folk Tales class. The princess kisses the frog, who
then transforms into a handsome prince. The various
princes in all the folk tales were interchangeable;
they didn't even get names. The stories objectified
males. The prince wasn't a character but rather a
reward for the heroine.

Hope couldn't see anything the heroine did that warranted a whole prince as a prize, but that's why she used the word *princess* in her own tags. She used a variety of tags and changed them often so the authorities couldn't trace her. But she always included the word *princess* in some way or another. Today, she was PrinSays.

*PrinSays: Hey, you free?*
*SalaciousFrog: One sec.*

She watched the display and waited. The net was filled with creeps who tried to learn things—personal things—and then they'd become sexual and gross. SalaciousFrog was never like that. He—she allowed herself to think of SalaciousFrog as a he—only wanted to take her to new places or to show her how to do new things. Unlimited challenges awaited online.

Playing out another scene in her mind, SalaciousFrog would ask her how her first day back at school was. She'd tell him about Dawn Perkins.

A shiver rode up her spine. *No.* She would never be vulnerable. She wouldn't bare her feelings for others to spit on. SalaciousFrog didn't try to get inside her, he didn't probe, he didn't have expectations, he didn't bait her, he didn't push his needs on her; he only wanted to give and to share. She desperately wanted a vidcomm with him to see what he looked like. No way. A vid stream was far more difficult to secure than a simple chat session.

*SalaciousFrog: I'm back.*

*PrinSays: What do you have for me today?*

*SalaciousFrog: Remember when I showed you the code to make your messages secure? I know a better way. It's the same technique the government uses. That's why I never have to change my tag. I'll show you how.*

||0 ||0 ||0

"TAKE A SEAT."

Marine Lance Corporal Juan Rodriguez evaluated his commanding officer's tone and inflection. It was strange enough that he was ordered to receive his next mission briefing in person, but stranger still to be invited to sit down. As instructed, he took the seat across from his CO.

"The Brits are making a change to their MI8 program, and we're making a change in the Omega Force to match. I'd like you to be a part of it."

"A change, sir?"

"Engaging solo is too limiting."

"Limiting?"

"Not to you as an agent but the missions. We have enough agents now. Teams are possible." He looked down at his display. "Your psych eval shows an exceptional aptitude for teamwork." Leaning back in his chair, he said, "We're forming a quick-reaction force made up of four agents working together. One team will cover the eastern half of the country, the other the western half, designated Echo and Whiskey, respectively."

He leaned forward again and tapped the display. "Rodriguez, you have an excellent cutting score, and that's why you're getting this opportunity. But your leadership rating is outstanding. I want you to lead Fire Team Whiskey."

Rodriguez's genetically enhanced brain processed all information, good or bad, with detached efficiency. With heightened curiosity, his only response was, "Yes, sir."

"Our modus operandi to date has been one of clandestine infiltration. That will not be the case here. The new teams will be a combat force. You'll lead three marines with specific skills: a sniper, a heavy-weapons expert, and a cyberspecialist."

"Combat, sir?" asked Rodriguez. "Why me? I mean, why the Omega generation? Why not wait for the Nu generation?"

"Cornelius's progress on the Nu generation is unpredictable, but your analysis is correct. Without armor, you'll be vulnerable. The plan is to outfit each of you with powered armor." He smirked. "Listen, son, I've been doing this a long time. Poker face or not, I know exactly what that super brain of yours is telling you. This ain't your granddaddy's powered armor, boy. I think you'll be pleased."

"Yes, sir. What's the deployment plan?"

"You'll be stationed on a specially configured scramjet. You'll cruise until needed and then inserted at the target LZ. We'll have enough fire teams trained to keep a Whiskey and Echo force in the air 'round the clock."

"Mission planning will also be adjusted, sir?"

"Yes. Major Nolan's signal experts will identify enemy activity and evaluate the threat. If the threat warrants the use of a fire team, tactical plans will be designed for four."

Something wasn't right. This was a clear escalation in power.

"What's bothering you, marine?"

"Permission to speak freely, sir?"

He nodded.

"You said our MO has been clandestine, but our existence is no secret. Quite the contrary, the public has glorified our activity. Vids portray us running around like some kind of modern-day James Bond. Our work is serious. In a combat role, even more so. Sir, the public image … it's unprofessional. It adds risk."

"Get used to it. The impact of the Omega Force goes beyond tactical victories against the Hoods. It's strategic. The keyboard jockeys over in psych warfare have been manipulating the public's perception of the Omega Force since the program's inception. It provides a psychological rally point for the public. You're right. James Bond was the model used for Omega Force agents. This time around, for the new fire teams, they're using the Untouchables."

"From the early nineteen hundreds."

"In those days, mob bosses were popular figures, romantic and exciting. Law-abiding citizens began to view organized criminals as the good guys and the police as the bad guys. The authorities needed an even more popular image for law enforcement to win public trust."

"The Hoods are popular with the restless unemployed."

"Bingo. Fighting thousands of Hoods is one thing; fighting millions of Pogers—well, that sort of conflicts with our sworn oath. Ever hear the term *gangbuster*? Like I said, get used to it."

||0 ||0 ||0

"HOW WAS SCHOOL?" LAURA ASKED.

"Great!" said Chris, coming in the back door.

"How do you like your teacher?"

"Mrs. Gonzalez is jazz, Mom. She likes history just like me. She has all these dioramas around the room. A diorama is like a one-room dollhouse showing a scene from history. They show the Lenape Native Americans, how they dressed and how they lived. We get to make one too."

"Sounds like fun." Laura set a sandwich and glass of milk on the table.

Chris washed his hands, sat down, and started to eat.

"What else?"

"Brad Evans said there was a lockdown at Preston Academy. An Omega Force agent came and killed a bunch of Hoods."

"I think Brad is making up stories."

"No, his cousin's friend goes there. They have lockdown drills all the time."

"Yes, but that doesn't mean there was an incident."

"Why don't we have lockdown drills, Mom?"

"Well, buddy, that's not an easy question to answer. We're fortunate that your dad and I have good jobs at the university. Most families aren't so lucky. So—"

"Like Al's and Katie's?"

"Yes, but it's rude to bring that up, so you shouldn't ask them about it. Now, I was saying—"

"Is that why they come over for dinner all the time?"

"No, they have plenty of food, Chris. Now, do you still want me to answer your question?"

He took another bite.

"There are some very rich families in the world. Very few, but very rich. Some people believe they got that way by not following the laws written for everyone."

"The Robin Hoods believe that?"

"Yes, among others, I'm sure. So these people feel it's OK to break the law to try to make things more equal. Making trouble at a rich kid's school might be one way to put pressure on a rich family. But I don't think the Robin Hoods caused the lockdown."

"Why?"

"The Robin Hoods aren't like an army. They don't fight with fists or guns. They've never used something like kidnapping. They use computers."

"Mom, the Hoods are terrorists; everybody knows that."

"You shouldn't believe everything you see on the screen. It's more complicated than that."

"How do you know?"

"Because I'm a professor of political science, that's how." She tilted her head. "What did Brad say about the Omega Force?"

"They're superspies, Mom!" He cocked his thumb, pointed his index finger, and fired imaginary bullets. "You know, in the vids." He took another bite.

"If you say so. Listen, I got a comm from Al's mom today."

"Yeah?" he said without looking up.

"Yeah. Mrs. Fuentes had an idea for you three, and she wanted my opinion before we mentioned it to you. Your dad and I think it's a great idea. And Katie's parents are on board too."

"What is it?"

Laura had his attention now. "Well, you know how you like those martial arts vids? How would you like to take lessons? Like karate or something?"

"Wow! Really? The three of us together?"

"Yes. You know, you can learn self-defense."

"Jazz!" He reached into his pocket.

"No percomm at the table! Finish your snack. You can find out their reaction when you're finished. I'm sure it will be the same as yours."

"Me too. Wow. I can't wait! Thanks, Mom!"

*KNOCK, KNOCK.* THAT WAS THE SOUND OF THE TREE AGAINST THE old house, Chelsea knew, not a knock on the door of her bedroom. Still, it made her heart leap.

Seeing now that the loop had slipped off the needle, she pulled the yarn to remove the dropped stitch and restarted. *It wasn't a knock at the door, for sure, but was it really the tree? Maybe he's out for exercise.*

She went to the window and pulled open the drape. Light streamed in, and she squinted as she scanned the grounds. It'd been over a month since she last caught a glimpse of him. *Or was it longer?* The knocking sound had to be the tree—the branch of the dead tree. It was a windy day. No sign of him, just the guard vehicle at the far edge of the estate.

She was safe as long as the guards protected them. *That's what Evan said.* She and Evan would always be vulnerable, but not their son. He was special. Dr. Cornelius even said so. *If only they would let me see him.*

She recalled the first year or two. She'd nursed him and saw him several times a day then. When she was a young girl, she'd overhear conversations between ladies, complaining about taking care of their babies, about the lack of sleep and making their husbands get up in the middle of the night to feed with formula. *Ridiculous.* She'd cherished that time with her son, watching him as he suckled from her breast. Dr. Cornelius had made her a harness to rest him in, so her arms wouldn't tire.

She remembered Dr. Cornelius's riddle: what's heavier—a pound of iron or a pound of cotton balls? Of course, the answer is that they both weigh the same. He said that was only true on Earth because of gravity. Dr. Cornelius said that density was similar to weight but didn't change in the presence of gravity. Iron is denser than cotton balls, and so that's why armor is made with iron instead of cotton. He explained how medieval armor smiths used tiny rings of iron and wove them together like fabric so the men could move easily yet still be protected. Dr. Cornelius said their son would be safe because the very tissues of his body were dense, denser than anything else on Earth. But Dr. Cornelius didn't have an explanation for the eyes.

Chelsea had missed all ten of his birthdays.

Presently, she stitched the last row of the sweater, cast off, and delicately snipped the yarn with a pair of scissors. She examined her work before pulling the drape closed and then walked to the wardrobe. Inside were ten sets of child-sized sweaters—one set for each year of his life. Very carefully, she placed the new sweater on top of the smaller, eleventh pile.

# CHAPTER 22

"**W**ELCOME TO MODERN POLITICAL SCIENCE 211."

The lights around the semicircular auditorium dimmed. Laura stood at the bottom of the bowl-shaped room—the point where all the seats faced, like a stadium. The illumination intensified where she stood, while at the same time, the light over the seats faded. Two jumbo screens on the back wall displayed the words Modern Political Science 211, and underneath that, Prof. Laura Richards.

She waited for the class to settle down. Several students put away percomms. The lighting made it difficult to make out individual faces. Stragglers found seats. The room could hold almost three hundred, and she judged it to be almost full. *Not bad, especially for an 8:00 a.m. class.* She tapped a button on her percomm, and a montage of epic scenes began playing on the jumbo displays while orchestral music started to build.

"During the term, we'll cover political dynamics of recent history and the effect they had on global events to shape the world we live in today. We'll begin with the Spring Uprisings and the Occupy Protests at the start of the millennium, followed by the wealth redistribution attempts in the West and the resulting failures. We'll examine the stances of formal world governments as well as those of organizations with nontraditional political boundaries wielding de facto control, including the Robin Hood movement. We'll compare these groups with similar groups who struggled for political voice in world history. For example, we'll compare the rise and fall of violence-based groups such as Al-Qaeda in contrast with the Black Panthers of the mid-1900s. Then we'll compare nonviolent groups such as the Robin Hoods in contrast with the civil rights movements in America and South Africa. Independent of race or fortune, we'll investigate the political philosophy behind nonviolent activism as well as the definition of nonviolence itself in the context of cyberdisobedience and civil disobedience. We'll examine the ethical implications of physical violence, threats of physical violence, and terrorism aimed to promote political change in contrast with the ethical implications of economic destabilization, threat of economic destabilization, and cyberterrorism aimed toward the same goal. By the end of the term—"

All the lights came on. The images and music stopped. The students turned around as the main doors opened and the dean of students entered with two campus security guards.

"Class is canceled for today," announced the dean.

"What? What's going on?" Laura's question became lost in the sound of shuffling feet.

"Everyone out. Let's go. Now. Professor Richards, please stay here."

Laura started to protest, but the dean simply raised his hand. The security men waited until the last student was out and then followed behind and closed the doors. It was just the two of them.

"Now. What's going on?"

He walked down the center aisle steps but still kept his distance after reaching the bottom. "I'm here to ask you for your resignation."

"What!"

"I'm sorry I didn't get here before you started the first class of the term, I—"

"You're sorry about the timing? You're firing me and you're worried about the timing? But why? I don't understand."

"A sister of a student you taught last term has gone missing."

"So? I mean, I'm sorry to hear that, but what does that have to do with me?"

"Every time a girl goes missing, the FBI questions you. And each time the university gets a formal notice. Laura, there were dozens after Lisa and then even more after Marsha. Fifteen years now, and no end in sight."

"Sixteen years," Laura mumbled. *Same as Chris's age, impossible to forget.*

"The regents feel there's too much risk."

"I don't know this girl. They'll question me, and nothing will come of it, just like every time before. Lisa and Marsha just happened to be my students."

"This time, the regents asked for an internal investigation. It seems you exchanged messages with Marsha just before she was declared missing."

"She went on a diving trip. Think about it. Dive plans were filed but lost? All evidence of the trip lost *except* my message to her? If I was the diabolical mastermind responsible for all the disappearances, would I leave that behind?"

"Framed? That's just as ridiculous. The point is, there's too much coincidence. A sister of your student is one relationship away. The regents have decided. There won't be another coincidence."

Laura fingered her wedding ring. *Coincidence?* She remembered Ben's story about photons and rolling dice. She knew she had nothing to do with the disappearances, but something about the word *coincidence* wasn't entirely off the mark. *Seemingly random events creating a pattern? An intelligent force causing an unlikely connection?* She stopped fiddling and formed a fist.

"Huh," he said, staring at her.

"What's 'huh'?"

"The Laura Richards I first met twenty years ago would be bawling in the corner right about now." He squinted. "But not you. You're pissed."

"Yeah. I'm pissed."

IT HAD TO HAVE BEEN A GOOD NIGHT'S SLEEP; BEN HADN'T HEARD Laura leave. He rolled out of bed, taking his percomm from the bedside table. There was one message from Raj, asking him to comm at his earliest convenience.

"Good morning, Ben." Raj's image was on the basement lab's wall display. "Thanks for jumping on so early."

"No problem. What've you got?"

"Well, the satellites go through a scheduled diagnostic program every six months. During the attitude-control test, the satellite detector faces the wrong way, toward Earth. Normally, instead of turning off the detector during the test, we simply delete the data. The guy who performed the last cycle is new, and he neglected to delete the data before sending the batch."

"Oh, no problem. I can strip the data before I run the batch."

"Well, interestingly, we reviewed the results, not realizing what happened, and a number of dark energy flares showed up."

"Probably just skewed readings," said Ben. "The detectors are designed to scan deep space."

"Right, that's what we thought. But there's something else." Raj paused. "We noticed one of the flares is located in eastern Pennsylvania. We plugged the coordinates into the geospatial mapping system. Ben, one of the flares is right on your house." Raj paused again. "I remembered your breakthrough analysis technique was related to some medical complication with your son. I thought that was resolved. Anyway, I thought you should know."

"Thanks." *Maybe there are others like Chris?* "Raj, the other flares—where were they located?"

"Mostly, clustered in one area. Nevada, around Las Vegas."

||0 ||0 ||0

CHRIS SAW AN OPEN SPOT IN THE FRONT ROW OF THE CLASSROOM. It was the first day of the last term of his junior year of high school, and now was no time to be slacking.

A boy whacked him on the arm as he passed. "Migo, *you* can't take this class; you'll have your mom do all your homework," he said, grinning.

"Hey, don't say that. I finally got the prerequisites done. I thought I'd never get in here." Chris slapped hands with him and kept moving.

"Chris!" another kid called from the back. "You up for *Sim Shooter 3* Friday night? I need one more player for my clan."

"Sure, count me in." Chris passed through a few more desks and then plopped down in the front row. He set his percomm on the desk, and the entire desk surface lit up, displaying his personal information and course material for the class.

Then he saw her, Hope Avenir, sitting right next to him. *She never sits in front!* She didn't look up.

She was wearing a baggy brown sweatshirt, and her jeans looked like the kind workmen wore. Her hair went every which way and covered her face like it was the hood of the sweatshirt.

But her hair was beautiful, dark brown with thick cords of natural waves that curled and criss-crossed, hiding her face but also flowing around her shoulders. Her clothes were baggy, but even that couldn't conceal the shape of her body.

Chris knew he was a late bloomer, and he knew girls matured faster than boys. He was well aware of the changes that had been occurring in the bodies of the girls, especially back when he had started middle school. But baggy clothes or not, she was incredible. When she walked or moved, the baggy material betrayed the curves underneath.

"All right, get to your seats; let's get started."

The announcement gave him a start, and he realized the trance he was in. *Good thing Katie and Al aren't here to make fun of me.*

"Welcome to Political Science," said Mr. Muzaffar. Their teacher continued the introduction. Chris heard the words, but he wasn't listening.

He stole a glance. If only he could see her face. *Why is she sitting in front? She never sits in front. Maybe because she knows I always sit in front, and so—*

"Isn't that right, Mr. Lumière?"

The whole class was looking at him.

"I said you might have an unfair advantage." Mr. Muzaffar's smirk faded as Chris struggled for com-prehension. "Sorry, just some inside humor. I didn't mean to embarrass you."

"Oh, right!" Chris smiled. "Sure. 'Cuz of my mom. Political science and all. Got it."

To the entire class, Mr. Muzaffar continued, "It's a challenging subject but brings together much of your learning to this point."

Chris slumped in his chair. He wanted to steal another glance but resisted. If the whole class had looked at him, she probably did too.

*How can I talk to her?* Even though they lived on the same street, he'd never really spoken to her or even properly introduced himself. He knew who she was only because his mom knew who she was.

When class ended, everyone started to stand up. She stood up too.

He caught her eye. "Hi. I'm Chris Lumière."

She stopped and looked right at him. Her face was stern, almost sneering. "I know who you are." She turned and walked out.

||0 ||0 ||0

"WHAT DID HINKLE SAY?" BEN ASKED LAURA AFTER SHE CAME home and told him about getting fired.

"He said my students posted vid clips even before they left the auditorium. *And* he said the look on my face was priceless." To this point, Laura had kept it together pretty well, but now her chin started to quiver.

"Nice." Ben held out his arms.

She went to him, and he gave her a squeeze and a kiss. She hugged him back, extra tight, and relaxed.

"So what's your next move?" he asked.

"I need to know what happened to the missing girls. I know I've said that before, but I was afraid to give the authorities any excuse to connect me. What's to lose now? Since they won't stop questioning me, I *am* connected." She stayed close to him with her head against his chest. "Remember what you said about forces beyond our understanding? What if the desperate pleas from the missing girls could somehow reach me, like there's a way I can help them?" The day had started off so horribly, and she'd built up so much tension. Now, in Ben's arms, she felt energized about the future and her life's purpose. "I want to find out more, but I don't want to attract attention."

"I can create a special log-in for you on my university account. My credentials are military grade. It won't trigger any alert to the police, not even the FBI."

"Really? You would do that for me?"

"Sure." He chuckled.

"When I struggle, you always step in and take action. Thank you. I love you, and I always will."

"I love you too."

She moved her hands down the small of his back, slipped them into his back pockets, and then pulled him close as she pressed against him. "Chris is going to karate practice after school," she said.

"What are you saying?"

"Take me to the bedroom," she whispered.

"Now?"

She squeezed her hands. "Right now."

"HOW'S IT GOING WITH THE HEAVY BAG AT HOME?" CHRIS ASKED AL in the men's locker room of the karate studio.

"I shredded it," said Al.

"Really? You've only had it about, what, three months?"

"I know. Master Cohen coached me about rotating my hips for more power." Al pushed his duffel bag into the locker and slammed the door shut. "I feel bad, because he bought it for me. But he said not to worry. He's getting me another one. He said it'll be my reward for the hard work. Anyway, how are you coming on your new kata?"

"I haven't even started yet. I still need to find the right music to go with it."

"I wish I was as good as you in forms competition. I'd love to have a tenth of the trophies you have."

"I'd love to kick like you."

Katie joined them outside the locker room. "What are you guys going to work on today?"

"Master Cohen asked me to lead the lower belts in forms practice," said Chris.

"I'll be in our regular black-belt class," said Al.

"Me too," said Katie.

"Great, you can be my partner."

"Fine, but just for self-defense practice, not the kicking and punching drills."

"What? Oh, come on."

"No, seriously, it's too much."

"Come on. I'll go easy on you."

"Al, wake up, migo," said Chris, "You're huge. What are you, two hundred pounds? You're like two Katies. Pick on someone your own size."

When class ended, Chris joined Katie and Al for some stretching before changing back into street clothes. One of the lower belts, a green belt named Tim from Chris's forms group that day, approached the three black belts sitting on the floor against the wall.

"Thank you for the tips on my form today," said Tim to Chris with jacked-up enthusiasm.

"Uh, sure. My pleasure," said Chris. "You've got a nice technique. Don't forget to work on your foot placement."

"Oh, I won't," he said, excitement on the verge of goofy. "I want to be just like you."

Chris was at a loss for words.

Katie buried her face into her crossed arms over her knees. "Oh, please. Spare me."

Chris elbowed her. "Uh, thanks, Tim. Keep up the good work."

"Yeah, I want to be great at forms like you."

"You've got to be kidding me," said Katie, face still buried.

Al elbowed her this time.

"Tim, that's a worthy goal," said Master Cohen, overhearing from his office. He walked over. "Just don't forget about the other aspects of your training."

Tim's fawning smile dwindled. "What do you mean?"

"Well, martial arts embrace the notion of balance. That includes the development of your training. Just as being off balance on your feet can make you vulnerable, the same is true about focusing on only one aspect of your training, thereby allowing another aspect to be incomplete. You become unbalanced."

"But Chris is awesome. He's not vulnerable," said Tim.

Katie's body began to jiggle with stifled laughter.

"Tim, I'll share some criticism of Chris's performance with you because this is an important concept for you to understand right now. And I know Chris can take it," said Mr. Cohen. "Chris is indeed awesome at forms. Forms are important for perfecting body placement and timing. Chris has excellent body placement and rhythm. But the martial arts are about self-defense—in real situations. Skills perfected in forms practice are important, but alone, they won't help much against a real attacker. Frankly, Chris has work to do on his striking power and speed. Comparing him to his two friends, for example, Chris would never have a chance to defend Katie's attack, because he can't block fast enough. She's incredibly fast, faster than I am. And Chris wouldn't survive the first blow from Al, who's got a one-hit KO. Al has a weight advantage, but he's also learned to channel that power. Now, it's good that you want to be like Chris, because Chris works hard to achieve balance. He works on his power and speed as well as his forms. You should do the same."

"Yes, sir." The kid seemed to understand, but now he looked like he'd been left out in the rain too long. He slunk off to the locker room.

"Chris," said Mr. Cohen, "I hope you'll think about my offer to make you an instructor here. The students really respond to you." He went back to his office.

"You should do it, migo," said Katie. "The kids are attracted to you, like magnets."

"Did you say *magnets* or *maggots*?" asked Al.

"Nah," said Chris. "I spend a lot of time here already. I need time for other stuff."

"Like what?" asked Katie.

"Never mind," said Chris. "Anyway, what Master Cohen said is true. I have a lot more to learn."

"Maybe," said Katie. "I never want to get in a real fight. So maybe it's better to have a bunch of trophies."

"Yeah, right," said Chris. "Admit it. Both of you can kick my ass."

"Did he say *kick* or *kiss*?"

||0 ||0 ||0

IN THE DARKNESS OF HER BEDROOM, HOPE LAY IN BED AND TRIED to ignore the yelling. Her dad had started drinking early. His unemployment wasn't her mom's fault, but that didn't matter. In his mind, it was, along with everything else.

Hope squeezed her eyes shut and tried to push the sound of his rant out of her mind, forcing her mind to other thoughts. She replayed the events of the day, her political science class. *He sat right next to me! Argh!*

Tomorrow she'd have to find another seat. *So annoying. Finally, for the one class I'm actually interested in, I find the courage to sit in front. Then he has to go and sit next to me.*

But it was wonderful. She couldn't quite see his dreamy azure eyes, but his hands were in plain view. *He's so sure of himself. His hands glided over his desktop display, tapping to advance the page. His hands are gorgeous, with long fingers, yet very masculine and strong looking. So many guys have dirty, crusty, nasty hands. His hands looked smooth and soft.* Her imagination took the tangent. *His hands.*

She thought back about the hour sitting next to him, how it had made her feel. Oddly, she felt so comfortable then. At first, she'd wanted to move to another seat, but as she tried to find the nerve, the urge to run seemed to melt away. Sitting next to him then, she'd felt the least amount of anxiety she could remember. But it all came crashing back when he spoke. All her defenses had snapped back in place. *I know who you are*, she recalled her own words. *Brilliant, just brilliant. He was only being nice.*

*On second thought, I don't have to move. What if I stay at the same desk? What if I stay next to him? For once, to have what I want.*

Suddenly, her bedroom door swished open, and her thoughts snapped back to reality.

His silhouette painted the floor inside a trapezoid of light until the door closed behind him. Darkness.

Her hands made asterisks in the linen. She could hear him breathing … then the sloppy steps across the carpet to the bedside.

After fumbling for the covers, he pulled them slowly, taking his time … until they cascaded to the floor. More breathing … open mouthed. The smell, landing like mud—time, suspended.

Then the mattress creaked under his weight, and her body tilted, the depression pulling her to him like a black hole. He was fully clothed and reeked of liquor.

"Don't you make a goddamn sound this time."

# Chapter 23

CHRIS WALKED WITH AL DOWN THE HALLWAY THROUGH the throng of students passing between second and third period.

"Hi, Chris!" It was the Queen's voice, Dawn Perkins, from a group of royals they'd passed.

The group parted. Dawn was standing at the center with a calculating smile and the class president pin prominently displayed on her blouse. Each girl in the group could have been a model. Each was dressed in sophisticated and sexy styles that girls a few years older would wear—rich ones, anyway.

Chris had to admit these were the hottest girls in the junior class. The Queen picked them well. He knew the situation at the homes of most of them—their parents never had steady work. The clothes, makeup, and salon visits must make the "royal invitation" irresistible. And, once inside, the fear of rejection controlled each of Dawn's pawns.

The group advanced on Chris as if he were at the end of a fashion runway. Long legs with each step placed directly in front of the other as if on an invisible tightrope. The rhythm of their hips made him wish he could watch from behind. Judging by the look on the Queen's face, she knew exactly what impact it had. Chris forced himself not to back up. They were like jackals moving in on startled prey.

"You know, Chris—" She was about a foot shorter, so she had to look up when she stopped in front of him, her perfume passing over him like stepping through beads on string. "My friend Victoria here is having trouble in history, and she was wondering if you had some time to help her."

Victoria, standing next to Dawn, casually flipped her hair and adjusted an earring with both hands. The tip of each finger had a perfect French manicure with a wet-ice shine. A delicate silver bracelet slid from her wrist partway down her slender arm. Her eyes were coy, but the glossed lips—slightly parted— were pure vamp. The whole maneuver was highly practiced and expertly performed.

Chris swallowed. "OK." He wasn't sure if the answer came from his mouth or his groin.

"Wonderful!" said Dawn. "The two of you will get along just fine. I know—" Dawn's eyes darted to something past him, over his shoulder. The smile dropped from her face. "What are *you* looking at, bitch?"

It was Hope, watching the scene from the end of the hall. He lost sight of her as students crossed between. Once they passed, she was gone.

"Sorry, where was I? Oh yes, I know the two of you—"

"Forget it," said Chris. "Let's go, Al."

"Oh, come on," Dawn stammered. "Victoria's super nice."

Reaching the end of the hallway, they rounded the corner. Chris pounded out his steps. He angled for the wall, letting the crowd pass around them. He didn't need to explain. Al might've given him a hard time when they were younger, but not now. "Something needs to be done about the Queen," said Chris.

"Agreed," said Al.

"But it can't be malicious. We can't—she has to. She has to do it to herself," he said. "Are you up to it?"

"Always," said Al. "One regime change, comin' up."

||0 ||0 ||0

THE ROOMS OF THE OLD HOUSE WERE OFF LIMITS TO CHELSEA except those on the top floor and the kitchen. With great anticipation, she waited for the daily pubcomm notification signaling lunchtime.

11:59:58. 11:59:59. Stepping out from her bedroom, she tiptoed down the hall to the adjacent room and paused outside to listen for her son. *No sound.* She moved to the next door. Listened.

Chelsea recalled the few occasions when they let her see him. It was always in the afternoon. She'd heard them getting one of the rooms ready.

One other time, she'd seen marks in the carpet pile leading to one of the rooms. They had wheeled in vid-recording equipment. They never said why they wanted to record her with her son. She wanted to ask if she could see the vid. It wasn't a home movie. It was more like the kind Selby Hancock made—technicians and wires and display screens. She'd wondered, at the time, if it might be posted online, but it didn't matter either way. She wasn't allowed online, ever.

*Maybe today?* No sound came from the room.

After listening at the last door, she placed her hand on the railing down. That's when she heard it. *A voice. Someone ... someone on the floor below.* She crept down the sweeping circular staircase. The sound was coming from the hallway to the kitchen. Her heart throbbed as she took a few more steps and then recognized the voice. *Ingrid. Maybe he's with her!* After a few more steps, she could see Ingrid on her percomm in a hushed conversation.

"No, sir. It won't be released from customs for another six hours ... No, sir ... No, sir, I checked that ... Yes, sir. I'll be there as soon as it's released ... Yes, sir. Out." She tapped commands on her percomm.

From the bottom of the staircase, Chelsea peered at Ingrid in the shadows with only her face illuminated by the percomm. Strange that the nurse never dressed like a nurse anymore; it was a uniform of some type, but without insignia.

"You shouldn't spy on people, ma'am," Ingrid said without looking up, still tapping.

"Oh no, I wasn't spying. I—I was just on my way to lunch."

"Well, then, move along."

Chelsea tiptoed past Ingrid to the kitchen. The kitchen staff was attentive as usual and had her lunch prepared and waiting. She sat down.

The kitchen door opened, and Ingrid walked in. "I might as well join you. I've got some time to kill." Ingrid spoke to the kitchen staff, and they began to pull together another sandwich. Ingrid sat at the staff table across from Chelsea and continued to flip through information on her percomm.

They didn't permit Chelsea to sit in the dining room—she ate all her meals at the staff table in the kitchen. They didn't let her have any guests, and she wasn't to engage in small talk with the kitchen staff. She always ate alone. Except when Evan visited about every other month. With his grandfather aging, the responsibilities of Venizelos Shipping consumed nearly all of Evan's time. At least, that's what he always said.

The sandwich was placed in front of Ingrid, but that didn't draw her attention away from the percomm. This woman had far more contact with her son. Ingrid was some kind of teacher or helped with his training somehow.

Chelsea couldn't stand it any longer. "How is he?"

Ingrid didn't look up. "Fine, ma'am. He's just fine."

"What's he doing today? Is he near?"

*Tap, tap, swipe, tap, tap.* "You know I can't tell you that, ma'am."

*Yes, I know. No harm in asking, though.* Chelsea watched Ingrid with fascination. All the time and effort the nurse devoted to her son over the years. She recalled the day on the street outside their London flat, how Ingrid had protected him even before he was born. "Why do you do it?"

Ingrid looked up this time. "Do what?"

"Why do you care for him? Why do you give so much time?"

"It's my job, ma'am."

"No, it's more than that," said Chelsea as she looked into Ingrid's eyes and searched for that woman-to-woman connection.

Still holding the percomm, Ingrid took a bite. "I do it for Dr. Cornelius."

Chelsea's eyes conveyed her confusion.

"He's my father. I mean, I don't have a mother or a father, but Dr. Cornelius is the closest thing we have to a father."

"Everyone has a mother and father."

"I don't." Ingrid took another bite.

After a moment, Chelsea asked, "Who's *we*?"

"What?"

"You said, 'Dr. Cornelius is the closest thing *we* have to a father.'"

There was no change in Ingrid's expression. Like rock. But somehow, Chelsea could almost feel the alertness. The woman-to-woman connection was there and seemed to give her a sixth sense.

"Ma'am ... Chelsea, your family and other families like yours are under a tremendous threat from the Hoods. The Hoods claim they want to close the gap between the rich and the poor, but they don't understand how the rich drive the world economy. They claim to fight for the poor, but if they succeed, there will no longer be rewards for hard work and ambition. No job creation. The economy is bad now, but if the Hoods win, it'll collapse completely, globally. Food distribution and medical services will collapse. A new dark age. The Hoods of today are like the barbarians of the past." Ingrid pushed the plate away. "Chelsea, in order to beat the Hoods, we need to be stronger and smarter. Dr. Cornelius has devoted his life to make a group of us stronger and smarter than the enemy."

"You're one of them. That day in London—that's how you were able to protect us?"

Ingrid nodded.

"What does my son have to do with this? Why isn't someone like you out battling Hoods?"

"He's the next group, Chelsea. He's better than we are. He's amazing. We're going to make an army like him. I'm honored to help train him. Dr. Cornelius is taking good care of him. We all are." Ingrid looked down at her percomm again, purposefully, even though there was no vibration or chime. "Sorry, ma'am. I have to get to the airport."

||O ||O ||O

THE OPEN SEAT IN THE BACK OF THE CLASSROOM BECKONED TO Hope like an oasis. People who sat in the back didn't care enough to pick the same seat each day; it didn't matter who you sat next to.

From the back, she stared at Chris and the seat next to him, unoccupied. *What was I thinking, sitting in front?* She would never be a part of that crowd. A boy like Chris was part of a different world. He had friends, close friends. Everyone liked him. *Especially the girls. Who could resist those blue eyes? He can be with any girl he wants, even that centerfold, Perkins. That's the kind of girl the Lumière kid wants.*

||0  ||0  ||0

"THIS IS WHERE YOU'LL LOAD THE CAGES ONTO THE TRUCK," SAID the animal shelter manager to the group congregated in the shelter's loading dock. "Any questions? OK, great. Thank you all for volunteering. There's coffee and cookies in the lobby. See you all here on Saturday."

The volunteers filed out.

"Chris, can you help me close up? Can you get the door?" asked the manager.

"Sure." Chris pressed the button to close the loading dock door. "Seems like we have a good bunch this year."

"Yeah. I think it's the biggest group so far. You know, other churches sponsor adopt-a-pet events but usually only get two or three volunteers. Thanks so much for all your recruiting efforts."

"I didn't do any recruiting. I just tell people how much fun it is."

"Well, keep it up, whatever you're doing." The manager turned off the light in the loading dock area.

Chris followed him back toward the front of the building. Passing through the kennel, the barking and yapping grew louder. Cages lined the walls, with even more cages stacked with aisles in between.

"Can I look at the puppies?" asked Chris.

"Of course."

Chris went over a few rows to the right to the smaller cages. One puppy, with a cream-colored coat, was up on two legs with its front paws on the metal cage and licking through the grate. A male, Chris could see clearly. The puppy's tail wagged happily— the kind of wag where its whole back end goes back and forth too. The little guy was trying to get as close to Chris as possible and kept licking through the cage. Chris put his hand up against the cage, and the puppy licked his hand as best it could.

"Pretty cute, aren't they?" asked the manager.

"Yeah. What's his name?"

"When they're this young, we don't give them names. And he's a yellow Lab, very desirable. Lucky for him, we won't have trouble finding a home. His brothers and sisters are already gone. No point in naming them. It's the old, sick, or injured ones that are hard to place. But we need to make sure that the family that adopts this little migo understands the obligation. Too many of the older ones here were once puppies just like him. Dogs can be a challenge to raise—furniture, clothing, and carpet all take a beating. You know how tough things are these days … a pet is one more expense. Anyway, there's no federal food program for puppies. And while I certainly think all dogs are cute, there's no denying that they're just not *as* cute after they grow up. The owners need to be in it for the long haul." The manager watched for a moment. "Want to hold him?"

"Oh yes!"

The manager began to undo the latch.

Chris had helped with the event every year for Father Arnold. He'd cared for many dogs, cats, puppies, and kittens, yet he never imagined himself adopting one. There was something special about this dog.

Chris held him close, high on his chest. The puppy licked and licked. He licked Chris's face and started to chew on his shirt. Chris pulled the soft rubber toy from the open cage and let the puppy chew on it instead. He knew it was important to train them early about what was OK and not OK to chew on. The key was to have a lot of things OK to chew on and to be there when the puppy strayed from those things. Chris understood how it could be a lot of work. "So this little guy will be at our event next Saturday?"

"No," said the manager, "I think someone will adopt him before then."

At home later that night, Chris argued his case. "Seriously, Mom, I'll take good care of him."

"You have school all day," she said.

"Only the rest of this term. Then it'll be summer break, and I'll have all day."

"So wait and get a dog then," said Ben.

"No, I really want this one. Mom, can't you help me for the first few weeks?"

"Honestly, I've prepared myself for this conversation every year since you started volunteering for the event. I'm surprised you didn't get the notion sooner. And now that I'm unemployed, I guess I have the time."

"Can we really? I mean, there's stuff we need to buy. A kennel, bowl, food—"

"Yes, I think we can still afford those things."

"I've got a whole list. Can we go to the store after school and then get the puppy?"

"You have karate practice," she said.

"I know. I'll have to miss that. But I want to show Al and Katie. Can we pick them up at the studio so I can show them?"

"Well, you certainly do have this planned out."

||0 ||0 ||0

*Puurinsez: I need a favor.*

*SalaciousFrog: You're up late. Past midnight your time, isn't it? What's up?*

*Puurinsez: I need a summary of the cyberdefenses at a comm provider.*

*SalaciousFrog: Which one?*

*Puurinsez: Here are the specifics … Sent.*

*SalaciousFrog: OK, let me track it down. What's the target?*

*Puurinsez: Just a friend's percomm account. I want to know what he's up to.*

Hope had been thinking about the Lumière kid liking one of those royal girls. Did he have a girlfriend? It'd been a long time since she'd hacked his percomm message log. Back then, there wasn't anything interesting, just the constant chatter between him and his two friends.

*SalaciousFrog: Got it. Sending now.*
*Puurinsez: Thanks.*

As usual, she planned her penetration with meticulous attention to detail—before sending a single byte—to eliminate any chance of detection. Each step had a backup step, and every plan had a backup plan. The security experts at the comm companies were very good, some of the best in the world, and they changed security protocols on a regular basis. She had to stay several steps ahead of them. SalaciousFrog and the others online knew months in advance what the companies would change.

Once inside, she reviewed his percomm message log but found nothing of interest. Apparently, he was getting a dog. His friends were all excited for him— blah, blah, blah.

*SalaciousFrog: Now, I have a favor to ask you.*

*Puurinsez: OK.*

*SalaciousFrog: But I don't want to text.*

*What? Meet? Could he know where I live?* The flash of fear subsided, but the tingle of curiosity remained. *Maybe a vidcomm? I'll finally get to see him and talk to him.*

*Puurinsez: Vidcomm?*

*SalaciousFrog: No. Just audio. I'm sending you the code to decrypt on your end.*

She downloaded the file, installed the code, and started the program. She put on her headset so the sound wouldn't wake her dad and tapped the button to accept the comm.

"I've known you by so many tags over the years," came the voice over the headphone speakers. It was definitely not his voice. It had a robotic quality—like computer-generated speech or digitally altered some-how. "So what should I call you?"

She moved the headset microphone as close to her mouth as possible. As quietly as she could, she replied, "Princess. Call me Princess."

# CHAPTER 24

"HEY, THERE YOU ARE," SAID KATIE. "SEEN AL YET?"

"No," said Chris, scanning the bleachers as students filed into the high school gym for the assembly. "Wait, there he is. Sitting behind Mr. Muzaffar."

They crossed the gym and sat down where Al held seats for them.

"So you'll pick us up after karate?" asked Al.

"I can't wait to see the puppy," said Katie. "You lucky dog."

A few girls passed in front of them looking for open seats and spotted Al. One of the girls called to him, "Thanks, Al!" And then another, "Great idea, Al!"

"What's that all about?" asked Chris.

"Beats me," said Al.

Chris noticed his mischievous expression and was about to press further when the principal took center court. After announcements about activities and events happening before the end of the school year, their principal finally got to the part they were all waiting for: the elections for class presidents.

Across the gym, Chris could see the entire group of the royals with the Queen in the center. Half a dozen of the girls held up big signs that said VOTE FOR DAWN and CONGRATULATIONS, DAWN.

The freshman election went first. The principal tapped his percomm, and the voting began. A buzz swelled as freshmen cast their votes on their percomms. After a minute, the principal proclaimed the polls were closed and announced the winner. Everyone applauded. The same kid was reelected. He shook hands with the principal before returning to his seat.

The process repeated for the sophomores, except the sophomores elected a new president. The old president transferred the pin to the winner. More applause.

"Before we begin the junior class election," said the principal, "I want to thank Geraldo Fuentes for the gracious adjustment to the election rules for the junior class."

Chris looked over to Al, as did most of the people around them. Al cringed; he hated his formal name. Katie patted him on the back.

"What's he talking about?" asked Chris.

"The petition Mr. Fuentes circulated," continued the principal, "received sufficient signatures to allow a change to the voting procedure. With so many girls in the junior class, Mr. Fuentes reasoned that there should be two presidents to give other students a chance. The juniors will elect two presidents."

"What?" said Chris. "What petition? I didn't get any petition."

"Well, I easily had a majority without your signature," said Al. "So I thought I'd make it a surprise."

"Juniors, please cast your single vote for your two class presidents beginning ... now. The two students receiving the most votes will be your new class copresidents."

The cursor blinked in the search box on Chris's percomm. *A boy doesn't have a chance with so many girls voting for girls.* Chris voted for Katie, as he had done every year before.

The Queen came down from the bleachers for the pinning. The principal handed her the second pin because another would be needed—one for each copresident. She had the gall to leave the other one pinned to her blouse.

"Thank you. The polls are now closed. And the two junior class copresidents are ... Chris Lumière and Julia Torres." The gymnasium went wild.

Stunned, Chris looked to center court. Dawn had both hands over her mouth. The principal tried to quell the pandemonium, but the students started to stomp their feet, as well. At the other end of the bleachers, kids mobbed Julia Torres with congratulations. The whole class liked Julia—who was smart, kind, and very involved, a great pick for class president.

"Get up, ding-a-ling!" said Katie as everyone around them was congratulating Chris too. Katie gave him a big hug, and Al shook his hand.

Julia and Chris stepped from the bleachers as the gymnasium erupted in thunderous applause. The Queen's expression hadn't changed, as if time had stopped where she stood.

The principal prompted her to take the pin from her blouse, but she didn't move. He removed it himself, put the pins on Chris and Julia, and shook their hands with enthusiasm. The Queen offered her hand. It was like shaking a piece of string. The applause got even louder when they returned to the bleachers. It wasn't just the junior class cheering; it was the whole school.

"What happened?" Chris asked Al once the clapping died down. "There should've been two girl presidents, Dawn and someone else."

Before Al could answer, Mr. Muzaffar turned around. "Very clever, Mr. Fuentes."

Al grinned. "I didn't break any rules."

"I don't get it," said Chris.

"The students assumed Ms. Perkins would win," explained Mr. Muzaffar, "just like previous years. But with the possibility of a second winner, the students—especially the girls—concentrated their votes on who they thought should be the second winner. It split the girls' vote. I probably shouldn't tell you this, Mr. Lumière, but you've always been near the top of the list. You never had a chance—that is, until Mr. Fuentes's little maneuver here. But I think the real upset was Ms. Torres beating Ms. Perkins." To Al, he said, "I immediately saw through your scheme to allow Mr. Lumière to be elected—ingenious, I must say—but the impact on Ms. Perkins was a complete surprise. I didn't see that coming." Mr. Muzaffar returned his attention to center court as the principal completed the senior class election and closing remarks.

Chris just looked at Al.

"What?" said Al. "You said she had to do it to herself—that it couldn't be malicious. I swear, I was just splitting the girls' votes. I had nothing to do with you getting elected; that was all you, migo."

||0 ||0 ||0

"PETE, MY GOD, WHAT'S WRONG?"

Sitting on the floor against the hallway wall, Pete Rasmussen lifted his head from between his knees.

His wife came to his side and knelt. "Honey, what is it? How long have you been sitting here?"

She was in her bathrobe. *Must be morning.* He ran his fingers through his hair and tried to process her question. "I don't know what he wants from me."

"Who, honey? Who?"

"Anderson." He felt her body stiffen at the sheer mention of his name.

"You can't keep going like this," she said. "The therapist wants—"

"That shrink has no fucking idea what I'm going through!"

"Keep your voice down; Tina's still sleeping. We talked about this—"

"We don't talk about anything. Nobody understands. If I fail, my whole team is out of work."

"We *did* talk about this. You can't put all that on yourself. It's irrational."

"Irrational? Try real!"

They both heard the whimper. Tina stood outside her bedroom door, tears in her eyes.

"Go back to bed, sweetheart," said his wife. "Mommy and Daddy are just talking."

"It's gone," Tina said.

"We'll talk about it later. Now go back to bed."

"No!" Tina screamed. "You said the tooth fairy would bring me a surprise. My tooth is gone, and there's nothing!"

Pete got up. "Go to bed! *Now!*"

His wife tried to hold him back.

"But I put it under the pillow like you said and—"

"*Now!*" Pete pushed his wife out the way. Tina ran into her bedroom.

His wife grabbed him again.

He stopped pulling away; he didn't have the energy.

"We can't continue like this," she said.

He slumped against the wall and wiped his face. "I know."

||0 ||0 ||0

"NOW, THIS IS THE MOST DELICATE STEP IN THE PROCESS," SAID THE manager of storage systems for TerraStore.

With arms folded, Anderson watched as the technicians on the other side of the glass assembled a new bank of quantum memory units. His two aides waited patiently behind him. Each technician wore a full-body gown and breathing apparatus to prevent particulate contamination of the air inside the vault.

"The performance of the Faraday shielding is dependent on the geometry at the corners," said the manager, who kept glancing at Anderson, looking for any reaction.

Anderson's percomm vibrated, and he peeked at the display. "I'm finished here."

The manager nodded, relieved.

The aides escorted Anderson from the memory system vault's observation deck to the waiting cart and whisked him through the tunnel network to his office. At the administration wing, the aides opened doors for him along the way. As he entered the anteroom of his office, two people inside stood up: his assistant, behind the desk, and Pete Rasmussen, reporting as ordered.

"You have a priority-one communication," his assistant said.

"I know," he said, and then he looked at Rasmussen. "I'll deal with you in a moment."

At his desk, Anderson tapped the surface display of his desk, and Skotino's face appeared.

"If this is about the haoma," said Anderson, "I have the situation under control. The unbihexium production will be back on—"

"No, we have a new development." *Even after so many years, the rumble of Skotino's voice is unsettling.* "The boy," he continued. "His sleep cycle has changed. Talk to Cornelius. Find out what he knows." The comm ended.

Anderson reviewed his schedule. *First things first.* At the touch of the intercom button, he said, "Send him in."

Rasmussen looked pale, like he hadn't slept in days, with eyes downcast.

Anderson leaned back and interlaced his fingers. He let the seconds tick by. "Unbihexium production," he said finally. "You don't seem to understand the gravity of the situation."

"I do understand," Rasmussen whined.

"Even if you don't care about your team or their families, you should at least care about your own family."

Rasmussen looked up, struggling to connect the dots.

"Do you realize what will happen to them if you fail?"

"Of course I do."

"No. You don't." Anderson reached into his pocket and tossed the tooth onto the desk.

Rasmussen's eyes widened, and his mouth opened, but nothing came out.

"If you fail me, I'll give your daughter her surprise—one she'll never forget. And you won't, either. Because I'll make you watch."

||0 ||0 ||0

"OH, HE'S ADORABLE!" SAID KATIE, HOLDING OUT HER ARMS IN THE karate studio's reception area. "What did you name him?"

"Lucky," said Chris.

Good thing there wasn't a class in session when they arrived, because the puppy made quite an impression; everyone wanted to see and have a chance to hold Lucky. Chris passed the puppy to Katie. Lucky's tail wagged furiously, and about a dozen kids crowded around.

"Mrs. Richards, hello," said Mr. Cohen, coming out of his office. "What do we have here?"

"Well, the brainwashing at the shelter finally took effect," she said. "It's a big commitment, but I think we're ready to have a pet."

"You know, Chris," said Mr. Cohen, "I've told you before about my volunteer work." He added for Laura's benefit, "I'm a member of a canine search-and-rescue team along with my own dog. Mostly, we spend our time training and practicing, but inevitably there's a crisis somewhere in the world. A group of generous donors fund the travel to wherever the disaster may be. The work isn't without danger, but it's extremely rewarding." Mr. Cohen turned to Chris. "Would you and Lucky be interested in joining our team? You have to start the dog training soon—the sooner the better. It's a great leadership opportunity."

"This is one of your leadership speeches, isn't it?" said Chris.

"That's right. You're a natural. You should exercise your talents. And you've got a Lab. That's one of the top breeds for search and rescue."

Katie passed Lucky off to another kid. "You should do it, Chris."

"Yeah, do it, migo," Al chimed in. "It sounds totally jazz."

*It does sound pretty jazz. As Katie would say, top jazz.* "OK, how do I get started?"

"Well, since you're a minor, we actually need your mom's approval."

"Oh, sure, make me the bad guy," Laura said playfully. "Well, we'll talk to your dad, but I think it's a great idea. I'm sure he'll agree. Let's assume it's a go."

"Thanks, Mom!"

"I'll make the arrangements for you and Lucky to start the puppy training class," said Mr. Cohen. "They call it puppy training, but it should be called human training. It's the owner who needs to learn the proper behavior and consistency of routine that dogs respond to. Later, you can join the rest of the team for search-and-rescue training. That's the real dog training."

Chris couldn't wait. He looked over at Lucky. The excitement seemed to finally get the best of him. He was passed out in the arms of one kid while three others stroked his fur.

||0  ||0  ||0

FROM THE KITCHEN, LAURA TAPPED THE DISPLAY FOR A VIDCOMM connection to the laundry room where the kids were setting up Lucky's bed and bowl. "Hey, you two want to stay for dinner?"

"I thought you'd never ask," said Al.

"Yes, please," said Katie, and she gave Al a whack. "Thank you, Mrs. Richards."

"How did it go?" asked Ben, coming into the kitchen as she unpacked the other items from the grocery sack. He kissed her. "I stopped by the laundry room on the way up. The kids look pretty excited. The dog is very cute."

"Yeah, it all went smoothly. It'll take all of us to work with the dog. I'll go over it with you later."

"OK. Say, I've made some adjustments to the chamber, and I was hoping to get a scan of Chris if there's time before dinner."

"Sure. By the way, Mr. Cohen invited Chris and Lucky to join his canine rescue team. Chris is very excited, but Mr. Cohen did mention the work can be dangerous." She explained the details. "What do you think?"

"I agree. It's a great opportunity. Chris will face risks his entire life. We all do. Better it be with the benefit of training and preparation," he said. "Mr. Cohen is Chris's Krav Maga instructor, right? That guy knows how to handle situations. He'll look out for Chris."

"I've heard that term—Krav Maga—since Chris started," she said. "I have to admit, I don't know what it means."

"It's one of the martial arts taught at the school, like karate but different. It was perfected by the Israeli military. Security forces all around the world use it. It's different from other martial arts because there's no sport aspect—no competitions or tournaments. Its purpose is to survive life-or-death encounters. The philosophy is to drop your opponent in the shortest amount of time—no holds barred. A kick to the testicles is considered unsportsmanlike in other martial arts, but not Krav Maga, where groin strikes are common, as are strikes to all the most vulnerable parts of the body, including lethal strikes."

"You mean, to actually kill?"

"If that's what it takes. Better him than you, right? But the goal is to incapacitate your opponent to either escape or fend off the next attacker. If incapacitating permanently is the fastest alternative, well, then …"

"I guess I never thought to ask about what he was learning. When we made the offer to Katie's and Al's parents to pay for the lessons, I didn't think the kids would stick with it. And I didn't think they'd be learning things like that."

"Bruce Cohen's bio is posted online. He served in the Israeli security force. I assume the training Chris receives is pretty authentic. Anyway, I'll round up the kids and get the scan going." He hesitated. "What is it?"

She realized she'd stopped unpacking. "I'm not sure. It all makes me think of the missing girls." She looked at him. "Would training like that have helped those girls?"

"Well, we don't know what happened to them," he said. "Have you had a chance to try any searches since I set up the secure account? You were so charged up about it, but that was months ago."

"No," she said. "I figured I'd start in a couple of weeks, once school ends." She leaned back against the kitchen counter. "It's just such a strange feeling."

"What?"

"I feel apprehensive about searching for the missing girls—which is probably the root of my procrastination—but then I feel a sense of determination, like courage is trying to win over the fear." She shook her head. "Anyway. What about the scan? Something new?"

"Yes. I think I've figured out a way for us to actually *see* the presence inside Chris."

IIO IIO IIO

BEN HEARD THE KIDS' BANTER COMING FROM THE STAIRWELL outside the lab on their way down.

"At least I'll have something to do," said Al. "I'll take care of Lucky while you guys do all the work. Oh yeah—I'm taking the Lab to the lab!"

"Sure, right after the funeral for your sense of humor," said Katie, sitting down at the console and tapping commands to prepare the software.

Ben was amazed at Katie's confidence and at how much she'd learned over the years. Her understanding of the underlying physics surpassed even that of the graduate students enrolled in his university courses.

"So what's different this time, Mr. Richards?" Her fingertips danced across the input surface. "I see some changes to the detector cycle."

"Correct." After explaining what had happened during the satellite maintenance, Ben said, "So I adjusted the detectors inside the Compton chamber to work the same way, to see the dark energy. The information is three-dimensional, and the computer generates a 3-D model. See?" He pointed to the wall display. "It looks like a regular vid image of the chamber, right? But there's no camera."

The three kids looked at the image on the display and then back to the chamber.

"Now, watch as I demonstrate." He walked to the chamber and sat down inside. "The detectors are sensitive enough to register the position and movement of particles smaller than the atomic scale—at the quantum scale, in fact. The image looks completely photo-realistic. Don't you think?"

"Riveting," said Al. "Lucky thinks so too." The puppy was sleeping in Al's lap.

"Yeah, it's like a regular vid," said Katie.

"Yes. The image looks normal because there's nothing in the scanned data that your eyes can't see." He stepped out. "Now, it's your turn, Chris. Just walk inside and have a seat. Just like I did."

Chris looked to Al, sitting on the floor with Lucky, and then to Katie at the console.

Ben gave Chris an encouraging nod. "Go on."

Chris stepped to the chamber door. The vid image began to turn white, as if a brilliant light was being carried toward the door.

"Whoa," said Katie.

Chris stopped instinctively.

"Yeah, why is it getting so bright?" asked Al.

"I'm not sure," Ben said. "It looks similar to the flares from the satellite imagery. Keep going, Chris."

Chris took another step, entered the chamber, and sat down. The display shimmered and went completely white.

"What happened?" asked Al. "I don't see anything."

"Hmm," said Ben. "The detectors are—"

"I got it! I got it!" said Katie. Her hands flew across the input display as she adjusted settings. "The detectors are saturated from the signal. The filter needs adjustment to compensate. I got it."

Ben smiled. "Yes, that's what I was about to say."

"Here we go," said Katie, looking up at the wall display.

The blinding white slowly faded, and the image of Chris returned. As the image stabilized, there was an unmistakable luminescent cloud. It surrounded Chris's head and partway down his back.

"Wow," said Al.

Ben marveled at the sight. "Chris, try standing up and just turn around, slowly."

As Chris turned, the cloud followed. It wasn't only around his head and back but seemed to be *in* his body.

"Well, Chris," said Ben, "this is what your little hitchhiker looks like. The cloud is visible as a thin layer around your entire body, just over your skin."

"Something weird is happening!" Chris called out. "I'm not sure how I know this. I'm not even sure how to say this, but … Dad, have you been talking to it?"

Al and Katie looked over.

"Well, sort of."

"You've been talking to it, and you didn't tell us?" asked Al.

"Well, I've been asking questions, and I get answers. Or at least responses on the display, like the mind-reader game. I wouldn't call it talking."

"Anyway, it wants you to do that now," said Chris.

Ben thought for a second and then said, "Katie, would you run the program we've been using to play mind reader?"

"Got it." A text window appeared on the wall display superimposed over a corner of Chris's image. "Ready."

Ben hesitated. "What do you want me to ask?"

But before anyone could answer, the word *Watch* appeared on the display.

"What does that mean?" asked Al.

"I don't know," said Ben. "Something having to do with time? Time always seems to be a source of confusion when interpreting the meanings. Or maybe it just wants us to observe. Maybe something's going to happen."

The word *Watch* appeared again, but the image remained the same.

"Or maybe it's already happening," said Ben. "Katie, would you turn on the recording function, please?"

"OK. Got it; it's on now."

The display repeated the word *Watch* yet again.

"What does it mean, Mr. Richards?" asked Al.

"I'm not sure. If we're supposed to be seeing something, it may be that the detectors aren't tuned properly to register it. I'll need to analyze the recording."

||0 ||0 ||0

"HAVE A SEAT, DOCTOR," SAID SKOTINO.

Spire and Vega escorted Cornelius into Alexander Venizelos's office in Greece.

"Unfortunately, your usefulness to the project has … expired," said Skotino, sitting at the desk. "We no longer require your services."

"Excuse me?" said Cornelius. "This is my project."

"Actually, Doctor, it's an MI8 project."

"Quite," said Cornelius. "I don't work for you. I'll decide who is attached to the project, not you American bollocks. The Nu generation will be the defenders of Britain. If you obstruct my work, His Majesty will have *you* sacked. Permanently."

"Yes, funny you should phrase it that way; that's exactly what I had in mind for you."

Spire and Vega grabbed Cornelius.

"Outrageous! You can't—what do you think you're doing?"

"It's simple, Doctor. You know too much."

"*I* know too much?" said Cornelius. "You're damn right I do. I know everything. You know nothing. You need me."

"No, Doctor, that's where you're wrong."

"You don't understand," said Cornelius, doubt creeping into his voice. "This is a critical time in the boy's development. He's becoming a man. There are dramatic changes occurring in his physiology!"

"Yes, we're well aware of that."

"You have no idea. You need me to foster the transformation."

"No, Doctor," said Skotino. "Your involvement really has had no impact on that. You see, the boy was born with a particular genetic alignment, the second of such alignments. It's not the simple kind of genetics that your science understands. What you call *genetic code* is merely the surface of the programming that governs all life. You see, humanity's first genetic alignment occurred fifty thousand years ago. Your anthropologists call it the Upper Paleolithic Revolution, when humans advanced beyond other hominoids. The alignment brought on dramatic physical changes to the human body and brain. But what your scientists don't understand is how that change transcended physical reality. The same is true for the second genetic alignment the boy is now undergoing. Thousands of years from now, all mortals will be born with the second genetic alignment. It's a stage that occurs eventually in the evolutionary course of all cognate life, regardless of origin within the universe."

"Universe?" said Cornelius. "What are you talking about?"

"But there's a missing ingredient, a catalyst. Nature ensures that the catalyst becomes available only when life is ready."

"The compound you supply ... the parahaoma."

"Yes. As you know, Doctor, elements are created inside stars. The carbon in your body—the foundation of all life—was forged in the stars of this galaxy. Stars die an explosive death and spread newly created elements through space as dust and gas. The dust falls to planets like Earth. Unfortunately, Doctor, Earth's galaxy is young, and few stars are large enough to create a particular heavy metal, unbihexium. The dust containing unbihexium is not due to reach Earth for another six thousand years—and, well, we simply don't want to wait that long."

"But why? What's it doing to him?"

"A simple example is royalactin, used by worker bees to trigger the morphology that produces a queen. In the case of parahaoma, the second genetic alignment allows carbon to bind with unbihexium, sparking a spectacular phenotypic variation."

"The expression of the genes as observable characteristics," said Cornelius. "What will he become?"

"Enough talk. I just wanted you to know how insignificant your contribution has been. We are perfectly capable of handling things in your absence. And I know this is probably difficult for you to believe, but what is about to happen to you now is preferable to life with the boy once he awakens from his hibernation as a man." Skotino stood and walked to the end of the desk. "On his back."

"What? No!" Cornelius struggled, but the old man gave no real resistance as Spire and Vega flipped him off his feet and onto the desk like a fish about to be cleaned.

Skotino dragged Cornelius to the edge of the desk so his head extended over the side, tilting back, nearly upside down. He pulled out the knife—the one with the six-inch blade, serrated on both sides—and then pinched Cornelius's nose. The old man was already short of breath and immediately opened his mouth with a gasp. Skotino slipped the tip of the blade into Cornelius's mouth, setting the razor-sharp edge between the doctor's two front teeth.

Cornelius's eyes widened.

"From your medical training, Doctor, you'll recall that human flesh and bone form in the womb, starting along the spine then wrapping forward and around to join at a seam called the Hulse line of symmetry. That's why you have the medial cleft in your chin and the infranasal depression on your upper lip, the philtrum. But what you may not know, Doctor, is that those same tissues split easily across the Hulse line—including the skull—like opening an oyster."

Skotino forced the blade between Cornelius's teeth, pressing, until the knife jerked through, slicing into the gum. Cornelius screamed, but the sound was muffled by blood pooling in his throat. Blood danced in the air over choking coughs.

Spire and Vega held Cornelius's body as Skotino shoved the blade deeper into the gum, slicing the upper lip, nose, and base of the nasal cavity. *Snap.* The blade lurched into the soft matter, ending the struggle.

"Now, get the nurse."

# CHAPTER 25

I T WAS DUSK, AND THE TREES CAST LONG SHADOWS ACROSS the Avenir house. Hope sat in the corner of her garage. The space was empty; they'd never owned a tran as long as she could remember. A shaft of setting sunlight peeked through the open garage door, creating a golden glow on the far wall. The summer day was coming to an end, and she watched as fireflies began to flash in the backyard.

The door to the house swished open, making her flinch.

"Get in here." He held his liquor well but was pretty far along for so early in the evening.

She didn't move.

He walked over. "Get in here, now!"

Still, she didn't move.

He grabbed her by the arm and pulled, strong but sloppy. She lost her balance as he dragged her across the wall, toppling a basket of cleaning rags from the shelf.

Regaining her footing, she yanked her arm from his grip.

"Get inside!" He reached again, but a voice from outside made him stop.

"Back off."

It was the Lumière kid, standing at the top of the ramp, the setting sun at his back.

Her dad raised a hand to block the sun, squinting.

In the glare, she saw a second silhouette at his side. The dog looked practically full grown now. Amazingly well behaved for still being a puppy.

"You talkin' a me?"

"Back off."

"Listen here, boy—"

Hope dashed up the driveway ramp, past Chris, out of the yard and kept running. Only after reaching the park did she glance back. *No one followed*. Slowing, she followed the path to the play area with the swing set. She picked a swing, kicked back, and swayed back and forth.

Another night to survive. If she waited long enough, he might pass out, and she could sneak back into the house. If she went back too soon, he'd be waiting for her. Sometimes he was waiting, anyway. She looked back again. *Still clear*. The streetlights had come on, and moths were swirling in the glow.

*The Lumière kid was either brave or incredibly stupid*. The squeak of the chain marked time, like a metronome. *Argh! I hate having the sick mess of my life dragged out in the open*. Back and forth, back and—

The dog startled her, appearing from nowhere, silently, standing right next to her. *That must mean …*

Sure enough, there he was, the Lumière kid, on the path about thirty feet away.

She continued to swing. The dog was magnificent. Pale ivory fur. Black nose. And black around the eyes, like eyeliner. He had to be a hundred pounds. The tail was thick, like a baseball bat. She could just imagine how it might clear off a coffee table with a single wag. The eyes watched her, and his ears were perked up, head tilted, like she might pull a treat from her pocket.

Finally, she said, "You just going to stand there all night?"

"If I walk over, are you going to run away?"

She smiled and almost laughed. *All those times before.* "No," she said as if the question were ridiculous.

Taking the swing next to her, he kicked back.

The dog moved to a spot in front of them, sat, and then inched his paws forward until he was lying down facing them. With his head on his paws, his eyebrows seemed to hop back and forth as they swayed.

"You should have him on a leash, you know. There's a law."

"He's in a search-and-rescue program. He's registered. I have a permit."

"Oh."

Minutes passed. "How did you find me?"

"Lucky's pretty good at that sort of thing."

She looked back again.

"What are you going to do?" he asked.

"Hang out here."

Another minute passed. She looked back again.

"I know a place where he won't find you."

She let her feet drag her to a stop and actually looked at him. Not stopping at a sip, she drank him in. Though her eyes were fully adjusted, all the colors were muted in the darkness. She couldn't make out the blue of his eyes, but she could see the contour of his body. He was gorgeous in his shorts and T-shirt. He'd grown over the past year and looked to be in great shape, cords of muscle rippling along his arm as he gripped the chain. After only a few weeks of summer vacation, he had a golden tan. *The outdoors type.*

Her own skin was as white as the walls of her bedroom. "You don't want to get mixed up in my problems."

His feet hit the ground, grinding him to a stop. "You have no idea about what I want."

She looked away from him, even though her gaze was still thirsty. "Where?"

"I'll show you." When he stood, the dog jumped to his side and heeled.

Together they walked along the path to the far side of the park, along the tree line. He stopped at a small gap in the bushes. The dog stopped too, sat, and waited. Chris made a hand gesture and pointed into the bushes. The dog crawled through.

"Lucky goes first to make sure there're no unfriendly animals," he said. "You'll have to crouch down. OK? Just follow me."

"OK." On all fours, she followed to a small enclosure where the branches of the bushes arched over top.

"It seemed bigger when I was little," he said, "but I still like to come here now and again. It's private."

The tension she felt was evaporating, replaced by confidence, safety, and trust.

Chris lay down on his back, looking up. The moon had come up, and beams of moonlight filtered through the branches. "A clear night," he said.

When she lay down, her shoulder bumped against his. The sudden feeling of anticipation surprised her. She held her breath and tried to hold on to the feeling.

The dog stepped across and forced himself between their legs. "Ouch. Jeez, Lucky."

The dog turned in a circle, the rough pads of his paws scraping against her bare thigh. "Ow." He circled again and plopped down at their hips.

Chris shuffled over to make room. "Sorry. He does that. I guess he likes you."

Lucky's back leg jerked one last time before he was settled.

Quiet and still at last, only the sound of the crickets remained.

*Chris is so patient. With no expectations. He's not asking for anything. Why? Why should he care?* She felt her defensiveness melting—her constant guard, her shield, it wasn't needed now. "My dad's been like this for as long as I can remember," she whispered.

*Why explain? Why share anything?* She felt like Atlas after holding the heavens for eternity, setting the tremendous weight aside for a brief respite.

"My mom says it started after they were married. He lost his job and never worked again. She says the problem wasn't that he couldn't find work but that the government tells you how to spend the credits. They tell you what food you can buy, what medical procedures to have. They give you a prefab to live in, but each night under its roof reminds you that you can't support your own family. It drains your dignity." She glanced over. "Do you know they make you have an annual physical or they turn off the credits? If you get type 2 diabetes, you have to have it treated or they turn off the credits. Of course, you'd want to be treated, but the point is they make you. They cut the food credits if you weigh too much. You've seen him. He's fat. Twice they cut us off completely. So now, a week before the clinic scan, he eats nothing at all. Still manages to drink, though. No idea where he gets the liquor."

"How do you deal with him?"

"The same way my mom does, I guess. She and I don't say much to each other. It's weird, though; even in silence, I can sense a thin thread of connection to her. We both share the need to survive one more day. Each day, we fight to survive another day with him. Each day, each hour, each passing minute is a challenge to avoid a confrontation. Yeah, just survive.

I don't have to exchange words with her. There's an invisible bond, an invisible strength somehow. Mutual empathy without sympathy. I suppose I learned how from her."

Chris didn't say anything right away. He seemed to be thinking about it. Then finally, he asked, "How does it make you feel?"

The question hung in the air. Listening to the crickets, she could see the stars in the sky above through the leaves. *Why does he care?*

"That's the most horrible part," she said. "I don't have feelings. I think I lost my ability to feel a long time ago. I'm dead inside."

After a while, he said, "Help me understand."

*How? In your perfect life? How could anyone like you understand me?* "We're under his constant threat. The relationship with my mom isn't mother-daughter but more like cellmates. Everything's backward. He treats her like she's his child; he scolds her and belittles her. Then he treats me like his wife. He argues with me—they're like adult arguments. He wants me to be with him—you know … I resist, but he bargains. He promises to be lenient with my mom or me about some stupid thing or another. A sick negotiation. Sometimes I give in just to get it over with. Or to protect my mom. It's all backward. It's all screwed up." She let it sink in. *Can you understand? Why do you care?*

Finally, she said, "I think it's been long enough."

"OK."

"And you probably need to get home too."

"Yeah, I think there'll be fewer questions that way. Will you be all right?"

"I think so. He should be asleep by now." *I'm not sure that's true, but I'm not going to burden you by saying it.*

Following Lucky and Chris, she crawled back through the bushes. At the end, Chris stood, turned and offered his hand.

*His hand.* She stared, just inches away. *What is it about his hands?* In the moonlight, she could see clearly: masculine and strong. Beautiful. She was paralyzed by her fantasies, often late at night—the softness, the caressing. Her hesitation became awkward. His fingers spread ever so slightly, the subtlest of invitations. *My choice. Voluntarily. Inviting me. Inviting me to touch him.*

She slipped her hand in his—her most sensuous fantasy now mediocre by comparison. He gently pulled her up, effortlessly. Her eyes darted to his lips momentarily.

He conveyed no expectation, no demand. He just turned, his hand slipping away.

She held on tight.

He looked at her hand and then at her, and he smiled. Lucky at their side, he walked her home.

110 110 110

"WHAT DO YOU MEAN YOU CAN'T FIND THE NURSE? TRACK HER!" Skotino said to Spire and Vega.

"We can't," said Spire. "She's off the grid."

"Tyvold can find her."

"We contacted him immediately. Tyvold confirmed she's off the grid. She knows how to avoid capture."

"Keep looking. She'll make a mistake."

"There's more. Tyvold said that—just before she went off the grid—she was monitoring Cornelius's percomm. Apparently, she did this regularly."

"So she knows the doctor's fate."

"Right," said Spire. "She knows we're looking for her. She's not going to give us the satisfaction of making a mistake and letting us find her. She's MI8. She can elude our search."

"She also has abilities—formidable abilities that threaten our plan. Find her!"

||O ||O ||O

"AT THIS POINT, I DON'T KNOW WHAT WOULD CONSTITUTE PROOF," Ben was saying to Chris when Laura entered the kitchen.

She poured herself coffee. "Don't let me interrupt." She sat down with them, but they stayed quiet. "What did you learn this time?"

"I concentrated on communication," said Ben. "It's as if the computer can interpret the analytical side of the being's thinking, and Chris can perceive the intuitive side. We surmise the being's origin is outside our galaxy. I wasn't able to figure this out before because its understanding of time and distance are interconnected somehow. Once we separated those two concepts, we made more progress. It claims to be a life-form far more evolved than we are. There are billions of them, apparently.

"I was able to look more closely at the scanned data from the chamber. The being has a body, so to speak, but the body is made up of a tiny fraction of atoms as compared to a human body. The atoms are held together by dark energy, creating the equivalent of molecules, but there are so few atoms spread across such a relatively far distance that the being can pass straight through an object that we consider solid, like a wall, by taking advantage of the natural vibration of the atoms. Just as air molecules get pushed out of the way when we walk, the being can pass through solid objects. Its atoms are inside Chris's body—interwoven, if you will—or superimposed."

"Is that why the medical scanners never worked?" she asked.

"Yes. The being's body contains atoms of an element that doesn't exist on Earth. The experimental name is unbihexium, a heavy metal with atomic number 126. Theoretically, unbihexium is very unstable. But the isotope I'm detecting, unbihexium-310, seems to be completely stable. The presence of unbihexium throws off the scanners."

"Did you learn what *feral emergency*—or whatever—means?"

"Not really. It has something to do with the evolutionary progression," he said. "Do you know what separates humans from our closest cousin, the chimpanzees?"

"Uh, higher-level thinking and problem solving or something like that, right?"

"Pretty much. There's a point in the fossil record when a sudden change happened that separated humans from apes called the Great Leap or the Upper Paleolithic Revolution. The being suggests it was a genetic reconfiguration. The *feral emergency* phrase has something to do with the next leap in human evolution."

"What do we do now?"

"That's what Chris and I were just talking about. I want to go back to Major Nolan and present this evidence. But we're not sure we actually have any evidence. I mean, it still sounds like a farce. If Nolan's position is that this is all some kind of schizophrenic hysteria, then what evidence do we really have?"

"What about the un—the unbi—whatever that element is called. Isn't that evidence?"

"Maybe," said Ben. "It's just a set of readings from a scanner that could be easily manipulated, like a picture of a UFO doctored up by some nut case. I bet that's the kind of thing Nolan gets every day. It's irrefutable if you actually have the UFO parked in your front yard. In our case, it would be nice to actually have the unbihexium. But it's all part of the being's body. I don't know."

"What about the word *watch*? Did you find anything unusual in the recording?" she asked.

"I think so. I was able to detect a slight decrease in air pressure around Chris's skin, as if the being were able to push some of the air molecules away from his skin. But I don't know why that's important. All the questioning is very tedious."

"Why tedious?"

"Every question has some response, like the *feral emergency* phrase, that just gets repeated. For example, when we try to find out more information about the air-pressure change around Chris's skin, the display shows the word *malt*."

"Malt? Like what's used in brewing?"

"Yeah, dried grain. Nothing that would lead you to believe it's not a completely random word. And lately it's been showing up as *galactic malt*. Crazy. It takes time to dig through the computer results for the semantic roots. But phrases like *galactic malt* seem like gibberish. The interview pattern that eventually works is to rephrase questions using a different line of thinking. Extremely tedious."

"You know, this reminds me of something," she said. "Ben, do you remember? Around the time Chris was born, I went to see Father Arnold. Remember that he talked about how science can substantiate how our spirituality affects our physical world?"

"Yes!" yelled Chris. "Yes, it's like I remember that conversation—but I couldn't, right?"

"No, I don't think you were born, or maybe you were a baby," she said. She watched Chris just looking off into space. "Uh … maybe we should make a visit to Father Arnold," she said.

"Yes!" Chris said again. "Good idea. I mean—it wants us to do that."

THE KNOCK FROM HER BEDROOM DOOR SURPRISED CHELSEA. *A real knock, or the tree against the building?* She turned the knob of the old-fashioned door.

"Mrs. Venizelos, please come with us," said one of the two guards.

"Where? Where are you taking me?"

"To see your son."

*What? I checked all the rooms, no sound, no marks in the carpet.* "I don't believe you," she said.

"Nevertheless, you're coming with us." The guard extended an arm.

Wearing her terry cloth robe—the one with the frayed pocket—she tucked away the loose threads. *I don't want him to see me like this.* "I'll be just a minute." She started to close the door.

The guard pushed the door open and pulled her by the arm.

"No, wait. I only need a minute to change."

Walking between them, she examined each door they passed. *He was just down the hall, and I had no idea!* But the guards didn't stop at any of the rooms. They escorted her downstairs and through hallways she'd never been before. At one point, they passed a hallway mirror. The sight of her own reflection made her gasp. The dark circles under her eyes were prominent. She reached up and raked at the straw-like strands of hair.

"How do I look?" she asked the guard holding her arm as she gave him her best smile.

"Fine," he said without even a glance.

Ahead, bright light spilled from an open set of double doors. When they reached the spot, the guard let go of her. She massaged her arm and stuck out her tongue at him before looking inside.

*Oh my.* She'd seen Mr. Skotino only once before, shortly after the birth of her son. She didn't know anything about him other than that he was in charge. Even Dr. Cornelius deferred to him. She thought she knew the designer of his suit—she used to know all the fashion designers. Though Skotino was tall and wide at the shoulders, the suit framed him perfectly. Nothing was out of place. The pressed white shirt set off his light brown skin and black hair. Chelsea couldn't quite guess his ethnicity. Maybe Indian, Latino, Native American, or even Greek. His complexion was refined but somehow swarthy at the same time.

"Mrs. Venizelos. Chelsea."

The sound of his voice gave her the most unusual sensation. It was rich and deep, like the tube station when a train passed below. She gathered the collar of her robe, snug, under her chin. *Where's my son?* She scanned the room. *There.* Across the room, lying naked in a kind of silver bed.

"I'm making a change in your arrangements," said Mr. Skotino.

The bed had a glass cover. There was a blue light shining down. The bed was high off the floor, on wheels, like a gurney. Or, on second thought, more like what a coroner uses to transport caskets. He was inside the silver bed—on the other side of the room, so far away. She couldn't really see him. She stood on her toes, but it didn't help. *I want to see him up close, hold him. Why is he sleeping? I'll wake him and ask him how he's doing. I'll—*

"Chelsea, do you understand me?" Mr. Skotino said. "Look at me."

She pulled her attention away from the bed. "I'm sorry." She forced herself not to look back.

"I was saying I'm going to move your son to America. I've decided to allow you to go with him."

"What? What about everyone here? Evan? Dr. Cornelius? Ingrid?"

"No, just you," he said. "Evangelos's work requires him to stay. He'll make visits when he can."

"What about Dr. Cornelius and Ingrid?"

"No. Your son is older now. He no longer needs their help." Without taking his eyes off her, he checked the knot of his red silk tie. "He needs *your* help now, Chelsea."

"Really?" *At last!*

"Yes, Chelsea. You've neglected him long enough." The gravelly resonance of his voice was less melodic now, more grating.

"No!" she said. "No, I *wanted* to be with him. They didn't let me!" The proportions of the room began to warp. Her throat became dry. Skotino's face filled her vision.

"You neglected him, Chelsea. You've been a horrible mother. He needed you, and you abandoned him."

"No. You don't understand, I—"

"You've hated him from the moment of his birth. You're disgusted by the sight of him. The feel of his skin appalls you. You're ashamed to even admit he's your son."

"No!" she begged. "No, I love him! I adore him. I love every part of him."

Mr. Skotino didn't say anything. The silence was like knives flying through the air. *I'm a horrible mother.* Thousands of knives, stabbing. *I abandoned him.* Knives still stabbing, agony overwhelming, until the utterance of his next words.

"Even his eyes?"

"Yes!" she pleaded. "I love all of him. Even his eyes."

"Then you'll have to prove it to me, Chelsea. You'll have to do better."

"Yes! I swear it! Please, just let me be with him. Please! I'll be a perfect mother. You'll see. Please!"

The room returned to normal proportions. Tears streamed down her cheeks, and she pressed her hands together, up to her lips as if praying. She waited, motionless, searching his face for any acknowledgment or approval.

"All right," he said finally.

She squeezed her eyes closed tightly in relief, a tear falling from her cheek. Opening her eyes, she let her gaze focus on her son. *My boy! No, he's a young man now.* "Can I wake him?"

"No, Chelsea. He's going to be asleep for a long time."

"How long?"

"As long as he needs. Maybe a year."

"Why so long?"

"He's changing, Chelsea. Getting stronger. When he wakes, he'll be a full-grown man. And he'll be completely safe then. Our work will be complete. The Hoods won't be able to hurt him, Chelsea. Never again will the future of the Venizelos family be threatened. Alexander is thrilled. Evangelos is too. You should be thrilled, Chelsea."

"Yes, yes, of course, I am." Her eyes remained fixed on the bed capsule. "Can I at least see him up close?"

"You can approach, but don't touch the hibernation pod."

She walked up to the hibernation pod, as Mr. Skotino had called it. Looking through the glass, she could see a moist film on his skin, some kind of milky white excretion surrounding his body.

"What is that white stuff?" she asked.

"He's forming his hibernaculum—a cocoon, you might say."

# CHAPTER 26

"**M**OM, I'M HOME."

"I'm in here," Laura called back to Chris from the family room as she heard him and Lucky coming in the back door.

When he came in, she gestured to mute the audio of the broadcast she was watching. "How did dog training go?"

"Great," said Chris. "So Mr. Cohen opened registration for the summer search-and-rescue training simulation for Lucky and me. You know, the one held in Calexico. I need your permission to go."

"OK. Is there a cost?"

"No, donors pay all expenses. Some of them are pretty rich, I guess. One of them has a private jet and lets the team borrow it. It's a scramjet, Mom! We go from Philly to Mexicali in less than an hour!"

"Wow. I've never been on a supersonic flight. I don't think your dad has, either," she said. "Lucky goes in the plane with you?"

"Yup. Oh, one more thing, Mr. Cohen is having a planning meeting at his house for the whole rescue team tomorrow afternoon. Can I go?"

"Sure," she said. "You keep calling him Mr. Cohen. You used to call him Master Cohen."

"Oh, I still do, but he said I don't have to call him that outside the studio." Chris turned to go and then added, "I can't wait to tell Dad that Lucky will have a supersonic flight even before he does!" He ran off.

She swiveled the input display around to her lap and tapped for a connection to the basement lab. "Hey, Ben, sorry to interrupt. It's time for Chris to get permission to go to the training in California. You OK with it?"

"Sure. No problem," he said. "By the way," he said, glancing over to his own computer screen, "another one of your anarchist newsletters got caught in the message filter. I've taken it out of quarantine for you so you can stay up to date with your rebel army friends."

"Very funny. OK, thanks."

"Which reminds me, have you tried any searches for the missing girls using the anonymous account I set up for you? You said you were going to once summer break started, but that was weeks ago."

"No. I guess I'm still procrastinating." She sat up straighter in the chair. "You're sure they won't be able to trace it?"

"I'm sure."

"OK." She pursed her lips together. "Well, no time like the present. Thanks."

She ended the comm, pulled up the link that Ben had sent her, and followed his instructions to log in with the special account. She created a query with the names of the missing girls she knew: Lisa, Marsha, and her student's sister. Then she added keywords for the publicized cases of the others from over the years and tapped the search button.

After spending an hour sifting through the results, nothing seemed to tie the cases together. About to give up, she examined the list of accounts that had accessed the case files. For each file, the account list included all the divisions of law enforcement involved—from local police, county sheriff, and highway patrol all the way up to the FBI. But a few addresses were just a jumble of numbers and letters. She noticed, too, that all the letters were at the top of the alphabet, and none of the letters went past F:

52657669766572205B3F2D3F5B204C6576656C203E3A2D3A3E20546972726974
4D75726472756D6D203B5D3B205265646976696469572203A3E3E3A20536F6C6F6F73
4E756E6E6E6570205D3A5B3B5B3A5D204D6F6D20262A3E3C3C3E2A262044656966696564
03A303BA03BF03C403B503B903BD03CC03CC03BD03B903B503C403BF03BA03A3

She tapped the hyperlinks and found that each led back to the same account, like a master account. The account details made no sense; all the fields were filled with more numbers and letters. The only piece of English she found was in the field indicating where the data was stored. It listed TerraStore, LLC.

"Hey, Ben, sorry to bug you again," she said over a new comm. "Does the name TerraStore mean anything to you?

"Yes, but I don't think that will help. That's the company that stores most of the data in the global network. Even Ben-U contracts with TerraStore. I think any account you look at will show TerraStore," he said. "I'll be up in a few minutes to start dinner. I can help you then if you like."

"Nah, I think I'm at a dead end. Thanks."

Before logging off, she did a search on TerraStore. *Headquartered in Nevada. The name of the CEO is Rick Anderson—and the parent company is TerraHoldings, also in Nevada.* Tapping again, she found little information about TerraHoldings except for a few old press releases announcing a charitable donation attributed to Aeron Skotino, TerraHoldings' executive director.

"Mom, when's dinner?" Chris yelled from the kitchen.

"It's your dad's turn," she yelled back, and then she heard him rummaging through the refrigerator. He'd grown so much recently. He was in hunter-gatherer mode now; he'd start eating the furniture in a few minutes. "Hold on, I'll be right there."

||O ||O ||O

BEFORE GOING UPSTAIRS TO MAKE DINNER, BEN HAD ONE MORE thing he wanted to get done.

"What can I do for you?" asked Raj over the vidcomm to Australia.

"You're coming up on another satellite maintenance period, right?" Ben asked. "I was wondering if you could save me the images from when the detectors are aimed toward Earth. Like before?"

"Sure, no problem," said Raj. "Did you discover the source of the dark energy flares? The one at your house?"

"Uh, maybe. Maybe not. I need another data set."

"How about the flares in Nevada?"

"No, I haven't looked at those yet."

"OK. As soon as the file's ready, I'll send you the link to the storage location."

|ıo |ıo |ıo

"WHAT'S WITH ALL THE MYSTERY?" KATIE ASKED CHRIS AT THE masstran stop for the ride to karate practice. "A private meeting? Just you and me? What's going on?"

"Thanks for getting here a few minutes early. I just wanted to ask you something before Al gets here."

"We don't have secrets."

"No, no, it's nothing like that," Chris said. "It's just—well—you're a girl, right? I mean …" *Argh, how should I say it?*

"Yeah, last time I checked. Thanks for the compliment, Mr. Flatter Master. Come on, out with it."

"Well, it's about Hope. I was able to spend a little time with her—by accident … sort of. Anyway, it confirmed a lot of feelings I've had—"

"Yeah, you don't need to explain, migo; you've worn that on your sleeve in flashing neon since I can remember."

"That bad, huh? Well, I want to see her again, and I don't want to wait for another chance meeting."

"Hey, I'm no expert on the boy-girl thing."

"Yeah, but—"

"Look, you should ask Al. He can give you ideas."

"Usually, all I get is a hard time."

"He deserves more credit than that. He's grown. Trust him," she said. "I'll help too, but ask him when he comes, OK?"

"OK, I'll give it a shot."

Chris had a hard time looking at her now. He felt like she could see inside him.

"Here," she said. "Try this one." She handed him a piece of gum.

"What flavor is it this time?" He unwrapped the blue chunk and popped it into his mouth.

"Key lime pie."

"Not bad," he said after a few chews. "But you gotta stop making them blue. I know it's all in my head, but blue just doesn't work for lime."

"I know. My uncle gave me a huge supply of the blue food coloring for the kit, because I like blue. But I realized the same thing. Sorry. I need to use it up."

"Why the long faces?" Al asked after Katie handed him a piece of gum.

Chris explained about Hope.

"Wow! Casanova is ready to strike!"

Katie whacked him on the arm and gave him the evil eye.

"Sorry," said Al. "OK, uh. Look, I'm not trying to pry—no more kidding around—just tell me a little bit about the last time you were together."

Chris didn't go into the details of Hope's personal situation, but he described his chat with her.

"So it sounds like she did all the talking," said Al.

"I guess so, yeah."

"Maybe it's time to share more of yourself with her."

Katie made an I-told-you-so face.

"Occam's razor," said Al.

"What?"

"Occam's razor," Al repeated.

"Uh," Katie jumped in to explain, "it's a principle of philosophy. Roughly, it means that the simplest or most obvious solution is often the best one."

"So?" Chris asked.

"Ask her out on a date, migo!" said Al. "It doesn't have to be complicated. Like if you had to find a way into a locked house, you'd just knock on the front door."

"Ask her out? You make it sound easy."

"That's my point. It's all attitude. It *is* easy," said Al. "Like if I wanted to spend time with Katie, I would just ask her."

Katie's mouth opened for a second, and then she turned away. Not anger, more like surprise. Al didn't notice.

"OK," Chris said, "but what *exactly*? What would I ask her to do?"

"What do you have in common? What interests do you share?"

"We don't have anything in common." *No, that's not true. Hmm.* "Well, she did go to one of the animal-shelter events. She always notices Lucky. I guess she likes dogs."

Al nodded and looked to Katie for her reaction. She'd turned back around but seemed distracted. Before Katie said anything, the masstran rounded the corner and pulled up to the curb.

"Easy," Al said decisively. "Ask her to go to the shelter or something."

The door opened, and Chris followed Al up the steps.

As Al looked for open seats, Chris turned back to Katie. She had one hand on the rail. "You coming?"

"Yeah," she said. "Sure."

||0  ||0  ||0

"WHAT IS IT?" SKOTINO ASKED FROM HIS OFFICE IN THE MEGARON via comm link to the security substation in the oubliette below.

"I'm not sure," said Tyvold. "Anderson sent me a report from TerraStore. The artificial intelligence software detected unusual activity and issued an alert, level six."

"A threat to the Circle."

"Yes," said Tyvold. "First, the AI quarantined an account with high-security clearance that searched the case files of our pharmakoi."

"Go on."

"Second, it flagged a file containing a set of geo-spatial coordinates of high precision—extremely high precision, really, within centimeters."

"Relevance?"

"Several of the coordinates point here. Right here, at this very spot."

"Someone knows our location."

"Not just that. It's as if the coordinates are us. I looked at the time stamp on the data, and as far as I can tell, the locations match where we were standing at that exact moment," Tyvold said. "Exactly where we were standing."

"I heard you the first time."

"Well?"

*True, it's a significant threat. But something's different. Beyond luck. Beyond coincidence. For the chance of reality's path doth tip. Divine prophecy unfolded. Dextral guidance. But how?* "Who owns the data?" asked Skotino.

"The query was submitted by a Professor Laura Richards. The account is associated with a project at the Benjamin Franklin University in Philadelphia. I made a cursory search of the university's records. There're many references to Laura Richards, but the employment directory lists only one Professor Richards with, oddly, Benjamin as the first name, which I assume is an error, mixed up with the name of the university. Professor Richards is an astrophysicist as well as an expert in advanced computing. It all fits."

"So ... some rocket scientist bitch is putting the puzzle together." *That's no coincidence.* "Host of my god's brother, convene the Circle."

"I hear and obey."

WITH TWO OTHER MEMBERS, CHRIS WAITED IN MR. COHEN'S LIVING room for the rest of the team to arrive. The two guys on the couch seemed like they'd known Mr. Cohen for a long time. One was tall and skinny, and the other was tall and big. Both looked fit and about the same age as Mr. Cohen. They were loud, yakking away, practically yelling so Mr. Cohen could hear them from his kitchen.

Chris didn't feel comfortable sitting down. He felt that if he did, he was supposed to join in on all the loud reminiscing. When Mr. Cohen had invited him over for the planning meeting, Chris felt grown up, but now he wasn't sure how to react to all the backslapping and smack talk. To kill time, Chris admired the photographs on the living room wall. One was a picture of four men and a woman kneeling down with a building in the background. They were dressed in what he assumed was some kind of army uniform. Each held a gun, and they all looked pretty intense, hard core, like they'd been through a lot— dirty and scraggly. The guns weren't handguns, more like some kind of strange rifles. One of the men was Mr. Cohen, but younger. The building and the sur- roundings could've been somewhere in North Africa, Chris guessed. The men in the picture all had beards, and the woman's face was covered in cloth.

"Are you sure I can't get you a soft drink, Chris?" asked Mr. Cohen, walking in from the kitchen. He handed bottles of beer to the two guys on the couch. "Juice? Water?"

"No, I'm fine. Thank you. Say, was this picture taken when you were in the Israeli military, Master Cohen?"

The two men roared with laughter.

"You don't have to call me that here, Chris." He smiled.

"I know, sorry." *An impossible habit to break, especially to his face.*

"Yeah, maybe you oughta take that drink, boy," said one of the men. "We got some stories to tell you about your instructor."

Both men laughed.

"No, no, he doesn't need to hear any of those stories," said Mr. Cohen. "Listen, the others should be here in a few minutes, and we can get started."

"What's that gun you're holding?" Chris asked. "It looks huge."

"See, Bruce?" said the man. "The kid wants to hear the stories." Then to Chris, he said, "A long time ago, your master here took down a lot people with that gun. Over a thousand, I'd say." The two men cracked up when they saw Chris's reaction.

"Don't listen to them, Chris. They're just having fun with you. That picture was taken when I was in riot control, early in my career. That's a suppression tool called a BSS. It's not an offensive weapon. So yeah, it's true, I took down thousands of people with it. They all lived."

"What does it do?"

"BSS stands for blind, stun, and snare. It doesn't shoot bullets."

Chris was disappointed; he'd always thought of Mr. Cohen as a gun-wielding soldier mowing down the enemy, like an Omega Force agent. But the BSS seemed to fit Mr. Cohen's philosophy of martial arts: match the technique to the task.

"Are you excited about the supersonic flight?" asked Mr. Cohen.

"Oh yeah! I can't wait. It's so nice of the donor to let us use it."

"Donor?" cried the man on the couch. "What did you tell the boy, Bruce?" Then to Chris, he said, "It's a Hillite handout, boy, pure and simple."

"Knock it off," said Mr. Cohen. "It's a donation— of sorts. So that makes him a donor. It's a win-win for everyone. Now, clean up your act, please."

"Oh, there's the master-speak," said the man. "I knew it wouldn't be long."

"It's just one person? One donor?" asked Chris. "Who is it?"

"You don't want to know that, kid," said the man, genuinely contrite now.

"Visitors arriving," announced the female voice from the seccomm. "Quantity three."

"They're here," said Mr. Cohen. "We'll get started in a minute."

Chris looked back to the picture on the wall and tried to imagine what stories Mr. Cohen could tell about his past.

# Chapter 27

"**V**ISITOR ARRIVING," ANNOUNCED THE SECCOMM OF THE Richardses' home. "Quantity one." The bedroom lights switched on as part of the security program, triggered by a visitor outside a door at such a late hour. Laura looked at the clock. *Just past 1:00 a.m.* "Visitor arriving. Quantity one," repeated the announcement, adding, "Emergency vehicles arriving. Quantity three."

"What's going on?" said Ben, getting out of bed. He cleared the sleep from his eyes and went to the seccomm panel. A vid image from the outside security camera appeared. "It's a woman—or girl—at the back door."

"That's the Avenir's daughter, Hope, from across the alley." In the background of the image, trees and homes flashed red and blue. "Oh my god, what on earth has happened?" She put on her robe and followed Ben.

In the elevator, he asked the seccomm, "Specify emergency vehicles."

"Law enforcement. Quantity two. Paramedic. Quantity one."

*What could've happened? I should've been a better neighbor. I should have helped Sue. The warning signs were obvious.*

As the elevator doors opened, Laura pushed sideways, and Ben followed.

"What's going on?" asked Chris, standing at the stairwell door, his hair sticking up.

Laura opened the back door to see Hope, red in the face but with no tears. Her expression was odd, like she'd been frightened and her face stuck that way.

"I'm sorry," said Hope. "I didn't know where else to—"

"Come here, sweetheart." Laura stepped out, put her arm around her, and brought her inside.

Ben and Chris stood out of the way.

Laura guided her to a seat at the kitchen table, sat down next to her, and kept her arm around her. The girl's body was sending a bizarre mix of signals. Her face reflected total shock, but her eyes were dry, and she didn't respond to Laura's embrace. Her body seemed full of tension, like a volcano ready to erupt. "Are you all right? What's going on?"

Hope nodded. "It's my dad ... he went after my mom. It's never been like this before."

Laura gave her a tissue but then realized she didn't need one.

"It's never been this bad. I was sure he was going to kill her. I called the police. I didn't know what else to do. He's still got her, I think. I was able to get away. The officer asked if there was a safe place I could wait. I didn't know where else to turn." She had an anguished look but still no tears.

"Oh my goodness, sweetheart, you came to the right place," said Laura, squeezing her shoulder. *Like hugging a mannequin.* "You did exactly the right thing."

Ben and Chris looked dumbfounded. They shared no DNA, but both had the exact same Neanderthal look on their faces. *Must be a Y chromosome thing. Emotional situations need subtitles so they can follow along.*

"You know," said Laura, "I made a commitment to your mom just after you were born that she could come to me anytime and I would help her. I knew the situation over there was rough. Your mom's a strong and proud woman, but I knew there was trouble. Well, it's about time I help."

Ben and Chris stood like statues.

"We'll *all* help," Laura prompted.

"Of course," said Ben. "You can stay here as long as you need. You'll be safe here. We'll make sure of that."

Chris started smoothing down his hair.

"Come with me," said Laura. "I'll show you the guest room."

Ben and Chris stepped aside as if Hope were radioactive.

Laura gave Ben the look.

"Right," he said. "I'll go out there and find out what's going on."

"Thank you," said Laura as if it were his idea.

She got Hope settled, and after a while, Ben returned. Sue Avenir would be going to the hospital, and Hope's dad would be in jail until charges were filed, certainly until morning but probably longer.

Over the next several days, Hope visited her mom in the hospital and started to adjust to the normal routine of the Richards home. She was reserved at first, clearly embarrassed by her situation. Laura made sure Ben made a conscious effort to make her feel welcome and safe. Chris was quieter than usual but seemed to be trying hard to be helpful. Even Al and Katie made her feel at ease, and the four kids got along well.

The following Saturday, Al and Katie came over for dinner, as was the tradition. Laura and Ben were already sitting down at the dining room table when the four of them came in. Katie, Al, and Chris took their usual spots. They all seemed unusually quiet, and Chris looked anxious. Instead of asking why, Laura waited—the body language was too captivating. Entering last, Hope took the open chair next to Chris. *Atmosphere, thick as molasses*, Laura thought. Chris gave Hope a quick smile when she sat down and then hastily grabbed the platter and passed it to Hope first. *Clockwise? He knows better.*

Still, no one said a word. *What's that phrase? Deafening silence?* Laura realized her frustration with Chris's lack of empathy was unfair. *His emotions are probably on overload.*

Laura took the opportunity to really look at Hope with a fresh perspective. Her style of dress, the dark-colored, oversized clothing, how her hair covered much of her face. *She's a beautiful girl, but who would know?* Katie wasn't a girly girl, but still, the contrast was striking. Having Chris as a son was wonderful, and she'd never wanted another child. *But a daughter would be wonderful too.*

"So," said Al, ending the silence, "did you get a chance to ask Hope out on that date?" He grinned at Chris.

Katie gave Al the evil eye. Chris looked bloodthirsty.

"Excuse me?" said Hope, swallowing hard.

"Yeah," said Al, still grinning, "Chris said he got to know you better but didn't talk about himself much."

"You are such an idiot," said Katie under her breath.

Chris blushed and looked ready to rip Al's head off.

"Well, I for one haven't had the chance to get to know Hope as well as I'd like," said Ben. "What do you like to do in your spare time?"

Everyone seemed to relax a bit, but Katie still glared at Al. He mouthed the word *what* with an expression of false accusation.

"Well," said Hope, "I spend a lot of time online."

"Oh," said Ben, "well, you may have trouble reaching some sites. The house is connected to the university's network, and the security policy is pretty strict."

"Yeah, it's government. Class four, military grade," said Hope.

"Whoa, miga," said Katie.

"Uh, that's correct," said Ben. "How do you know that?"

"Like I said, I spend a lot of time online. I hope you don't mind me using the pubcomm."

"No, of course not," said Ben, still a little off balance.

"I'd like to get to know you better too," said Laura. "Maybe you and I could go shopping together."

"That sounds terrific," said Hope. She seemed genuinely pleased by the idea, not just being polite.

Al started eating in his happy-go-lucky fashion. Katie still looked disgusted with him. Chris looked wilted. Hope glanced over to Chris, caught his eye, and gave him a smile. That was all Chris needed. He smiled too and appeared instantly restored.

There was something about the interaction between Chris and Hope that was startling. Growing up, Hope had been as quiet and withdrawn as her mother. *What was it?* Not the attraction between two teenagers—that was textbook. Then Laura realized it was the first time she'd ever seen Hope smile.

||0 ||0 ||0

KATIE DRIBBLED THE BASKETBALL AND TURNED FOR THE BASKET. Chris reached to block, but Katie's move was a feint. She pumped once and took the shot. The ball teetered on the rim, and Al jumped up to tap it in.

"Isn't Hope supposed to be back by now?" asked Al.

"Yeah," said Chris. "She's with my mom, so who knows."

Lucky was lying in the shaded grass. The tip of his nose twitched casually, sniffing the summer air.

"Finally!" Chris said, seeing the Richardses' tran coming down the alley. The ball had rolled to the grass around the driveway. He picked it up and took the ball to the back line. "Let's get Hope in the game! It'll be two on two." Chris heard the tran door open behind him. He passed the ball to Al, but it just hit him in the chest and then dropped to the ground and bounced away. "Hey! Migo! Wake up!"

Al's attention had apparently been hijacked by something. His mouth fell open.

Chris turned to look. There was his mom and—

"Wow!" said Al.

*Wow is right*, thought Chris. Hope had completely transformed. The baggy pants and shirt were gone. She was wearing a white skirt, short but not too short. Chris had spent many hours imagining what was under the baggy clothing but never guessed her legs could be so long. The top she wore was a bright turquoise, but it wasn't the color that caught his attention. His imagination over the years seemed to have no limit yet was no match to reality. *She's amazing.*

"You look fabulous!" Katie called out. She ran to Hope, hugged her, and stood back to admire the change.

"Do you really like it?" Hope turned to the side. She seemed unsure, self-conscious, and as if she were seeking approval.

"Oh my god! Yes!" squealed Katie.

"It's not too much? It was all Mrs. Richards's doing. She picked it out."

"Me next!" Katie said. "And your hair and makeup too!"

Chris hadn't noticed. Her hair was smooth and shiny in large relaxed curls flowing down her back and on one side. On the other side, her hair was up behind her ear. He could see her face. Was she wearing makeup? Hard to tell. It looked natural. He could see a contrast around her eyes and lips. The whole look was stunning. She was stunning. *She's beautiful, and now everyone in the world can see it too.*

"Yes, we did a little makeover," said Laura, beaming, clearly pleased with her contribution and admiring the change too.

"Wow, you look great," said Al, very sincerely. "Even the navigation computers will be rubbernecking!"

Everyone chuckled, so Chris laughed too, but too late and way too loud. He couldn't take his eyes off her. Her smile was such a rare treat. He cherished it. *What was that vocabulary word of Katie's? Demure?* He managed a smile in return. Then he heard the sound of dry leaves crushed under tires as a tran swerved into the driveway.

Hope's smile shattered.

The vehicle skidded to a halt. It looked like a rental, and it was clearly under manual control. Hope's dad stumbled out. It was a hot day, granted, but the man was sweating like crazy. The look on his face was familiar, just like the night outside the Avenirs' garage.

Lucky stood up, tail straight, head low, eyes on the man, and with a defined strip of hair rising along his back.

Suddenly, Chris felt the presence. In the deepest part of his mind, he was no longer alone. A rush of sensations registered in his mind. Smells. Mr. Avenir ... sweat ... alcohol. Chris recognized the smells as if he'd known them forever. Then the sensation faded.

"It's time to come home, young lady!" His tone was all syrupy.

Hope's eyes darted about as if she were looking for an escape route.

Laura put her hands on Hope's shoulders, and that seemed to give her confidence.

"No," said Hope.

"Get your ass home *now!* Or I'll drag it home!"

Hope's shoulders flinched at the sound, but she didn't move.

"You don't have the authority," said Laura. "She's here under Sue's authority—and yours has been suspended. In fact, you can't be within a hundred feet of her."

"My daughter won't bother you again," he said. "I'll make sure she learns her lesson." He moved toward Hope.

Chris and Al were the farthest away. Laura stood behind Hope, and Katie was beside her. Chris took a step to intercept, with Al right behind—but they both stopped when they saw Katie's subtle hand signal to halt. *Katie has this under control.*

Mr. Avenir seemed to expect Katie to move out of the way, but she didn't. He angled to go around, but Katie sidestepped into his path. He stopped and stared at her with surprise and then reached to push her out of the way. The motion of Katie's counter was graceful, but the joint lock was ferocious. Mr. Avenir went down, hard. His cheek smacked down on the cement. Katie stood over him, holding his wrist from behind, keeping him pinned to the ground. What had barely started was now already over.

"Come inside," Laura said to Hope. "I'll comm the police."

"Let me go, you bitch!"

Al called out, "I've been in that hold. I wouldn't call her that if I were you." Then to Chris, he said, "I guess Hope gets her smarts from her mom, huh?"

# CHAPTER 28

AFTER LUNCH, BEN RETURNED TO HIS UNIVERSITY OFFICE. He sat down and tapped the keyboard to bring up the results of the morning's computer run. It still hadn't completed. *That's odd*. He tapped several more commands to check on the progress. *Not even close to done*. A few more taps and the cause became clear: the computers in Australia were offline and weren't contributing to the parallel computations. He looked for the server logs, but the entire directory was gone.

"A fire?" Ben asked when he reached a technician at the network operations center.

"Yes," said the technician. "That's what we're assuming. It's the middle of the night over there, so information is trickling in. The alarms are environmental. The vid feed from the intact cameras show smoke and flames. Local authorities are on the scene, but we don't have a formal report yet."

Ben ended the comm and then found Raj online.

"Are you all right?"

"Yes. Everyone had gone home for the night. No injuries that I know of, thank god."

"The NOC says it's a fire."

"Hardly."

"But I saw the camera feed. I saw flames."

"Ben, think about it."

"I don't understand."

"We have a halon fire-suppression system."

"But I saw the flames."

"Oh, it's on fire, that's for sure," said Raj. "I retrieved a backup log from Heinrich's data center in the UK. It shows the environmental sensor alarms going off right from the start. But it was two explosions, one at the data center and the other at the satellite dish. Ben, it's not just the data center; the dish is gone too."

"What!"

"The damage is catastrophic. As far as I can tell, the explosions went off simultaneously."

"Simultaneously? Then it was deliberate. But who would do such a thing? Hoods?"

"Impossible to say at this point," said Raj. "But it's someone with access. The halon system was disabled seconds before the explosions."

# CHAPTER 29

CHRIS COULDN'T SLEEP. HE AND LUCKY WOULD BE LEAVING in the morning to go on his search-and-rescue training trip. He had a sense of foreboding. When Hope came to stay with them, he remembered his dad telling her that she'd be safe with them. "We'll make sure of that" were his exact words. After the confrontation with Mr. Avenir, he didn't want to be away from her. In fact, she was all he could think about.

He knew his feelings were common for teenage boys—or teenagers in general—but there was nothing common about Hope. No one else in the world could make him feel this way. *Love? Infatuation?* Infatuation was mostly about physical attraction. There was no question about that. Looking at her— or just picturing her in his mind—created a hunger deep down inside. But not cheap lust. *OK, fine, lust.* But not cheap. Was it just infatuation? Infatuation was sudden, intense, and fleeting. His feelings were intense, but he'd felt this way about her for as long as he could remember, and there certainly didn't seem to be any end in sight. It had to be more than infatuation.

||0 ||0 ||0

*"AHHH!"* HOPE SAT UP IN BED AND REALIZED IT WAS HER OWN scream. She was in the guest room at the Richards home. *Safe. Just another nightmare.* She wiped her forehead.

There was a tap at the door. "Are you all right?" came the whisper from the other side. It was Chris's voice.

"Yes," she whispered back. She got out of bed and went to the door.

As soon as it opened, Lucky pushed through and rubbed his head against her legs, almost knocking her over.

"Sorry, just a bad dream," she said.

Chris didn't come in, but he looked relieved.

She scratched Lucky behind the ears. There was nothing for her to say. She could close the door and go back to bed, but every moment the door stayed open was like oxygen. She didn't want to close it. She wanted the door open forever.

The moonlight, shining through the window, made his eyes look spectacular, filled with compassion. She wanted to rush into his arms and have him hold her. Would he accept her? He was so perfect, and her life was so screwed up. *My dad—the vio-*

*lations*. Did that matter to Chris? His eyes were so inviting. Looking deeply into them, she searched for any shred of judgment. It wasn't just compassion she saw but also outright passion.

She realized then what she was wearing: one of his oversized T-shirts that she'd been using for pajamas. It wasn't revealing, but with without a bra, the T-shirt might as well have been wet. Shame flashed through her mind. She crossed her arms and turned away. Her dad had told her it was because of the way she looked, that she had asked for it, that he couldn't help himself. *It's my fault. I should shut the door.* Her body didn't obey. Chris's very presence seemed to drive away her fears.

"It wasn't your fault," he whispered, behind her.

"What?" she said and stepped to the middle of the room, away from him. *Can he know what I'm thinking?*

"He's to blame. You have nothing to be ashamed of."

She went to the window. The moon was bright. Across the alley, she could see her own house. Deep down, she knew he was right. His very presence seemed to drive away the shame too.

"How could you know that?" she asked, still looking out the window. She didn't get a response. Just silence. She waited.

*Is he still there?*

"Because …"

The whisper was right behind her now. She could feel the warmth of his body. Goose bumps surfaced from the heat, her skin tingling from the back of her scalp and down her spine. She closed her eyes as the word hung in the air, waiting for him to continue.

"Because it was his choice not to love you as a father should."

The words enveloped her, purified her, as if she'd been dipped in cleansing water and then raised high into the air. The shame and guilt were stripped away, discarded like an oily film.

Then she felt his touch, fingertips at the nape of her neck, just behind her ear, gliding down over her shoulder. With her eyes closed, she savored his touch. His hand wandered down her arm, first across the cotton and then crossing to bare skin, caressing as it went, leaving goose bumps in its trail. Then, almost as quickly as it came, the hand was gone, passing across her elbow and away. *More.* There was absolutely nothing in the world she wanted more than his touch at that very moment.

Then she realized she couldn't be more wrong. *The trip!* It was some kind of training thing, right? She didn't know anything about it. She hadn't cared to ask, so self-absorbed. Now she needed to know. Her eyes snapped open, and she spun to face him. "This training. What is it?"

"For the search-and-rescue team. It's sort of a simulation. Lucky and I work as a team."

"Is it safe?"

"Don't worry, I'll be fine. But promise me you'll let Katie and Al look out for you while I'm gone."

"OK," she said. "There's just so much I don't know about you."

"It'll have to wait. It's late, and I need to get some sleep. And I think we should find another place to talk. The two of us alone, late at night, is really testing me." He stepped back.

She wanted to kiss him. She wanted to be kissed. She wanted to be kissed *by him*. She wanted to be kissed by him *now*. She couldn't hide the anticipation.

"Another time. Another place," he whispered, and he walked out.

Lucky pressed his head against her leg and wagged his tail.

"I know," he said to Lucky. "Come on."

And they were gone.

| |0  | |0  | |0

"HOST OF MY GOD'S BROTHER, WHAT REMAINS OF OUR THREAT?" Skotino asked Tyvold.

Tyvold sat against the sanctuary's circular wall, facing him, with the podium for the sacrifice at the center, between them. The sacrifice was yipping relentlessly, pawing and scratching at the corner of the box. Even in the candlelight, Skotino could see toenails pop out through the holes of the box at every scratch, like digging under a fence.

"Host of my god's brother," said Tyvold, "the satellite facility is destroyed. Laura Richards can no longer track us."

"And what of the data file revealing our locations?"

"The copy at the Australia data center was destroyed," said Tyvold. "Two locations remain, one in Britain and one in Philadelphia. Of course, we control the original."

The yipping and scratching continued. Tyvold had fed it the carcass of the previous sacrifice, as the ritual demanded. Usually, the big meal would make the bitch sleepy, but it didn't always work. "And what of the inquiries about our pharmakoi?"

"The searches originated from a point very near the Philadelphia location, domicile of Laura Richards," said Tyvold. "Host of my god's brother, we gather at your call. Pronounce thy condemnation."

Skotino raised his arms into the air.

> *Hear me, god of gods, once one of twelve, now ruler over six*
>
> *Mortal's prophecy perception, in truth, my god's willful tricks*
>
> *In thee, the end of nature's works is known*
>
> *Presently, all judgment is absolved alone*
>
> *O chthonic power, into condemnation's drink, lace thy verdict's spit*
>
> *For the chance of reality's path doth tip*

"The god of gods has ruled," said Skotino. "Death alone is insufficient. We must inflict the six layers of death upon Laura Richards. Before she dies, she must witness the death of her loved ones. But before we kill the loved ones, they must witness the death of *their* loved ones. And before that, their loved ones. We must record each death. Death layered between witness of death. The circle of death extending six layers, each witness of death worse than death itself. Only then can we take her life. Only then will the threat—with its tentacles of interference—be truly dead."

The six responded together, "We hear and obey."

Skotino brought his raised arms together above the box, hands over the plunger, spikes looming. The sacrifice was still scratching ... relentless high-pitched yipping. "The emergence has begun. With fecund fetuses—those with the genetic alignment—we nurture with parahaoma to spawn our demon hordes." Skotino slammed his hands down, the incessant barking finally over, ending in the echo of a final yelp.

# CHAPTER 30

CHRIS LOOKED OUT ACROSS THE CALEXICO VALLEY. AS FAR as the eye could see, debris filled the landscape in every direction, remnants of shanty houses, each little more than a simple lean-to. The entire area was the site of the Great Mexican Emigration following the financial collapse of the US economy. The Mexican government had agreed at the time to accept US emigrants. The Mexicans had constructed a temporary camp in Calexico to handle the processing of persons for entry into Mexico at Mexicali.

Unfortunately, news spread. Too many US citizens—in a state of severe desperation—made the trek to Southern California. Nearly half a million people had converged on the camp and quickly overwhelmed the accommodations that had been planned for a mere sixty thousand.

Chris recalled the lesson from history class describing the catastrophe that followed. The Coachella Canal was the only freshwater source in the area, and a cholera epidemic quickly developed. Mexican authorities had constructed many structures in the camp for housing, dining, and medical treatment, but panic swelled, and the emigrants-to-be looted and ravaged the facilities. Masses fought. When the chaos ended, all that remained was a holocaust-like wasteland.

The Mexican government had no choice but to close the border. It took months for the United Nations to organize a relief effort to air-drop food and clean water. Survivors constructed shanty houses from material stripped from the buildings, anything that provided protection from the blistering sun and heat. By the time the UN was able to safely enter, two hundred thousand people perished. Thousands of individuals remained unaccounted for, their bodies lost in the broken structures and rubble. There was never adequate funding to clean up the site.

Mr. Cohen had explained that the search-and-rescue training was held at the Calexico site to simulate a real disaster. Volunteers, posing as disaster survivors, entered the area each day and hid. The crumbling buildings and residue from the human squalor provided a very challenging environment for the dogs' noses. But Lucky had proven to be exceptional. Mr. Cohen couldn't get over how well Lucky was doing. Chris had to agree. It was as if Lucky could find people by sensing their need for help even before picking up their scent.

On his percomm, he examined a map of the area. Based on Lucky's body posture—sniffing along the ground in a consistent direction—he was zeroing in on something. The terrain was rough, mostly rock and dry brush. Lucky was heading for the warehouses originally built to receive supplies. Long stretches of corrugated metal buildings bordered fields of intermodal shipping containers, the kind hauled by tractor trailers and cargo ships.

Chris kept to the top of the surrounding ridge as he followed. The offices had been built into the ridge and overlooked the cargo receiving area. Stepping onto the rusted metal roof of the first building and looking for a path down, he heard the sound of sand and dirt raining down in the room below.

He was halfway across when *snap*. Falling, he flailed his arms for purchase, but the corrugated metal roof crumbled like crackers at each grasp. The structure creaked and boomed as support beams separated from the ridge. He'd fallen through two floors before scraping to a halt. The violent shifting finally subsided.

He was pinned. Dust poured in rivulets from some black location above, filling the air with a choking powder. He kept his eyes shut as chunks of debris rattled down. Cascading sand sprinkled over his forehead and face. He struggled to breathe, testing the air with staccato sniffs and then coughing.

His left arm and leg were trapped in a pile of cinder blocks underneath him. He wasn't quite lying down, but he wasn't fully upright, either. Something sharp—glass, metal, jagged wood?—stabbed at his left side where it supported his weight. He tried to move, but pain shot through his left leg.

Just then, his mind filled with an image. The perspective was from only a few feet above the ground. He saw the other members of his rescue team and heard barking. *Lucky!* From the image in his mind, he saw his team members leaning over, looking right at him, saying, "What's the matter, boy? Where's Chris?"

The image faded.

*Good. Lucky will bring them. But how could I know that? How is that possible? If only I could reach my percomm.*

Searing pain shot through his body along his left side. The building shifted again. Sand began to fill around his neck. The pain was unbearable.

Then he felt a familiar sensation: he wasn't alone. *The warden.* Forgetting about the dust, he instinctively opened his eyes. Strangely, the sand wasn't falling on his face now. Dust swirled in miniature tempests all around him but not on him. He could even breathe. Then he felt a tremor around his trapped leg and arm. The vibration intensified until the gripping pressure cracked away. His body jerked up, free. The pain was too much; he blacked out.

||0  ||0  ||0

"DID YOU SEND YOUR MOM ANY PICTURES OF YOUR NEW OUTFITS?" Laura asked on the drive to the women's shelter.

"No," said Hope, completely engrossed in whatever was on her percomm.

The pertran exited the freeway; the shelter must be close. Laura peered out the window. Several shops on the corner were boarded up.

"When can she return home?" Laura peered out the other side.

"They said anytime. She doesn't seem ready yet." *Tap, tap, swipe, tap.*

"Is she comfortable there?"

"I guess." *Swipe, swipe.*

*What an infuriating habit! What's so important you can't even look up? Thank god I raised Chris better. Two can play that game.* Laura reviewed her own messages. *Ugh.* A message from Ben saying he needed to stay at the university even longer. *Someone else can worry about the explosion. We have our own emergency! His attention should be on Chris and getting him back home.*

"Arriving at destination." The pertran pulled to the curb.

The shelter had a security entrance and iron bars over the first-floor windows. Hope was looking at the front entrance but hadn't gotten out.

"You'll be fine." Laura took another hard look at the neighborhood.

"I need to ask you something," said Hope, turning.

"Of course. Anything."

"If Chris is OK, why can't he come home tomorrow with the rest of the group?"

"Well, the doctors want to do more tests."

"That makes no sense. And when I ask him, he won't explain."

"You're right. I don't know what to tell you. Maybe I'll know more when I pick you up in a few hours." Laura gave her the most genuine smile she could manage.

Hope looked down, nodded, and tapped the door button.

Watching her walk up the path, Laura wondered why Hope hadn't worn one of her new outfits to show Sue. *Maybe she only wore them for Chris.* As soon as he'd left, she'd gone back to her old style.

Laura waited until Hope was safely in the building and then set the destination for home.

"Can't someone else handle things?" she asked Ben when he picked up. "I need you. I can't handle all this alone."

"No. There's no telling how long it will take," he said. "What's the latest?"

"The hospital in California contacted Dr. Williams. He told them to give up on getting a scanner to work. They're going to run the tests through a lab. It could take weeks, Ben! Williams tried his best, but they won't release him. Ben, what if—"

The pertran stopped at a traffic light to the freeway entrance. Two men on the corner glared at Laura; one had his hands jammed in his front pockets. She pressed the door-lock button repeatedly, ignoring the chime that said the doors we already locked. The traffic light turned green. The one man kept his eyes on her even as the pertran sped away.

"Ben, what if he has internal bleeding or something? You need to go get him."

There was only silence. She tapped the button to put him on vid. He was wearing the same clothes he'd been wearing the day they got news of the incident in Australia. It looked as if he hadn't slept since. She could almost see the wheels turning in his head. "You need to go get him. *Now!*"

He wiped his mouth and stubbly chin, making a sandpaper sound. "I've got an idea."

"An *idea*? Enough with the *facts*, *ideas*, and *information*! You said Cohen would keep him safe! I'm stuck here taking care of the girlfriend. I've a mind to tell her it's a shelter, not a spa."

"What? You said she could stay as long as she needed."

"That was before."

"Before what?"

"Never mind. She's asking about Chris. She's not stupid. I can't keep putting her off. You need to go get our son!"

"Hold on now. Listen. I have several scanners in the basement lab. They're kind of old—from the testing when he was little—but otherwise fine. I can modify one to send the scan data to my computers and then transmit the computed results. They won't know the difference. We can have Dr. Williams send the scanner to California. Just a few hours by scramjet."

"When? *When* are you going to do all this?" She saw her own image in the corner of the screen. The woman in the image looked hysterical, but she didn't care. "You're *busy*!"

"I know, I know. I'm sorry. Let me think."

Think? *How about* feel? *Chris is so far away. Am I the only one who can feel or care about anything?*

"Katie can do it," said Ben finally.

"Are you kidding me? Our son's life is at stake, and you're going to let Katie handle it?"

"No. I mean, yes. I mean, I'll write myself a reminder to comm Katie. Sorry, I have to get back to work. Try to relax."

# Chapter 31

"I'M FINE. I'M FINE," CHRIS INSISTED. "MOM, YOU CAN LET GO now."

Laura held him tightly. Her head only came up to his chest, he was so tall. She kept both arms wrapped around him. At that moment, she felt certain she'd never let him out of her sight again. Ben had gone to get Chris from the airport once they received word that the modified scanner had worked. The wait with Chris's friends had seemed an eternity. *He's home now.*

"Really, Mom. I'm fine." Chris started to pry her arms away, so she let him.

"Yes, yes, that's enough," said Ben. "Everyone, sit down. Chris, we all want to hear what happened."

Laura gave him one last rub on the arm before going into the living room.

Chris sat down, and Lucky plopped himself down under his feet. Katie and Hope sat on the love seat. Al sat on the floor next to Lucky. Lucky rolled over and opened up like a Fifth Avenue flasher. Obliging, Al started scratching his chest.

"Laura," said Ben. "You too." He patted the spot on the couch next to him.

She joined him but couldn't stop glowing. "Katie, thank you so much for fiddling with the scanner thing."

"It was easy," said Katie. "The scanner's really just a portable computer. Like a big percomm."

"Yeah," said Chris. "Thanks. I didn't think I was ever going to get out of there. I kept telling them I was fine, but they wouldn't believe me."

Laura took Ben's hand into both of hers. "And you are my man of action. Your brilliance saved the day—and our son."

"Whoa, Mrs. Richards," said Al. "The sappy meter just blew a gasket. OK, Chris, get on with it. What happened?"

"You heard it all already. Lucky was tracking a scent. We worked our way over to some buildings by the depot. The building collapsed. They rescued me. And here I am."

Nobody said a thing. He was selling, but no one was buying. Laura looked at the polite but mystified expression on Hope's face.

"Uh, Chris?" said Laura. "We need to talk about what happened to you. I mean, what *really* happened to you? Have you shared your, uh, *condition* with Hope?"

"No," said Chris sheepishly. "You know … what am I supposed to say?"

"It's part of you, buddy," said Laura.

"Condition?" asked Hope.

"I know it's hard to believe," said Chris after explaining everything. "It claims to be an alien from outer space and calls itself a warden—*the warden* or just *warden*." He shrugged. "Little kids talk about having an invisible friend, but mine's for real. I know I've been slow to open up. I just didn't know how to explain it. Maybe I never will. In fact, it's fine if you don't believe me."

"No, I believe you," said Hope without reservation. "You probably think I'm just saying that, but as long as we're making confessions, I have one of my own." She looked around the room. "Thank you all for being so open with me and taking care of me. Coming here has been the best thing to ever happen to me. I've never felt safer or more welcome." She paused. "But I need to be completely open with you. I've been monitoring your communications."

Everyone exchanged glances.

"I'm sorry. I know it's not right. Over the years, I picked up fragments here and there. You kept talking about a presence. It didn't make any sense. Until now. So, yes, I believe it. Somehow, it's easy for me to believe it."

"I don't understand," said Ben. "How could you possibly? The security—"

"The security is crap," said Hope. "And the false sense of security it creates makes it even worse than crap." Her tone was forceful and confident. "With all due respect, Mr. Richards, the security systems used by the university, the government, and the military can be easily hacked."

"And this is something you're capable of doing?" asked Ben.

"So now it's my turn to convince all of you," she said. "I guess—I guess I had a lot of time on my hands growing up. Practice makes perfect, right?" She managed an awkward smile. "I don't want to keep secrets."

Chris nodded.

"OK," said Ben. "Let's get it all out on the table. Chris, tell everyone what you told me on the way home from the airport. Tell the story. What happened? What *really* happened?"

"Now we're getting somewhere!" said Al.

"Well, after the roof collapsed, I couldn't move. The pain was horrible, but it made a connection to the warden. You know, sometimes I get a vague sense, but this was really strong, like never before. Somehow the connection extended to Lucky. I was able to see through Lucky's eyes." Chris reached down and scratched Lucky's ear. "I could see out his eyes, and I could hear what he was hearing."

"How did you get out of the collapsed building?" asked Laura.

"That's the part I don't know. I think I passed out from the pain. But just before that, the air around me was swirling. The rocks, dirt, and sand were roiling about, but I didn't feel it against my skin. It got stronger, and the air acted like a cushion. Then the outside started shaking, like a jackhammer, until my leg broke free. The last thing I remember—this is going to sound crazy—I think I was flying. Or at least floating up. Maybe it was a hallucination. Anyway, the next thing I knew, I was surrounded by paramedics. They said they found me lying about thirty feet from the point where I fell through."

"Weren't you hurt? How's your leg?" Laura asked.

"Bruised and scraped, but otherwise, I'm fine."

"Can't you use the chamber thing to talk to … the warden … and ask it what's going on?" asked Hope.

"Yes, after all that's happened, we should plan to spend more time in the lab," said Ben.

"You know, Mr. Richards," said Al, "Chris has to drop everything to go down there. It takes for-ever to set up. It's a pain in the neck. I was thinking, now that we have the medical scanner sending data to your computer, can't we show the results of the mind-reader program on the scanner too?"

"Of course!" said Katie. "That's a great idea. I can reprogram the system to transmit the text from the mind-reader program back to the scanner's display." Katie bolted out of the chair.

The kids jumped up and dashed after her. Lucky barked and chased too.

Laura heard them crashing down the flights of stairs to the lab.

"Something else we need to do," said Ben.

"What?"

"Remember we said we were going to visit Father Arnold?"

"Yeah."

"That seemed to really resonate with Chris—the warden too. I'll get that scheduled."

Laura hugged him. "You are my man of action. I love you."

||0 ||0 ||0

"CHRIS, ARE YOU SURE YOU'RE WELL ENOUGH TO COME TO PRACtice?" asked Mr. Cohen.

"Sure. The doctor forwarded the exam results to you, right? I passed with flying colors. All systems go."

"Well, the fact that there's no evidence of head injury is the important thing. Honestly, I didn't think your mom was ever going to forgive me."

"Yeah, I heard she was pretty cranked there for a few days. But I'm home now. She forgives you. I'm fine. She let me come to practice, right?"

"Still, I want you to take it easy. Just work on blocking. Don't push it. Katie, you work with him."

"Yes, sir, Master Cohen," said Katie.

"Great," said Chris flatly. "I wonder how long *this* is going to last?"

"Oh, don't pout, you big baby. And stop thinking about yourself all the time. Al gets to be in our regular class today, but I have to babysit you. Come on, this is always good practice—for any of us."

"Fine," he said, unconvinced.

They bowed before stepping onto the mat and then bowed to each other at the center of the practice ring and took the ready position. Katie began with some easy fist strikes as they warmed up. Chris matched her rhythm with fluid blocks. Still frustrated, he wasn't sure this practice was *always* good, more like a waste of time. Practicing with Katie was predictable. She would get faster and faster until he couldn't block anymore. She'd get a few taps on him and then lecture him about how to improve, as if she could simply *teach* him to be faster.

She picked up the pace and began to mix in a few kicks.

Chris kept up mechanically and prepared for the eventual humiliation. He remembered Hope's words about practice makes perfect. He'd been eating Katie's dust his whole life. She was always faster. If it was possible to *learn* to be faster just by practicing, he would've done it a long time ago.

The blows came more quickly. At this speed, she would usually find an opening if she had the right combination.

He tried his best to concentrate and keep his mind from wandering, already wishing it was over.

She began to use more of the mat and increased the travel distance between strikes to try to catch him off balance.

He managed to fend her off.

She seemed satisfied that he was in good shape. That's when she came at him with one of her signature wheel kicks. Spinning on one leg, her foot sailed up and around, aiming to tap him on the ear.

Instead of blocking the kick, his hand met her foot as it whipped around toward his head, and he pushed it faster still, sending her flying through the air.

Sitting on the mat, she scowled at him. No one ever blocked that kick. She used it regularly during sparring to remind everyone who was boss. She was probably just going easy on him. But from the look on her face, not anymore.

In a flash, she was back up and on him, throwing a flurry of strikes.

He backed away, blocking each thrust. It was almost if he could see where her next strike would land even before she threw it. He kept up easily. In the pummeling blur, he started to work in his own strikes. She countered. He pressed. Giving ground, she backed up until she was at the edge of the painted ring on the mat. He saw several openings then, as if she were moving in slow motion. He went with a combination: two to the chest and one to the chin, scoring a tap with all three. The force was light, just enough to demonstrate intention, but it knocked her off her feet. She fell back on her butt.

Panting, she said, "What was *that*?"

He smiled. "I don't know. It's like my limbs were being propelled through the air—or pulled—or pulled and pushed at the same time. I don't know."

"Wow."

||0  ||0  ||0

"SO HOW CAN I HELP?" ASKED FATHER ARNOLD.

Laura, Ben, and Chris and Lucky had dropped Hope off at the women's shelter for a visit before continuing to the church. Katie and Al had stayed back at the basement lab to prepare the mind-reader program.

At the church, Ben had turned on his per-comm's room speaker so Katie and Al could listen while Chris told the story about the warden. Just like Hope, Father Arnold's acceptance of Chris's tale seemed uncanny.

"We're not exactly sure," said Ben. "Chris is able to let us know if we're on track with our interpretations of the warden's answers, but there are entire areas of questions we can't get answers to. Chris thinks you can help." Ben held up the portable scanner. "We can use this to see the responses from the warden."

"Of course," said Father Arnold. "What questions?"

"Well, we want to know what it is and why it's here, but it keeps repeating the phrase *feral emergent urgency*. We don't know what to make of it."

Father Arnold thought for a moment. "I'm sorry. I can't think of anything. That doesn't make any sense to me, either."

"Mom, ask Father Arnold about the conversation from when I was a baby."

Laura nodded. "Father, you asked me years ago, around the time Chris was born, to think about how my life had been up to that point. You said, at some point in the future, I should compare it to my life after living with Chris. Do you remember?"

"Yes, of course. You came to me asking about what it meant to be a godparent. I knew caring for

Chris would answer all your questions, and I wanted to cement the memories for when you were ready."

Chris had that faraway look. He seemed to be trying to sense the warden's reactions.

Laura looked back to Father Arnold. "Well, I guess I'm ready now."

"OK. Looking back on your life then and comparing it to now, what's different?"

"Well …" *Everything's different. But also perfectly average.* "Well …" *What stands out? What's special?* "Ah! All this pressure. I've been thinking about this question the whole ride over here, and only the obvious stuff comes to mind. I don't know what to say. I feel like you all expect me to have a magic answer, but I don't."

"Try expressing the obvious stuff," suggested Father Arnold.

"Well, it's been wonderful to have Chris, of course. What more can I say? I think my life has been much better since he entered our world. I think our life *together* has been better." She pulled Ben's hand to hers, interlocked her fingers with his, and squeezed. "Ben too, I mean." She felt him squeeze back. "The three of us. I think our life has been fuller because of Chris. I love Ben—and I did before Chris arrived, certainly—but there's something about the vulnerability of a child that brings people together. It made me realize how much I need Ben and he needs me. Our marriage was a partnership, but it was only after Chris arrived that we truly became partners."

Her mind, no longer blank, flitted from memory to memory of Chris as a child, the arguments with Ben over silly things and then making up. "There's something special about when the person you love is dependent on your care. I mean *care* in the biggest sense of the word, not just changing a diaper or saving for college expenses. I think everyone needs someone to love in that way, to need and be needed. If you can't have kids, then adopt. If you can't adopt, get a pet. If you can't afford a pet, love somebody else's kid."

Laura stopped there just to experience the feelings she had. It felt wonderful to express them. No one said a word. They were all being so respectful to hear her out. The sheer peace of the moment soaked in. She let the feelings—

"Nothing on the screen here," said Al. "But the sappy meter blew another gasket." Sounds of a scuffle came over the speaker. "I'm not an idiot—am not—stop hitting me."

"Enough, you two," said Ben. He tilted the display of the scanner so they all could see. It continued to repeat *Feral Emergent Urgency*. "Keep going."

"What's different about the love when the other person needs you?" Father Arnold asked. "You can love many people, right? What's different?"

"No, I think a special bond is created when the mutual need exists. It can take time for that to develop, for example, in an adult relationship. But then sometimes it's immediate, like when a newborn is dropped on your doorstep."

"What is it that changes? When does love become that more intense kind? How is it different?"

"I guess when it's unconditional."

"That's it!" yelled Chris.

The scanner flashed with a string of phrases: *Paleolithic Revolution Saoshyant Übermensch Parthenogenesis Speculum Naturale Pantheism Dextral Beltane Suda Feral Emergence Urgent Advaita Galactic Malt Psychopomp Genocide Frashokereti Parthenos Samhain Trinity Aka Mainyu Dirac.*

"You seeing what we're seeing?" asked Al.

"Yes," said Ben. "Chris, we've seen some of these words before, but some of them are new."

Chris was looking off into space.

"Chris, what are you sensing?" asked Laura.

"The Paleolithic Revolution thing," said Chris. "When humans stopped acting like apes, it was more than that. It was the point when human beings became capable of unconditional love." He paused and then added, "To love is a choice."

Laura waited for more, it sounded like he would continue.

Chris seemed to reflect, and then his expression changed, like he'd had an epiphany, but not a pleasant one—more like a horrible nightmare. He looked right at her. "There are others here."

| | 0 | | 0 | | 0

BIG VEGA SAT IN THE BEDROOM OF DR. HEINRICH MILLER'S COUNTY Durham cottage. The place was in shambles. Miller and his wife hadn't put up much of a fight, but Vega had enjoyed chasing them through the halls. Not that they were hard to catch; it was just part of the fun. The cottage was strewn with overturned furniture and smashed belongings. Miller's wife had to go first, of course. Her death was slow, and Vega had made Miller watch, recording it all the while—the first layer of death. Presently, Miller's wife lay dead, her usefulness exhausted. It was down to Miller himself now, naked, facedown on his own bed. *Separate beds? What a pitiful life.*

Vega had used nylon ties to secure Miller's arms and legs to the bedposts. Next, he'd ripped a long section of molding from the wall and then snapped off one end, creating a jagged edge. He'd positioned the blunt end of the long wooden board in the corner of the ceiling where it met the wall and put the sharp end on Miller's back. Then he'd positioned the bed—and Miller's body—close to the wall, creating a large isosceles triangle. He'd pushed the bed toward the wall, letting the point of the plank dig into the skin covering Miller's spine, precisely between two vertebrae.

Now, Vega sat directly in front of Miller. Waiting. Holding his percomm. Waiting for the signal from Spire. *Nothing worse than waiting.*

Vega put his foot on the edge of the bed and pressed. The bed creaked forward a fraction, and the board trembled under the pressure.

Miller screamed in agony.

Vega glanced at his percomm. Still nothing. Spire was good at waiting; it took him forever to do anything. Skotino always said Spire was painstaking. *I say he's lazy. How long does it take to plant a bomb?* More waiting. *Skotino and his damn sense of timing.*

Vega pressed on the bed frame again. Miller screamed, and his body shuddered. The old man's flesh had bunched and torn where the board made contact.

The percomm vibrated. *Finally!* Spire had successfully detonated the incendiary explosives at England's research center. Another data-storage location gone. Only one data center remained that held the file that showed the whereabouts of the Circle of Six. So now the fun resumes—another layer of death.

Vega activated the vid function on his percomm, propped it up in front of Miller, and tapped the record button.

The old guy was exhausted.

*Pathetic.* Vega pressed on the edge of the bed. "All right, just like we rehearsed it. And don't worry, I'll get your good side."

Miller hesitated.

Initially, the old geezer had tried to be tough and refused to say the words Vega had told him to recite. So Vega had made him practice. Over and over again. Miller had begged for mercy, for Vega to finish him, blubbering all the while.

On the first practice run, Miller had tried to blurt out a hasty description of Vega—thinking the practice recording was live. Such a brave attempt to get information out about his attacker—to avenge his wife's death. *Or some bullshit like that.* Vega had roared with laughter. *Scientist! Ha! Tyvold says this guy designs satellites. The old geezer's a rocket scientist. Spire calls me a dumbass, but I'm smarter than a rocket scientist. Now, it's time for the final performance, or more importantly, the closing curtain.* Vega pushed again. "Now! Say the words!"

Miller had no choice; the words poured out.

*Now for the really fun part. Skotino wants the message to be convincing.*

Vega pressed the bed to the wall with finality.

Miller shrieked. The board buckled, the sharp edge digging into his back. The board quivered and suddenly straightened as the tip sliced into the spine.

Vega let the percomm capture the final moments—the perfect message for the troublemaker lady in Philly, each layer of death coming closer and closer to home. Literally.

An astonished smile appeared on Miller's face. Still very much alive, he seemed to be reconciling this apparent miracle.

*What? The board must have cut the spinal cord.*

Miller kept smiling. He took a deep breath. The pain seemed to be completely gone.

"Oh, hell," said Vega, standing. He put his hand on the back of Miller's head and shoved the old man's face into the mattress. So comical the way his arms flailed around, but not his legs—nothing moved below the cut in the spinal cord.

It didn't last long. When it was all over, Vega stopped the recording and sat down to watch it from the beginning. *It needs a little editing.*

"THERE ARE OTHERS? YOU MEAN, OTHERS LIKE THE WARDEN?" asked Ben.

"Yes," said Chris, still in his faraway voice. "But not exactly the same. They choose, no—I mean, they *chose* not to love. Or maybe they can't. They're feral, returned to the wild. They ..." Chris seemed to struggle to maintain the connection.

"What's the matter?" asked Laura.

"I can't tell if they lost the capacity. Or choose not to—I can't quite—" He became agitated.

"It's OK. It's OK," said Ben. "Think about something else. Uh, how many others?"

Chris relaxed and thought a moment. "Sorry, I don't know that."

"Mr. Richards, look at the scanner!" said Katie over the comm.

"Oh, right," said Ben apologetically. "When I ask an analytical question, I need to look at the text translation."

The display showed *1+6*.

"One plus six," said Ben. "I guess that's seven, but why is it displayed as one plus six?"

"We have to stop them," Chris said flatly.

"Stop them? From doing what?" asked Laura.

There was a long silence. Chris was looking off into space again. "The warden used the word *genocide*, right?"

"Yes," said Ben.

Everyone waited for Chris to say more, but he just had that glazed look.

"What does the word *malt* mean?" asked Father Arnold.

"We're not sure of that one, either," said Ben. "The terms *Malt* or *Galactic Malt* appear when we analyze the movement of air around his skin. The effect is strong enough to amplify his movements. Air molecules are swept from one side of a limb, leaving a vacuum, and then pushed to the opposite side, producing high pressure. His movements have surprising speed and force."

"The screen!" said Katie.

Ben read the phrase out loud. "It says *Galactose Maltose*."

"Those are sugars," said Katie. "Galactose is the sugar in milk, and maltose comes from grain that starts to germinate."

"Yes!" yelled Chris.

Father Arnold jumped at the intensity of Chris's response.

"Interesting," said Ben. "Uh, I guess we should pick some up on the way home."

Chris seemed to snap out of the trance. "From a store? What would we do with it?"

"For starters," said Ben, "I think you should eat it."

"Yes!" he yelled again, like a marionette on a string. He shook his head and seemed frustrated by his own answer. "Argh."

Father Arnold leaned over to Ben. "You know, I was prepared to accept all of this on faith, but I have to say, it's quite disturbing when he does that."

"Yeah, I haven't seen him so connected like this before."

"Eat it?" asked Chris, ignoring their side conversation. "I don't want to eat germinated grain."

"I don't think you have to. Galactose and maltose are sugars, like Katie said. Galactose is milk sugar, but maltose is harder to find. I think you can still buy it, but not with food credits." Laura noticed Ben was getting authoritative, like when he dished out wisdom either at home or while lecturing in front of his grad students. "Chris, the financial collapse was triggered by the health-care crisis—the result of widespread obesity during the early part of the century. The government banned high-calorie foods containing scant nutrition. Malt is another name for a milk shake prepared by mixing ice cream with malt powder. I remember as a kid, we used to eat foods like that all the time. We added malt to ice cream—it was like adding sugar to sugar. No wonder everyone got fat. Anyway, I think you can still buy malted milk powder. It contains both sugars."

Chris just looked down in silence and nodded.

"Is that right, Chris? Eating it?" asked Laura.

"Yes, that's right. The pain I felt in the Calexico accident allowed a connection to the warden. The warden was able to direct the air around my body and get me out. The galactose and maltose will create the connection too, without the pain." Chris looked up and smiled. "It's clear to me now."

Ben's percomm jingled. "Sorry, it must be urgent to get through." He looked at the message and then went completely white.

"What is it?" asked Laura.

"I have to get to the office."

"What is it?" she repeated.

"There's been another explosion."

| | 0 | | 0 | | 0

BEN WAVED GOOD-BYE TO LAURA AND CHRIS AS THE TRAN PULLED
away from the front drive of his university office
building. He passed through the checkpoint at the
main entrance and then headed down the hall to the
high-security wing of the building. He placed his
percomm against the panel and leaned to the side for
the retina scan.

The door swished open. "Afternoon," said the
janitor, who seemed to be waiting on the other side,
and he pushed past Ben.

"Oh yes, good afternoon." *What is he doing here
at this time of day?* "Hey, is everything all right?"
Ben called out.

The janitor didn't look back as he hurried away.

Once inside his office, Ben checked on the status
of his good friend and colleague Heinrich Miller. *Still
unaccounted for.* Then he read through the reports
coming in.

The authorities believed the UK explosion was
no accident—but echoing the incident in Australia,
there was a shocking lack of physical evidence. No
ruling of criminal involvement or terrorist influence
had been made—the investigation was completely
mired in chaotic bids for control and accusations of

jurisdictional overreach. After decades of terrorist attacks, it was inconceivable that events like these could transpire without an organized government response. The British and American governments had taken the unusual step of limiting the distribution of information, blocking any possible coordination between agencies.

Ben found Raj online and contacted him via vid-comm. "Thanks for letting me know, Raj. Have you heard from Heinrich?"

"No. The records indicate he left the building long before the explosion, but it's very concerning that he doesn't answer."

"Our government isn't going to do anything but lock down communications," Ben said. "The facility manager here has reduced the staff to essential personnel only. People are dropping everything and leaving. Hopefully that will save lives if they strike here."

"That sounds like a very intelligent thing to do," said Raj. "So why are you still there?"

"I know. I know. Just a quick question for you. Did you save the satellite image from the last calibration cycle?"

"I assume so. But don't worry about that now; all the data is backed up at TerraStore. You can access it from your lab at home. You need to get out of there."

"OK, OK, I'm leaving." He ended the comm, accessed the directory containing the satellite data, and scrolled through the files. *Where is it?*

"Evacuation procedure initiated," said the computer voice from the seccomm panel. "Please proceed calmly to the nearest exit."

The evacuation program would begin cutting power to the office systems one by one. He scrolled frantically. *It's not here!*

The shrill sound of the evacuation alarm blasted the office space. He covered his ears involuntarily but then forced his hands back to the keyboard. *Where is it?* Page after page of query results flashed across the screen.

The sound was too much. He put his hands over his ears again. It was impossible to concentrate. The sound was so loud it almost hurt.

*They said they would save it!*

Then he remembered. He switched to the directory of discarded files. *There it is!*

He opened the file and calculated the locations of the flares. A picture of the earth appeared, and he dragged his finger, rotating the model. Just as he feared, two flares were in the vicinity of the County Durham research park.

His office lights went dark as the blaring alarm continued, and then the emergency lights kicked in from a box on the wall. His computer terminal would go next.

He flicked his finger across the screen, rotating the globe to North America and then zoomed in on the East Coast. He was relieved to see only one flare. That would be Chris, or more precisely, the warden.

"Please proceed calmly to the nearest exit."

He rotated and zoomed to the southwest and saw several flares around the Nevada-Arizona border.

*Others. Where are you now?* The data was old; they could be anywhere.

The screen want dark along with every other device in his office. He ran for the door, hustled through the darkened hallways illuminated by emergency lights until he reached the lobby, and then exited through the security checkpoint. Looking back, he realized he must have been one of the last people out; he hadn't seen anyone along the way, and the grounds looked deserted. The alarm was still going off. *Where is everyone?*

He headed for the transit area. On his percomm, he requested a pubtran. The display said the taxi would arrive in six minutes.

Checking for messages, he noticed one from a sender he didn't recognize. When he opened it, a vid started playing automatically.

IIO IIO IIO

"DID YOU FIND SOME?" ASKED AL.

Laura set the grocery sack on the kitchen counter. Chris and Hope followed her into the kitchen. Al rummaged through the sack and pulled out the canister.

Katie yanked the canister out of his hand and examined the label. "Yup, this oughta do it."

"What about the explosion?" asked Al.

"We dropped my dad off at the university," said Chris. "It's all top secret." He sat down at the kitchen table. He looked tired.

"Not top secret, actually." Hope sat down across from Chris. "Just LIMDIS—meaning limited distribution. The only reason your dad can see it is because of his military-grade credentials."

"Yes, well, in any case," said Laura, "days passed before Chris's dad learned what happened in Australia. There's no telling how long he'll be there."

Al yanked the canister back from Katie. "Let's give this a try!"

"No, I think we should wait for Ben," said Laura. "It's getting late. I'm sure your parents are expecting you for dinner."

Katie pulled the canister away from him and set it on the counter. "Yeah, come on, Al. We should be getting home."

"Aw. Can't we—"

Katie pulled him by the arm. "Come on. You can walk me home."

Laura waited until they were out the door. "Chris, do you just want to go to bed?"

He shook his head. "Maybe Dad will find out sooner this time since they know what to look for."

"Maybe." She put away the sack and sat down between them. "I'll see if I have new messages." She tapped the pubcomm display in the table's surface. "Nothing."

"Do you want to watch a program?" asked Hope. "I'll even try one of those karate vids."

Chris shrugged. "Maybe later."

"How's your mom doing?" Laura asked.

"Pretty good," said Hope. "There's still a lot to get worked out, but she might be ready to come home. My dad is locked out of the house for good. He's still being held for violating the restraining order."

Chris didn't seem to be listening.

"Oh, maybe you'll like this," said Laura after a new message popped up. "It's a newsletter from a student group at the university. It has some pretty edgy political views."

"Edgy?" asked Hope.

"Yeah, controversial. It even gets stopped by the message filter," said Laura, trying to build intrigue.

Hope leaned over. "This one didn't."

"Oh. Ben must've fixed it."

"It sounds very interesting," said Hope, helping to encourage Chris.

He still wasn't interested.

"It has a cartoon you might like," said Laura. "Ever heard of *Poge and Loyd*? Here, let me show you." She tapped the screen to open the message.

"Fine," said Chris. He leaned over too.

What appeared on screen was not the newsletter. Instead, a jerky vid began to play.

"Oh my god." In the image, Laura recognized Ben's colleague Heinrich Miller.

"What *is* this?" Chris asked.

Hope leaned in closer.

"Hey, scientist lady. Think you're pretty smart, huh? Trolling around the network? Looking at other people's stuff?" It was Heinrich saying the words, but in a monotone, his voice trembling and weak. Laura could hardly believe the look on his face. The entire scene was helter-skelter. "You're going to die for your snooping," said Heinrich, the words coming out flat, like a kindergarten play.

"This is horrible," said Laura, reaching to stop it.

"Don't!" said Hope. She pulled out her percomm and started recording it.

"Keep going," demanded a voice from off camera. They heard a creak.

Heinrich winced. "But before you die, your loved ones will die, and you will witness. But before they die, their friends will die, and they will witness. And before their friends die, their loved ones will die, and they will witness. Like my beloved, Connie." Heinrich choked on his own words. Another creak. He cried out. "Witness your six layers of death."

"Reality's chance doth tip." Heinrich and Chris spoke the words in unison.

Laura screamed.

Chris's eyes were glazed over.

A loud scraping noise came from the vid, wood against wood. Laura couldn't watch. The sound alone made her sick. "Enough!" she cried. "Chris, snap out of it!"

||0 ||0 ||0

AS THE COMPUTER-CONTROLLED PUBTRAN PULLED TO THE CURB, Ben was still stunned after watching the hideous recording on his percomm. *Could it be real? Is Heinrich really dead? He said "scientist lady." Political science? That could only mean Laura.*

*Boom!*

The shock wave of the blast slapped against the back of his shirt. Clouds of smoke billowed from above the trees in the direction of his office building.

Ben jumped into the pubtran and rattled off his home address.

"I'm sorry," said the navigation computer, "please repeat your destination. Please speak clearly and enunciate."

Another boom rocked the pubtran. Enormous balls of flame swelled inside clouds of smoke mushrooming into the sky. Debris hit the sidewalk and the vehicle like tiny meteorites.

Keeping his voice under control, he repeated the address.

Once the pubtran pulled from the curb, he commed Laura. "Are you all right? I got the most terrifying message. Then my office blew up. I think it's—"

"I know. We saw the vid. Ben, it's Chris!"

"What?"

"I can't describe it—and Hope says not to say anything specific over the comm. Please, Ben, just come home!"

# CHAPTER 32

LAURA THREW HER ARMS AROUND BEN THE MINUTE HE stepped in the back door.

"What's wrong with Chris?" he asked.

"Nothing, at the moment. But I was so scared." She pulled him into the kitchen.

Hope was still working at the pubcomm with Chris watching over her shoulder.

"I didn't mean to scare anyone," said Chris. "It was just the warden telling us about the others. It's all connected somehow."

"We have to comm the police," said Laura. She waited for them to agree, but Ben and Chris were looking at Hope typing away at the pubcomm.

"Hmm," said Ben. "I bet Hope is going to tell us that's a bad idea."

"Just one sec," said Hope, typing until a final tap on the Enter key before looking up. "Yeah, our communications are being monitored. I'll need more time before I can fix that, but for now, I have a way to secure our comms on a case-by-case basis. You have to tell me before any comm so I can set it up. I mean *any* kind—voice, vid, or text."

"Good. So we can comm the police?"

Again, nobody agreed.

Ben walked around the kitchen table and sat down across from Hope. He cocked his head. "Now I bet you're going to tell us that your magical comm trick doesn't change anything—that we still shouldn't comm the police."

"Right. I don't think it will do any good," said Hope. "Mr. Richards, you said your office exploded?"

"Yes, they evacuated the building. I was lucky to get out in time."

"And they were already on alert for a bomb threat. Notice anything odd?"

"That's it! That's what was so strange. The place was deserted when I came out. No bomb squad, no fire engines, nothing."

"Yup. I've been monitoring the response from the authorities. Everything's messed up. From what I can tell, each agency thinks another agency is handling it."

"But who could do that?" asked Ben.

"I'm tracing it back. I'll need more time. I have to make sure I'm not detected."

"What about the awful message? The vid? Heinrich?" said Laura. "He said you were snooping around, Ben. They tried to kill you."

"No," said Ben. "Heinrich used the words 'scientist lady.' Political science. He was talking about you."

"No. It's you. I haven't been snooping—oh no! The missing girls, the special account you set up for me—the files I found with all the funny codes."

"Whoa, whoa, whoa. What funny codes?" asked Hope.

"Here, I'll show you."

"Wait, wait, wait. Please," said Hope. "Look, there's way too much going on here. I need to hear everything. Then I need to do some investigation. But I have to avoid detection. It's going to take time. Until then, don't access anything."

"But we don't have *time*," said Laura. "They could be coming after us right now."

"Hope's right," said Ben, "Any action we take will give them more information. We need to know what we're dealing with. Let's get a good night's sleep and let Hope work on it tomorrow."

"Mr. Richards," said Hope, "this is where I agree with Mrs. Richards. I need to get to work right now."

"Work through the night?" asked Chris.

"Night is the best time for this type of work."

Laura tossed and turned all night. She forced herself to wait until Ben got up, and she went with him to the kitchen. Chris was already up and sitting next to Hope.

"I found out how they manipulated the information to the authorities," said Hope. "In each case, a different account was used. At first, the only similarity I could find was the technique used to hide any trace of the manipulation. It's a sophisticated technique—whoever did the tampering knows what they're doing. But the software tool they used is also sophisticated—and rare. I correlated the access times of the tool with the access times of the files about the missing girls, and I discovered that it's the same account. The owner of the account's domain is TerraStore."

"That's the name in the files," said Laura. "The ones with the codes."

"That's right," said Hope. "Those files were completely encrypted."

"But that doesn't mean anything," said Ben. "Practically all the data on the planet is stored there."

"Right again," said Hope. "But whoever did the encryption wasn't so careful about obfuscating the tool access."

"Someone who works at TerraStore?" asked Ben. "But why? What would—"

"Visitors arriving," announced the seccomm. "Quantity two."

Laura looked out the kitchen window and saw Al and Katie coming to the back door. Lucky barked as he greeted them.

"Morning," said Al, zipping into the kitchen. He went straight for the canister of malted milk powder. "Breakfast, anyone? I suggest a milk shake." He tossed the container in the air like a basketball.

"Were you able to learn anything more?" asked Katie.

"It's not safe outside," said Laura.

"What? Nonsense," said Al. "I walked with her. Besides, she can take care of herself, trust me."

"No—the looks on your faces," said Katie. "What happened?"

"We'll fill you in," said Chris. "But Al's right; we need to test the malt."

"OK," said Ben. "But let's use the chamber. I want to analyze what happens. We may not be able to see the effects."

||0 ||0 ||0

HOLDING THE MILK SHAKE, CHRIS STEPPED INTO THE CHAMBER, closed the door, and sat down.

"OK, I started the recording," said Katie, at the console. She had the computer-generated vid feed up on the wall display with the text window of the mind-reader program. Al and Hope were watching with Laura. Lucky lay on the carpeted area where he always waited while Chris was in the lab.

Chris took a sip of the mixture. "Hey, it tastes like chocolate milk. With all the talk about dried grain, I thought it was going to be disgusting."

"Do you see anything happening, Katie?" asked Ben.

"No," said Katie. "Oh, wait, there's the word again."

The word *Watch* appeared.

"Oh!" Chris felt a heightened awareness, like walking alone in a forest but feeling that someone was watching from the distance. His inner self was no longer alone. The feeling was familiar and pleasant, like finding a favorite toy that had been lost for many years. His mind felt alert and capable of stretching beyond normal. Every memory of his life was available with perfect recall. He could remember the verses of any song he'd ever heard from beginning to end—any face, name, school lesson. Anything. His mind explored the memories; they were incredibly clear. He could linger on the most minor detail—dropping a fork from the dinner table, falling in slow motion in his mind's eye, taking many minutes to tumble gently through the air, bouncing off the carpet, and twisting in the air.

Chris realized that exploring his memories took no time all, as if everything around him had paused. More than ever before, he felt a clear connection with the warden. Then he sensed a thought that was not his own. It wasn't language, exactly—more like perception.

Chris set down the cup. "The warden wants me to stand up. It wants you to watch."

Yielding to the force directing his body, he felt his arms begin to rise from his sides. He trusted the warden and let it guide him. The sensation was like the magic trick he did as a kid—pressing one arm against a wall for a minute and then stepping away. He knew his arms were rising, and he had control if he needed it, but he just let the warden direct him.

Bits of dust began swirling around the chamber floor. He sensed a force pushing his arms up, especially at the palms of his hands. To compensate, Chris held his arms stiffly, as if on parallel bars, opening his palms downward. The force became strong, and air raced around the chamber. The chair fell back behind him. The force increased further, and the chair slammed against the back wall. The cup tipped, spilling the milk shake, and then it rolled and smacked against the corner, becoming pinned. Oddly, Chris felt no turbulence against his clothing, skin, or hair.

The word *Watch* flashed on the display.

Chris felt his heels leave the floor, and then his toes.

"Whoa!" said Al.

As Chris rose from the floor, he felt the force under his feet also. The force under his feet began supporting the majority of his weight while the pressure on his hands lessened but still enough for balance. He was standing on a cushion of air.

It didn't last long. His body drifted back to the floor. The swirling air slowed, and the cyclone of paper bits, dust, and dirt spiraled to the floor.

"Migo, that was incredible!" said Al.

Stepping out of the chamber, Chris felt another, even more foreign sensation. He tilted his head back slightly and passed a hand through the air. The air passing over his skin intensified the new sensation.

"What is it?" asked Ben. "You look like you're sleepwalking."

"I can ... I can smell you. All of you. Not with my nose—I can sense what's in the air. It's easier when I walk through the air. There're a lot of scents in air. Did you know that? A lot! It's staggering." He waved his other hand through the air.

"Wait." An image formed in his mind, like the road on a hot summer day materializing from behind a mirage. "The vision thing with Lucky is happening again. You know, when I could see out his eyes? After my fall?"

Lucky was still on the carpet but now sitting up attentively as if waiting for a command. From Lucky's point of view, Chris could see himself standing outside the chamber. "I can switch the images back and forth at will ... to my eyesight or his. Like when you cross your eyes and your vision goes in and out of focus." He stepped forward with both hands outstretched. "And the scents: I think it's me sensing the smells in the air, but somehow I know what the scents are. I can smell the circuit board manufacturing odor from the server cooling fans, Styrofoam packing peanuts, and ammonia cleaning solution—but underneath are more subtle scents ... ones we brought in with us—fresh-cut grass, asphalt, honeysuckle, the gum on the bottom of Al's shoe."

Al bent his leg. "Oh, real nice."

Suddenly, Chris felt a looming loneliness. "Wait, I'm losing it!"

The display flashed *Galactose Maltose*.

"I'm losing it!" He looked at one arm and then to the other.

"Amazing," said Ben. "The sugar seems to amplify the effects we've witnessed before—the ability to manipulate the air molecules around the skin and the connection to Lucky."

"Let's do it again!" said Al.

"Yes, I agree," said Ben. "But I think we should try it outside. Obviously, the chamber is too constraining for a good demonstration."

"I'll bring up the scanner," said Katie, "so we can see what the warden has to say."

"I'll make another milk shake," Laura said as everyone went upstairs.

"My assumption is that your connection to Lucky isn't just the vision but also his scent memory, as well," said Ben.

"That must be it," said Chris. "The richness was fantastic. If I could see the smells, they would be like ribbons of rainbow color flowing through the air. Each scent is clear and distinct. I still sense it now, just not nearly as strongly as when I sipped the milk shake."

"Katie, would you turn the scanner on now, please? I might be able to predict the duration of the effect based on the sugar metabolization rate."

"Sure," said Katie. "OK. Recording."

"So why is this all happening now?" asked Al. "After all the years of trying, why is Chris suddenly able to interpret the clues so much better?"

"Well, I have theory about that." Ben crossed his arms and started tapping his chin. "Chris, have you noticed an increased interest in the opposite sex?"

"*What*?"

"Do you have coarse dark hair growing—"

"Dad! Holy cow!"

Al busted a gut, and Hope had to look away.

"Do you know what I'm getting at?"

Al was laughing so hard he was almost purple and then managed to say, "You forgot to ask about nocturnal emissions."

"I'm going to rip your head off," said Chris.

"OK, Mr. Richards, we get the picture," said Katie. "Puberty."

"That's right. I think the changes brought on by puberty allowed the warden to shape Chris's development to be more symbiotic. Chris is seventeen now—completing the morphologic changes. It might explain the connection to Lucky too, since we got him as a puppy."

"Hey, look what popped up on the screen," said Katie. "It says, *Canine Paleolithic Revolution*."

"What does that mean?" asked Al.

"Why guess?" said Laura. "The malted milk is ready."

"Chris, this time, drink more than a sip. We need to see how long it'll last," said Ben. "Katie, are you recording?"

"Yup. Lights, camera—"

Chris gulped it down. "OK. Now, let's go in the backyard and see what happens."

"We'll need a big, open area," said Hope, looking out the kitchen window. "Mom!" Hope pointed and then ran to the back hallway. "My mom's home from the shelter!"

Chris followed her with everyone behind.

Hope dashed out the back door toward her mom's open arms. "Mom!"

What happened next was almost too fast for anyone to see. Chris raced from the back step to Hope's side and yanked her back just before the embrace. Spinning in the air, he delivered a wheel kick to Sue Avenir's head.

The woman's body hit the ground, and as it rolled, the slender white woman morphed into a sleek and muscular black man. He rolled to a stop, got to his feet, and said, "Don't worry, you'll witness your six layers of death soon enough." He locked a gaze on Laura and then ran.

"She … she changed … right before my eyes. But it *was* my mom! It was!"

"No," said Chris. "She didn't smell right."

||0 ||0 ||0

"WHAT DO YOU MEAN, *UNSUCCESSFUL*?" ASKED SKOTINO FROM his office in the megaron with Spire on the other end of the comm.

"I posed as her son's girlfriend's mother. It was perfect. She was watching, witnessing. They were all watching."

"You said unsuccessful."

"Her son saw through the deception. I don't know how. Knocked me on my ass."

"I'm losing patience. What *exactly* is the problem?"

"The kid's movements—his speed, the kick—it wasn't … mortal."

"And?"

"Host of my god's father, after feeling the pain from the kick, something became clear to me. I'm not sure what it means—"

"Out with it!"

"Just one word. It sounded like: *sow-shy-ent*."

*Saoshyant! The warden! Of course! But how did he escape? Released? No matter; his meddling is obvious now. The mother's life just happens to be intertwined with the lives of our pharmakoi? She just happens to have security clearance to follow the trail? She miraculously develops satellite-imaging technology that can pinpoint our whereabouts? Manipulation of events is evident now. Based on the depth of interference, the warden has been at work for decades. Maybe longer.*

"What does it mean?" asked Spire.

"You'll know after your next clarity," said Skotino. "Our plans have changed. Apparently, the son is Saoshyant's host. Only the hex-minyan ritual can return Saoshyant to his prison: Saoshyant must witness the death of the host's mother. Kill Laura Richards. Record it. Make sure her son lives to see it."

"Vega won't be happy; he's giddy about the six layers of death."

"Let him have his fun. Just make sure the son lives to see his mother's death. Only then will the warden be returned to his shackles for eternity."

"Host of my god's father, I hear and obey."

| 0  | 0  | 0

"EVERYONE INSIDE," SAID CHRIS.

"Let's go after him!" said Al.

"We don't know what we're dealing with," said Chris. "We're not ready for a confrontation. Now get inside."

Hope, with her hands over her mouth, didn't budge.

Laura walked her in.

Katie and Ben followed.

Chris glanced down to Lucky.

Lucky snapped to the ready with front legs spread and chest low to the ground, as if Chris was going to throw a ball, and then he tore out of the backyard and down the alley.

"Oh, so he gets to go after the guy?" said Al.

"He'll follow from a distance."

"Did you see the way that guy looked at your mom?" said Al. "Who needs a middle finger when you have a stare like that?" He followed Chris to the house. "Migo, we gotta do something."

"I know," said Chris. "That's your department. Give me a plan."

Inside, everyone was huddled around Hope.

"What's wrong?"

"If they know what my mom looks like, then that means they were there—at the shelter," said Hope, her voice strangely calm.

"Oh, sweetheart, we don't know that," said Laura, holding her.

Chris didn't know what to say. It was strange the way Hope didn't cry exactly, like some kind of emotional pressure cooker. He wasn't sure what to do or how to help.

"I've been thinking," said Laura. "I was thinking about Father Arnold's question about what's different about life with Chris. Well, for one thing, *I'm* different. I'm less afraid. Chris, come over here."

"What? Why?"

"Just get over here." She had that look.

He didn't have a choice. He walked over.

"Hold her."

"What?" *Not like this*. He remembered being alone with Hope that one night. He regretted not hugging her then. It didn't seem like the right time. Now he really regretted it. *Ugh*.

"Yes! Come on, she won't bite. Give her a hug, for god's sake."

It wasn't a first kiss, but it was a first hug. *This is all wrong. Everyone's watching.*

Hope wasn't looking at him. That made it easier. She seemed to know what he was struggling with.

*I'm just administering medicine.* It's not the personal and private thing he desperately wanted to share. He put his arms around her.

"Don't you wreck it," he heard Katie whisper to Al. "Don't you say a single word."

Chris didn't care what Al or anyone said. He could feel the tension empty from her body. She was warm. It felt so natural. Part of him had been yearning for this. *Giving is better than receiving.* It wasn't about him; it was about her—giving her what she needed when she needed it.

"Feel better, sweetheart?" Laura asked her.

"Yeah," said Hope. "It's like chocolate cake."

Chris started to pull away.

"Don't let go," said Hope. "Not yet."

"What happened out there?" asked Laura. "One minute we were welcoming Sue, and the next minute, I saw a stranger on the ground."

"It had the ability to change its appearance," said Katie.

"I don't think it was a physical disguise," said Ben. "I was looking right at her—him—when the change happened. I think our minds were influenced somehow to see him as Sue Avenir. We simply believed it."

"Yeah, it's weird," said Hope. "My mom was smiling, and she was going to hug me. Seriously? I should've known. But in that moment, I had no doubt it was her. Where did he go?"

"Lucky caught up with him," Chris said, watching the scene in his mind's eye. "He got into a vehicle. I have a pertran identification number. Hope, can you track it?"

"Uh, yeah." She let go and sat down at the pubcomm. "Yeah, I can try. OK, I'm ready."

"E29296A-3899596," said Chris. "It's a Pennsylvania plate. I'm bringing Lucky back home."

"OK, let me see what I can find."

"Just in time too. I can feel it wearing off."

"What good will it do to track them?" said Katie. "They're going to keep coming back."

"We have to assume the warden can stop them," said Chris. "So if they keep coming back, all we have to do is be ready. We need a way to make the connection last longer."

"I got it!" said Al.

"You got what?" said Katie.

"An idea! Katie, your gum-making machine—it has some special way to make the flavor last longer, right? Micro—"

"Yes, I see. The machine uses microbeads to time-release the flavor. We can use the malted milk powder as the flavor. I'll get the machine!" Katie went for the back hallway.

"Oh, my goodness, no," said Laura. "You can't go out there with those things running around."

"We can't just sit here," said Katie.

"Hold on, hold on," said Al. "It's true, we need help. We're totally vulnerable right now. But we can't assume we're safe anywhere. Our best strategy is to not be a target. In fact, I think they're trying to paralyze us with fear. Remember? The six layers of death?"

Hope winced with a wounded look on her face.

"Sorry, sorry, sorry!" said Al. "Don't listen to me. I'm an idiot. Anyway, Chris can't be everywhere at once. We need help."

"I keep saying we need to comm the police," Laura said yet again.

Chris saw Al was still stewing. "What are you thinking, migo?"

"We need help. But who can we trust?" Al started to pace.

Lucky barked outside the back door until Chris let him in. Lucky crawled under the kitchen table and lay down at Hope's feet.

Al stopped pacing. "This is a long shot, but what about Master Cohen? He was in the army or something, right? Chris, you said you saw pictures of him with guns."

"But what do we say?" said Katie. "He won't believe us. Aliens?"

Hope looked up from the keyboard. "There's no doubt in my mind. Like when Chris explained it to me."

"That's right," said Ben. "It was the same with Father Arnold."

"No doubt," said Hope. "It's not just the chocolate-cake feeling; Chris has a way of talking that makes you accept whatever he says."

"Yeah! Like the stock-market people," said Al. "Hook, line, and sinker, baby!"

Chris shot Al a stern look. His mom and dad had quizzical looks on their faces.

"Or the kids at karate," said Katie. "Chris doesn't try to be persuasive, but everyone follows his lead."

"Still, I think I should go with you, Chris," said Ben. "We should ask him together."

"OK, so maybe by some miracle, Master Cohen happens to own an anti-alien ray gun," said Katie. "If these nasty things can disguise themselves, who is he going to shoot? Hope's mom? How will we even know it's Master Cohen when he shows up?"

"I've been thinking about that," said Al. "When Hope's mom came to visit, we didn't get a seccomm announcement."

"That's right," said Ben. "Just like Chris. They must be invisible to the scanners."

"Yes," said Al, "but—"

"I see!" said Katie. "We can use the modified medical scanner! Let me look back at the readings ... Here we go. You're right! I can make some adjustments so we'll be able to detect them." She looked at Al. "You're brilliant!"

"Yeah, a brilliant idiot."

"Hope, if you can set up one of your secure comm links," said Ben, "we can reach Mr. Cohen and find out where he is, and then Chris and I can go meet him to ask for his help."

# CHAPTER 33

FROM THE KITCHEN WINDOW, KATIE WATCHED BEN AND Chris drive off to meet with Mr. Cohen. "Hope, can you monitor their progress, in case— well, you know," said Katie.

Hope was hunched over the keyboard and looked exhausted.

"Sorry, miga. I shouldn't put all that on your plate."

"It's OK. You're right. That's a good idea," said Hope. "I will. I just have to concentrate while I track down the vehicle ID. It's a rental. The credentials for the renter turned out to be fake, so I can only assume it'll tie back to TerraStore. But I can't let them know I'm accessing the files."

"Well, they're off," said Laura, coming into the kitchen. "I hope Bruce will agree to help us."

"I should be off too," said Katie. "I have to get my gum-making machine."

"No, you stay here," said Al. "You have to tweak the scanner. I'll get it. Tell your parents I'm coming. Hope, can you—" Even Al could see how tired she was.

"Sweetheart, you look exhausted," said Laura. "You've been up all night. You should rest."

"Maybe," said Hope reluctantly. "I don't want to make any mistakes. I'll set up the secure comm to Katie's house, and then I'll lie down for a bit."

Once Al had left the house and Hope had gone upstairs, Katie sat down at the kitchen table and got to work on the scanner.

"It's going to be a while before they get back," said Katie.

"I know," said Laura, standing at the sink and looking out the window. "I'll just keep you company." She looked out again.

"Was it hard for you to deal with the scanner problem while Chris was growing up?"

"No, not really. Chris's dad adjusted the seccomm in the house. And Chris's doctor—actually Chris's birth mother's doctor—agreed to act as his pediatrician even though he's a gynecologist. That helped a lot. You kids have always been good about it, you know, at school and so forth. There're more old-fashioned doors in the world than you might realize."

"Yeah, I guess."

She glanced out the window again. "What is *he* doing?"

"Who?" Katie got up and joined her at the window.

It was a man—a very big man—carrying an aluminum baseball bat, standing in the alley looking around.

"Maybe he lost his ball," said Laura. "That guy looks like he could hit it out of the park, literally."

The man looked in both directions and then marched toward Chris's house.

"I don't think so," said Katie. She waited for the seccomm to announce the visitor. "What the heck?" The man was nearly to the back step. "Computer, lock down!"

"Panic mode acknowledged. Security lockdown initiated. Complete. House secure."

Laura grabbed Katie's arm. "Oh my god, it's one of them!"

Katie leaned forward, keeping the man in view as he walked up the steps until her head bumped against the window and she lost sight of him.

"Stay here," said Katie, prying Laura's hand from her arm. Cautiously, she stepped to the hallway leading to the back door and peered around the corner. She could see him now through the back door window. "What does he think he's going to do out there?"

"Trying to kill us!"

"Shhhh. Mrs. Richards, try to stay calm, please."

Katie watched as the man took out his percomm and tapped on the display. Suddenly, the door lock clicked open.

"Panic mode canceled."

"Hey! What?" The red flashing PANIC MODE on the seccomm vanished, and the back door swished open.

The man charged in.

Katie saw the glint of the aluminum bat as it sliced through the air, smashing into the wall above her head. She managed to duck and scramble out of the way. Drywall dust and paint particles sprayed from the point of impact. *Draw him away*, was her only thought. She darted to the opposite wall, away from the kitchen.

The man raised the bat high into the air, and the chandelier exploded in a shower of glass shards. As broken pieces rained down, Katie's feet slipped and scraped, trying to get traction. Like a samurai, the man brought the bat down with both hands. The bat cracked the floor, and tile chips peppered Katie's legs. Off balance now, she scrambled back.

He jumped forward, and Laura screamed when he landed in the doorway. The man turned to her, and she looked completely paralyzed.

Katie took advantage of the moment to get better footing. *Draw him away*. With the man's back to her now, Katie searched her instincts. *Something's wrong. Who would take their eyes off their opponent? Why is he stopping? He's careless, like he's missing me on purpose, like he's more interested in smashing the house, playing with us.*

"Hey, scientist lady," the man said. "I got one of your loved one's friends here. You watching?" He turned back to face Katie.

"*No!*" screamed Laura.

Katie dodged his lunge and felt his fingertips slash down the back of her shirt as she pivoted around the corner—the front door in sight.

The bat smashed into a mirror on the wall behind her. Without slowing down, he pulled the bat from the hole and kept coming.

The front door began to slide open. *Thank god!* She angled her body to slip through the opening.

He grabbed her shoulder, the force knocking her into the doorframe. He grasped her shoulder as she turned and ducked under his arm. He squeezed, trying to hold on, but his hand only tightened further around the twisting fabric.

Rotating, she channeled the momentum into a chop on his wrist, breaking his hold. She thrust the palm of the other hand up into his nose—the blow had no effect.

He laughed and slapped her with the back of his hand, sending her through the door, over the front steps, and onto the ground.

"Enough fun," he said. "Time to go back inside so Mommy Dearest can watch."

Katie rolled and bolted like a sprinter out of the blocks.

He leaped from the doorway after her.

Pumping her arms, she picked up speed and put distance between them, finally having the advantage. He was fast, but not fast enough. Sprinting down the street, she pulled her percomm from her pocket. *Come on, pick up!*

"Hey, this isn't secure, you shouldn't—"

"Al! I need you! Where are you?"

"Getting the machine now. I stopped at my house first to get my—"

"Come outside now!" she screamed and ended the comm. She needed both arms.

She dashed between houses as she moved toward her house. The man wasn't far behind. Instead of running along the street or sidewalk, she ran across the front yards, easily navigating the berms and landscaping, but the man took more time.

*There he is!* Al was on the old red bike he'd long since outgrown. He was pedaling like crazy. He popped the front wheel over the curb ahead and rolled into the yard. When he was close enough, he jumped off.

Katie ran to his arms.

"Who is he?"

"It's—" she gasped. "It's—" That was all she was able to get out before the man raced up to them. They both ran, but Al more slowly, drawing the man's attention.

Katie circled behind, creating two fronts.

Al moved backward across the street and maneuvered toward a tree.

Katie stayed on the man's flank, kept her distance, and caught her breath.

Al veered around the tree, using it as an obstacle. The man swung the bat wildly. It bounced off the tree, making a ringing sound. Al dodged, keeping the tree between them. Another wild swing and miss.

Al planted his feet, chambered his leg, and side kicked the man just under the rib cage. The kick pushed the man off balance, but he was still able to stab at Al, using the bat like a fire poker.

"Holy crap!" Al stumbled back and fell to the ground.

The man gripped the bat like a lumberjack—raising it high into the air, his elbows up to his ears and the tip of the bat touching his butt—then heaved it down.

Al rolled, and the bat cracked the sidewalk. As the ringing sound echoed off the houses, he dashed from the ground. "New plan!" he yelled to Katie. "Follow me!"

||O ||O ||O

"MRS. RICHARDS? WHERE ARE YOU?" CALLED HOPE FROM THE elevator door after hearing the crashing from upstairs. She was afraid to step into the hallway, because it looked like a cattle stampede had passed through.

"He's going to kill her!"

Hope crossed the hall as broken glass crunched under her shoes.

Laura was cowering in the corner of the kitchen.

"Who? Who's going to kill who?"

"Katie! One of them got in."

||O ||O ||O

KATIE FOLLOWED AL ALL THE WAY TO THE PARK. HE TOLD HER HIS plan as they sprinted.

"Are you sure you can hold him off?" he asked her.

"Yes! Now go!"

Al ran off, and Katie tried to think of how she was going to stall the guy. She didn't have much time; the big man had pursued steadily. Now he was only a block away. She looked around to see if other people would be in the way. Some kids and parents were by the swings, but they wouldn't be in danger.

Like a bull, the man plodded straight for her. He wasn't fast, but he didn't look winded, either. When he was close, Katie called to him, "Who are you?"

No response.

She backed up and circled.

He adjusted course, always heading directly for her.

She backpedaled across the park lawn and picked a tree to get behind, like Al had done.

He went around and kept coming.

Trotting backward, she lined up another tree in his path. "Who are you? What do you want?"

Still nothing.

She found a particularly large tree and maneuvered behind it. The man veered to one side, but this time, she circled, keeping the tree between them. The man reversed direction. So did she. He slowed a bit and then suddenly doubled back to catch her on the other side. She saw the feint and reversed back herself. He bobbed back and forth behind the tree with his arms out, trying to trick her. She kept her eyes on his waist and wasn't fooled. He lunged to one side. She scooted around easily.

Finally, he stopped and peered at her from one side.

"Who are you?" she repeated.

"You left her," he said.

"What?"

"You left her all alone."

"Who?"

"The scientist lady. You left her alone."

Her perception of the world began to fold in upon itself. The man's face seemed to grow to fill her line of vision. "I—I *didn't* leave her," she said. *Did I?*

"You left her alone, unprotected. How could you? How could you abandon your friend's mother? It's your fault she's dead."

"She's—she's not dead. She's—" In Katie's mind, she saw images as if a simultaneous event were playing out. She saw Hope's mom walking up to the back door of Chris's house with the back door still wide open and then transforming into the black man. A chill crossed Katie's body as she watched the images in her head. Like an out-of-body experience, she watched him turn to the kitchen. In the corner, Mrs. Richards was screaming a silent scream, like an Edvard Munch scream—her gaping mouth contorting in slow motion, shrieking inaudibly. The man inched closer with his hands, reaching for her throat. Katie felt the guilt and remorse flood over her. *It was my fault!*

The warped perception in Katie's mind shattered when the big man lunged around the tree. She instinctively backed away, sluggishly, stunned by the images and feelings. Tripping on a tree root, she fell backward.

He swiped at her, but she scooted, rolled, and ran. *That was close! What happened? I must never underestimate my opponent!* She gained distance and looked for another tree to get behind. Then she felt her percomm vibrate—the signal from Al. *Finally!* Running, she headed for the opposite side of the park.

The man charged after her.

At the far side of the park, she jogged along the tree line and then dove down, right at the gap in the bushes and scrambled through.

He rushed up behind her. "Got you now!"

An earth-shattering boom rang out across the park. A mist of blood and pulverized flesh mushroomed back across the grass. The man's body flew back six feet and rolled to a stop.

"Nice shot!" Katie said, crouching behind Al, who himself was crouched behind the coil gun aimed out the entrance of their childhood hideout.

Katie crawled out. "Yuck, that is the grossest thing I've ever seen. The hole in his back—it's the size of a basketball."

"I wasn't sure if it would stop him, so I loaded the rod with the blunt end first."

"Like a hollow-point bullet."

He nodded.

"Where did the rod go?"

"Who knows? After the last round of design improvements you made, it's probably in the next county."

"Thanks," she said. "Thanks for saving me."

"Sure. I mean, I was saving myself too. That guy was unstoppable. At least we know they can be killed."

"Look, we gotta get out of here. People are going to notice. We have to warn Chris. And I need to make sure his mom's OK."

"Mrs. Richards?"

"I had some kind of hallucination. It was so real. I'm afraid it *was* real. Come on. We'll get the gum machine on the way."

# CHAPTER 34

"**M**OM, ARE YOU SURE YOU'RE OK?" ASKED CHRIS.
Everyone seemed unhurt, but his mom was still frantic. He kept one arm around her, just to be sure—*Like chocolate cake*, he remembered. The house looked like Calexico.

"Yes. But I owe Hope an apology. She came down when she heard the commotion, and I was completely panicked. I thought the man had caught Katie and was coming back."

"I think that was his plan," said Katie. "Thanks to Al, we don't have to worry about that one anymore."

"They're coming for us, all right," said Chris. "We have to hurry. We have to make the gum so the warden can maintain the connection longer."

"Wait," said Ben. "We have another problem. There's a dead man in the park."

"I'm on that," said Hope. "I figured out how they hacked the seccomm. I've made sure that won't happen again. But when I traced the account back, I noticed it had a tap on police communications. You're right, Mr. Richards. One of the neighbors reported the incident at the park almost immediately. The public vid network caught everything in living color."

"But if that's true, the police should be here by now," said Ben. "They'll want Katie and Al for questioning."

"Right again," said Hope. "But as I was monitoring the police response, I saw the orders were changed from *interrogate* to *arrest*."

"But we didn't do anything," said Katie. "It was self-defense."

"Yup, based on the recorded evidence, they should have no reason to arrest you. So I traced the change in orders back to its source. It's the same account that hacked the seccomm."

"So the police are going to arrest Katie and Al?" asked Chris.

"Well, I didn't know what else to do, but something needed to be done, and quickly," said Hope. "Mr. Richards, I noticed the authorities flagged all your communications as LIMDIS because of the university explosion. Well, I couldn't think of anything else, so I flagged the park incident with the same classification."

Ben smiled.

"What! What does that do?" asked Chris.

"Slows things down," said Ben. "Prevents communication between agencies—just like the investigation into the bombings."

"Yup. The police think it's under federal jurisdiction. And the feds think the police are handling it."

"Jazz," said Al. "Flies will be swarming over the body even before they string the yellow tape."

"But they'll keep coming," said Laura. "The threat in the vid message—he called me the scientist lady and then said I had to witness all of you die."

"We have to make the gum and test it before Mr. Cohen gets here," said Chris. "So the warden can help."

"Bruce Cohen agreed?" asked Laura.

"Yes," Ben told Laura, "just like Hope predicted. And he has weapons. He's getting them and bringing them here."

"But remember, the warden is our only defense until then," said Chris. "How long will it take to make the gum?"

Katie didn't answer. She looked worried, and Al was frowning.

"What?" said Chris. "We have the scanner to identify them, right? They'll come to us. That's what you said. That's the plan."

"The problem is," said Al, "we can't assume we know all their little tricks."

"Yeah," said Katie. "When the guy was trying to get me at the park, I got careless, and he said something—well, he said something, and then something happened. He blamed me for leaving your mom alone, and I began to imagine the worst. I started second-guessing myself, and that's when he made his move. He almost got me."

"We can't sit here like targets," said Al. "It's only a matter of time."

"Then what, exactly?" said Chris.

"We need a new plan." Al crossed the kitchen floor and turned. "Occam's razor!"

"Huh?"

"It doesn't have to be complicated. We go on the offensive. *We* go after *them*. We take the warden right into their nest."

"How?" said Chris. "We don't know where they are."

"The ID from the car," said Al. "Remember?"

"Actually," said Ben, "I think I have information that pinpoints their exact location."

Everyone looked at him.

"Yes. The satellite image. You know, the one that gave me the idea that we could use the Compton chamber to see the warden? It shows a flare on our house. But it also shows flares in other locations, primarily in Nevada near Las Vegas. I only have two images, but both show a congregation in Nevada. Here, let me show you. I've got a copy backed up."

"Whoa, whoa, whoa," said Hope. "Let me guess. TerraStore?"

Ben nodded sheepishly. "Don't tell me I led them right here."

"No. You never accessed the file from here," said Hope. "They traced our location from the searches about the missing girls."

"Do you think they're responsible for the abductions?" asked Laura. "Do you think the girls are there? Alive?"

No one said anything; no one had to.

"Anyway," said Hope, "I can access the file without tipping them off, but how do we get there? Just drive to Vegas? Talk about complicated. All the toll scanners and cameras between here and there? Forget about it. I can't hide a trail like that. Even if we rent a tran or buy a plane ticket under a false account, there're too many surveillance systems."

Al walked across the kitchen and back. "Chris, what if we ask to borrow the scramjet you used for the training in California?"

"How's Master Cohen going to explain why he needs it?" said Katie. "Ask him to lie about a disaster somewhere?"

"Chris," said Laura, "you told me a wealthy person donated the use of the plane. Do you know who?"

"No. Mr. Cohen seemed to avoid the subject. One of his buddies said the owner was a Hillite."

"So the owner's filthy rich," said Al. "That makes sense."

"Well, it's more than that," Laura said. "Chris, remember when we talked about the school lockdowns and the wealthy families?"

"Yeah. You said they're afraid of the Hoods."

"Yes, well, afraid of terrorists in general. Think about it: the people we're up against, the bombings, Heinrich—" She shuddered. "We wouldn't be lying to describe them as terrorists. I think Mr. Cohen might find the plane's owner to be very sympathetic if you explained the truth, or a version of the truth."

"We should ask right away," said Chris. "No telling how long it will take to convince the owner."

"I can set up a secure comm to Mr. Cohen," said Hope.

"OK," said Al. "In the meantime, we need to get the gum machine working. The warden has been trying to help us all along. We need that connection. Let's get on with it, people. Here comes Operation Occam's Razor!"

# CHAPTER 35

KEN BARRISTER TOOK THE ELEVATOR UP FROM THE UNDER-
ground level of his office building, where the
company gym was located. He loved this time of the
morning after exercising—the way his body felt. His
skin glowed from the heat of the shower. His muscles
were sore, confirming he'd had a great workout—
upper body today. After all, he had a reputation to
keep up: his buddies called him the Bear, and the
chicks called him the Banister. "Hold on for the ride,
ladies," went his favorite pickup line.

The elevator stopped at ground floor, and half a
dozen coworkers piled in for the ride up. A few of
the women were pretty hot. They all shifted body
positions to make room, but he didn't budge.

When the door closed, he took a good look at
the hottie next to him with an obvious head-to-toe
inspection. He'd seen her around. Married. But she
was aware of him. *Oh yeah*. The sexual tension was
definite. She didn't look his way, but she moistened
her lips, and he saw a bit of a smile. Maybe.

He recalled the splash of cologne after his shower. *The fragrance is arousing her, that's right. Thinkin' about my chiseled body at this very second, aren't you, hon?* His biceps were still gorged with blood from the workout. He loved to wear short-sleeved polo shirts to work and had them tailored to accentuate his massive guns. He flexed his arm casually—to brush back his thick brown hair—and then paused and held the pump for her benefit. *Oh yeah.* He caught her glancing. Maybe. *Teasing me, huh?*

The elevator door opened. *Later, babe.*

At his desk, he saw the message immediately. *Finally! The boss is announcing the promotion today.* It'd been six weeks since his boss had told the team about the position. It was perfect. He'd slaved away at his tax-consulting position for years. This was his chance to move up. The others were idiots—his boss admitted as much. But he also said Ken needed to work hard during the six-week evaluation period before the decision to prove he could handle the new position. He'd showed him, really showed him. Early to work, late nights, even on Fridays, and a few weekends too, just to be sure. A slam dunk, his boss had said. But the six-week period was required to make the promotion fair. Sure. No doubt to make it obvious to everyone who'd earned it. The whole team was working their asses off. But he was the best. Slam dunk.

In the conference room, the team gathered and waited for the boss to arrive. They left the seat at the head of the table unoccupied.

His boss entered and crossed the room. But so did another guy Ken didn't recognize.

"Thank you all for coming," his boss began even before taking a seat. "I know you're eagerly awaiting the announcement of the new team leader. So without further ado, let me introduce you to Terence Fishbocker."

The new guy smiled and gave a little wave.

*Son of a bitch!*

"Now, I know what you're thinking," he continued. "But hiring from the outside is a brilliant move, and I'll tell you why." Then to the new guy, he said, "Terence, have a seat." The boss pointed.

Terrence sat at the head of the table and surveyed the group.

*He's gloating! Like a fucking sea captain!*

"Yes, a brilliant move," his boss droned on.

Ken heard none of it. *A slam dunk! All the work I did! The whole team. A trick!* Ken watched his boss—his mouth flapping and waving his arms around Fishbocker like a bikini-clad model showing off a new tran at the auto show. *A trick. A goddamn trick! Nobody fucks with the Bear, not my sniveling boss and not this skinny-assed Fishbocker. The first thing I'm going to do is—*

The sensation hit hard. Pain—like a smack on the elbow at the wrong place, but all across his body. The room began to rotate. The pain intensified around his head and hair, as if his scalp were being ripped off. Then the pain vanished.

Now he felt exhilarated, powerful. The feeling filled his psyche and stripped away all the thoughts from his mind—except one. *That goddamn smirk on that fuckin' Fishbocker's face. I know exactly what will wipe it off. Fear. And pain.*

# CHAPTER 36

"ALL SET UP?" CHRIS ASKED KATIE.

"Yeah. Your dad cleared this spot for me." She indicated a few feet of counter space in the basement lab. Chris thought it looked like his dad had taken his forearm and shoved all the junk to one side. Katie's contraption had a set of plastic hoppers on one end and a roll of wax paper at the other, ending with a little conveyor belt over a basket of finished gum.

"How does it work?"

"The secret to the long-lasting flavor is the way it's prepared," said Katie, being pretty animated, reminding Chris of his dad in professor mode. "The machine divides the flavor into eight portions, each encapsulated into tiny digestible microbeads that act as a time-release system. The first portion has a thin coating that dissolves quickly. The coating gets progressively thicker until the last portion, which takes a long time to dissolve, even after significant agitation."

"Agitation?"

"Chewing."

"Oh." Chris picked up a piece. "It's blue."

"Yeah, sorry. I still have a lot of blue left over."

"So all I have to do is pop one of these in my mouth and chew?"

"Exactly. It's hard to say how long it will last, but it should be at least an hour or so," she said. "Did you get a hold of Master Cohen? Can we use the plane?"

"Sure enough. I guess the owner has a fleet of them. Mr. Cohen still has a few things to take care of."

"Seriously? Like what? Water his flowers? We don't have time."

"No, no. Hope was working on a way to make the flight plan secret. Once he found out what she can do, he said he wanted to get a special piece of equipment that might help. I didn't really understand what they were saying at that point. Anyway, he'll be here in the morning, and we'll leave for the airport together. We have to defend ourselves until then; hopefully the warden will know what to do."

"OK, everyone," said Al. "Let's go outside and see how this flying thing really works."

"I'm not sure outside is a good idea," said Hope. "If anyone sees him, it'll be on every network in seconds."

"He needs a big area," said Al.

"We can do it right here." Chris moved to the middle of the lab and held out his arms for perspective. "Good, huh?"

"No way. Look at all the stuff," said Katie. "The force of the air is strong. The boxes, the papers, my gum machine—everything will get knocked over."

"The garage?" asked Ben.

"The stairway!" said Al. "It goes all the way to the top floor."

"Not much room in there," said Katie. "It's just for emergencies if the elevator doesn't work."

"No, I think that's good," said Chris. "Let's try it."

They waited at the bottom of the stairwell until Laura collected the picture frames from the landings above.

Chris trotted up the steps to the first landing and turned to face them. "OK, here goes." He unwrapped the gum and popped it into his mouth. "Chocolate? Chocolate gum that's blue? That's just not right."

"Shut up and chew, you big baby," said Katie.

He felt a sharpening of his senses. The subtle presence of the warden he'd experienced his whole life suddenly intensified. Seclusion to solidarity. Separation to unity. Dissension to harmony.

"What's happening?" called Laura. "You've got that look on your face."

"Uh, the odors are back."

Lucky wagged his tail.

"And I can see through Lucky's eyes. It's working perfectly."

"Try the flying thing," said Al.

More confident this time, Chris levitated off the floor in a whoosh of air.

Everyone protected their eyes from the
blast of air.

He went higher, up the first set of stairs, banking
around and up the entire stairwell until he reached
the top landing.

*Bang!*

"What was that?" Laura yelled from below.

"You missed one of the picture frames, that's all!
It didn't break." Chris hovered over the frame and
rotated his body. Like an acrobat held by wires at the
hip, he picked up the frame and then spiraled back
down, coming to rest on the first landing.

"Chris, I checked the time when you took
the gum," said Ben. "We need to know how
long the gum lasts, so keep us informed on what
you're feeling."

| | 0   | | 0   | | 0

SKOTINO EMERGED FROM THE CLARITY COMMUNION.

"Oh, god, *please*!" Regina screamed.

As Skotino's mind cleared, he knew now that
his god's son—the one who had occupied Erik
"Big Vega" Mathers—had claimed someone named
Ken Barrister as host. He also knew the warden,
Saoshyant, was coming.

Skotino's attention returned to the present.
Regina's left hand was still in the vice, and he still
had the pliers clenched around the pointer finger.
He continued the twisting motion that had triggered
the clarity. The finger ripped away with a crescendo

of tiny pops and snaps, difficult to hear over all the screaming.

Finished, Skotino closed the door to Regina's room.

Tyvold was waiting in the security substation at the entrance of the oubliette, eager for information. "Do you know the location of the sinistral host of my god's nephew?"

Skotino nodded. "I'll get the new symbiont and bring him here. His urge to commune will be overwhelming. Any delay will just make it more difficult to clean up."

"I hope your god's son chose a better host this time. Vega was such a moron."

Skotino grunted. "The gods know. It's someone as strong as a rhinoceros and just as stupid. We've seen the same pattern for millennia on this forsaken planet. No creativity, that one."

"And the warden?"

"Saoshyant will come for us."

"Here?"

"You will protect the boy while I'm away."

"He's in the hibernation pod, quite vulnerable."

"Yes, the timing is to the warden's benefit. His temporal manipulation continues."

"What do you have in mind?"

"Let the mortals deal with the warden. Have Anderson alert the military that we have reason to believe the traitor who killed their beloved Dr. Cornelius is on her way here and bringing a group of Hoods to destroy what's left of the good doctor's project."

"And what of the hex-minyan?" asked Tyvold. "To return the warden to the chains of eternal bondage, his dextral host must witness the death of the host's mother."

"Just make sure Spire records Laura Richards's death. Instruct the mortals to apprehend the terrorists, not kill them. We'll simply replay the recording," said Skotino. "The host is a teenager, right? Probably likes vids."

"Host of my god's brother, I hear and obey."

# Chapter 37

"AT FIFTY-SIX THOUSAND FEET, CORPORAL RODRIGUEZ, Omega Force fire team leader, sensed the course change. The team had been on station for only a few hours. The course change could only mean that they were about to receive mission orders.

Number Two and Number Three—call sign designations, of course—were sitting in their jump seats. Number Four was performing a systems check but sensed the course change too and was now returning to his seat.

The incoming vidcomm popped up on every display in the scramjet's cabin. "Corporal, this is a priority mission directive. Target of opportunity. Hood interception. Not just any Hood, boys, the traitor that killed Cornelius."

Cornelius—father to them all—had been murdered, betrayed by one of their own. All leads had dried up.

His commanding officer continued, "The civilian assets who provided the intelligence believe they themselves are now targets. Your orders are to apprehend. Be advised, the compromised agent is still MIA. Your mission is to protect the civilians and their infrastructure. The accumulated knowledge of Cornelius's work is contained in the minds of the civilian personnel. Our next generation of marines is at stake, your future brothers and sisters. The laboratory and equipment must not be damaged. Your primary contact is one Victor Tyvold. He has security authority over the compound. ETA, eighteen minutes. Prepare for insertion."

"You heard the man. Hustle up. Let's go," said Rodriguez.

"Ready for inspection," said Number Two.

Rodriguez examined Number Two's gear before sealing him into his tube, including the ghillie system of the sniper's powered suit. Tiny liquid crystals covered the suit's surface, creating near invisibility. Effective, but fragile. "Good. In you go." Rodriguez tapped the button next to Number Two's tube pedestal. A transparent cylinder descended from the ceiling to surround Number Two and seal around the pedestal. One by one, indicator lights changed to green.

Rodriguez stepped over to Number Three. There was nothing fragile about the suit of his heavy weapons and explosives expert. His rifle fired explosive-tipped, armor-piercing rounds and sported a grenade-launcher attachment. Rodriguez made sure the mortar kit, grenades, and breaching explosives were secure.

With Number Three sealed in, Rodriguez moved to Number Four. The communications and cryptography specialist only carried a pistol as an offensive weapon. Even the grenades he carried were only capable of zapping electronic systems.

"Listen," said Rodriguez, "don't forget about the traitor. Watch for her involvement. She knows our tactics. You see something odd, you report it to me immediately."

"Aye-aye," said Number Four.

With his team all tucked in, Rodriguez stepped to his pedestal and checked his own gear. His armored suit had a VTOL thruster for vertical takeoffs and landings, essentially a jet pack that only carried fuel for about thirty seconds of flight. His automatic rifle had a unique hinge in the middle. The front half of the gun (with the barrel and the targeting camera) could be angled, allowing him to see and shoot around corners.

He tapped the button on his wrist, and the tube glided down around him. Ready.

With no intel on when the Hoods would strike, there was no way to know how long they'd have to wait. Their suits were fully self-contained, holding enough power, air, food, water, and waste capacity to last seventy-two hours. *Better not take that long.*

"Insertion cycle activated. Combat release in twenty-nine seconds," announced the aircraft's computer.

He felt the aircraft roll and dive. It plummeted to earth on a direct course to their insertion point. He checked the LZ from his helmet display. *A location in the Nevada desert.*

The braking engines kicked in, and he felt the sudden jerk as the aircraft transitioned out of super-sonic flight.

"Release in fourteen seconds."

Rodriguez watched the image on his helmet display, fed from the cameras on the underside of the aircraft, that showed the civilian's compound. *Odd. It doesn't look like an industrial complex—more like a resort.*

"Release in three, two—"

The powerful engines fought gravity, slowing the aircraft to a point sixty feet above the desert floor. At the exact moment before the aircraft began to rocket back, sphincter seals on the bottom of each tube snapped open like the shutter on an old-fashioned camera. Propelled by the remaining momentum, the soldiers shot from the bottom of the aircraft, their descent controlled by tethers attached to each helmet. When their boots touched the sand, the tethers detached, and the aircraft blasted up and away.

"Secure a perimeter," Rodriguez ordered. "Number Four, connect me with Tyvold."

# CHAPTER 38

"VISITOR ARRIVING. QUANTITY ONE."

"Bruce is pulling up," called Laura.

At the back door, Katie checked the reading on the portable scanner. "Yup, it's really him."

"Time to go!" said Al.

After an uneventful night, Laura had worried that bad weather might be a problem, but fair weather was expected all the way to Nevada.

Ben led the way to greet Bruce, and the two men shook hands.

"I can't thank you enough," said Laura.

"Well, I'm doing it for myself too. I knew Chris was special from the moment I met him. It explains a lot, actually. I saw the way my karate students responded to him. I have to admit I felt it too."

"Let's see the guns!" said Al.

Katie and Hope didn't seem quite as excited.

Bruce opened the trunk of his pertran and pulled out a small case, popped two latches, and opened the lid. Inside was a device of some kind, nestled in gray sponge. It looked like a big percomm.

"That's a gun?" asked Al.

"No, but you might say it's a weapon of sorts. This device can receive and transmit any kind of wireless communication. If we can tap into their signal, we might have a shot at cracking their encryption. It's standard issue for the Israeli army. Pretty old, but I thought it was worth a try. What do you think, Hope?"

"I don't know how it works, but I have friends online that probably do," she said. "I'll connect with them during the flight and see what I can learn."

"Is that a good idea?" asked Katie. "No offense to your friends, but can we trust them?"

"I'm not sure we have a choice," said Hope.

"That's all?" said Al. "That's the gun?"

"Holy cow," said Katie. "Have some manners. You're like a toddler over a cookie jar."

"I don't know what you were expecting, Al. You might be disappointed." Bruce put away the small case, pulled out a long one, and opened it.

"That's the SSB, right?" asked Chris. "From the pic?"

"BSS," he corrected, and he lifted the strange-looking rifle from the case. It certainly looked big. It had several barrels sticking out the front, not just one. There were a lot of buttons along the middle.

"It looks like a jackhammer," said Al.

"BSS stands for blind, stun, and snare. Designed for riot suppression. It's old too. But I'm pretty handy with it." He put it back in the case. "Sorry, Al. I know you wanted a rocket launcher or something."

"I don't mean to be ungrateful," said Al. "It's just that the guy who chased us was relentless."

Bruce closed the trunk. "Seven people and a dog. Are we taking two trans?"

"Laura and I are staying here," said Ben. "We know we won't be safe, not really, but we'll only slow you down."

"What will you do if they come while we're gone?" asked Bruce.

"They can't override the seccomm programming anymore," offered Hope. "I'll be monitoring communications. If I notice anything unusual, I'll warn you. Maybe that will give you time to escape or ... or something."

Laura could tell from her voice that she knew the futility. Hope was so sweet. The reality was obvious. They all knew.

"Mom," said Chris, "maybe there's another way."

"It'll be OK," she said. "Easy for me to say now, I know. The real test will be when you're not around to give me courage." She smiled and hugged him.

"Can I hold the gun?" asked Al.

Katie whacked him on the arm. "Ho-lee-cow! You've got the emotional sensitivity of a brick. Go get Lucky and let these people have a moment."

# CHAPTER 39

MISSION TIME: T PLUS TWENTY-TWO HOURS.
Rodriguez's genetic engineering allowed him to function without sleep, but still, waiting was the worst part of the job. Number Two was covering the front of the civilian compound, and Number Three was covering the rear. Number Four was in the security station with the civilian liaison, Tyvold.

The only excitement was when two of the civilians returned completely unannounced. Rodriguez had then explained how close they came to a disaster and warned them to coordinate all travel. One of the arrivals was the owner of the compound, Aeron Skotino. The man had a voice like tectonic plates grinding underfoot. From his dossier, Rodriguez learned that he owned the firm with the contract to develop the Nu generation. *Deserves some latitude.*

Rodriguez looked out over the desert from the vast wall of windows along the back of the building. The opulence of the compound was unnerving. *With so much unemployment across the nation, how do these people sleep at night?* Sunlight poured into the living space. He caught his own reflection in the glass—in his powered armor, holding his weapon, surrounded by the plush carpet, swank sofa, and delicate coffee table. A viper coiled in satin.

He walked along the back hall to a door leading to—according to his mission blueprint—the gestation laboratory. Maybe there were little supersoldiers running around in a playroom on the other side of the door. He remembered his own childhood. It wasn't a real childhood, just a period when he was young. No playroom, only training classrooms. He felt no resentment—no good or bad judgment—just memory. *What's childhood like for the next generation?* The rumor was that they had genetically enhanced skin, dense like armor but otherwise indistinguishable from normal.

"Number One, Tango acquired," came the comm transmission in Rodriguez's helmet earpiece. "Vehicle approaching on the front-entry road. It's slowing to turn."

"Just like the vehicle earlier this morning? Confirm with the civilians that this isn't another unscheduled visit."

"Aye-aye. Stand by, please," said Number Four. "Confirmed. Vehicle is not authorized. It just turned onto the entry road."

"Number Two, come in," called Rodriguez. "You have a vehicle on approach, presumed hostile. Repeat. Tango is hostile."

"Copy that. I have a dust cloud in the distance."

Rodriguez flipped through the vid channels in his helmet's heads-up display to see Number Two's sniper scope feed. The vehicle was almost in range. "We need to keep them as far from the compound as possible. Stop the vehicle at all cost." He watched the vid feed as the sniper aligned the crosshairs on the vehicle's window between the heads of the occupants, and then he heard Number Two take a quick breath before holding it. *Psssst!* The bullet exited the silenced muzzle.

||0 ||0 ||0

*KSHHH! KSHHH!* THE FRONT AND REAR WINDOWS EXPLODED. Chris ducked instinctively and bumped heads with Hope on the way down. Warning tones sounded, and lights flashed from the control display of the rental tran. The vehicle slowed as a preprogrammed cycle brought the vehicle to a safe stop on the side of the road.

*Kshhh!* Another window in the back exploded into cubes of glass. Lucky barked.

"Hang on," said Mr. Cohen. Keeping his head down, he accelerated off the road toward some rocks to the right. A third shot hit the left rear tire. More alarms sounded. Mr. Cohen fought to keep on course as the rim of the rear wheel spun wildly in the dirt. Another shot flattened the front tire on the same side. "Come on, baby, hold together!" Dust sprayed up from the flat tires along the left side. In a grinding arc, the tran plowed to a stop, still twenty feet from the boulders.

"Get out!" yelled Mr. Cohen. "Run for cover!"

| | 0   | | 0   | | 0

"VEHICLE DISABLED," REPORTED NUMBER TWO. "MULTIPLE OCCU-pants have taken cover."

"Number of occupants?"

"Uh, four. No, five."

"Which is it?"

"Their exit was shrouded by dust clouds. Uh—"

"What's the problem, marine?"

"Number One, are you sure they're Hoods?"

"What do you mean?"

"The occupants, they look like—well, they look like tourists."

"Of course they look like terrorists."

"Negative. I say again. They look like tourists, repeat tourists."

"Copy that. Stand by. Let me review the log." Rodriguez accessed the recorded feed from Number Two's targeting camera. It showed the vehicle turn off the road and swerve to a stop, and then figures exited. The dust made it difficult to see. He froze the vid at a point where it was possible to make out the figures. They looked like young people, and their clothing didn't match anything he'd experienced before. The Hoods didn't conform to any type of dress, yet Number Two's description of them as tour-ists fit pretty well. Shorts and T-shirts? A dog? Could this be the band that murdered Cornelius? *It must be a decoy.*

"You have new orders, Number Two. If they emerge, shoot to kill. I'll have Number Three take them out with a mortar round. We have no time for this."

Then Number Four broke in. "Number One, I've got cybercontact."

"Specify."

"I was monitoring the vehicle's approach via satellite when I lost the feed. It's not a malfunction; the transmission is jammed."

"Well, get it unjammed. Now."

*Time for that mortar shell. Adios, decoy.*

"Number Three—" Rodriguez called.

No response.

"Number Three, come in." He waited. "Number Four?"

Still no response.

"Break-break, this is whiplash-actual calling any Oscar Foxtrot. Please respond."

Silence.

*All communications must be jammed.* He hustled to the security station to find Number Four and figure out what was going on.

|I0 ||0 ||0

"HOLY CRAP!" YELLED AL, KEEPING HIS HEAD DOWN WITH EVERY-one else huddled behind the rocks. "Who are these people?"

Hope tapped on the display of the wireless transceiver. After a moment, she said, "Mr. Cohen, does the term *Oscar Foxtrot* mean anything to you?"

"That can't be right. Where did you hear that?"

"Listen." Hope replayed the recorded audio.

*Number Three, come in! … Number Four? … Break-break, this is whiplash-actual calling any Oscar Foxtrot. Please respond.*

"What does it mean?" she asked.

"It means we're up against the Omega Force."

"Are you serious?" asked Al. "Like in the vids?"

"Wake up, Al," said Chris. "This is serious."

"Chris is right," said Mr. Cohen. "We're facing the elite counterterrorism force of the United States Marine Corps, not Hollywood actors. Not good."

"I don't understand," said Katie. "They're the good guys. Can't you tell them to stop shooting at us?"

"I don't think that'll work. They have their orders. They won't stop. You have to convince their leadership. That takes time, and we don't have time." Mr. Cohen took a peek above the rock. "If only we could block their communications."

"We can," said Hope. "I mean, I did."

"What? No. The transceiver can't do that; it can only decode their transmissions."

"Actually, it couldn't even do that," said Hope. "Mr. Cohen, the transceiver is ancient. But during the flight, I updated the firmware, and now it's picking up the signals perfectly. Anyway, you're right. It can't jam their communications. But my friends have been monitoring our progress—running shotgun—and blocked their communications from inside their own command and control network."

"Really? Impressive," said Mr. Cohen. "That explains why we're still alive."

"Yeah, well, my point is, the jamming probably pissed them off. Not exactly an olive branch."

"We need to do something," said Al. "And fast!"

Mr. Cohen hefted the BSS gun. "Once they get close, I can neutralize them with this. But their attack will be coordinated. I can only handle one at a time."

"You said the B in BSS stands for blind," said Chris. "Can it blind them so we can approach the house?"

"Normally, yes. The special scope here can locate the target's face. The BSS fires a laser precisely into the target's pupil. The blindness lasts for several minutes."

"That's perfect," said Chris.

"Well, I said *normally* because it's usually used against rioting crowds. These marines have helmets with visors that protect their eyes. Even the lenses on their scopes turn opaque when they detect the laser energy."

"But they can't see while the laser is firing?"

"Right."

"That might be just long enough." Chris unwrapped a piece of gum and popped it into his mouth.

NUMBER TWO CONTINUED TO WATCH THE ROCK FORMATION FOR any movement.

*What's taking so long? Hit 'em with the mortar already.* Number One was taking a big gamble by countermanding the apprehension order. But it still seemed odd. *Like attacking a school bus.* He'd feel more comfortable knowing this was indeed a decoy attempt.

*Ah, movement!* He spotted a head pop up above the rock. He aimed, but the image in his helmet went black, and the laser-threat warning sounded. *What?* He waited a moment, knowing the laser couldn't harm him or his equipment. The image of the rock formation returned.

His threat-assessment computer confirmed the use of an Israeli BSS. *Hoods using a BSS?* This mission was getting more bizarre by the minute. He kept aim on the rock formation and wouldn't let any of them get away alive.

After a minute passed, his motion-detector warning flashed, and the proximity alarm sounded. *A second enemy group?* He switched his helmet display to show the location and direction of the new threat. The glowing dot was in the center. *Right here?*

He risked a look around. Nothing. Then he noticed the shrubs around him quivering in the breeze. *Breeze? There's no breeze.* It got stronger, and streams of sand started swirling around. *Above?* He looked up and saw two men hovering in an embrace.

One looked like an Olympic gymnast performing the iron cross. The other was hanging on and pointing the BSS directly at him!

Number Two saw the shot, but it was too late to react. The tiny device hit, and his armor went limp. He knew the situation was bad, but close-quarters combat in an unpowered suit was part of his training. His genetic engineering gave him superhuman strength to move even under the weight of the unpowered armor. He stood and removed his helmet, ready to fight. That's when he felt the needle in his neck just before his field of vision tunneled, and he lost consciousness.

||0 ||0 ||0

MR. COHEN HELD ON TIGHT WITH ONE ARM AS CHRIS TOUCHED down next to the soldier, sprawled on the ground.

"What was that?" asked Chris.

"A tranquilizer dart. And before that, a round that fries the electronics of anything it hits. The nasty thing about these guys is that they continue to fight even when faced with catastrophic failure of their equipment. But their training also makes them predictable. He has to take off the helmet to see. The dart will continue to administer the tranquilizer, like a wasp's stinger. It can keep a normal human unconscious for an entire day. But his genetically engineered body will metabolize the tranquilizer at an accelerated rate. We may only have a few hours before the dart is empty."

"What now?" said Chris.

"We need to find and neutralize all the marines. Remember Hope's recording? They used numbers as call signs. That means a fire team of four—a combat squad, not what you're used to seeing in the vids. This guy here is very specialized. He's the eyes. We need to make sure there are no more marines outside before Al, Katie, and Hope can leave the protection of the rocks. Then we need to find a way inside, and once—"

Chris heard the whistling sound of the mortar shell too. The rental vehicle exploded. The rock formation would be next.

Mr. Cohen yelled, "Run! *Run!*"

| | O | | O | | O

NUMBER THREE DIDN'T KNOW WHY HE WASN'T ABLE TO COMMUNI-cate with his team members. He had started to move to the front of the house to check with Number Two. He initially thought he'd made contact with the enemy when his motion detector identified a target approaching, but it was only a dog. *Somebody needs to tell the civilians to keep their dog in the house.*

Then he'd seen the disabled rental vehicle and realized the compound was under attack. The communications failure had to be the result of enemy jamming. If the jamming was local, the device causing it might be in the disabled vehicle.

Number Three's mortar shot had been a direct hit on the vehicle.

He tried his radio again. "Number One? Come in. Do you read me?"

No reply.

He saw three targets emerge from behind a set of rocks and run for the house. From his position, he could easily hit them with another mortar round. He adjusted his aim to intercept.

*What the—*

He felt the nudge against his equipment belt. *The dog again.* The dog turned and dashed off like a cheetah, but not so quickly that Number Three's genetically enhanced eyesight didn't catch a glimpse of the hand grenade pin in the dog's mouth.

The explosion was followed by multiple secondary explosions as his remaining ordnance detonated.

||0 ||0 ||0

"A BUNCH OF YOUNG PEOPLE? I DON'T GET IT," SAID RODRIGUEZ IN the compound's security station. Number Four stood over the shoulder of the civilian, Tyvold, watching the security monitors as the enemy shattered an outside floor-to-ceiling window and entered the building. The group tiptoed over broken glass and peered down the hallway.

"The guy with the BSS is no youth," said Number Four. "And I'll bet he knows how to use it."

As if on cue, the vid image showed the man with BSS look directly at the security camera and raise the BSS, and then the picture went black.

"He shot out the camera," said Tyvold.

"No, we'd see an error message," said Rodriguez. "The BSS fires ink beads."

"How did they get past your man out front?" asked Tyvold.

"We have to assume the worst," said Rodriguez. "Number Four, once you get communications back online, alert Number Three and have him join me. I'll take care of the intruders. Our priority is the guy with the BSS."

"You will not kill them," said Tyvold. "You will capture them."

Rodriguez stepped directly in front of Tyvold. He took a long, hard look at this character. Normally, he'd rip into him about who was in charge. But everything about this mission was wrong, backward somehow. "No guarantees. The safety of my team comes first."

| |0 | |0 | |0

FROM HIS OWN DISPLAY IN THE SUBSTATION AT THE ENTRANCE OF the oubliette, Skotino watched and listened to the soldiers talk with Tyvold. He messaged Tyvold to come down so they could talk privately.

*The warden is indeed formidable*, thought Skotino. *However, this—Omega Force—seems completely unprepared to deal with the situation.*

"Did you hear?" asked Tyvold when he arrived. "They'll kill the son if they have to."

"Tell his superior to order capture."

"Communications are still jammed. I don't even know Spire's progress," said Tyvold. "Their communication expert—they call him Number Four—is watching everything I do. I need time."

"And *I* need the vid from Spire," said Skotino. "The chains of Tartaros will bind the warden only when the son witnesses the mother's death." Skotino tapped again on the console. The display showed the intruders moving defensively with their backs to the wall. *Two of them are female.* The man raised the BSS, and the image went black. *Another camera rendered useless.* "The warden must behold: *estrus lordosis a priori libidinal matricide.*"

"I need more time," said Tyvold.

Skotino slammed his fist on the console, and the noise elicited moans from the reaches of the oubliette. *An inspiring sensation.* "Work here. Our intruders need something to occupy their time. I will prepare a room for a very special young lady. Tell Barrister to move the hibernation chamber into the transport vehicle and wait there with Chelsea."

"Host of my god's brother, I hear and obey."

||O ||O ||O

MOVING SILENTLY TOWARD THE END OF THE HALL, CORPORAL Rodriguez raised his rifle and released the hinge, creating a ninety-degree angle. He inched the barrel around the corner while watching the vid feed from the gun's scope.

Nothing.

He proceeded to the next corner and repeated the process.

*There!* He could see one of the intruders peering around the corner at the end of the hallway. He fired a three-round burst. Chunks of drywall exploded from the point of impact. He rushed the corner and again angled his rifle around the corner.

*Splat!*

He pulled the rifle back. The scope lens was covered with ink. *Damn that BSS!*

||0 ||0 ||0

"WHAT DO WE DO?" WHISPERED HOPE.

They had retreated back, almost to the point where they came in. The soldier was going to force them right back outside.

"Well, for one thing, stop screaming at every noise," Mr. Cohen whispered back.

"Sorry. His gun is so loud."

"I only have one more sticky-stunner. It's the only way I know to immobilize them long enough to get the helmet off, but I think it's our only option. When he comes up the hallway, I'll blind him first and then fire."

Chris crept behind Mr. Cohen. He could hear the soldier around the corner stepping across the debris on the floor.

"On three," whispered Mr. Cohen. "One … two …" He stepped out and pulled the trigger, and laser light flashed across the visor. The soldier backed up and shot blindly, shattering the wood floor. Mr.

Cohen dove across the floor, rolled, and fired the sticky-stunner.

The soldier pushed himself out of the line of fire, and the device smacked uselessly against the wall. He regained his footing and, with his visor clear now, leveled his rifle at Mr. Cohen.

In a blur, Chris flew between them and pushed the rifle up. Like parkour in zero gravity, he snatched the device from the wall, pushed off in midair, and slapped it on the soldier's armor.

The soldier crumpled to floor like an octopus out of water.

Chris flew on top of him. "How do I get it off?"

Mr. Cohen released the helmet latch and fired the tranquilizer dart at point-blank range. In a hushed tone, he called to the others, "Over here."

Hope, Katie, and Al stepped from around the corner.

"Nice work, migos," said Al.

"He might not be alone," said Mr. Cohen. "Hope, have you heard them use any other call signs?"

"No. They're still trying to reestablish communications. No designation higher than four."

"One to go," said Mr. Cohen. "I'm out of stunners. We need a plan; he could come any second."

"But we're here to find the bad guys and the missing girls," said Al. "Are these soldiers the bad guys?"

"No," said Katie. "I got a reading on the soldier outside and this one, but I don't know about the one that Lucky took out—not that there's anything left to scan."

"Then let's just avoid the last soldier," said Al, keeping his voice down.

"Maybe," said Mr. Cohen. "But how?"

"What about scent?" asked Al.

"I've been trying," said Chris. "Either we haven't crossed his path or the suit blocks the scent. I thought about using Lucky for an extra nose, but he's patrolling the outside. I don't want to get surprised."

"The tranquilizers are wearing off," said Mr. Cohen. "We have no choice but to search. Chris and I will take point."

Every room along the way was empty. Each was perfectly decorated, and none of them seemed lived in, like a museum.

"Uh-oh," said Mr. Cohen, examining the next door.

"What?" asked Chris.

"This isn't a room; it's an elevator."

Chris stepped around for a closer look. Hope, Katie, and Al caught up.

"Oh, great," said Chris. "There must be more levels below. This is going to take forever."

"Notice anything strange?" asked Al.

"Like what?"

"It has a button to open it. Just like your dad installed for you at your house."

"Hey, that's right," said Katie. "All the doors had handles."

"We're on the right track," said Chris. "But let's find the stairwell instead."

The levels below were furnished less like a house and more like an office building. They continued to check rooms, reaching the lowest level, until they came across a door that looked very different from the rest, like an outside door.

"Could it be another elevator?" whispered Chris.

"Beats me. But we have to—"

The door swished open. A soldier, pistol in hand, took aim on Chris.

Chris ducked to the side, away from his friends.

The soldier jumped from the doorway, turned, and aimed at Chris.

Chris bobbed as he backed up.

The soldier pursued, his pistol arm wavering, trying to get a fix.

From behind the soldier, a series of long strips like wire flew through the air and hit the soldier's running legs, sticking. The powered suit emitted a mechanical whirring sound as it strained against the bindings. More strips soared through the air and attached.

The soldier went down like the loser of a three-legged race. He rolled onto his back.

As Mr. Cohen fanned the BBS, strips landed across the soldier's pistol arm and the floor on either side.

The whirring noise grew louder until the arm popped from the floor. Chunks of wood splintered into the air from where the strips had made contact.

Mr. Cohen pulled the BBS back.

*Empty? Jammed?*

The soldier's pistol arm—seemingly adorned with the guts of a broken piano—wavered, trying to zero in on Mr. Cohen.

Chris jumped forward and lifted the helmet.

Mr. Cohen brought the barrel back down and fired, and the soldier slumped forward.

"So I'm guessing that's the snare part of the BSS," said Chris after everyone gathered around the sleeping figure.

"Yup," said Mr. Cohen, catching his breath. "Fires strips of carbon nanotubes reinforced with a dual-polymer hydrogel. Nearly unbreakable. Each strip gets coated with an epoxy as it's ejected. One man can stop the rush of fifty rioters."

"That was close," said Chris. "Let's check the room he came out of. Empty?"

Mr. Cohen peeked inside. "Whoa."

The walls were covered with display screens and computer consoles below.

"Looks like a command center," said Mr. Cohen. "Hope, do you think you can—Hope?"

"She was right behind me," said Katie.

Chris ran back to the hallway.

At the end of the hall, a tall man was holding Hope in one arm with his other hand over her mouth. She dangled a full foot off the floor, helplessly.

"Welcome to *my* world, warden."

The sensation from the sound of his voice felt like a passing locomotive.

He disappeared through an open door, taking Hope with him.

Chris heard footfalls. A stairwell down to yet another level, no doubt—a level even below the ones marked on the elevator buttons.

"Where did that guy come from?" said Al.

"Not that this will come as any surprise," said Katie, holding the scanner. "No reading. Just like Chris."

"Also no surprise, he's clearly using her as bait," said Al. "That means he's ready for us."

"We need to get her back." It wasn't just fear. Somehow, Chris could sense the future unfolding, like memory in reverse. Now-ness—shooting through time like a firework. The present moment was exploding into fractals. "Before he has a chance to hurt her." He ran to the open door and dashed down the steps three at a time. At the bottom, he came to a corridor. The door was open, and he could see a similar door at the far end, but that one was closed. The doors were small, more like hatches, like ships have to seal off compartments.

Mr. Cohen, Katie, and Al came up behind him and looked inside too.

"What do you think?" asked Chris.

"Can't be good," said Al. "You were right to avoid the elevators. This looks worse. A trap for sure. But..."

Chris nodded. "I know. No choice. Well, here goes." He stepped into the corridor. The door shut behind him instantly. He pounded on the door. "Hey! Hey, can you hear me?" He pounded more but heard nothing.

All six walls of the corridor were completely featureless except for the doors on either end. Light seemed to be coming from nowhere and everywhere at the same time. He crossed to the far door and ran his hand along the seam. He tried to force it open, but it wouldn't budge. Then he noticed a tiny hole in a corner by the ceiling. *A camera lens.*

He removed the gum from his mouth, looked into the lens, smiled, waved, and then jammed the wad into the hole. He unwrapped a fresh piece and popped it into his mouth.

The lights went out, and he heard the far door swish open.

He considered using his percomm for light. *No, I have the advantage.* The man's scent lingered in the air, strong and recent. Chris crouched and passed his hand over the floor. The scent was easy to detect, almost as if each footstep glowed in his mind.

On hands and knees, he crawled out of the corridor to a hallway. It was completely black. It wasn't the kind of darkness where his eyes eventually adapted; there was not a single ray of light. Following the scent trail, he crept forward, reaching out into the void until he discovered more scents—many more—like a high-traffic area. *A door.* He groped for the door seam. *A doorknob! Like the doors in the upper levels.*

He opened the door just a crack, and the smells that rolled out nearly made him sick: burned clothing, kerosene, alcohol, acid, bleach. But the worst were the organic odors of rotting flesh, blood, urine, and feces. He shut the door and crawled on.

After a few feet, he sensed Hope's presence somehow. Somewhere up ahead. The feeling intensified.

He could sense her. No, not her, exactly—it was her fear. Waves of fear, making him light-headed, as if pulled into a dream. He could sense the specific type of fear: fear of retribution, a fear reinforced by the memory of pain. *She's in pain!* The rhythmic waves triggered vertigo. He struggled to know up from down and clung to the floor—surrounded by blackness—feeling he might roll up the wall to the ceiling, like tumbling in a barrel. Waiting for the vertigo to pass, infinite futures seemed to explode out from the present.

IIO IIO IIO

"PANIC MODE CANCELED."

Laura screamed. She ran for the pubcomm. "My god, Ben, get up here! Now!"

"Panic mode acknowledged. Security lockdown initiated. Complete. House secure."

"Panic mode canceled."

"Panic mode acknowledged. Security lock—"

"Panic mode can—"

Laura ran to the elevator. It was still on the basement floor. *It'll take forever!* Then she heard Ben coming up the stairwell. *Thank god!*

"Panic mode ackno—"

"Panic mode canceled."

"Ben!" She pulled his arm as soon as the door opened. "Come on!"

"Panic mode acknowledged. Security—"

"Panic mode canceled."

"Panic mode acknowledged. Security lockdown initiated. Complete. House secure."

"Wait," he said. "What's going on with the seccomm?"

"Who cares? We have to go now!"

"Look—the doors are still locked."

She tried to listen to what he was saying. "No, the panic mode was canceled. They're getting in."

"I don't think so." Ben leaned over and looked down the back hall.

Looking too, she couldn't see anyone through the back door window.

"Let's check the front," said Ben, tiptoeing to the front hallway. "Ouch. You're squeezing the blood out of my arm."

"Sorry." She loosened her grip.

He leaned around the corner. "Aha."

Through the front door window, she saw Sue Avenir with a percomm.

"Panic mode canceled."

"Panic mode acknowledged. Security lockdown initiated. Complete. House secure."

"What's happening?" Laura asked.

"I'm not sure. I think he's trying to get in, but someone is overriding his override."

"Who?"

"I don't know."

*Tshhhhh!* Glass sprayed into the living room, and a rock skidded across the floor. Sue Avenir vaulted through the broken window.

Laura screamed. Ben pulled her. She held on, unable to concentrate on where he was going, anticipating a grab from behind at every turn.

They reached the garage, but the garage door was already up. She followed Ben to the tran. All four tires slashed. "Now what?"

Ben took her by the hand, and they ran up the ramp.

Laura screamed again when she saw Sue Avenir across the alley in her own backyard.

"What? How?" said Ben.

The scream must have caught Sue Avenir's attention, because she turned and gave her modest little wave.

"No, Ben, it's really her. She's back from the shelter. It's our only chance. Come on!"

||O ||O ||O

CHRIS TRIED TO SHAKE OFF THE NAUSEA AS THE WAVES OF FEAR dissipated, and he tried to concentrate on Hope.

The man's scent was still clear. He continued forward on hands and knees. After passing four more rooms, he froze at the threshold of the next. Hope's scent lingered, as if he had put her down before taking her into the room.

Chris eased the doorknob down, inch by inch, until the latch popped. He smelled her immediately. And the man.

He could hear her calling to him, but only from her chest and throat—gagged—and she was struggling, restrained somehow. He still sensed the emotion from her, the fear, but it had changed somehow. The fear was less for herself and more for him.

He pushed the door open fully and scanned for any spot of light. The blackness was unnerving, like swinging in ink. From her muffled pleas, he knew Hope's general location and tried to estimate where the man was from the scent trail.

"Sacrifice." The man's voice reverberated around the room, seeming to make the walls shake.

The sensation made Chris's abdomen constrict, clouding his thinking, as if his own fear had joined with Hope's. "Sacrifice?" It was the marionette feeling again. Did the question come from him or the warden? He fought to maintain his own thoughts and feelings. "She's not your sacrifice."

"Oh, I don't mean your little friend here."

The deepness of his voice was so distracting, Chris had to concentrate on the words.

"Although," he continued, "we did have some alone time. She let me see things much more clearly. Warden, I must say, you have truly outdone yourself."

"I don't know what you're talking about. I don't care—" Chris felt his own consciousness get shoved to the side. "Sacrifice?"

"Yes, Warden, it's time Chris Lumière learned the truth."

"Sacrifice?" The word came out again robotically.

"Yes. Your mother, of course."

"Leave her alone."

"Oh, I don't mean Laura Richards. No, she's just a pawn in the warden's elaborate deception. I had it all wrong. Laura Richards searching for missing girls,

Benjamin Richards searching for dark energy—I had the two mixed up. I don't make mistakes. What are the odds? The warden's manipulation is obvious now, as plain as the tattered corner of a playing card in a gambler's deck. But your lady friend here helped me clear up the mystery."

"Sacrifice?"

"Yes, I'm talking about your real mother—your birth mother."

Chris felt new emotions swirl inside him.

"Marian. You never knew her. She was murdered."

Chris's emotions screamed for attention. "She wasn't murdered. She died during childbirth. My biological father died before that."

"Father? Oh, how very interesting. Then you don't know?"

Conflict raged in Chris's mind.

"You don't have a biological father. That thing inside you, that thing that's taken residence in your body, that controls you even now—it used your mother to make you. Your real mother was nothing more than a petri dish to spawn you as sinistral host."

The phrase splintered across Chris's psyche. Again, his consciousness was kicked to the side. "No! Dextral!"

"Fine. Dextral host, yes. It doesn't matter. You are a vessel, a slave, a tool. And, as the final step in the elaborate plan, it murdered your mother."

"She wasn't murdered!"

"Oh yes. In fact, her death was a critical part of the ritual."

The vertigo returned. Chris felt as though the room was rotating around him. Even in the complete blackness, the man's face seemed to fill his inner eye. The man's mouth seemed to open, showing fangs—moist and glistening—about to snap.

"It killed her," the rumbling voice repeated.

Chris realized the voice was now coming from behind him. Disoriented, he rolled to sit and face the voice. *How did he get behind me?* Chris heard gagged pleas from the same direction. *Hope! He's taking her!*

"Didn't that thing tell you? The bond to your body requires clarity. A clear path, you might say. A path created through pain and fear. The warden performed the tri-minyan ritual to take control of you. The pain of childbirth alone would have been enough. But no, that thing ravaged her womb, creating more pain than any human has ever endured. Then combined it with the ultimate fear for any mother—the fear of losing her unborn child."

"No!" Chris's mind thrashed.

"Oh yes. But here's the best part. And I must say, the warden's brilliance amazes even me. You see, the warden is here to stop me. Fortunately, it's easy for me to banish him to eternal bondage. It's a simple ritual, similar to the one used to take control of you. But the ritual requires a key—the death of your true mother."

"No!" Chris leaned over and vomited, inconsistency writhing inside.

"Brilliant, don't you agree? It sacrificed your mother to eliminate its only vulnerability."

"No!"

"Let me guess, they rushed you away before she died? You, as an infant, didn't see her die? The warden killed your mother simply to ensure its own invulnerability."

"No!"

"The time I wasted pursuing your adoptive mother—a red herring. Masterful."

"No!" Chris swallowed hard, holding down the acid in his throat. Then a light flared at the end of the hall. Shadows danced along the wall from the glow of a percomm back by the entrance. Chris staggered to his feet and saw Hope twisting in the man's arms as he struggled with the device. Suddenly, blinding light flooded the hallway from the corridor. Chris covered his eyes and stumbled forward. He heard kicks against the wall as Hope was carried through. Squinting, he ran after them and bolted up the stairs. *Which way?* He extended his arms and followed the scent to a stairwell up. Hearing footfalls from above, he raced up.

On the upper level, windows stretched floor to ceiling the entire length of the building. He tracked the scent to where it ended at a door. *Locked!* He smashed through in a single blow, sending fragments of doorframe through the air and emerging on the other side to find a most disturbing scene.

"That's far enough."

It was an enormous garage, half the length of a football field. The man was standing in a stall directly across from Chris, still holding Hope, but now with a gun pointed at her head. She wasn't struggling anymore.

The room was a series of garage stalls, several of which were occupied by luxury pertrans. The walls were lined with storage cabinets and tool benches. All the garage doors were closed except for the stall across where a hearse-like vehicle was parked. Two men and a woman stood by. The two men were guiding a glass crate, moving on a conveyor into the back of the vehicle. One of the two men was cradling his arm. The woman looked frail, and she was fixated on the crate. Inside the crate was a white mass. It looked like a mummified body, except wet.

One stall over, Mr. Cohen, Katie, and Al were standing like statues.

"Sorry, Warden," the man continued, "I guess it's a stalemate this time. But I really need you to stay where you are for a few more minutes." He pressed the gun into Hope's temple.

The loading door on the back of the vehicle closed, and then the two men and the woman got in.

"Yes, a stalemate for now, Warden. But I don't want to leave you without a farewell present. Are you watching?" The sound of the gunshot reverberated across the room.

"No!" Chris yelled.

Under a flash of ivory fur, Hope fell to the ground and rolled.

"Argh!" The man fought back as Lucky yanked and thrashed on his arm until a kick made Lucky yelp and release.

Chris flew forward as the man jumped in the vehicle. It raced out of the garage, leaving behind plumes of blue smoke and the smell of burned rubber.

||0 ||0 ||0

SKOTINO BORE DOWN ON THE CONTROLS WITH HIS LEFT HAND, HIS other covered with blood oozing from beneath the saturated cuff of his starched white shirt. *The canine's timing was too perfect, like it knew when I would pull the trigger—the chance of reality's path doth tip. The warden's tentacles of interference reach far, wide, deep, into the past, present, and future indeed.*

The vehicle accelerated down the long entry road, speeding past the smoldering rental tran. After a glance over his shoulder, Skotino called back to Tyvold, "What happened to your arm?"

"Broken. I was bringing the parahaoma when I came across one of them. The girl. I went after her, but she moved like lightning. She took off around a corner, and there was her big friend. He side-kicked me. I blocked it, sort of. Hurts like hell. I managed to get away, and they chased me. When I reached the garage, Barrister was ready for them."

"Yeah, I took them at gunpoint and waited for the guy with the BSS," said Barrister. "When he saw our two hostages, he didn't put up a fight." To Tyvold, he said, "I told you to call me the Bear."

"Just shut up. What about the chamber?" asked Skotino.

"Vitals are all green," said Tyvold. "Once we reach—"

The compartment window exploded as an arm reached through for Skotino.

Chelsea screamed.

"The warden!" yelled Tyvold. "He's on the roof!"

The vehicle swerved as Skotino struggled to maintain control, dodging the swiping hand. A roar erupted underneath as pebbles ricocheted inside the wheel well. He jerked the controls back toward the road.

Against the force, the arm stopped swiping, and the elbow hooked at the window frame.

Hitting asphalt, Skotino jerked the controls again, and the tires screeched as the vehicle swerved back on course. The arm flailed for grip but then vanished, yanked from the compartment.

Skotino accelerated to maximum speed and looked back. *He's flying!* But the speed of the vehicle was more than a match. In the rearview mirror, the figure in the air became smaller and smaller, finally coming to rest on the highway, watching them as they drove away. Just watching.

"*Antio sas*, Saoshyant."

# EPILOGUE

"**V**ISITING HOURS ARE OVER."

Laura noted the time before closing her percomm. It was 2:53. Officially, visiting hours ended at three. She was going to object but then saw the look on the nurse's face—a you're-keeping-me-from-my-next-task type of look. Chris had commented how welcoming the hospital staff was when he visited in the mornings. Laura wished she had the same effect on people.

"Maybe she'll see you tomorrow." The nurse offered a plastic smile, but her eyes still said, *Get up already.*

Laura obliged, and the nurse escorted her to the elevator across from the nurse's station.

"Are you allowed to tell me when Hope will be discharged?"

The nurse had wasted no time getting behind her console. "No."

"After discharge?"

"Trust me, I wouldn't want you to be here any longer than necessary." Another plastic smile, and then she made a real show of being busy.

Laura took the elevator down. Everyone except Hope's mom was persona non grata. Sue hadn't offered much information and seemed worried about her daughter's reaction if she shared too much. Chris was convinced that Hope blamed him for what had happened.

"Mrs. Richards?" asked a different nurse when the elevator doors opened.

"Yes?"

"I'm glad I caught you before you left. Miss Avenir has agreed to see you. Do you still have time?"

"Yes, of course."

"Wonderful. This way, please." The nurse went to a room down the hall on the right. "Here we are," she said, letting Laura go first.

Inside, the solitary bed was empty. *What?* Laura felt a sting on her neck and she slapped the spot as if to kill the offending mosquito.

The door closed, and the nurse stood in front. "Relax, ma'am, I'm not going to hurt you."

"I ... I ..."

"Come, sit down."

Laura went along easily and felt less dizzy. She rubbed her neck. "That hurt."

"Sorry, just a little truth serum and short-term memory blocker. It'll wear off in a few minutes."

"I don't like you."

"Seems to be working."

"I just want to know if Hope is all right."

"I actually don't know. Apparently, she has some disconnected friends in well-connected places. There's a very effective information barrier around her. In fact, it extends to your family. Awfully convenient if you want to avoid the authorities. A broken finger doesn't warrant a hospital stay. But then again, I'm not sure the trauma was limited to just physical."

"I'm not going to tell you anything about what happened."

"That's not true, but you don't have to; I was monitoring everything during her Vegas excursion."

"Then let me go."

"I just have one question. Your friend Marian Lumière—when did the medical scanner stop working?"

"A few months into her pregnancy. Why?"

"Three weeks ago, an OB/GYN submitted a search query listing the same condition."